Contents

List of Quick Guides

List of Figures

Preface and Acknowledgements

Several explanations may be useful at the outset of this book. The quotations that illustrate the discussion come from a variety of sources. We are very grateful to all those who filled out our questionnaire asking about contraception; they provided us with plenty to think about as well as interesting quotations. We are particularly grateful to the readers of *Cosmopolitan, Women's Weekly* and *Spare Rib* who took the time to write to us about their experiences of fertility and contraception. We have quoted widely, and even where we have not been able to use letters directly, have been influenced by their content in the writing of this book.

The title, *The Fertility and Contraception Book*, may appear misleading to those looking for a book on subfertility or infertility. Sadly, the problems of infertility and its treatment fall outside the scope of this book, except where they are directly related to contraception or part of the pattern of naturally declining fertility which occurs with age. The chapter on natural family planning explains how to discover the most fertile part of a cycle, but we have not been able to discuss fully problems of conceiving. There are now several excellent books available that deal particularly with sub- or infertility, some of which are listed in the reading list at the back of the book.

While writing this book we have had help from many directions. Roger Osborne of Faber and Faber has been a constructive and supportive editor throughout. Robert Snowden provided invaluable access to the library in the Institute of Population Studies at Exeter University. Anna Flynn gave up time to provide inspiration on the subject of natural family planning. The staff of the resource room of the FPIS were generous with their time and help. We would like to thank all who read and commented on various drafts of the manuscript at different stages, in particular Francis Grier, Tammy Kohn, and Michèle Wood, who provided many of the detailed examples in the natural family planning xiiPREFACE AND ACKNOWLEDGEMENTS

chapter. Special thanks to Bruce Fairbairn for the loan of a computer in the critical last stages and to Bill Raeper, Janie Hampton and Ben Driver for accommodating such a disruptive invasion during the completion of the manuscript. Josephine would like to thank Carol, Claire, Helen and especially James, without whose help combining motherhood and writing would have been impossible. Julia extends many thanks to Arokiyah Mary and Salat Mary for their care and hard work, and to David Mosse, without whose support, understanding and insight this book would have been very much harder to write.

Finally, our thanks to Sarah Dyson for providing the woodcuts and to Leela Sanadi for some of the illustrations.

Introduction

I, too, beneath your moon, almighty Sex, go forth at nightfall, crying like a cat . . .
                                        Edna St Vincent Millay

Why a book on fertility and contraception? Technical information on contraception abounds, so why another book, and moreover one that puts an accent firmly on fertility as the context in which any discussion of contraception needs to take place? This is a book about *fertility* and contraception because the images of contraception that most of us inherit run so counter to the potential resources of fertility that the human body offers. Fertility, the capacity of our bodies to create the seeds and to nurture and sustain the earliest lives of our children, has for most people throughout most of history been the mark of adulthood and the one significant definition of maturity. We have long since abandoned an awareness of the importance of fertility in western societies. How much of that awareness is yet reclaimable, should we wish to do so, is one of the questions that we ask in this book. In place of an emphasis on fertility, western society has erected a multimillion-pound contraceptive industry. The role that contraception plays in our lives is the other focus of this book.

Contraception is most often talked about in terms of rubber and copper, thrombosis and pelvic inflammatory disease, gels and creams. Diagrams of women standing with one leg up on some kind of box and line drawings of unrolled condoms are pretty unedifying to most people, yet these are the stuff of most discussions of contraception. Contraception has become as uninspiring as the instructions on packets of the pill, written with one eye on the legal establishment, one on the medical and both on the potential financial gains to be had from a successful contraception product. And because this is the way that contraception is sold to us, manufactured by chemical giants, packaged by pharmaceutical companies and delivered by doctors or chemists, this is the way in which we think about fertility and fertility control. Occasionally a condom advert breaks out of this mould and risks a hint of sexuality; most of us never see the adverts for the pill, IUD and diaphragm since they are directed at doctors. The images they peddle are those of good health. Contraception is seen as an extension of good medicine.

But contraception, used as it is at some time or another by almost 90 per cent of adults in Britain, actually has as its context the astonishing complexity of the fertile body and the multifaceted experiences of heterosexuality. Contraception exists within the web of bodily events which go to make up human fertility; it also exists within social, political and cultural constraints. Most books on contraception take it entirely out of context, presenting it as a series of mechanical actions, such as unrolling a condom properly, or taking the pill in the right sequence. This book is an attempt to fill in some of the background to contraceptive behaviour, looking at it from physiological, social and cultural perspectives, as well as examining its practical aspects. We hope to show how our understanding of contraception is the product of our social conditioning, including our attitudes to authority, to babies, to our bodies and to our sexuality.

Sexuality, for example, as it pervades the media, is inherently non-contracepting. Passionate couples on TV simply don't stop to ask about it. This is just one of many ways in which we are taught that contraception is something that really ought to be taken for granted, or invisible. We shall argue that this view has its roots in a negative attitude to the human body – particularly the female body. This attitude is apparent in the whole development of contraception which was fuelled primarily by eugenics, financial gain, the quest for scientific fame, population control and a host of other factors. We will argue that least among the motives for developing contraception has been the desire for women and men to live in harmony with their fertility without doing harm to their bodies. Proof of this is the large number of ugly episodes perpetrated in the name of contraception, some of which we describe later in the book.

But, despite this background, women and men still have to live with their fertility. We would argue that contraception, far from being merely a denial of the body and its capacities, or a necessary evil that gets in the way of the real pleasures of sex, can be a way of understanding human bodiliness. By 'bodiliness' we mean that fluid awareness with which women and men experience and conceptualize their own physical well-being – their sense of process and movement in the physiological changes their bodies undergo, month by month, year by year.

Seen in this wider context, contraception needs to be understood in relation to its opposite pole: conception. And this raises questions about the value we place on our fertility, and what fertility means in an age in which it is no longer a potent symbol of well-being. Contraception always assumes one thing: a fertile body. Most people take their fertility for granted until confronted by the spectre of infertility, that haunts more and more couples. But what is fertility, and why does it matter? There are at least two answers. One is to be found in the physiological functions of women and men which go to make babies. The other lies in the social meanings that these things carry. We hope to show that both are equally important.

PART ONE   FERTILITY

CHAPTER I

The Fertile Body

The physiology of fertility

In the natural world, when the ecological balance is holding, most animal pairs leave behind them only two offspring that are capable of breeding and sustaining their own offspring into the next generation. This is equally true of the starling, which lays only sixteen eggs in a lifetime, and the codfish which lays 40 million. Historically it has also been true of the human race. While a woman may have had many pregnancies it was likely that only two or three of her children would survive long enough to reproduce successfully themselves. This accounts for the relatively slow growth in population that has characterized most of human history. The large surviving families of the Victorian period were a historical anomaly and a unique phenomenon in the history of Britain. Until recent historical times in the West, the cycle of fertilization, gestation, birth and lactation was, and still is for the majority of the world's women, the dominant means of measuring out time. Figure 1.1 shows how women's lives have changed. Contraception now controls a major part of the time which in the past would have been filled by successive conceptions and long periods of breastfeeding. In Western Europe the population has once again returned to achieving more or less biological replacement; on average each woman will be replaced by another one who will reproduce in the next generation. Once the average number of children per woman drops below 2.1–2.4 a population is no longer replacing itself, as is currently the case in West Germany.

How fertile are human beings? Before we can assess the need for contraception it may be useful to have some idea of what we are up against. We know that in traditional societies fifteen conceptions were not unusual, though only two or three children would have survived to reproductive maturity. There are different ways of assessing fertility; we can look at an individual's fertility or we can look at the fertility of a

Figure 1.1 Changing patterns of fertility

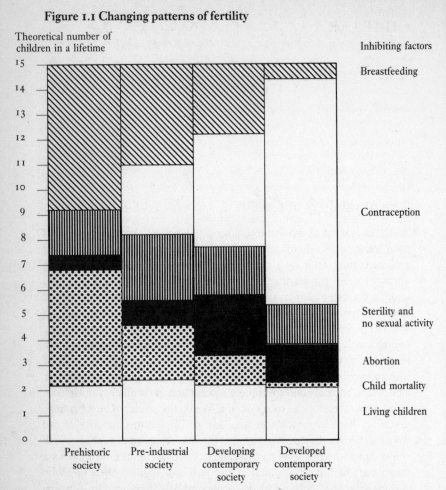

Theoretical number of
children in a lifetime

Source: Modified from Bongaarts, J. (1980), *The Fertility Inhibiting Effects of the Intermediate Fertility Variables*, Center for Policy Studies, Working Paper No. 57. New York, The Population Council.

whole society. Globally the population continues to expand. Apparently twenty-seven 'extra' babies, over and above replacement level, arrive every ten seconds: 200,000 every twenty-four hours. Humans are fertile enough to have become the most populous vertebrate that this planet has known.[1] And yet, in terms of individual fertility, human reproduction is a far more hit and miss affair than in the rest of the animal kingdom. A farmer expects his animals to have at least one offspring as a result of one mating. But human beings rarely achieve this feat. Different studies suggest different levels of fertility, but it seems likely that a fertile couple making love at the most fertile time of a woman's cycle have only a one

in four chance of conceiving that month. The chances of actually
producing a baby are more like one in five. Other studies suggest that if
a fertile couple makes love daily it will take on average three months for
the woman to become pregnant, while if they make love ten times or less
a month it may take at least six months. The probability of conceiving
on any one day of the month is shown in Figure 1.2. It is interesting that
peak fecundability, or the best chance of conceiving, occurs well before
the ovum is released, because the sperm is already in the fallopian tubes
waiting for the egg to arrive.

Human pregnancy is a chancy business. The fallopian tube has only
one chance every month of catching an egg as it bursts from the ovary.
Recent research suggests that as many as four times out of ten it misses.
In 15 per cent of cases the ovum itself is defective and cannot be
fertilized; in 25 per cent of cases fertilization takes place but for one
reason or another implantation fails to take place and the ovum silently
aborts. In only 20 per cent of cases do sperm and egg successfully meet
in the right place at the right time.[2]

The number of babies a couple chooses to have will be determined
by social and economic factors as well as by their fertility; things like

Figure 1.2 Probability of conception by day of intercourse

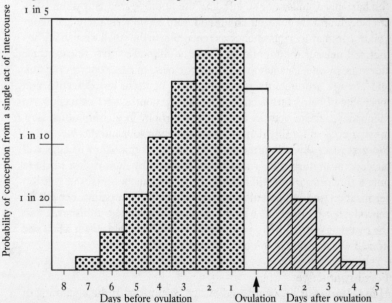

Source: Dixon, G. W., Schlesselman, J. J., Oru, H. W., and Blye, R. P. (1980), 'Ethinyl estradial and
conjugated estrogens as postcoital contraceptives', *Journal of the American Medical Association*, Vol.
244, p. 1336. Copyright 1980, American Medical Association.

money, peer behaviour, pressure from families, career plans and so on will all contribute. But in considering 'natural' fertility it is interesting to look at areas where there are still pockets of culturally determined *high* fertility. The best known modern example is the American Hutterite community which refuses all birth control but takes full advantage of modern medical facilities. Dedicated to multiplying and being fruitful, the women average 8.1 children each, with two thirds of them having between seven and fifteen children. What is particularly interesting is the fertility of older women, some of whom are still producing children well into their forties.

Fertility in women

Fertility in women has a dramatic way of announcing its arrival and a correspondingly clear way of indicating its exit around the age of fifty. The intricate processes that result in a small amount of blood being expelled from a girl's body have their roots in some of the very first developments of the female fetus. In the earliest weeks and months of gestation the lifetime supply of eggs is laid down, and the fetus has many millions of potential eggs in her tiny ovaries. At six months' gestation she has only a million or so left, and the number gradually diminishes after birth and throughout childhood until by puberty there are about 300,000 immature eggs or oocytes remaining in the small whitish ovaries that will tick off the months of fertile adulthood as they release their store one by one. By menopause only 300 or so of these oocytes remain, and already around fifty years old, most of these are defective and incapable of being fertilized. From only six months after conception to menopause, these oocytes develop and atrophy in a continuous, slow moving cyclical fertility dance, hence the enormous number needed in the first place. In a lifetime only 400 or so of this store of eggs will succeed in maturing fully and being released by the ovaries; of these only a tiny proportion will survive the hazardous processes of release, fertilization and implantation and form new human beings capable of reproducing themselves. Many a mother is surprised to discover that the ova that formed her daughters and sons were laid down when she herself was growing in her own mother's womb.

Fertility and age
Quite clearly fertility is affected by age. As we saw at the beginning of this section, by the time a woman reaches the menopause she is likely to have only 300 or so sub-standard eggs left in her ovaries. Peak fertility has dropped long before. As many women choose to begin childbearing

at later ages, there is considerable interest in the age-specific decline in fertility. Some would argue that subfertility or infertility that seems to be running at an epidemic level afflicting around one in ten couples has much to do with the age at which women begin to 'test' their fertility. Other estimates of subfertility put the figure higher, at one in six couples. Subfertility that comes to light at thirty-five is much more difficult to treat than subfertility discovered at twenty-five simply because by thirty-five 'natural' fertility has begun to decline anyway. Lowered fertility may be caused by many different things, but how does the figure of one in ten compare with 'natural' infertility? It seems likely that much infertility today is caused by widespread sexually transmitted disease leading to pelvic inflammatory disease (PID) and subsequent abdominal investigations. In this sense infertility is not so much 'natural' as produced by the circumstances in which we live. Some researchers looked at twenty-five seventeenth- and eighteenth-century French communities and an early twentieth-century Hutterite community. The assumption made was that these communities were unlikely to have been affected by abortion, contraception, PID and other potentially sterilizing circumstances. Women classified as infertile were those who had not given birth after five years (though obviously it was possible that their partners were to blame). In all communities there was a dramatic rise in the rate of infertility after the age of thirty-five (see Figure 1.3). Under thirty-five the rate rose only slowly.

What does this tell us about a woman's natural fecundity by age and the chances of subfertility and infertility? A woman's fertility peaks between the ages of twenty and twenty-eight. A number of factors are responsible for this; unsettled hormonal patterns and consequent annovulatory cycles (where no egg is released) tend to have smoothed themselves out by eighteen and between eighteen to twenty and twenty-eight the cycle tends to be as regular as it is ever likely to become. A woman's ova are as old as she is, so that a woman who conceives at thirty-six does so with an ovum of the same age. Eggs cells deteriorate over time, so with increasing age the ova produced are more often defective, with spontaneous abortion and failure to fertilize becoming more common.

One study recently conducted in France suggested that fertility begins to decline at thirty rather than thirty-five. Two thousand women were impregnated with frozen sperm by means of Artificial Insemination by Donor (AID). After a year, failure to conceive was much more common in women over thirty than younger women, with 39 per cent of the thirty-one- to thirty-five-year-olds failing to conceive, but only 26 per cent of those under thirty having no success. While it has been pointed out by

Figure 1.3 Age and female infertility

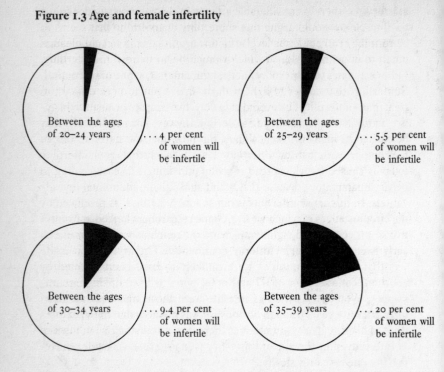

Between the ages
of 20–24 years   ...4 per cent
                        of women will
                        be infertile

Between the ages
of 25–29 years   ...5.5 per cent
                        of women will
                        be infertile

Between the ages
of 30–34 years   ...9.4 per cent
                        of women will
                        be infertile

Between the ages
of 35–39 years   ...20 per cent
                        of women will
                        be infertile

Source: Bongaarts, J., 'Infertility after age 30: a false alarm', Family Planning Perspectives, Vol. 14, No. 2, p. 76.

critics of the study that the use of frozen sperm creates higher infertility rates, it is none the less interesting that the relative failure rate was higher in the older age-group.[3]

Aside from any considerations of a natural age-linked decline in fertility, it is certainly arguable that with time a woman has more opportunities to have had more sexual partners with the corresponding risk of infection. A study in America estimated that a single new sexual contact brings with it a 15–20 per cent risk of pelvic infection, while three new encounters raise the risk to a six in ten chance of contracting something. Obviously not all sexually transmitted disease leads to pelvic inflammatory disease, and not all pelvic inflammatory disease leads to infertility; but several attacks can severely alter a woman's chance of conceiving successfully, because once the delicate fallopian tubes become scarred their fine hair-sized diameters close up, preventing the egg from travelling down and the sperm from travelling to meet it. Finally, the amount of sex a couple has over the years tends to decrease; this in itself may have a significant effect on the time it takes to become pregnant. We look more specifically and practically at patterns of fertility in Chapter 3 where we examine childbearing decisions and age.

One interesting fact seems to work against the idea of a rapid decline in fertility after thirty. Unidentical, or dizygotic twins, are those resulting from the fertilization of two eggs rather than one. Far more unidentical twins are produced by older women, the number rising by a factor of five to peak between the ages of thirty and forty. It may be an indication that the ovaries compensate for the other factors leading to a fertility decline by producing extra eggs. Certainly the ovaries reach their maximum size later, rather than earlier in reproductive life.

Fertility in men

Until relatively recently it was popularly assumed that all men were more or less fertile, that fertility problems were a woman's affair and that every man produced enough sperm in every ejaculation to populate the whole of North America. In fact in 35 per cent of couples attending infertility clinics it is the man who has the problem whether from lowered sperm count, a varicocele, a hormonal imbalance or one of a number of other recently recognized problems. It is now generally understood in literature on subfertility that 35 per cent of the time it is the woman who has the problem, 20 per cent of the time both have problems and 10 per cent of the time nothing can be identified. On average boys begin producing sperm at around thirteen years old and carry on producing sperm vigorously into old age. Once the sperm production has started up it continues to be produced at the rate of around 1000 sperm per second in each testicle! The androgen or male sex hormone levels in men peak at around thirty, but continue to sustain masculine features in men (beard/muscle development, etc.) until well into the sixties.

In the 1950s two American scientists analysed the sperm of 1000 new fathers. As a result of their investigation they defined the normal sperm count as around 125 million sperm per ejaculate. Some men produce many more than this – up to 300 million sperm in the 3–5 ml of their ejaculate. In fact it has been suggested that only 3 million sperm may be enough in some cases to cause a pregnancy, which would be contained in a virtually invisible drop of seminal fluid – hence warnings about the potency of the first drops of ejaculate proper which contain the majority of sperm. Once ejaculated into the vagina the majority of sperm are killed off rapidly by the acidic environment which is peculiarly lethal to sperm. Maximum survival time in the vagina is thought to be about six hours. But for the sperm which make it through the cervical canal, into the protective environment of the uterus and fallopian tubes, survival time can be anything up to six or seven days, though the average is more likely to be around three to four days. Sperm survival is, as we will see, highly dependent on the point reached in the woman's hormonal cycle. Sperm ejaculated around ovulation have a far better chance of surviving than those deposited at either end of the cycle because the cervical mucus produced by the woman at this time protects the sperm from the vagina's hostile climate.

One interesting fact has recently emerged from research on fertility in America. There is an increasing incidence of lowered sperm counts among men. A significant number of men attending clinics for vasectomies (and therefore presumably fertile) have been found to have sperm counts of 60 million per ejaculate, or less. It is possible that factors such as environmental pollution, alcohol, overcrowding in cities and high levels of stress may be working together to lower sperm counts. As a result the average 'normal' sperm count has been adjusted downwards and a man with a sperm count of at least 60 million per ejaculate is considered fertile – almost half the level that was expected in the 1950s.

A perfect conception

Contraception is all about preventing conception, or preventing a successful conception from implanting itself in the uterus. But what is conception? We have already seen that a fertile couple have only a 20 per cent chance of conceiving in a given month. What are the mechanics of conception that make it such a chancy business? The following picture is what happens when all systems are working perfectly, and a man and a woman make love at the most fertile time of the woman's cycle.

Conception is an incredible chance encounter. It is the culmination-point of two systems that evolved together millions of years ago. Perfectly complementary, one is hidden in the secret recesses of a woman's body; the other, less secret but equally vulnerable reproductive system, is closely guarded by the male. From puberty onwards, the bodies of men and women take part in the most intricate sequence of events, the complexity of which we are only just beginning to understand.

The female process
The woman's external genitals, the labia, protect her internal reproductive organs and are designed for pleasure. The pudendal nerve which carries the exquisitely sensitive nerve fibres responsible for arousal and orgasm divides into three, with branches going to the clitoris, the vulva and vagina, and the anal area which means that all these are potentially orgasmic. Her internal organs of reproduction are protected during

childhood by the hymen, a uniquely human part. They begin with the
potential space of the vagina, whose sides lie collapsed and still unless
sexually aroused. Its walls are lined with tissue not unlike that found in
the mouth but more ridged and elastic to enable it to expand during
childbirth. High in the vault of the vagina lies the cervix, with the os
cervix, its opening, lying in its centre. In women who have had no babies
the cervix feels something like a nose; after childbirth it feels more like
a small chin. The cervix is the gateway to a woman's uterus, and its role
is to protect this inner space from infection, to let sperm in and menstrual
blood out, and to expand, miraculously (and often painfully) during
childbirth.

The uterus itself is like a small, unripe pear suspended in the pelvic
cavity, and is built of some of the most powerful muscle tissue in the
body. In its non-pregnant state it holds only about a teaspoon full of
fluid, though during pregnancy it expands to forty times its normal
length. Never completely still, the uterus, cervix and fallopian tubes are
in constant motion, contracting and relaxing throughout the month. The
fallopian tubes with their velvety lining lead to the ovaries, lying like two
white unshelled almonds on either side of the uterus. The ovaries reach
maximum size at around thirty, but over the years the smooth surface
becomes pitted and scarred from the release of ova during ovulation. As
the body reaches menopause and the levels of oestrogen drop, the
ovaries shrink back to their prepubescent size. Figure 1.4 shows a
representation of a woman's reproductive organs.

A perfect conception starts in a woman's brain. Around the first day
of every new menstrual cycle the hypothalamus – the part of the brain
that controls basic bodily functions like hunger and thirst – sends signals
to the pituitary gland in the form of a chemical message known as luteinizing hormone – releasing hormone (LH–RH) to tell it to start manufacturing the hormone known as follicle-stimulating hormone (FSH). This
hormone makes its way to the ovaries through the blood supply. Under
its influence hundreds of follicles – small balls of cells with an immature
egg in the middle – begin to grow and ripen, releasing the hormone
oestrogen as they develop. Each growing egg contains forty-six chromosomes, like every other cell in the body. Before it can be fertilized it
must somehow lose half of these chromosomes, which it does through a
process of cell division known as meiosis. Each maturing follicle divides,
passing half of its chromosomes into a twin cell. This twin cell remains
attached to the egg, but shrivels up; it is known as a polar body, and it
seems to be completely useless though it travels along with the ovum on
its journey down the fallopian tube. Gradually under the influence of
FSH, one follicle begins to surge ahead, possibly by some 'survival of

Figure 1.4 Female reproductive organs

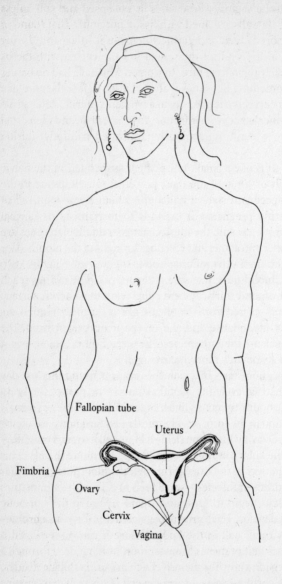

Figure 1.5 An ovary showing the different stages of maturity of an ovum

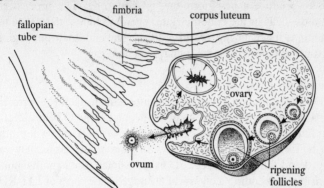

the fittest' mechanism, and the other follicles simply atrophy and die. The rapidly ripening follicle, now known as the graafian follicle, produce copious amounts of oestrogen which is poured into the blood stream. This in turn stimulates the cervix to begin producing the wet stretchy mucus that is characteristic of the fertile phase of the cycle; it also causes the lining of the womb to thicken ready to receive a fertilized egg.

As the level of oestrogen rises in the blood stream, it in turn acts as a messenger to the pituitary gland, telling it that enough FSH has been sent. The pituitary gland immediately shuts off production. The peaking levels of oestrogen in the blood stream trigger the hypothalamus in turn to instruct the pituitary gland to produce and send another hormone, called luteinizing hormone or LH, to the ovaries. Everything is ready for ovulation. The LH travels through the blood to the ovary where the follicle has risen to the surface and now bulges against it. The arrival of the LH causes the wall to rupture and the egg to burst out. Ovulation has taken place. Some women experience a sharp pain or cramping sensation around ovulation called Mittelschmerz (middle pain). It can be quite severe, and doctors have been known to hospitalize women suffering Mittelschmerz for suspected appendicitis.

The egg falls through space; no bigger than a grain of salt, the delicate feather-like fimbria at the entrance to the fallopian tubes must catch it if conception is to have a chance of taking place. Four out of ten times the egg falls into emptiness and is lost. But when the fimbria are successful, the egg is gently conveyed into the fallopian tube, which is lined with microscopic hair-like projections called cilia. The cilia wave backwards and forwards in an endless dance, and waft the egg along their surface in its journey towards the sperm. The egg is the biggest cell in a woman's body, and has a thick, sticky outer coating. As the egg is conveyed gently down the fallopian tube the yellow-coloured empty follicle left behind by the egg, at this stage called the corpus luteum, begins to produce a new hormone, progesterone. The progesterone enables the cells in the endometrium, or womb lining, to finalize their preparations for receiving a fertilized egg. The endometrium begins to store sugar and proteins in its spongy, wet lining.

The male process

Meanwhile the woman's partner continues to manufacture sperm. The process whereby sperm come to be made, and come to bear either the X chromosome that will result in a daughter or the Y that will produce a son is, like the production of ova in women, an exquisitely well-balanced and intricate process. As in the woman, the hypothalamus is responsible for sending a chemical message in the form of LH-RH to the pituitary gland which in turn sends FSH and LH through the blood to the testes, anatomically the equivalent of the ovaries. The testes are hung in a soft skin pouch, the scrotum, which keeps them 5°F lower in temperature than the rest of the body. When the testes receive the hormonal signal, they begin to make sperm. Unlike the woman's cycle the male hormonal axis is not cyclical but linear; once it is turned on and the pituitary gland begins pouring FSH into the blood stream, only extreme old age turns it off.

The testes are composed of a mass of tiny tubes called the seminiferous tubules, inside which are millions of reproductive cells, known as 'mother' cells or spermatogonia. Each mother cell, like each unripened ovum, has forty-six chromosomes which include an X and a Y. Responding to the FSH, each mother cell generates a duplicate (also with forty-six chromosomes). This takes about sixteen days. The new cells move forward, leaving the mother cell behind to continue the process; each new cell or primary spermatocyte divides again, but this time it splits its chromosomal material between itself and its new half. These two new cells, called secondary spermatocytes, have twenty-three double stranded chromosomes, but the X goes with one cell and the Y with another. In order for the double strands to become the single ones needed for fertilization, each cell divides once more, leaving four new cells or spermatids, two of which have X chromosomes and two of which have Y. These further two divisions also take about sixteen days each and at the end of this process these spermatids move on down the epididymis where they spend the next twelve days or so maturing. The epididymis is a long hollow tube measuring up to fifteen feet but packed into a tiny space. Swimming through its labyrinthine twists and turns the young sperm develop the strength, energy and experience that they will need to navigate their journey through the cervix and fallopian tubes.

Sperm accounts for only 2–5 per cent of semen. The sperm swim in a rich fluid that is secreted by the prostate gland, the seminal vesicles and Cowpers glands. It contains proteins, enzymes, citric acid, zinc, magnesium, fructose, prostaglandins, potassium and various other compounds, some acting as fuel to power the sperm, others as protection. A healthy man produces about 50,000 sperm a minute, or 72 million sperm a day, and forty hours after ejaculation the sperm count is back to its peak. For the perfect conception we will assume that the couple make love frequently, so that the sperm in the semen are new and fresh. Men who ejaculate only infrequently tend to have a higher level of abnormal sperm in their semen; men who smoke or drink heavily can also lower the quality and quantity of their sperm though even in what is classified as good sperm up to 40 per cent may be pretty abnormal with two heads or no tail, or even dead on arrival.

The moment of conception

Around the twelfth or thirteenth day of the woman's cycle (assuming that this is a perfect cycle) the couple make love, and 60–100 million sperm are deposited high up in the vagina, near the cervix. Some of the sperm die instantly, but for others the environment is more welcoming. The thick mucus plug that usually blocks the cervix has thinned out; the mucus is thin, clear, stretchy. A flotilla of sperm launches itself into this abundant, fluid stream that pours from the cervix. A journey of some five to twelve inches lies in front of them – indeed an epic journey; the sperm must navigate the inner spaces of the woman with as much accuracy as any salmon or eel that travels thousands of miles to spawn. The sperm swim against the tide, relying on the downward contractions of the uterus and fallopian tubes to guide them in the direction of the waiting ovum. The journey is hazardous. White blood cells may lie in wait to consume the unsuspecting sperm. The interior folds of the cervix are composed of many branches known as the 'arbor vitae', the tree of life, and sperm can easily get lost in these labyrinthine crannies. Even the sperm that reach the entrance to the two fallopian tubes have an impossible choice; those that swim down the wrong fallopian tube are inevitably lost.

Eventually some sperm find their way into the fallopian tube down which the egg is gently tumbling. Timing is everything; if the sperm arrive too soon they may die of old age while waiting for the egg. If too late, the ovum itself may have begun to deteriorate and die. In a perfect environment, the sperm may wait in the nooks and crannies of the uterus and fallopian tubes for up to five days. During their journey through the uterus the sperm have undergone a transformation. The invisible

Figure 1.6 Male reproductive organs

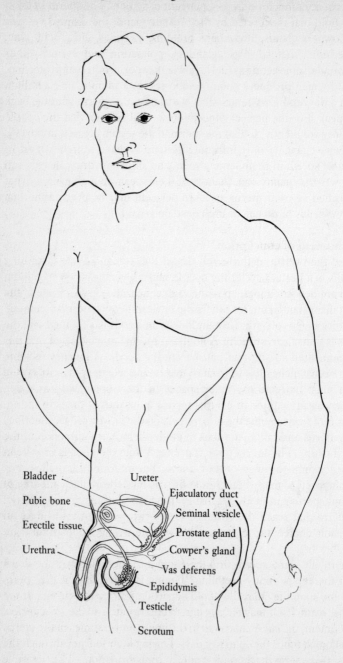

Bladder

Pubic bone

Erectile tissue

Urethra

Ureter

Ejaculatory duct

Seminal vesicle

Prostate gland

Cowper's gland

Vas deferens

Epididymis

Testicle

Scrotum

membrane that protects the head of each sperm is gradually worn away in a process known as capitation; sperm that fail to capitate cannot fertilize an egg. Sperm that make it as far as the fallopian tubes are well prepared. Suddenly the egg appears; dozens of vigorous sperm rush up to it, and in the force of their movement cause the egg to start spinning. The sperm begin to battle their way through the egg's tough outer coating, but only one sperm succeeds, locking itself on and spraying its chemicals against the egg's protection. Breaking through the protective shell it forces itself into the egg, and fertilization is complete. The membrane surrounding the egg forms a rigid barrier, preventing the entry of any more sperm. Two to three days later the cell divides and twenty-four hours later divides again. Seventy-two hours after ovulation an eight- to sixteen-cell embryo moves out of the fallopian tube and enters the uterus. Seven to eight days after ovulation the small cluster of cells, now called a blastocyst, implants itself in the fertile, blood-filled walls of the uterus. Meanwhile the progesterone has thickened the mucous in the cervix preventing the arrival of any more sperm, and preventing the pituitary gland from producing any more LH or FSH, ensuring that ovulation can occur only once in any one cycle. The fertilized ovum sends out signals to the corpus luteum telling it to carry on sending out progesterone. It is progesterone that is responsible for the tender, enlarged breasts and the feeling of engorgement that are common before a period. In fact these are the same feelings as early pregnancy and many pregnant women spend the first few weeks of pregnancy convinced that a period could start at any moment. As the blastocyst quietly embeds itself in the well-prepared endometrium, the remains of the follicle continue to pump out enough progesterone to sustain the pregnancy for the next sixty days or so. By then the placenta has formed and is mature enough to take over, and the corpus luteum dies.

This then is a perfect conception. If the egg is not fertilized, no early pregnancy signals are given and the progesterone and LH production tail off. As soon as the progesterone levels fall the thick lush endometrium begins to break up and the stored blood begins to ooze into the uterus. The continuous gentle contractions of the uterus intensify slightly and the lining is sloughed off through the vagina. This is menstruation. But as soon as the pituitary gland receives the message that the level of progesterone has fallen off, it begins pumping out FSH: the cycle repeats itself once more.

Figure 1.7 Conception and implantation

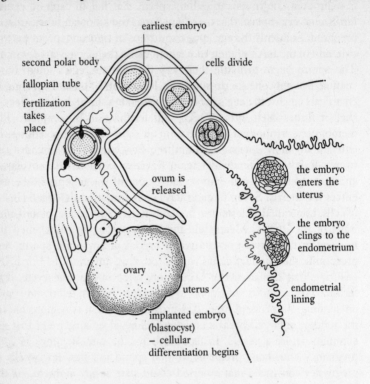

More than mere mechanism

These are the biological building blocks that go to make up the fertility of women and men – hormones and egg cells housed in structures as complex as anything else found in the human body. While women may experience these ritual cycles of hormonal triggers, ovulation and menstruation as entirely unconscious processes, the extent to which they are affected by the external circumstances of our lives is only now becoming apparent. Fascinating work is being done with couples experiencing difficulty in conceiving using hypnotherapy and deep relaxation techniques. Women who were apparently blocking their ovulatory cycle find that they can begin to ovulate again without powerful fertility drugs. Most women will have had experience at some time or another of a shift in the normal pattern of their periods: stress, bereavement, a new relationship can all affect the regularity of the cycle. The fact that a woman's body offers her such a strong, clear signal of her physical well-being, in the form of her ovulatory and menstrual cycles each month, may be taken for granted. But the cycle of fertility is a point at which a woman may experience her inner and outer lives touching very closely. This is why controlling fertility is more than a simple mechanical matter; it is why many women find the existing contraception on the market so inadequate. Only when a women has come to terms with what her fertility means to her will she be able to gain some perspective on the best way of living with it. Contemporary Western society encourages women to ignore fertility; it represents fertility only in the context of sex, as if the two were synonymous, which is one of the reasons why women sometimes feel that the contraceptives available to them have been designed by men with male sexuality, rather than women's fertility in mind. In the next half of this chapter we suggest that contraception is part of a much broader process of living with fertility, rather than something that is only attached to sexual intercourse, and that fertility is much more than having 2.4 babies in a reproductive lifetime.

The meaning of fertility

The denial of the female body

. . . female biology – the diffuse, intense sensuality radiating out from clitoris, breasts, uterus, vagina; the lunar cycles of menstruation; the gestation and fruition of life which can take place in the female body – has far more radical implications than we have yet come to appreciate. Patriarchal thought has limited female biology to its own narrow specifications. The feminist vision has recoiled from female biology for these reasons; it will, I believe, come to view our physicality as a resource, rather than a destiny. In order to live a fully human life we require not only control of our bodies (though control is a prerequisite); we must also touch the unity and resonance of our physicality, our bond with the natural order, the corporeal ground of our intelligence.

Adrienne Rich, *Of Woman Born*

The trouble with most books on contraception is that they put contraception in perspective only from one point of view – the technical and medical one. Diagrammatically, we can draw a picture of the female anatomy (which may bear little relation to a woman's own conceptual map of her body), and indicate with arrows the points at which contraception can intervene in the process of conception. Details (none of which are unimportant) about the biochemistry or mechanical action of contraceptives complete the picture. And that, it seems, is the story of contraception. From the perspective of a busy doctor trying to get through a list of patients, or that of a contraceptive researcher with a technical problem – how to prevent a sperm from meeting an egg – a

satisfactory technical solution is indeed the end of the story. But for
many women this perspective may be one more step down the path that
leads away from her sense of the autonomy of her body, leaving it, as it
were, 'uninhabited'.

How do Western women understand themselves, what do their bodies
mean to them, how do they interpret the bodily fluxes that characterize
the experience of being female? In order to make sense of contraception
we have to make sense of our fertility. Germaine Greer suggests that
the management of fertility is an essential aspect of adulthood.[4] But
clearly, for many people, managing fertility is something that can be left
to others and its meaning never fully appropriated. Many men, for
example, have little interest in controlling fertility, preferring to leave it
to their partners. Some women happily hand over responsibility for their
fertility control to the medical profession. Other women feel they
are never offered a real choice. This is not to say that medicalized
contraception does not have a vital part to play in a woman's decisions
about her fertility. But it is to say that much medical practice encourages
a passivity in women regarding their fertility, and that many contraceptive
acts may be part and parcel of a denial of the body which has its roots
in a basic fear and mistrust of the female body.

Where do women get their awareness of their bodies from? For an
answer we must look both at the history of ideas about women's bodies,
and at the personal history of the individual woman's own body. The
personal history embraces all the bodily experiences of a woman's life
which start from when she was born, or indeed from before she was
born, and include the process of being born, her earliest nurturing, her
childhood, puberty and adolescence, her experiences of sexuality, of
masturbation, and her experience of falling in love and giving and
receiving pleasure with another body. This history includes the experiences of menstruation and contraception, of trauma, perhaps of abortion,
rape, incest or illness; and it includes the cycle of conception and
pregnancy, labour and giving birth, the oneness with another's body in
pregnancy, and the vulnerability, openness and division of childbirth,
breastfeeding or not breastfeeding and the discovery of pleasure in the
body of a child. The history may also include the discovery of difficulty
in conceiving, of medical intervention and of involuntary childlessness;
or the decision not to bear children from choice. A woman's bodily
history circles onwards until the cycles stop and time thereafter may
seem more linear; she experiences menopause, ageing, the growth and
separation of her children and a different type of relationship with her
body. The history of the changes that take place in a woman's body are
inestimably rich and sensitive. Her bodily identity is not fixed and static,

but changes and returns in a constantly evolving movement of body and mind.

The way in which a woman interprets her own private bodily history is a consequence of a much broader set of historical circumstances. There is considerable evidence that in Western patriarchal societies as well as in other cultures throughout the world, women's bodies have been seen as something to fear, especially during the changes associated with puberty, childbirth and lactation. In patriarchal cultures women and their bodily processes have been regarded as both dangerous and powerful. They have been seen as more deeply involved in the organic aspects of humanity as against the social and cultural ones, and associated with natural forces which are potentially destructive of the organized cultural and social lives of men. Straddling at once both nature and culture, women become the chief agents or 'doorways' for the eruption of the biological into social life. Indeed in many cultures elaborate rites of passage marking puberty and childbirth contain the disrupting threat to the established social order which these physical events embody. But if on the one hand women's bodies are seen as dangerous, they are also the locus of reproductive potential and harbour an incredible power. Some feminist arguments suggest that childbearing in the name of the father, the emphasis on paternity and legitimacy, and the history of reproductive technology up to the newest developments in *in vitro* fertilization can be seen as an attempt by men to appropriate this reproductive power for themselves, or at least control it in their own interests. There seems little doubt, too, that women in the West were defined by this childbearing function at least until the twentieth century and, some would argue, until the present. If women succeeded in any other sphere it was considered to be despite their biology, and involved a sublimation of energy that might otherwise have been put into making babies. Ironically, however, until the twentieth century the very processes that defined a woman as a woman were often hazardous to her well-being.

A history of sickness?
Edward Shorter has argued in his book *A History of Women's Bodies* that until the twentieth century women suffered disproportionately from bodily crises such as traumatic labour and difficult childbirth, infections and fevers following childbirth, sexually transmitted diseases and a variety of other undermining conditions. Femininity was defined negatively and women themselves concurred in this definition, at least as far as bodily vulnerability was concerned.[5] Even enlightened feminists such as Mary Wollstonecraft, who herself died of an infection following

childbirth, wrote that she had been 'led to imagine that the few extraordinary women who have rushed in eccentrical directions out of the orbit prescribed to their sex, were *male* spirits, confined by mistake in female frames'.[6] Women writers, artists, scientists and explorers frequently chose to remain single, or if they married to avoid children. A constant succession of pregnancies may indeed have been debilitating to a woman's health, and coupled with childcare, housework and possibly work outside the house it would not be surprising if women found their fecundity a liability. Moreover women were likely to suffer some serious infection at some point in their lives, infection to do with their reproductive capacities that men were not even exposed to. Shorter argues that these terrible conditions were very much bound up with a woman's whole notion of 'femininity' or 'womanhood' in previous times, and if we wish to understand these women we must grapple with their injuries.

In fact Edward Shorter is one more in a long line of male exponents of women's bodies and though he would no doubt put himself strongly on the women's side he none the less sees the history of women's bodies in terms of sickness and disease. To be feminine was somehow to be sick. Women had to wait for the developments of technology to rescue them from this sickness. The 'natural' femininity of women was a liability which could only be overcome by the advances of modern, Western civilization. Technological advances are seen as a necessary condition for freedom. It is certainly arguable that with the advent of contraception to control the wayward fertility of women's bodies, the discovery of asepsis and the medicalization of childbirth, safer, though still illegal abortion, and the invention of drugs to cope with sexually transmitted diseases, the time was coming for a reassessment of femininity. The first wave of feminism between 1880 and 1918 successfully accomplished this in many spheres. The women who emerged from the First World War were likely to have had a very different sense of themselves, their physical capacities, their needs and limitations from the one their grandmothers had. In theory the door was open for women to enjoy the same unproblematic relationship with their bodies that men had always appeared to benefit from. In practice, despite the technological rescues, the reproductive life cycle of women has continued to raise questions and has been perceived as problematic to the present day. The idea that technical solutions to the problems of bodily existence are an automatic guarantee of freedom seems to raise more questions than it answers.

The medicalization of the body

What a Profusion of Fluids is the Female Form! Milk, Tears, Blood – these are our Elements. We seem to be for e're awash in Humours of divers Sorts. O we are made of Waters: we are like the Seas teeming with Life of ev'ry Shape and Colour.

Erica Jong, *Fanny*

One of the dominant factors in answer to the question 'where do women get a sense of their bodies from' lies in the rise of the medical profession and the hegemony of the medical view of the body. Schoolgirls learn about their bodies from their parents and biology teachers and their views generally speaking reflect the latest medical understanding of its various systems. We deceive ourselves however if we imagine that the knowledge received is entirely objective and value free. It is interesting to look back just a few decades to see how ideas about the female body owed less to objective science than to contemporary sexist and class prejudices. Citing biological factors, eminent scientists produced evidence to show why sexual equality could only be achieved at the cost of damage to women's reproductive functions. The evolutionary philosopher Herbert Spencer claimed that the involvement of upper-class girls in education led to a 'deficiency of reproductive power' which he attributed to the 'overtaxing of their brains – an overtaxing which produces a serious reaction on the physique. This diminuation of reproductive power is not shown only by the greater frequency of absolute sterility, nor is it shown only in the earlier cessation of childbearing, but it is also shown in the very frequent inability of such women to suckle their infants.'[7] In Manchester in 1884, a Dr Thorburn claimed that embarking on a university education was 'one of the most dangerous occupations of life' for a woman![8] She would be lucky to escape with her uterus intact. Scientists and particularly doctors of the day used the most recent scientific theories to keep women in their traditional roles. One such theory was that of the conservation of energy. It was argued that energy that was used up by one organ reduced by the same amount the energy available to the other organs of the body. Thus excessive brain work took away energy from the reproductive system. Janet Sayer shows how this belief was applied to menstruation. The prevailing medical belief of the late nineteenth century was that a girl's reproductive system developed primarily during menstruation and that therefore a girl must rest during menstruation to allow sufficient energy to be put into the development of this 'delicate and extensive mechanism within the organism – a house within a house, an engine within an engine'. Clearly the medical authorities' erroneous view of the body was not to women's advantage.[9]

In current medical practice it is still possible to document the ways in which scientific theories are used to project sexist views of women. Some would argue that the development of certain medical practices (aspects of gynaecology and obstetrics for example) are rooted in negative views of women. But even without being consciously or unconsciously sexist, the medical view of the human body may be problematic because these sciences do not discuss what the philosopher Mary O'Brien has labelled 'questions of reproductive consciousness' – in other words, what we think and feel about the systems that gynaecology describes in such detail, and how our culture shapes the way in which we perceive these systems. Modern medicine is about empirical signs. It reduces the body to a 'defective stimulus-response system', a reduction that clearly has consequences for the way we see ourselves. It presents issues of personal experience – sickness and health – in terms of abstract processes. Not surprisingly both gynaecology and obstetrics have been, and largely remain, male enterprises; they are part of the appropriation and control of reproductive behaviour that characterize patriarchal societies. Hence it is also not surprising if women feel that something is missing in the way in which these sciences handle women's bodies.

Diagrams and models of hormonal axes, such as we have included, present neat mechanical representations of the changes that take place in a woman's body; they do not indicate how a woman feels about these changes. There is nothing wrong with this, but it is simply not enough. As O'Brien points out, when we look at these models we learn nothing of the social relations surrounding a woman's reproductive life, nothing of the internal and external shaping forces, nothing in other words of reproductive consciousness. We need to find a way of drawing together both the biological and the thinking/feeling aspects of human behaviour. A small example will demonstrate what happens when the biological and conceptual levels are seen in isolation from each other.

A pregnant woman may build up in her mind a whole and highly detailed picture of the child she is carrying. She knows when it will kick and when it will sleep, what sort of sounds it responds to and, towards the end of the pregnancy, where to feel for its feet, knees and elbows. A relationship has already developed. If the same woman has an ultrasound examination late in pregnancy she may experience a profound dislocation between her conceptual picture of her baby, and the fetal image on the VDU. She sees the raw biology of the fetus. Instead of the baby she has come to imagine she sees the fetus as an unrecognizable dissected being. The ultrasound pictures of the working of its heart valves and kidneys, its stomach and bones, far from reassuring her, may disturb and upset her. Even when the fetus is pronounced to be in good working order she will feel that something is missing – the personality of the baby – the discovery of which is a major aspect of the work of reproductive consciousness during pregnancy.

Again this is not to claim that ultrasound is wrong or useless or shouldn't be done in late pregnancy. It is simply to say that it is not enough. Ultrasound pictures do not represent the 'truth' about pregnancy any more than diagrams about hormone flows represent the truth about a woman's ovarian cycle. Human beings, being always social creatures, cannot avoid bringing social interpretations to what they see and hear. The question of what something *means* is never far away. Many books that have been written from a feminist perspective on women's health (including the first part of this chapter) fall into the trap of presenting the biological facts without asking what they mean, and how they affect and are affected by the social and cultural web in which we live. The danger lies in simply presenting the latest medical dogmas about women's bodies; the fact that the authors may be women encourages us to trust them further because we believe that they will be on our side. By unquestioningly taking on board the latest medical view we perpetuate the belief that there are technical solutions to all the problems of female 'bodiliness'.

Feminist responses

Woman like man, is her body; but her body is something other than herself.
                                        Simone de Beauvoir, *The Second Sex*

We have turned away from our bodies. Shamefully we have been taught to be unaware of them, to lash them with stupid modesty . . . There are still so few women winning back their bodies.
                                        Hélène Cixous, *The Newly Born Woman*

How has the women's movement responded to questions of the body? There are at least two identifiable positions. One is summed up by Simone de Beauvoir and the other by a quotation from a more recent French writer, Hélène Cixous. Simone de Beauvoir was the first modern feminist to take the issue of women's bodies seriously; she certainly took issue with women's bodies. Her work is important because she confronted head-on the problem that women had always been defined by their bodies, that they were somehow more bodily than men. But far from denying this, or arguing that this was misplaced, she concurred with history's judgement that women's bodies were both fundamental to their lot, and pretty troublesome. She believed that many women found their bodies to be something 'other' than themselves, that their bodies, to a greater or lesser extent, got in the way. De Beauvoir's work has been very influential in the feminist movement because she was among the first to argue systematically that women's reproductive biology oppressed them, a view that has found exponents up to the present day, not least in the work of Shulamith Firestone, who states quite categorically that 'the heart of woman's oppression is in her childbearing and childrearing role'.[10]

The trouble with women's bodies, according to de Beauvoir, is that they enslave women to biology and to the needs of the species, so that although a woman's agenda may be entirely other, she is forced to live through a series of bodily catastrophes that far from enhancing her status as a free agent, subordinate her to her body: '. . . the individuality of the female is opposed by the interest of the species. It is as if she were possessed by foreign forces – alienated.' And what are these foreign forces? '. . . crises of puberty and the menopause, monthly "curse", long and often difficult pregnancy, painful and sometimes dangerous childbirth . . .'[11] Throughout this takeover, women fight, but fighting just makes it worse. This inexorable cycle, which involves the whole female organism, cannot be supressed or ignored. Instead it taunts her as an 'obscure, alien thing'; her body is 'indeed, the prey of a stubborn and foreign life that each month constructs and then tears down a cradle within.' Only with the onset of the menopause do women escape the iron grasp of the species – and only then by passing through yet another bodily crisis.

Inevitably de Beauvoir sees women's lives as very different to those of men, because men are not taunted by this alien inner life of eggs and uteruses. Interestingly, de Beauvoir denies that bodies lead to a fixed and inevitable destiny (her success as a philosopher and writer bears this out) but she does argue that the body, being the instrument of one's grasp on the world, inevitably affects the way in which males and females perceive the world. While men see the natural world as something they can transcend, women are more likely to see themselves locked into endlessly turning cycles of immanence, to break out of which demands a herculean effort. Most women don't try. Even fewer succeed.

Clearly de Beauvoir's provocative, forcefully expressed views demand some sort of response. While it seems undeniable that being female will affect the way that one sees the world, that this should automatically put women at a disadvantage is certainly questionable. Secondly it is questionable whether it is women's biology which is inherently at fault rather than the oppressive social structures in which women exist. Neither are inevitable. The philosopher Carol McMillan gives an interesting example to illustrate the differences between inherent biological conditions and social structures. She suggests an analogy with racism. For women to claim that it is inherently their female biology that oppresses them is equivalent to the black community claiming that the real difficulty with being born black is not that they live under racist apartheid regimes, but that their skin is black instead of white. If this were the case, then liberation for the black community could only be brought about by the free availability of skin lightening creams, hair straighteners and massive research into techniques for changing a person's phenotype. Clearly such a perspective would be monstrous. But the point of the example is to show the error of believing that women's bodies are an inevitable, 'natural' problem with a technological solution. Just as blackness is not a problem with a technological solution, neither is femaleness. It is social conditions that make being black a disadvantage in racist countries, just as it is social processes that make being a female a disadvantage in sexist society.[12]

What would the technological solutions to the 'problems' of women's bodies look like? For some feminists the priority of reproductive technology should be the liberation of women from the tyranny of the sexual-reproductive role. With the abandoning of sexually determined behaviour would come the abandoning of conventional social roles, and an end to the oppression of women. Shulamith Firestone suggests that '. . . we shall soon have the means to create life independently of sex – so that pregnancy, now freely acknowledged as clumsy, inefficient, and painful, would be indulged in, if at all, only as a tongue-in-cheek archaism, just as already women today wear virginal white to their weddings'.[13] But we are not really very close to artificial wombs, for all our celebrated test tube babies.

A further solution might lie in efficient contraception and early back-up abortions should the contraception fail. But seeing contraception as a means of controlling problematic femaleness – the tendency to have babies – can have oppressive consequences, such as the mass sterilization programmes that have occurred in some parts of the developing world; coerced abortions in women conceiving once too often for national population programmes; and even the peer pressure on teenagers to go on the pill in this country before their menstrual cycles have settled down. There is all the difference in the world between a woman choosing to control her fertility by using contraception, and a woman coerced into fertility control by an external agent, whether the state or an individual.

The real problem with the technological argument is that it simply takes on board a sexist view of women's bodies. If the supposedly unproblematic male body is the measure of freedom, then we will measure freedom as freedom from our female bodies. Freedom will become the degree of technical control we have over the natural process that defines femaleness. If men's bodies are the measure of freedom, then pregnancy, birth, and suckling will have no meaning other than as a lack of freedom. Thus, birth control, abortion, painless periods, safe, painless birth and safe, sterile baby milks will become the tools whereby a woman can take control over and intervene in processes that formerly defined her. With these technological means at her disposal, she will *ipso facto* discover her agency as a creative, active, free being.

But this analysis is fraught with problems. In the first instance, many of the technological offers of freedom have quite clearly not been in women's best interests. Secondly, this view of the female body has its roots in an internalizing of patriarchal views of the body, with a subsequent rejection of them (i.e. of the idea of female body as problematic). But the end result is a denial of the body altogether, and since to be human is to be embodied, this is hardly a satisfactory solution. Thirdly, in rejecting the view that women's bodies are their destiny, we risk rejecting them as a resource, thereby condemning ourselves to an unhealthy dualism in which body and mind lose their integrity.

In recent years some women in the feminist movement have begun to reassess ideas about the body. Totally rejecting the views represented by de Beauvoir and Firestone as a sell-out to patriarchal views about women, this reassessment stresses that woman's 'difference' and hence the ground of her liberation should be rooted in what is unique to her – her body. The mothering role, not as defined by patriarchy but as redefined by the women's movement, offers a new and fecund way of looking at the world. Women, oppressed because of their bodily differences, find a kinship with the rest of the oppressed natural world, hence the strong links between feminism and the ecological movement. But these views have come in for much criticism. Attempts to place female bodies and female biology in a more central position in women's consciousness are labelled as 'essentialism'. Critics of essentialism argue that such ideas dictate a belief that women's 'essential' unchanging nature is rooted in her biology and persists despite social, environmental and political changes. Furthermore, essentialists risk romanticizing nature, believing it to be benign and good, and so risk ending up where they have always ended up – defined by their bodies. Essentialists believe that women find greatest fulfillment when complying with the maternal role that nature has built them for.

There must surely be some middle ground to tread between ignoring one's body and being totally defined by it, a middle ground that takes into account social and political factors and at the same time chooses to believe that what takes place in the female body can have meanings which may be an enrichment and a resource for women. We need to define such a middle way. We must reject the idea that we have internalized, that our bodies are frail and capricious and need constant medical attention to keep them in order, particularly in reproductive processes. But we must avoid the equally dangerous opposite pole: the belief in nature as an all-embracing feminine good: the 'if it is "natural" it must be good' syndrome. For this romanticizing of nature fails to recognize that the intimacy with nature that is sought is predicated on a degree of separation from nature. Once we have 'civilized' nature, 'domesticated' nature into our culture, we are free to enjoy the natural life. The middle way which we seek, and which we want to establish as the context in which women live with their fertility, is not some naive back-to-nature rejection of contemporary medicine and all that it entails. We are not proposing a woman's culture based on the primacy of women and their special wisdom just because gestation happens to take place in the female body. Nor are we suggesting that women's freedom can be predicated upon the technical control of fertility.

We would support the view that the bodily events that occur only in women's lives can be understood not as a burden, nor as a destiny, but as a resource which can give women access to a web of meanings that may enable them to accept themselves more wholeheartedly. By accepting and affirming our bodily life unreservedly, both in health and in sickness, and in coming to understand its changes and returns, women may gain a stronger sense of themselves, and more confidence in their abilities. This bodily acceptance needs to be rooted in knowledge – not just the type of medical knowledge with which this chapter began, but an imaginative 'knowing', a conscious participation in bodily events, a willingness to explore what sexuality, menstruation, the ovarian cycle, pregnancy and childbirth mean for us in the context of our own particular lives. It is the totality of these events and the meanings that women ascribe to them that is the broadest meaning of fertility. Thus fertility, far from being simply a question of the number of children women have and how long it took them to conceive, becomes a term for their conscious appropriation of their whole reproductive cycle, which may or may not include children.

It is only when a woman's fertility is seen in its broadest possible terms – the totality of the reproductive story of her life so far – that we can begin to put contraception into a more meaningful context. Our fundamental argument is that many contraceptive acts represent an attempt to deny and ignore the body's fertility, to make ourselves in Germaine Greer's unforgettable phrase, female eunuchs. And in so doing we may do damage to our body's capacity to be fertile (by failing to protect it from damaging infections). Moreover, in alienating our fertility – in denying our bodily lives – we may miss out on a source of fecundity that spills out into the other areas of our lives too.

Moments in the reproductive cycle

What are the key moments in a woman's reproductive life cycle? Quite clearly a woman's experience of these moments is mediated by her culture and the social, educational and environmental circumstances in which she grew up. We are not suggesting an unmediated, 'pure' experience of the body. The idea of 'moments' comes from Mary O'Brien who suggests using the word to get away from the text-book physiological descriptions which move from well-marked stage to well-marked stage in a unilinear time sequence. She suggests the need to capture the determining, active factors which operate at both the biological and conceptual levels. The word 'moment' also conveys the sense in which these events are both 'momentous' and 'momentary'.[14] Some moments are voluntary, others involuntary, some conscious, others silent and not apprehended by consciousness. Moreover, the word 'moment' reflects a powerful idea in the work of one of the first women writers who explored the difficulties of writing about one's 'experiences as a body' – Virginia Woolf. Her phrase 'moments of being' is used to express intense moments of self-realization. The vignettes that we present here are designed not as comprehensive accounts of aspects of reproductive life, but rather as impressionistic pictures; they are essentially 'moments of being' in a woman's bodily life. O'Brien suggests a number of such moments, but we have taken out some, renamed others and added some of our own. For some women the circle will look very different, but we have drawn a classic cycle with most of the major reproductive life cycle events included. We will now look at some of these moments in more detail.

Ovulation and menstruation

Few women have not at some point in their lives referred to menstruation as 'the curse'. For many schoolgirls this is the only acceptable way of mentioning menstruation in a throwaway reference. And the meaning of 'curse'? According to the Pocket Oxford Dictionary it is a 'divine decree or human invocation of destruction or punishment on a person or thing'. And this is perhaps how some, maybe many women perceive their monthly bleeding. If a woman experiences severe premenstrual tension, affecting her mood as well as her body, painful heavy periods,

Figure 1.8 Reproductive moments

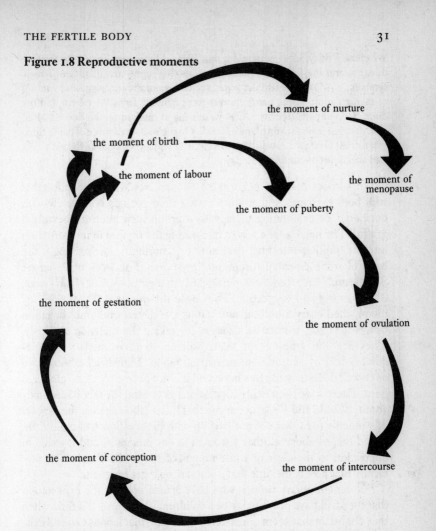

the moment of nurture

the moment of birth

the moment of labour

the moment of menopause

the moment of puberty

the moment of gestation

the moment of ovulation

the moment of conception

the moment of intercourse

and if she is disabled by this monthly ritual why indeed should she not see menstruation as a curse?

Feminist assessments of menstruation have taken a number of routes. Some have concurred with the judgement that periods are destructive and punishing and that the best thing we can do with them is to get rid of them altogether. Artificial hormones that prevent ovulation can suppress the worst effects of the cycle, and, if taken without a break, get rid of the cyclical aspects of fertility completely. Other women have gone in the opposite direction and tried to turn a negative taboo into a positive feminist symbol. In an attempt to see menstruation as connecting women to the rhythms of nature and each other, one group of American feminists held a 'Bleed-in'.

We chose Friday, July 13, 1973, for our 'Bleed-In' because Friday, the number
thirteen, and the full moon (it shone on us that night) are all ancient female
symbols . . . Mary Jane had decorated the bathroom with the signs and symbols
of menstruation. Large paper flowers were hanging from the mirror and the
door. Stained pads (tomato sauce) were lying at random on the floor . . . Red
yarn dangled from the rim of the toilet . . . On the wall was a piece of paper titled
'Menstrual Graffiti' . . . we all sat in a circle (a female, womb-like form) . . . We
told anecdotes of our first periods . . .[15]

We suspect that the majority of women would be uncomfortable
with both extremes, either suppressing their periods completely with
hormones or celebrating them with a group of women in menstrual
graffiti. The need is for a way of integrating the rhythm of menstruation
into life, neither rejecting, despising or ignoring it, nor making it the
basis of some essentialist feminine mystique. The work of Penelope
Shuttle and Peter Redgrove, particularly in their book, *The Wise Wound*,
is interesting and suggestive. They pose the question 'What does my
blood, shed every month, mean?' citing the distress that menstruation
brings for many women as a reason for taking the question seriously.
They see the attitudes of many women to their menstruation as
conditioned by centuries of menstrual taboo. Menstrual taboos have
been well documented elsewhere, and it is not necessary to go into them
here. There have been many suggestions as to what the taboo is actually
about. Shuttle and Redgrove argue that it is a taboo against the aspects
of women's lives that are not tied up with procreation and childbirth.
Blood means above all that a woman is not pregnant, and it exists in
opposition to the clear or white mucus of the fertile days which says
clearly that now is the time that a woman *could* get pregnant.

For contemporary women who have grown up with the expectation
that they will have only one or two children, if any, and at a time when
they choose, it may seem unreasonable to claim that taboos can still exist
against menstruation because it proves that a woman is fertile, but not
pregnant. But it is also hard to account for the fact that it is only the
negative aspects of the menstrual cycle that have been documented.
Women are supposed to become fiendish during their periods. Young
women are told that the negative symptoms of their cycles will disappear
when they start having babies. Doctors write papers about the adverse
effects of so *many* periods on a woman's health, which perhaps should
be relieved by more babies or hormonal repression of the cycle. Many
women grow up believing that menstruation is a negative event, the
funeral for the disappointed egg, while the womb weeps 'bloody tears
for its loss'. Added to this, most girls are not at all sure how to greet
their periods when they first arrive. There are no events to mark her

transition from girlhood into fertility. On the contrary she is usually encouraged to hide the fact that she is menstruating. On no account must the bleeding show; we need sanitary protection against its excesses. Whatever we may say in our secular age, many women and men grow up believing that menstrual blood is somehow dirty, unsavoury, insanitary.

Perhaps it is true that internalizing these attitudes has given women a disadvantage when it comes to a positive reassessment of their menstrual cycle. Yet why should the changes in a woman's chemistry throughout her cycle not offer the potential for different insights, a more subtle understanding of the mind/body continuum? Menstruation signifies that a woman is using her energies for something other than the cycle of procreation (or early nurture, since breastfeeding women frequently suppress ovulation and hence periods). It is true, that if left to 'nature' a woman might experience fifteen or so pregnancies in her reproductive life span. If she is not pregnant and nurturing she is clearly doing something else, concentrating her energy on work, on creativity, on the kind of body-transcending projects that de Beauvoir was so concerned about.

Accepting the fact that menstruation symbolizes a liberation from an incessant childbearing role – and contraception is clearly a part of that freedom – is one thing; living harmoniously with the ovarian/menstrual cycle is another. The human body has been submitted to a process of 'secularization' by medical technology and other political forces (in the sense that it has been demystified, our superstitious or religious views of it replaced by scientific ones); there is little scope to learn imaginative participation in its changes and cycles. Few women are encouraged to learn a sensitive perception of the different steps in their cycles. An example of the secularizing process can be seen in the shift of ideas about the centre of the self. What constitutes death, or the loss of self, is no longer the cessation of breathing; neither is it the stopping of the heart. Rather, the centre of the self has migrated to the head, so that death is brain death, regardless of when the heart (traditionally understood as the centre of emotions) stopped functioning, or when the last vital breath was breathed. We have submitted ourselves to the paradigms of medical technology where inventive, imaginative involvement in our bodily life does not fit easily. Yet women who have learnt to recognize the subtle differences in their hormonal cycles do record corresponding changes in their perceptions, their energy, their sexuality, their sensitivity. This is expressly *not* the same as being at the mercy of 'raging' hormones. It is simply the recognition that the cycle offers different potentials at different times – not madness at menstruation.

The majority of women are not aware of when they ovulate. Yet when a woman has learnt to recognize the signs of ovulation, they are hard to ignore. The pattern of red and white, of fertility and infertility, stamps itself on her sense of passing time. This is not simply the result of biological inevitability – after all it was not until this century that the moment of ovulation was accurately pinpointed – but the result of imaginative participation in the signs that the body gives her. The wetness of her vulva becomes apparent, she may become aware of a cramping pain in her abdomen; dreams or fantasies may occur with cyclical regularity. The brief hours of her fertility, her recognition of this, and hence her choice of what to do with it, may offer a peculiar sense of power. As the pattern between the red and the white shifts, new insights arise. The exquisite sensitivity of the uterus at menstruation and the corresponding emotional sensitivity that many women feel (and heightened sexual desire) can be welcomed and enjoyed.

One psychologist has described it like this:

At ovulation, a woman's body is receptive and fertile. She may then feel an emotional expansiveness, an abundance of sexual energy, a new potency in her creative ideas and insights. If her ego is not in touch with this phase of her cycle, she often squanders her energy . . . If she is related to what is happening in her body and psyche, this time of the month can give increased confidence and new certainty in her own capacities. Because this sense of herself is rooted in psychosomatic reality, it . . . [leads to] a real sense of her own strength. At menstruation, when the body passes its blood-food, a woman often feels an ingathering of her energy and feelings to a deeper centre below the threshold of consciousness. If estranged from that centre, a woman experiences this phase as a 'curse', as moodiness, as oversensitivity and pain and irritability. If she is in accord with herself, this phase can be a time of developing fertile insights, new relationships, or creative possibilities suddenly opened to her during ovulation.[16]

For any female reader who wants to take this further we would suggest an experiment. Try charting your cycle for two or three months, using the information in Chapter 4. Try to pinpoint the exact day of ovulation, but in addition to the information about temperature and mucus, record moods, dreams, sexual desire, energy levels and so on. At the time of menstruation, pay particular attention to the things that you feel over-sensitive about, working from the assumption that menstruation and its attendent feelings are not aberrations, but potential sources of insights. You may be surprised. (Women who are on the pill do not experience the same natural shifts in hormonal levels because the usual levels of oestrogens and progestogens have been heightened to prevent ovulation.)

We have not yet mentioned the meaning of menstruation to a woman who is trying, perhaps has been trying for a long time, to conceive. Here, indeed, a period may seem like bloody tears for the loss of an egg that has failed to meet with a sperm, or failed to implant. Quite clearly the pattern of red and white takes on an entirely new meaning; the value of the white, the fertile time, becomes unequivocably the positive pole, and the red the negative. Women who have difficulty in conceiving may rapidly come to perceive themselves only in terms of a quest for a baby, and menstruation becomes a time of particular pain and grief.

Intercourse

The moment of intercourse is but one point in the diffuse web of female sexuality. For too long sexuality has been defined in terms of sexual intercourse, but recent writings from the women's movement have begun to challenge this hegemony. Writers such as Sheila Kitzinger and Niles Newton have successfully questioned the dominant cultural view that sexuality for women means only copulation. Sheila Kitzinger writes that

For women sex is not something restricted to bottoms and breasts. We cannot talk about it with any sense of reality just in terms of what we do with our genitals. Whatever it is for a man, for a woman sex consists of a whole range of experiences that are not just genital. Sex involves the whole body and is expressed in different ways at different times in a woman's life, during her ovarian cycle and with the varied and complex bio-social experiences of pregnancy, childbearing, menopause and ageing. . . . One view of sex is that it is what a man does to a woman on a Saturday night in bed. We have been conditioned by a society that sees the be-all and end-all of sex as intercourse and that devalues all the other aspects of female sexual experience.[17]

Genital sex may be one part of the sexual or potentially sexual experiences in a woman's life. Reassessing its importance is not to downgrade genital sex; rather it is to upgrade other potentially sexual experiences. An adult woman may experience pregnancy and birth, suckling and nurturing a child as intensely sexual. In a long-standing relationship, the importance of genital sexuality may wax and wane, but the couple may none the less see their relationship as fundamentally sexual in nature. Writers have pointed to the similarities between sexual excitement and undisturbed, undrugged childbirth, and breastfeeding both for the baby and the mother. When giving birth in an undrugged state, a woman's breathing, vocalization, facial expression, uterine and cervical reactions, abdominal muscle and central nervous system reactions, sensory perceptions and emotional responses may be gross intensifications of sensations with which she is already familiar from sexual excitement. Certainly the potential for connection is there though in practice few women are able to make it. Some women may find that retrospectively they can interpret giving birth as in some way sexual even though they may not have perceived it as such while it was taking place.

Sexuality may be a diffuse continuum pervading a woman's life, her relationships with her friends, her children and with her partner. If this is so then it has implications for the way in which we look at contraception. The dominant image fed to us by the media is that sex means intercourse and therefore a woman needs to be prepared the whole time, just in case intercourse occurs 'spontaneously'. As a woman swoons on to her sofa, slayed by sexual passion, or is 'taken' totally unexpectedly while flying at 20,000 feet she needs to be 'protected'. But these images of sexuality are partial fantasy; obviously sex does occur spontaneously but not often as a complete bolt from the blue. The danger lies in confusing what happens in our dreams and fantasies, when we may indeed swoon on sofas, with what actually happens in our lives. Living happily with contraception means considering the facts of sexuality as it actually exists in our lives, not in some idealized representation. (We will look more fully at the way that women do and do not use contraception in the next chapter.)

As part and parcel of discussions on the place of genital sex in women's lives there has been a long and tangled argument about orgasms and where they occur, in the clitoris, in the vagina, in both, or indeed in neither. Many writers have dedicated many pages to the issue, and it has been seen as central to feminist understandings of sex, particularly lesbian sexuality. It is not our intention to enter the discussion here, except to comment on the unfortunate way in which an exclusive focus on orgasms, and where and whether or not they occur seems to duplicate a male view of sex and risks falling into the trap of believing that genital sex and orgasms are an end in themselves. Many health books for women, including the much acclaimed *Our Bodies Ourselves*, treat the body from an essentially functionalist point of view that either does or does not achieve orgasm. Sexuality is in danger of being reduced to the manipulation of a particular organ. The German feminist Barbara Sichterman provides a much needed corrective in her book *Femininity: The Politics of the Personal*. She suggests that orgasms always have a 'history', or a context, and that it is this history that determines the happiness or otherwise of a sexual relationship.

An orgasm is the last in a chain of experiences, of images, dreams, longings and anxieties: all sensations which unfold outside the bedroom. It is the last in a chain of impressions, expectations, disappointments, surprises, looks and touches . . . It does not have to be a long chain either. But it must exist, it must have a certain *significance*, and if it does so, genital satisfaction takes care of itself. If there is no chain, no history, then even the most patient and skilful stimulation of the clitoris will have no effect whatsoever, there will be no real satisfaction.[18]

Contraception, in order to be successful and to enhance a relationship, must take into account all these aspects of a woman's sexuality. It needs to fit into the history of the developing relationship. It must be appropriate to the woman and to the nature of the relationship. A woman who would prefer not to develop a friendship in a sexual direction but who feels she ought to be prepared 'just in case' may go on the pill and resent it. Because she is on the pill the relationship may drift into a sexual one, and she may resent it even more. She does not experience much desire in the relationship, and blames it on the pill. In a sense she is right to do this, but not necessarily because the pill is lessening her libido. Unfortunately the doctor who lays out the hardware on the table in the consulting room has no way of knowing anything about the sexual life of the woman who has come for advice. She may accept a diaphragm because of her doctor's enthusiasm for it but find that it undermines her sexual confidence in a new relationship; she may accept the pill and then regret the 100 per cent availability it seems to signify to her partner; or she may choose natural family planning because she really would like a baby and can't quite admit it to herself yet – but can blame it on the method when she conceives. We will look at these things in more detail in the next chapter.

Labour and birth

We have no . . . philosophies of birth.
Mary O'Brien, The Politics of Reproduction

Bearing a Child made me, i'faith, more philosophical than e'er before . . .; for what can be more mysterious and strange than to be one Person for all one's Life and then suddenly become two! To be doubl'd, then halv'd; to be one, then two, then one again.
Erica Jong, Fanny

When a woman becomes pregnant for the first time, she has little idea of what to expect; she can turn to the magazines and books on pregnancy and see pictures of blossoming women parading the latest in maternity wear. She can read accounts of what a fetus can do at this or that time and how big, how long and how heavy it is. She can decide what kind of birth she would like, weighing up the merits of epidurals and breathing, forceps and squatting positions. She can acquire more and more information, but the information will tend to be either medical or consumer-oriented. If she wants to ask questions of a different nature – what gestation, labour and birth *mean*, have meant in the past, may mean to her now, she is unlikely to get much help from existing sources.

We have seen how writers such as de Beauvoir, with their talk of alien foreign forces occupying the body, have based their ideas about birth on male philosophies which are inimical to women. They deny that there is any creativity or intellectual significance in human reproduction. But women who have given birth know this is not true. The problem is how to express it. The problem is indeed that we have no women-centred philosophies of birth. Philosophy may sound too pompous a word for what we are talking about. To put it another way: what language and images, other than medical ones, can a woman use to talk about the experience of being pregnant and giving birth?

Throughout pregnancy a woman attending an antenatal clinic carries with her a record of her pregnancy, the summary of vital information about her current state. But the parameters of this vital information are things like blood pressure, protein in the urine, fetal position and number of weeks' gestation. It is essentially bio-data. No one records how the woman felt when her baby moved for the first time; how she feels as she watches the familiar contours of her body soften and swell. And because no one else is interested, many women lose confidence in the importance that they themselves attach to such things. The focus on medical data to the exclusion of almost everything else perpetuates the myth that gestation and birth are medical events rather than cultural ones. Social meanings are replaced by physiological measurements; figures purport to explain what is going on, but may baffle and confuse. Does the fact that the bump measured 32 cm one week and only 32 cm two weeks later mean that the baby has stopped growing, or that a different midwife measured it from a different place? The woman who felt that she was rather good at being pregnant hesitates.

If the script is all about fetal monitoring, dilatation of the cervix and the appropriate doses of analgesics and anaesthesia, then the real actors in the drama are the doctors and midwives. The progression of labour is measured by traces on graph paper and the success of the birth by an Apgar score. Again, this is not to say that these things are wrong or unimportant or unnecessary. It is rather to say that as a record of the birth and its meaning they are not enough. Women themselves do not perceive labour and birth only in these terms. The experience of pain may be represented by jagged lines on a chart, but a woman does not experience herself in this way. One woman described the pain like this: 'I began to visualize myself, as each contraction approached, as a choc-ice melting in the sunshine as it lay on the beach, with my uterus rising up like a hovercraft into the ocean and leaving me . . .'. For her this was a distinctive and memorable aspect of labour, but there is clearly nowhere for such an impression to be clinically recorded! All too often a woman has to adopt medical language to describe what has happened, perhaps because even a 'natural' labour and birth has to be conducted by medical personnel. Indeed at its most extreme, medical technology prevents women from knowing what has happened to them other than in medical terms. Here is one account of 'good birth' in the 1930s:

Arriving [at the hospital] . . . she is immediately given the benefit of one of the modern analgesics or pain-killers. Soon she is in a dreamy, half-conscious state at the height of a pain, sound asleep between spasms. Though hours must elapse before the infant appears, her conscious self is through; the rest is up to the doctor and her own reflexes.

She knows nothing about being taken to a spotlessly clean delivery room, placed on a sterile table, draped with sterile sheets; neither does she see . . . the doctor and nurses, garbed for her protection in sterile white gowns and gloves; nor the shiny boiled instruments and antiseptic solutions. She does not hear the cry of her baby when first he feels the chill of this cold world, nor see the care with which the doctor repairs such lacerations as may have occurred. She is, as most of us want to be when severe pain has us in its grasp, asleep. Finally she awakes in smiles, a mother with no recollection of having become one.

For a medical profession dedicated to eliminating pain, the cry of a woman towards the end of her labour may, as Suzanne Arms has pointed out, be understood as 'Stop it', 'Intervene', 'Do it for me'.[19] But to want to experience an undrugged childbirth is not masochistic, or perverse. A woman submits herself to such an ordeal because she interprets it as meaningful. She does not want to become a mother with no recollection of the experience.

Of course, the process of interpreting the pain – the labour – will be different for each woman. But here we at once return to the problem of hearing women's voices through the hum of the machines. To see how differently women may interpret the birth process compare the following two passages. The first is by Edward Shorter, who heralded the advent of modern gynaecology and obstetrics as the first opportunity for women to interpret their femininity positively. He describes – without questioning it – the birth procedure in a modern Toronto hospital. The second extract is from Margaret Atwood's novel *Surfacing*. She, too, is Canadian, and might well be describing the same birth, but from the point of view of the woman:

. . . the mother checks in; her pubic region is shaved; if she is at all 'postdue', labor is induced and an 'oxytocin drip' started at the time time; she is placed flat on her back, her feet in stirrups; as the infant's head appears in the vagina, she is given an episiotomy; then forceps are routinely applied if the head promises to be at all delayed in popping out. . . . And at the end of what in the 1920s

would have been damned as 'this orgy of intervention' will appear a healthy
baby.

As far as Shorter is concerned, the case is entirely clear cut: 'In return
for surrendering their autonomy, women today receive pink, brisk
babies. *Nobody dies*'.[20] But compare this with Atwood:

After the first, I didn't ever want to have another child, it was too much to go
through for nothing, they shut you in a hospital, they shave the hair off you and
tie your hands down, and they don't let you see, they don't want you to
understand, they want you to believe it's their power, not yours. They stick
needles in you so you won't hear anything, you might as well be a dead pig, your
legs are up in a metal frame, they bend over you, technicians, mechanics,
butchers, students clumsy or sniggering practising on your body, they take the
baby out with a fork like a pickle out of a pickle jar . . . I won't let them do that
to me ever again.[21]

Shorter, it would seem, has missed the point entirely. The issue at
stake in many discussions of who controls birth is how far the woman
can appropriate the meaning of gestation, labour and birth. Of course
the well-being of the baby must remain central to the whole affair and
as long as any baby is damaged in the process of being born, the right
of the obstetrician to intervene in a labour that is not going well must be
respected. But a good birth experience (which may involve such medical
intervention; some doctors and midwives can offer intervention in a way
that does not hijack the labour) is one in which a woman develops a
sense of the creativity and significance of what she is doing. A good birth
experience may be a surprisingly healing event in a woman's life; her
body may seem to be more of a piece (a peace?) with her mind; and
although her vulnerability inevitably increases, so too does her capacity
for strong and powerful emotion. Sadly there are too few reflections
in print of the positive meanings women have found in their birth
experiences. To try and get some material for this book, we asked a
number of women who had recently given birth to write about it. We
asked them to describe giving birth not in terms of medical procedures
but to say what it meant in the context of the rest of their lives. One
woman sent us this reply:

Shortly after I had given birth after a long, painful, but strangely exhilarating
labour, I was struck that for the thirty-six hours or so of the labour I had been
on an inner voyage of discovery that I'd always longed to set out on. It wasn't
that I experienced this feeling when I was actually in labour, though the whole
outer world receded and I felt utterly centered in my body. It was afterwards
when I reflected on my experience that I saw that I had been on a symbolic
journey. I had, it felt, set off alone into the night (that was literally true at one

point, as my partner fell asleep); I alone felt the waves of pain that thundered over me. I faced all the strength that my body could muster to open itself. I journeyed into darkness, down to a place where the earth plates shift and move and open to give birth to new continents, new mountain ranges. I felt that I was joined to these huge movements of rocks and ocean and planets and that this connection was awesome. And like all heroes who set out on a voyage into the night I came back holding treasure in my arms and in my heart. What astounded me on reflection was in seeing in labour and birth so many of the symbols I had already encountered in myths and poetry. But in all of these the traveller was a man. Yet here in the heart of an experience that can be a woman's alone was the original epic journey. Maybe there is some residual memory of the journey lodged in the deepest unconscious of everyone who has been born. But it is only a woman who can consciously live the process of giving birth and of feeling the enormous strength that it offers. I could be accused of romanticizing the birth, but I would ask in response why women have failed to submit the experience of birth to their own imaginative interpretations, and let it offer a storehouse of symbols and a new way of looking at themselves, as voyagers and discoverers? For me, giving birth was the profoundest insight into myself that my life had yet offered.

We have dwelt on the moments of labour and birth at length because they clearly play a part of considerable significance in developing a woman's sense of self and enabling her to define the meaning of fertility. Far too often contraception is divorced from its opposite pole, conception and birth. Because of contraception women are able to choose conception. And because women can choose when and with whom to conceive, the entire birth process is open to new significance, new interpretation. We may be in a better position to appropriate the creative and intellectual significance of birth than ever before.

The moment of suckling, the moment of nurture
The French obstetrician, Frederick Leboyer, says in his book, *Birth Without Violence*, that the newborn child is looking for a lover, not only emotionally and spiritually, but physically. From being at an all-embracing oneness with the mother's body, the new-born infant experiences separation, gravity, light, air. The breast is his route back into communion with his mother and the mother becomes for the child his first, most responsive lover. The lover feeds, comforts, rocks, encloses, does and is everything for the baby, bringing the world to him and shaping the universe for him. Suckling is one of the most pleasurable sensations open to the newborn. A baby approaches its breastfeed with visible excitement, hands and feet moving rhythmically as he sucks, until satiated, relaxed and content, he drifts off to sleep. For the mother, too, suckling may be an intense sensual experience. As she feeds, her uterus

contracts, her nipples become erect, her breasts are stroked and stimulated rythmically, and the rush of milk that comes with the let-down reflex may be deeply pleasurable. Breastfeeding may be all this and more; or it may be perfunctory and disappointing, the woman eventually opting for the certainties of a bottle rather than the vagaries of her breasts.

The anthropologist, Margaret Mead, who shocked a bottle-feeding generation of American mothers by her uninhibited breastfeeding, made some telling points about the two experiences:

The failure of milk, the failure of the baby to nurse . . . are all natural enough in a setting where the new child is treated as if its health and well-being depended on the machine-like precision with which it is fed . . . The mother learns impatience with her milk, which is too rich or too weak, too much or too little, pouring through nipples that are inverted or sore or otherwise unobliging. She can turn with some relief to the bottle and the formula, the reliable rubber nipple with a hole that can be enlarged with a pin, the graduated bottle into which just the right formula, at just the right temperature, can be measured. No recalcitrant, individual, unregulated human body here, to endanger her baby's gain in weight, the chief criterion of its healthful existence . . . Most American mothers reject their own bodies as a source of food for their children, and in accepting the mechanical perfection of a bottle, reaffirm to themselves, and in the way they handle their babies, that the baby too will be much better the more it learns to use the beautifully mechanical bottle . . . the more it accepts an external rhythm, and abandons its own peculiar rhythms that it brought into the world.[22]

The important point here is the fear of the 'individual, unregulated body' that leads so many women to bottle-feed their babies. We return again and again in our discussions of fertility to the overwhelming distrust of the body and its capacity that characterizes so much western life. The body is a problem; it can veer from ridiculous over-production of milk to dangerously low supplies. A technical solution – the bottle – is turned to. Despite the beginnings of a swing back to breastfeeding, despite the fact that some hospitals pursue policies to make it as easy as possible to start successful breastfeeding, most women whose babies fail to show a suitable weight gain on the clinic scales will have to fight to keep a bottle out of their baby's mouths, when instead they should be offered counselling and support to help them build up their milk supplies. But, if the nurse and the doctor don't trust a woman's breasts, it will not be long before the woman too stops trusting them and opts for bottle feeding. The disappointment of a woman who wants to feed her baby and fails may be sadly underestimated.

Obviously the bottle and formula do have a useful place to play in contemporary life. We are not suggesting a Luddite boycott of baby-milk manufacturers (except when they abuse the International Code of Marketing of Breast Milk Substitutes). Women who want to go back to work, women who are uncomfortable with breastfeeding, women with all sorts of reasons opt to bottle feed their babies. There is always the danger of setting up hierarchies among women, with those who have a superabundant supply of milk coming out on top. The point we are making concerns the forces that undermine the confidence of women who would like to breastfeed. Women who feed happily for as long as they choose may feel differently about their breasts and their bodies afterwards, more confident, more relaxed. Many breastfeeding women feel proud of their ability to feed their babies. They value the relationship between themselves and their babies as yet unmediated by objects; so far, nothing stands in for the mother and it is this *conscious* act, with the gradual weaning that can follow, that consummates and gives meaning to the moments of gestation, labour and birth. In the act of breastfeeding, a woman consciously appropriates the nurturing that her body has offered the baby in the womb. The moments in the cycle of fertility merge so that suckling and gestation, conception and labour, far from being bodily happenings without meaning, can be understood as active, willed, committed.

What has this to do with contraception? Most straightforwardly, women who breastfeed uninhibitedly – through the night as well as through the day – may significantly delay the return of fertility. Any book on breastfeeding, however, will tell you not to rely on breastfeeding as an effective contraceptive, and for the majority of western women this is probably wise. It is true though that, in societies where babies have access to their mothers' breasts day and night, subsequent births tend to be well spread out. This may be partially due to cultural taboos on sexual intercourse, but it is also because very frequent suckling keeps the prolactin in the blood high, and, through a very imperfectly understood chain of events, prevents ovulation. Prolactin has been called a night hormone, and it seems that really effective suppression of ovulation demands plenty of night-time feeds.

More generally, however, breastfeeding as another moment in the cycle of fertility has much to teach us; we bring to it our whole conditioning as women, and its outcome reflects this.

Contraception

I am intelligent, I understand the methods of contraception, I have sat through countless discussions and demonstrations on the subject. So why have they all failed me? The pill makes me bleed and bloat, the IUD brings PID, the cap and condom make sex premeditated, are messy, and having failed me leave me insecure and anxious. Celibacy is not going to be the answer for ever. To enjoy sex fully again I'll have to wait until I want children, and when I do, who says my body will respond after my abuse of it?

Contraception is not a 'moment' in the way in which the other moments we have looked at can be understood. On the other hand, it clearly has a part to play in the reproductive cycle. We want to pose the question: what do the moments we have looked at suggest about the nature of contraception? Firstly, each had the capacity for enhancing a woman's sense of her own integrity, physical capacity, bodily well-being, or, conversely, for undermining it. The same is true of contraception. A good birth experience may restore to a woman a positive sense of bodily well-being lost at adolescence, or it may reinforce her belief that she is passive, entirely dependent on the professional expertise of others. Secondly, the moments in the cycle of fertility offer a woman an opportunity to experience her body on her own terms, or in the negative, hostile terms that a patriarchal system offers her (if she can separate out the two). This is equally true of contraception. The strong move towards lesbianism in the women's movement results precisely from a redefinition in these terms; and while some women feel uncomfortable with the lesbian alternative to heterosexuality, they have none the less embraced a belief in the goodness and the integrity of their own bodies. Thirdly, a mechanistic understanding of the cycles of fertility is not enough. Just because it is possible to show a woman that the inside of her baby's heart is working well before it is born does not mean that psychologically this will be acceptable to her. In other words, the fact that something looks technically feasible does not mean it will be good for women. The history of contraception with its high doses of oestrogens and Dalkon Shields makes this abundantly clear. And fourth and finally, the cycle of fertility is not a series of static, clearly defined incidents; nor is it not a linear process measurable through time, except by the crudest of measurements. Rather it is a fluid, fluctuating, cyclical, integrated movement that changes as a woman's experiences of life change. The moments that make up her life history are not separable from the continual changes and returns of her bodily fluxes; she will experience herself differently at different times. Relationships ebb and flow. Her body will offer her different meanings in the changes that it passes through, and all of these will affect the way in which she touches the world around her.

Contraception rarely takes any of the above into account. One medical friend, when discussing this book, asked what there could be to say. He commented, 'with contraception it's all pretty straight forward. I lay out the options on the table and the woman can choose.' But he failed to grasp the complexity of the background to a woman's choices about her fertility control. Based on the survey that we conducted for this book, we came to the conclusion that when contraception is taken out of the cycle of fertility and seen as a mechanistic way of stopping conceptions, women are invariably unhappy and frustrated with the method that they are using. Contraception is open to exactly the same abuse as the other elements in her reproductive cycle. It may very well not enhance a woman's sense of bodily well-being, her sense of integrity. Comments from our survey bear this out: 'I felt like a wind-up clockwork doll, dancing to an "ideal" femaleness while I was on the pill'; 'I was terrified of so much blood. It got everywhere, I couldn't go out.' This from someone with an IUD.

Contraception may reinforce a woman's sense of her own inadequacy. Women who wrote to us said how stupid and uncomfortable they felt when explaining a contraceptive failure to a doctor and asking for post-coital contraception. The scepticism of some doctors' response when a woman wants to try natural family planning is undermining. The apparent mechanical success of a method of contraception may be no guarantee of its psychological suitability. We know of women who were simply very unhappy while on the pill, and another woman who was so terrified of becoming pregnant that she simply could not bring herself to make love with only a diaphragm for protection.

Sadly we are not able in this book to suddenly reveal a wonderful new contraceptive that fits in perfectly with all the potentiality of a woman's reproductive cycle, that offers no bodily harm, and that is 100 per cent effective. We are stuck with the same old choices. What we are able to do however is to look at the way individual contraceptives may enhance a woman's sense of well-being by offering her conscious control over her fertility rather than a denial of it. In the end it may be simply a question of perception, or looking with new eyes at old problems. What we hope has become clear from this chapter is that there *is* a context for contraception outside the doctor's consulting room.

As we have researched this book it has been clear to us that there are much better methods of contraception waiting to be developed if only the developers of drugs and medical technology had the will to pursue them. So while we are currently left with the same old choices, we are not complacent; whether the future of contraception lies in carrot seeds (currently being researched in India) or in better barrier methods, the demand for gentle, safe and effective ways of living with our fertility remains paramount.

CHAPTER 2

Fertility and Contraception in Britain

Any reading of the history of the birth-control movement soon reveals that this subject was seen as being far more than just a medical matter affecting the health of mothers and their children. Indeed, the social, professional and political issues surrounding the topic are as obvious and relevant today as they were a century ago although the precise focus of these concerns may have changed.

Robert Snowden, *Consumer Choices in Family Planning*

The management of fertility is one of the most important functions of adulthood . . .

Germaine Greer, *Sex and Destiny*

Every act of contraception has a context, a history. In the last chapter we looked at the ways in which contraception fits into the whole of a woman's bodily history. In this chapter we will consider the other contexts, the other ways in which our choices about contraception are circumscribed. We will look at the way in which our choices are 'set up' for us in advance, examining the factors that have led to a situation whereby a woman can either control her fertility by sophisticated systemic contraceptives, or opt for methods that in essence have changed little in 100 years. We might call this the politics of contraception. Why is it that GPs cannot prescribe condoms, and that around 98 per cent of the contraceptive prescriptions they do write are for the pill? How are the contraceptive services set up in Britain? Who uses what and why? The first section of this chapter sets out the statistical context of contraceptive practice in Britain – how the birth-rate fluctuates, the age at which people begin having babies, and the shifts in these patterns. The second section looks at the historical context, outlining the various social forces – particularly the eugenic, medical and feminist arguments that eventually led to the establishment of the first free and universally available contraceptive service in Western Europe. Subsequent sections look at the social, political and medical factors that shape contraceptive usage.

In 1940 Norman E. Himes, a prolific writer on birth control, in his book, *Practical Birth-Control*, described the contraceptives available to the mothers and grandmothers of today's contraceptive users. He refers to many surprisingly familiar names – Durex condoms, diaphragms, cervical caps, Ortho-Gynol spermicides, KY jelly, and Durol, from the London Rubber Company. The book includes diagrams of all the then-available diaphragms, the drawings of which might have been taken from any contemporary medical textbook – as might the following description of a woman going for a diaphragm insertion:

At the clinic the woman is first interviewed by a nurse or social worker and this is followed by a medical examination. Answers to certain questions about the economic, marital, reproductive, and medical history of the patient will be required. If the patient is accepted for advice, a doctor, usually a woman, will make a vaginal or pelvic examination in order to determine the condition of the patient's organs and the type of method suitable for her. If the diaphragm is decided upon, then the size suitable for her will be selected. The patient will then be instructed in its proper use by the doctor or nurse. The patient will be asked to introduce and remove it several times to make sure that she understands clearly the technique before she leaves the clinic. Most women learn the technique of the method quickly. If the patient does not live too far from the clinic, the doctor will ask her to practise the method at home for several days without having sexual relations and then return to the clinic for a check-up on the technique in order to make certain that she knows how to use it correctly.[1]

While so much else has changed, especially in medicine, it is extraordinary that there should be such continuity in this area of contraceptive practice. It raises some interesting questions. The diaphram, which is safe, simple to use and relatively effective has always suffered from a bad press; it has always been labelled 'messy' and 'unspontaneous'. Why then has it taken almost a century to improve on it (and even these improvements, such as the vaginal ring, are not yet readily available)? Why, when it has been shown in study after study that well-taught, well-motivated women can achieve a extremely low pregnancy rate when using a diaphragm, has it remained a bit of a joke, something a woman has actively to ask for? Why is it that a method of contraception that remains linked to sexual intercourse, is in the control of the woman, is visible, requires anticipation of sex and an active commitment to use, is so far away from the so called 'ideal' contraception that we are all waiting for? What does this tell us about the way that we have been conditioned to think of sexuality and contraception? These are some of the questions we will look at in this chapter.

A statistical overview of fertility in Britain

In Chapter 1 we looked at the fertility of individual couples. For those apparently anonymous policy-makers who decide on what proportion of the health budget should be devoted to the supply of contraceptives, the concern is the significance of individual patterns of fertility on a national scale. This has been an issue for the last century and a half, first with anxieties that the British population was growing too quickly, and subsequently that the birth-rate was dwindling at an alarming rate. Then came the 1950s baby boom and everyone breathed a sigh of relief that British women had not given up breeding after all. By the 1970s the post-war boom was well and truly over, and the levels of births dropped off again dramatically. For the first time this century, excluding the two World Wars, the death-rate exceeded the birth-rate for two brief spells. In the 1980s babies are a little more popular again, though our birth-rate is still below that needed to replace the population in the long term.

What do fertility patterns look like at a national level? Despite the use of contraception and a declining birth-rate, the population of Britain continued to rise significantly from the beginning of the century until the 1970s, since when the growth curve has begun to tail off (*see* Figure 2.1). In 1986 there were 745,982 live births in the UK and 159,643 abortions. Interestingly, out of the million or so conceptions that occurred in that year, an estimated 340,000 to 370,000 were 'unintended'.[2] In fact, the decline in the *birth-rate* (which is measured by babies born per 1000 of the population) actually started as early as 1877. At this point the rate stood at 35.5 per 1000 of the population, but by 1914 it had fallen to 14.4. The birth-rate has continued to fluctuate until the present, but since 1982 there has been a slight upturn; it has risen from 12.6 per 1000 population in 1982 to 13.2 in 1986.

Another way of looking at birth-rates is to measure what is called the *total period fertility rate*. This is the average number of children that would be born to a woman if she experienced the age-specific fertility rate of the period in question throughout her childbearing life span. Since 1951 the total period fertility rate in Britain has told an interesting story (*see* Figure 2.2). For a population to replace itself over a long period of time the total fertility rate needs to be about 2.1–2.4. Below that – the most extreme example being West Germany with a rate of 1.28 (1985) – the population will begin to drop. This first happened in peacetime conditions in the UK during the early 1970s following the baby boom of the 50s and 60s where the total fertility rate had almost reached three children per woman. However the trend is again gently

Figure 2.1 Population changes and projections in the United Kingdom

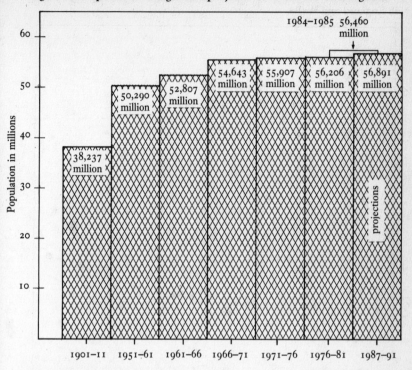

Source: 'Population changes and projections, social trends', 17, 1987, reproduced by permission of the Controller of HMSO.

upwards and is predicted to level out to about two children per woman by 2011. It may be significant that the 1960s saw the introduction of the pill, a new generation of IUDs and legal abortion. It is arguable that these helped to bring down the total fertility rate still further, though it is still not fully understood what other social and political factors affect the birth-rate. It is certainly not likely that it was the pill alone that was responsible for the 45 per cent fall in fertility in Britain between 1964 and 1977. After all, the even more dramatic fall in the crude birth-rate between 1877 and 1914 was achieved without recourse to any form of hormonal or intrauterine contraception.

Another interesting profile of the childbearing population emerges from official census materials. Figure 2.3 shows the change in the age at which women have the most babies. In 1985 the average age for a first birth was 24.8 and in 1986 it had risen slightly to 24.9. Most dramatic is the fall in the rate of babies born to women under twenty in England and Wales. The number fell by over 40 per cent between 1971 and

Figure 2.2 Total fertility rate since 1950 and the projected rate to 2011 in England and Wales

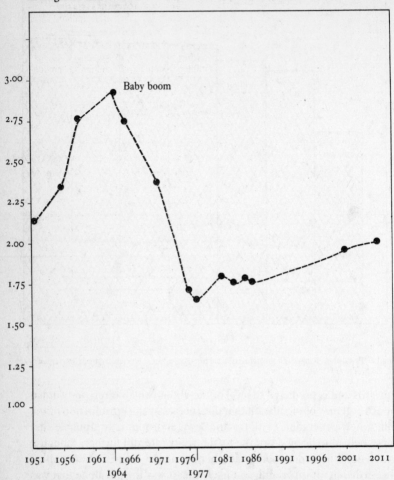

Source: *OPCS, Demographic Review 1984*, Series DR No. 2, HMSO 1987.

1985, while the rate for older women stayed more or less the same. This indicates the strong trend for women to delay starting their families till much later – particularly shown by the rates for the thirty to thirty-four and thirty-five to thirty-nine age-groups. If the trend established by 1985 continues it could mean that the rate of births (per 1000 women aged fifteen to forty-four) to women under twenty-five becomes *lower* than the rate of births to women of thirty to thirty-four. This would be an extraordinary turnabout, only achievable by long-term contraceptive usage backed up with abortion.

Figure 2.3 Live birth rates by age of mother in England and Wales

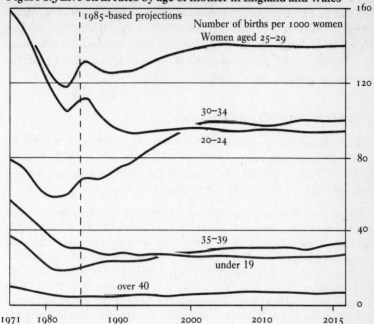

Source: 'Population changes and projections, social trends', 17, 1987 reproduced by permission of the Controller of HMSO.

The pictures that emerge from these statistics are highly significant. A woman who has only two children in her reproductive life span but is sexually active from twenty to the menopause may have anything up to twenty-eight years of fertility to take care of. Increasingly much of this time is before her first pregnancy. Many women choose not to have children at all. For them good contraception is paramount. But even the most effective forms of contraception have a failure rate. By 1986 the average number of abortions in a woman's reproductive life had risen from 0.16 in 1969 to 0.39, a significant increase. Equally important, unalleviated years of menstrual cycles may also have their implications, with a potential increase in various cancers of the reproductive organs. The literature on contraception suggests that future developers of contraception should aim to develop methods that are not only simple, reversible and have a minimum of side-effects, but which also forestall the pathologies associated with late childbearing and non-pregnancy. Potts and Diggory look forward to a time in the future when women will not only be using contraception to avoid pregnancy but 'to mimic those changes in the lifelong pattern of reproduction associated with protection against breast cancer and other forms of reproductive pathology which occur if pregnancy is delayed or never takes place at all.'[3] Some would see this as an unwelcome promise of future intervention in women's fertility. On current projections, according to the Office of Population Censuses and Surveys, the trend towards fewer children will continue; contraception will therefore continue to have a vital part to play in enabling women to chose when to have them.

A short history of contraception

The history of the struggle for effective and safe contraception has been told in many places and what follows is by no means a comprehensive account. We were struck by the extraordinary stories sent to us by women who experienced this struggle at first hand. One wrote:

After the birth of my baby in 1938 we found out about Durex, known as 'french letters', which was a dirty word. I had to go to the chemist when not many people were about and whisper what I wanted. The assistant would dive under the counter and bring forth, all ready-wrapped, the packet, and slide it across the counter. About this time I heard that 'clinics' had been opened but could not find out where. Having heard that a new clinic had opened in the town, I went along. When I said that I wanted to know about 'birth control' the lady screamed and told me to get out. This was a bone clinic. . . . Soon after this my sister was in a nursing home having a baby and one afternoon the matron sat down to chat with us while I was visiting. 'Ha', I thought, 'She will know about birth control, I'll ask her.' I did and was promptly told that they brought babies into the world, not murdered them, and would I please go as I was not welcome anymore. Oh dear, I never tried again, just stuck to Durex sheaths until I was 50. . . . We can laugh about all this now, but it wasn't funny at the time.

Human beings have always controlled their fertility. Well before the advent of modern contraception cruder methods of birth control existed. Like women today, if our forebears could not prevent an unwanted conception from taking place they practised abortion. There is also historical evidence to suggest that if they could not prevent an unwanted birth from taking place they practised infanticide. The desire for some form of limit to the excesses of natural fertility has driven many women into situations that have damaged their health and threatened their lives, but they have still been prepared to take such risks. The history of contraception is a messy one, full of prudery and moral sanctimoniousness, racism and classism, eugenics and self-interest. Fortunately it also has its heroes in the form of women and men who kept the issue of women's bodies and women's lives central to the discussion and insisted on a woman's right to control her own fertility. What follows is a brief outline of some of the major stages in the struggle for free and universally available contraception in Britain. Developments in other countries have been brought in only where they are important to the overall story.

There was an old woman who lived in a shoe
She had so many children she didn't know what to do.
Don't be like her. Ask the doctor for birth control advice.

Caption to wall poster in one of the first birth control clinics to open in
Britain, 1926

Prehistory Written records of barrier methods, used by the Egyptians, and coitus interruptus, used in a variety of cultures, exist. While the exact mechanisms of conception were not understood, the necessity of preventing semen from entering the vagina or uterus seems to have been well appreciated.

4th Century Some references to coitus interruptus exist. St Augustine, for example, wrote: 'If a man has not the gift of continence let him marry lawfully, lest he beget children shamefully or, still more shamefully, copulate without begetting. Though this is done even by those lawfully married: for it is unlawful and shameful to have intercourse even with one's own wife if the conception of children is avoided. Onan the son of Judah did this and God slew him for it.'

Middle Ages Only fragmentary glimpses of fertility control during this period are available for study.

17th and 18th Centuries Rise of contraceptive practice in France among the educated upper classes – either coitus interruptus or the vaginal sponge. Abortion was an important part of fertility control too.

18th and 19th Centuries Condoms made from animal membranes were manufactured and sold. They were usually seamless, with a silk ribbon tied around the top to keep them in place. London became the condom capital of the world. The most popular fabric for condoms was sheep's gut, which made condoms about half as thick as a standard contemporary British one. They were used not as contraceptives at this point, but as protection against sexually transmitted diseases.

1823   Francis Place, a Londoner, gave out handbills addressed to both sexes suggesting ways of family planning. He suggested that men could practise withdrawal and their wives might like to try the sponge, dipped in water, which needed to be 'as large as a green walnut, or a small apple' and would not 'diminish the enjoyment of either party'.

1826   Publication of Richard Carlisle's *Every Woman's Book* in which he wrote of an English Duchess who 'never goes out to dinner without being prepared with the sponge'.

1836   The first cervical cap was invented in Germany, made by taking a wax impression of the cervix to ensure a good fit. The idea of custom-fitted cervical caps is again causing some interest among developers of contraceptives.

1843–4 Vulcanization of rubber was first carried out. This had major implications for the development of contraceptives and three decades later rubber condoms were produced for the first time.

1876   Police arrested a bookseller for selling Charles Knowlton's book *The Fruits of Knowledge* in which he recommended the use of withdrawal and douching with a syringe. The book was accused of obscenity.

1877   Annie Besant and Charles Bradlaugh set out to challenge the backward step that this represented and published their own edition of the book. They were promptly arrested and the subsequent case against them raised the profile of the birth-control movement. They were acquitted on a legal technicality and the way was now open for major strides forward in the provision of family planning.
       The steady decline in English birth rate started. At this point the crude birth rate was 35.5 per 1000 of the population and it fell to 14.4 per 1000 by 1914. Illegally induced abortion was rampant and a major public health problem.

1880s W. J. Rendell, a London-based chemist, began advertising his contraceptive pessaries, thereby founding one of Britain's oldest contraceptive manufacturers.

1882   The world's first contraceptive clinic was opened by Dr Aletta Jacobs in the Netherlands. Most of the women who attended the clinic were offered a diaphragm, which subsequently became known as a Dutch cap. The name is still used today.

1886   Publication of *The Wife's Handbook* by Dr H.A. Allbutt. It carried advertisements for contraceptives, including one for the 'Improved Check Pessary', a type of cervical cap. Its manufacturers, Lambert and Son (who incidentally are still in business) described it as a 'simply devised instrument of pure soft medicated rubber, to be worn by the female (during coition) as a protection against conception. It is constructed on a common-sense principle, and strictly in accordance with the female organisation; can be worn any length of time with ease and comfort; is easily adjusted and removed, adapts itself perfectly and no apprehension of it going too far or doing the slightest harm need be felt, and with care will last for years . . . 2s 3d each.' It looks remarkably like a 'Today' contraceptive sponge and was probably reasonably effective. Dr Allbutt had his name erased from the Medical Register for his pains.

1887   Medical opinion remained strongly against contraception. A letter to the *Lancet* had this to say: 'You, Sirs, may easily plead that this subject is not one a decent man would care to handle with a pair of tongs; but I trust you will agree with me in the hope that . . . the medical profession . . . must never identify itself in this matter, however indirectly; and that . . . if this evil is to continue, at all events it shall never exist as a sidewing of the healing art.'[4]

1890s   Current contraceptive options were: coitus interruptus; the 'safe' period (though no one actually knew when this was); condoms; douching with alum and other substances; vaginal sponge soaked in quinine or some other substance; pessaries (including the cacao-butter and quinine pessary) and various rubber cervical caps and diaphragms.

1909   Development of an early IUD by Dr Richter of Waldenburg made from a loop of silkworm gut. Marie Stopes described early IUDs as 'freak instruments'. These IUDs remained a minority interest and it was not until a new generation of IUDs was developed in the 1960s that this form of contraceptive finally 'came of age'.

1914   The First World War. The war marked a turning point in British public opinion in a number of areas particularly sexual conduct,

the role of women and the use of birth control. The 1916 Report
of the National Birth Rate Commission provided assurances about
the safety of some contraceptive methods. Medical opinion was
slowly changing.

1916   Margaret Sanger opened the first American birth control clinic
in Brooklyn, New York.

1918   *Married Love*, by Marie Stopes, was published. Stopes, who was
a botanist, had made an unhappy and unconsummated marriage.
After her divorce she wrote her book, basically as a plea for the
right of a women to sexual satisfaction. Although contraception was
mentioned only briefly she received thousands of letters asking for
more details.

1921   The 'First Birth Control Clinic in the British Empire' opened
at 61 Marlborough Road, Islington. The Mothers' Clinic for
Constructive Birth Control, as it was called (or CBC for short) had
four aims; to help the poor with free advice; to test the belief that
the working class was hostile to birth control; to obtain hard facts
about contraception in practice; and to collect scientific data on the
sex life of women. The clinic mainly provided women with cervical
caps to be used with a dissolving pessary. In fact Marie Stopes
had a number of extraordinary ideas; she believed that during
intercourse the penis actually became interlocked with the cervix
which led her to reject certain forms of contraceptive such as the
diaphragm.
    She also shared with many of her contemporaries ideas that
would be quite unacceptable nowadays. A key to the direction of
her thinking lies in her contraceptive brand name 'Racial'. She had
clear ideas about the fit and the unfit and would like to have had
the unfit sterilized. Her book *Wise Parenthood* published in 1918 is
dedicated to 'All who wish to see our race grow in strength and
beauty'. In the nineteenth edition of *Wise Parenthood* printed in
1935 she is still writing about the reproductive habits of 'vicious
and feeble-minded people'. When they reproduce they do so
'recklessly'.
    Despite these views, Marie Stopes was seen as a champion by
the poor, and she responded warmly to requests for help, whoever
they came from, according to her biographer Ruth Hall. Moreover,
unlike many of her contemporaries who used the same rhetoric,
she was moved to do something about those submerged in what

she labelled 'a bog composed of the bleeding and tortured bodies of women and children'. Some of the letters she received make tragic reading – a salutory reminder today,when contraception *is* readily available:

> . . . what I would like to know is how I can save having any more children as I think I have done my duty to my Country having had 13 children 9 boys and 4 girls and I have 6 boys alive now and a little girl who will be 3 years old in may I burried a dear little baby girl 3 weeks old who died from the strain of whooping cough the reason I write this is I cannot look after the little one like I would like to as I am getting very stout and cannot bend to bath them and it do jest kill me to carry them in the shawl I have always got one in my arms and another clinging to my apron and it is such a lot of work to wash and clean for us all . . . I think I have told you all my troubles . . . yours truly . . .[5]

1928 E. Grafenberg developed his 'Grafenberg Ring', a small silver ring inserted into the uterus. This IUD is considered by some to be the mother of all many subsequent IUDs developed in the 1950s and 1960s.

1924 Founding of the Society for the Provision of Birth Control Clinics.

Eugenics began to give way to feminist ideas in some quarters. Feminists began to argue that control over reproduction was an essential aspect of women's ability to control their lives. The Worker's Birth Control Group was set up which stated that 'all women, rich or poor, have an equal right' to knowledge about contraception.

1926 Dora Russell secured victory over the National Executive Committee at the Labour Party Conference and established that birth control was a party issue.

Medical opinion began to change. In a letter in Guy's Hospital Gazette, 11 October 1924, a correspondent wrote: 'The complete omission of the spermicidal suppository and occlusive pessary from the orthodox medical curriculum and training must be regarded as emanating from a superstition if anything more idiotic than that which a few years ago forbade gynaecologists undertaking major pelvic operations by anything other than the vaginal route.'

The campaign for the provision of birth control by public health authorities intensified.

1930s   Development of the first latex condoms.

1930   The Ministry of Health decided that welfare clinics (mother and baby clinics) could begin to give contraceptive advice to married women whose health would be at risk from further pregnancies. This was a major step forward towards a State-funded contraceptive service, and the only one until the 1967 Family Planning Act.

1931   Thirty-six health authorities decided to take action under the Ministry of Health ruling. Some gave grants to women to go to clinics, others held special birth control sessions.

The National Birth Control Association which was founded in 1930 began to play a more prominent role in organizing the voluntary sector. While it was committed to local authority provision it none the less set up its own clinics in places where district authorities did not do so.

1935   There were now forty-seven NBCA clinics and sixty-six council clinics established, largely giving out spermicides and the diaphragm.

1939   The NBCA changed its name to the Family Planning Association (FPA) and it restated its aims which were now to provide advice on birth control to married women who wanted to limit or space their families, not just women whose health would be at risk from another pregnancy.

Throughout the 20s and 30s there was a continuing anxiety about the falling British birth rate. This anxiety continued until the start of the baby boom in the 1950s.

1946   The National Health Service Act empowered local health authorities to open clinics where advice could be given to nursing mothers on medical grounds. Few health authorities committed themselves to family planning and the FPA continued to do most of the work.

1950s   The FPA was now running 100 clinics which increased to 276 by the 1960s.

1951   Luis Miramontes working in the Syntex laboratories under the direction of Carl Djessari succeeded in making a synthetic progestogen known as norethisterone or norethindrone – the first step towards the contraceptive pill. Norethisterone is still used in some pills.

1961   The pill was made available for the first time under the brand name 'Conovid'. It was provided at FPA clinics. Doctors could prescribe the pill on medical grounds (or on private prescription). Within four years 460,000 British women were on one of the high dose pills, Conovid, Conovid E or Anovlar.

The 1960s also saw the introduction of a new generation of IUDs, for example the Lippes loop and Dalkon Shield.

1967   The Abortion Act was passed. Abortion became legal under certain conditions (see Chapter 11 for details).

The National Health Service (Family Planning) Act was passed. This enabled local authorities to provide advice and supplies to people seeking contraception. It was interpreted liberally to include single as well as married people and many were able to get their contraceptives free under arrangements with FPA clinics.

1973   The National Health Service Reorganisation Act was passed. This set up a completely free family planning service in clinics and in hospitals – the first universally available and free contraceptive service in Western Europe.

1975   General Practitioners were able to enter a contract with their Family Practitioner Committees to provide free contraceptive services to patients, and to people not registered with them for general medical care. The need for special training of GPs resisted.

1976   The Family Planning Association completed the transfer of its clinics to the NHS. Nowadays the FPA plays a role as an education and information service.

1984   Mrs Victoria Gillick obtained a ruling from the Appeal Court that except in an emergency, or with leave from the court, health professionals were deemed to be acting illegally if they provided contraceptive advice or treatment without the consent of the parents of a girl under sixteen.

1985   The Law Lords in the House of Lords upheld the DHSS appeal against the Appeal Court judgement and ruled that doctors acting in good faith could give contraceptive advice and treatment to girls under sixteen without parental consent providing the girl is of sufficient understanding and intelligence to give valid consent herself.

1990   The current system means that free contraceptives are available from District Health Authority clinics, from GPs (your own or another), from hospital clinics, and from voluntary sector clinics such as Brook Advisory Centres, which receive grants from central government or from health authorities. Women have freedom of choice as to where they go. Abortions are available either under NHS provision or from voluntary agencies such as the British Pregnancy Advisory Service. Financial machinery of the NHS has led to closure of many Family Planning Clinics. This saves money for health authorities but it costs more overall for service to be provided by GPs. It also limits choice for consumers.

A number of themes emerge from this history which are important to our discussion. The first is the attitude of the medical profession to contraception. From an actively hostile and negative approach to the whole business of fertility control, the medical profession as a whole has now become the gate-keeper to most forms of contraception. If a woman decides to opt out of the medical system she is left only with condoms, the sponge, spermicides or natural family planning (including coitus interruptus). Systemic hormonal contraception surely owes its prevalence to the medicalization of contraception in general, and the gradual professionalization of its status. This is a mixed development, from which women have both benefited and lost out.

Another significant thread that runs through this history is the desire of writers and thinkers on contraception to prevent the poor and the unsuitable from having too many children, a thread that runs into the early years of the twentieth century. Marie Stopes in *Wise Parenthood*, in its nineteenth edition in 1935, wrote: 'from a variety of causes our race is weakened by an appallingly high percentage of unfit weaklings and diseased individuals . . . when the vicious and feeble-minded people reproduce, they do so recklessly . . . only children with the chance of

attaining strong, beautiful and intelligent maturity should be conceived.'
Alcoholism, for example was considered to be hereditary, as were all
sorts of other so-called 'mental' deficiencies. The desire to protect the
race was as strong a motive as any other for the gradual development of
state provision of birth-control. Interestingly, though clothed in different
language, many aspects of this way of looking at class and race have been
carried into current contraceptive politics, particularly in the way that
the northern hemisphere worries about the over-production of babies
in the southern hemisphere. Certainly, it is true that if populations in
developing countries continue to grow in the way they are currently
doing, they will have more of a struggle to feed their people in the next
century. But the question is also one of resources. Far from recognizing
that the question *is* one of resources (an American baby can expect to
use up to forty times more of the world's resources than a baby born in
India), and often racist attitudes (the British, for example, are just
as tightly packed into Britain as Indians are into India), Western
governments continue to fund inappropriate and ineffectual family
planning programmes in developing countries. Above all, family planning
programmes cannot hope to be widely accepted until the problem of
child survival is lessened.

A further continuity in the history of contraception can be seen in the
role of the condom, which has moved from being seen largely as a
prophylactic against disease to a very popular contraceptive. Now, when
the spectre of AIDS confronts our sexual behaviour, we are witnessing
vigorous attempts to return the condom to its original prophylactic
role.

There are obviously many more themes that could be picked out and
discussed but we turn now to a fuller discussion of the social, medical
and political contexts which have determined the contraceptive options
currently open to us.

The context of contraceptive choice today

*The use of contraceptive methods is not a pleasant matter for most people. The regular
taking of hormones to inhibit fertility, the fitting of a cap, diaphragm or condom, the
'insertion' of an IUD and the prospect of a sterilization operation are not experiences to
which individuals look forward with any sense of pleasurable anticipation. Indeed, the
reverse is nearer to reality. The methods of fertility regulation from which most couples
choose represent a choice among unpleasant alternatives. This choice is not so much a
positive discrimination but a negative one, in that the methods not chosen are even more
disliked than the method that is chosen. The contraceptive methods most people use are
therefore the least unpleasant of an unpleasant set of alternatives. However, it is most*

*important that this realistic summary is set against the other reality that consumers
greatly prefer the available range of methods to no methods at all.*
                                        Robert Snowden, *Consumer Choices in Family Planning*

What are we to make of the institutionalization of our fertility? Given a
multimillion pound industry, controlled at one level by the multi-
nationals who manufacture and distribute contraceptives, and at another
by the doctors who prescribe them, and a corresponding sexual ideology
spread through the media, how are we to evaluate the freedom of
women's choices, their ability to make decisions that are in their own
best interests? What are the factors that undermine that process? In
order to consider this question more fully, we will start by looking at
how young people learn about sex and contraception and how women
in particular are encouraged to fall into line with myths about spontaneity
and appropriate sexual behaviour. Then we look at how gaining access
to contraception through the medical profession may reinforce these
ideas, how the medical establishment structures the provision of contraception, and, within its own ranks, the development of a 'contraceptive
career'. Finally we will provide a feminist critique of these issues and
show how prevailing ideologies may work directly against women's best
interests in the provision of contraception. In the pursuit of a particular
version of heterosexuality women may unwittingly participate in their
own bodily harm.

Learning about contraception
Contraceptive behaviour, like sex itself, is a learning process. Many
young people embarking on sex start off as risk-takers or use a risky
method such as withdrawal. In 1987 the Annual Report of the Brook
Advisory Centre commented on the overall poor awareness of contraceptive practice among teenagers. 'Some teenagers say they do not use
contraception because they think they are too young to conceive. Others
believe pregnancy is impossible if it is their first intercourse, if they have
sex infrequently, if they have a bath after intercourse, or if they have sex
standing up.' Quite clearly many learn to become efficient contraceptive
users quickly enough or the incidence of unwanted pregnancy in this
age-group would be higher than it is, but even so one half of all abortions
performed yearly are for women under twenty-five. Estimates of sexual
activity in the young are notoriously hard to get right and are highly
subjective. It seems reasonable to accept the estimate that 50 per cent
of teenagers have had some experience of sexual intercourse by the time
they are nineteen. Other surveys have suggested that one in five teenagers
have had some experience of intercourse by the time they are sixteen,

though only one in eight teenage girls. The law putting the age of consent at sixteen for girls which purports to protect them, could well be acting in the opposite way by exposing them to accidental pregnancy. Some girls under sixteen are (mistakenly) frightened of being prosecuted for having sexual intercourse, and equally frightened of getting their boyfriends prosecuted. For this reason they may be unwilling to seek contraceptive advice, despite the clarification of the legal situation since the efforts of Mrs Gillick. However, in a survey of contraceptive usage among a random sample of about 1500 teenagers aged 16–19, carried out in the mid-70s, only 8 per cent of the sexually active informants had never used any form of contraception. Twenty-seven per cent claimed to have used the safe period or withdrawal as their first method, while 52 per cent had used a condom first of all and 74 per cent had used condoms at some time. The pill had been used by 48 per cent of the sexually active sample.[6] A clear pattern emerged. Couples often began with a risky method, such as withdrawal or the safe period, and moved on to a more reliable method, such as condoms or the pill, once relationships became established. But what factors encourage or discourage contraceptive behaviour? And why do some people remain perpetual risk-takers?

For a large number of teenagers, as they become sexually active, the idea of a pregnancy is very remote. In the main their sexuality and their image of themselves is not constructed around any conscious idea of fertility or parenting. In an interesting conference paper on 'The Consequences of Teenage Sexual Activity' the agony aunt of *Woman's Own* outlined from her own experience some of the reasons that young people embark on sex. Discounting as spurious reasons such as earlier physical maturation, lack of moral guidance, a permissive society or emotional immaturity, she suggested that far more important are the quest for status, the bid to establish a sexual identity in the face of parents' attempts to pretend that sex doesn't exist until marriage, and above all, the quest for love.

Most of the teenagers who engage in sexual activity are in it for the same reasons that most adults are in it i.e. for the loving arms, and the warmth, and the reassurance that one matters, and the comfort, and the touching, and the skin-to-skin communication. For, once out of childhood, the only way we can find these things is in a sexual context, so strictly do we limit the word love to its sexual expression between two adults. Adolescents, so lately out of the age to be cuddled and hugged are particularly vulnerable to the sudden drop in temperature . . . a great deal of sexual adventure is a disguised search for warmth and love rather than a mate.[7]

This quest for love, for 'beautiful sex . . . the passionate embrace of masculinity and femininity'[8] is the driving force at whatever age we become heterosexually active. But with maturity it is easier to accept that sex is only as good as what gets put into it; and that *ipso facto* it cannot fulfil the longings and dreams that we invest there. It cannot offer meaning, identity, wholeness, unless those making love have already discovered meaning and identity outside their sexuality. For some young people sex not only fails to deliver the fulfilment they were seeking, but it also fails to deliver one of the more unambitious of their expectations: pleasure. In a recent interview with 150 young American women about their sexuality, not one of them mentioned pleasure. The best they said was that it didn't hurt. The meaning of their sexuality was tied up in the *relationship*, the story of what was happening to them in this particular drama of their lives. The socialization of girls ensures that most will look to a relationship with a man as the focus around which the rest of their lives will revolve. Often as long as the relationship holds together, young women will put up with an awful lot. One young woman explained to us 'When I went back to the doctor I told him that the pill had taken away all my feelings (libido). He half-jokingly said that it might be the relationship, which really upset me. But he was probably right. I still have all the feelings – for example if I see a sexy film, but I can't seem to feel like that when we do it. I feel a bit cheated.' Yet she had no intention of leaving her man, or discussing her feelings with him. The relationship will take priority over everything else that life has to offer.

One of the most important ways in which we learn about sexual roles and sexual behaviour is from the media and popular culture. Many media images of sex are both unrealistic and irresponsible. References to sex are extraordinarily frequent. On American TV viewers can expect three to four references to sex per hour of watching and in six out of seven encounters the couples are not married to each other. In six months one American soap opera had eight divorces, two bigamous marriages and twenty-one couples had sex out of wedlock. The average soap opera couple apparently has sex every 2.5 hours.[9] In the vast majority of television sex nobody mentions contraception. Nobody mentions the possibility of sexually transmitted disease or unwanted pregnancy *unless* this is the focus of the programme. Sex is, above all else, *spontaneous and romantic* which is another way of saying that the man initiates and the woman gets carried away. Obviously there are exceptions; the influence of feminist ideas, and caution in a post-AIDS era, has changed things to a certain extent, but in the main, the images of sexuality with which we grow up endorse the idea of heterosexual sex as beautiful, passionate, spontaneous and initiated by powerful men.

It is arguable that popular ideologies of sex have a direct bearing on pregnancy rates among young people. The lowest incidence of induced abortion in the world occurs in the Netherlands, with only 18,000 abortions per 180,000 live births a year. The pregnancy rate among adolescent women is only 14 per 1000, compared with 45 per 1000 in England and Wales and 96 per 1000 in the USA. Some of the literature on the subject argues that the low rate of pregnancies achieved in the Netherlands derives from the matter-of-fact way in which adolescent sexuality is accepted and the wide-spread provision of formal and informal sex education, counselling services and contraception, including 'morning-after' contraception. This contrasts strongly with attitudes in the USA where media-fostered romantic views of sex and the belief in mutual attraction that wordlessly sweeps young people off their feet are not backed up with proper sex education or easily accessible contraceptive services. The result is high adolescent pregnancy and abortion rates.[10]

Expectations derived from the media and popular culture are important factors that shape a young woman's first encounters with her own and another's sexuality. She may also have a background which has led her to believe that getting pregnant outside marriage is the worst thing that can happen to her, that sex before marriage is wrong, and that contraception is embarrassing and difficult to get hold of. In the latter case she may well be right. Robert Snowden describes the acquisition of contraception as 'a series of personal inconveniences'. The inconveniences are accentuated because 'there is no immediate benefit to be gained; the benefit of the prevention of a possible future pregnancy is not only a long-term one, but it is, in a sense, only a hypothetical benefit, as the pregnancy is only a possibility and not an actuality.'[11] For a young woman who has no proof of her fertility, no certainty that a relationship is going to become sexual and no confidence in negotiating the complicated institutional structures of family planning, acquiring contraception may be all but impossible. Even the term 'family planning' may put her off. After all, few young people think about their sexuality in terms of planning families.

What are the sources from which young people learn about contraception? Some people are lucky. They grow up in an environment in which contraception is a naturally acquired piece of knowledge. They know what their parents do, they have older brothers and sisters. Other people acquire information from the media – though often in the form of stories about pill scares and so on. The recently high profile of the condom will have helped many young people to feel more confident about this particular piece of contraceptive softwear. In the book *My Mother Said*, the author found that the main source of information for girls was another female friend (80 per cent had discussed contraception with their best girl friends), and 71 per cent of boys had discussed it with other boys. Mothers were most commonly cited as the person that girls had found most helpful to talk to (62 per cent of the girls had talked to their mothers, but only 31 per cent of the boys had). Forty-two per cent of the sample had been given some information at school, on average when they were fourteen. Unfortunately the survey doesn't record whether they found it useful at the time and in subsequent years.[12]

One fact emerges again and again from much of the available literature on young people and contraception. This is the very limited information that is easily accessible to them, especially those who are not used to turning to books as a source of information. Lack of information is compounded by the lack of easy access to medical facilities. For young people who live in large, anonymous cities the problem may be less acute, especially if there is a Brook Advisory centre or an equivalent that they can turn to. For others there may be a huge gap between where they currently are and where they want to get to – protected against pregnancy in a way that is invisible to their partners (so that they can be *spontaneous*), invisible to their parents (so they won't get found out) and preferably invisible to their doctors. If a girl is under sixteen, anxieties about telling parents and legality is another hurdle to cross. Doctors who have to help young people through the consequences of an unwanted pregnancy know just how difficult and traumatic the quest for contraception can be.

In the first place obtaining contraception involves confronting the fact that you have become sexually active, not only once 'by mistake' or as an experiment, but that you intend, deliberately to carry on. We well remember being told that nice girls get pregnant because they make mistakes and get carried away; bad girls don't get pregnant because they take precautions. In other words their sex is premeditated. Facing up to your sexuality is doubly difficult if you are treated as non-sexual by parents and teachers. This issue of being able to accept the fact of active sexuality is the key factor in early contraceptive or non-contraceptive usage and it goes right to the heart of our deepest feelings about our sexuality, volition, our rights to our own bodies. One university student described her own struggle like this:

I began to get closer and closer to my boyfriend; we were sharing the same bed most nights, and doing everything but having intercourse. It still didn't occur to me to begin to use contraception, since it was absolutely taboo for me to go all the way. Then my period was about a week late, and I realized that we had been close enough to risk a conception, however unlikely it would have been. I went to the local (anonymous) family planning clinic . . .

Secondly, obtaining contraception goes against the socialization of many girls. They need to be active and assertive about their own needs to go through the rite of passage of obtaining contraception for the first time. But girls grow up learning not to make a nuisance of themselves, not to ask awkward questions, even at great personal cost to themselves. To stop and say 'Excuse me but what about contraception' is very difficult for many girls who fear they will be rejected. Thirdly, by seeking out contraception one is acknowledging the fact of fertility and recognizing that it has no place in your life for the time being – that the sex you want is non-procreative. Some people have argued that this in itself is difficult for some women to accept, even when they know they do not want babies. In order to cope with the tension they need to feel that they are simply delaying a baby for a short time. Fourthly, logistical problems may finally deter some women. One doctor recalled how a sixteen-year-old had come to see her with an unplanned pregnancy:

She lived in a small village and had gone to her GP for the pill. There she met an elderly locum doctor; she told him she was engaged to be married because she thought this would ensure he would prescribe. He told her that the human race was wearing out its genital organs and she should learn to behave like the local wild deer and have intercourse very infrequently; he did not prescribe. . . . The patient considered going to the FP clinic. This was some miles away in the nearest town where, for the convenience of the majority of their customers the clinic was held in the evening. The last bus for this girl's village left at 4.30 p.m.[13]

The American edition of *Our Bodies Ourselves* gives a good summary of the reasons young people give for not using contraception. It includes most of those outlined above, but adds some others: embarrassment, shame and confusion about sexuality; inability to admit to having intercourse; unrealistically romantic ideas about sex. It has to be spontaneous and passionate, and contraception seems too premeditated; fear of 'inconveniencing a partner' – a sign of the inequality of many relationships; fear of a moralizing and disapproving practitioner; belief that it 'can't happen to me'; failure to recognize deep dissatisfaction with the method being used and using it haphazardly; submitting to the temptation to become pregnant to prove fertility, to improve a shaky relationship, or to have someone to care for.[14]

Overcoming these barriers to using contraception becomes much easier with maturity. Links with home are severed to some extent. Confronting institutions (even your local surgery) becomes easier with practice. Young women who already visit their doctors on their own for other things may find that they broach the subject of contraception anyway. Women who have gone away to college are in the easiest position, since students are expected to be sexually active and therefore to need good contraceptive services laid on for them. The temptation to resolve a relationship or a personal crisis through pregnancy may become less appealing when other resources are available to fall back on. More realistic ideas about sex and sexuality develop in time. Even so, the fact that abortions to women under twenty-five account for only 50 per cent of the total performed each year suggests that even with greater maturity people risk pregnancy for a variety of reasons.

Not all these unwanted pregnancies in older women can be accounted for by burst condoms, or lost IUDs. There are probably as many reasons for needing an abortion as there are women seeking them, but in *Sex and Destiny* Germaine Greer cites an interesting study of one aspect of unwanted pregnancy. The doctor carrying out this study of women who had a perfectly competent understanding of contraception and no problem of access to supplies coined the phrase 'wilful exposure to unwanted pregnancy'. It seems that all the women who became pregnant did so during a time of considerable personal stress. Somehow, in a way that is by no means understood, their fertility came to the fore, quite unintentionally, as a response to stresses in other areas of their lives.[15] Other women may deliberately risk a pregnancy to test their fertility. Fears about never being able to conceive a child, about growing old, about not finding fulfilment in life may lead a woman to see conception as reassurance or some kind of a solution. However, in time, the vast majority of sexually active women in Britain become users of contraception. This means, for about 4 million women a year, encountering a highly complex system of contraceptive provision.

The medical provision of contraception in Britain today
In order to understand the way in which the provision of contraception is organized in Britain it is necessary to know a little bit about the structure of the NHS and GP provision. Basically GPs are not employees of the National Health Service. Rather, each practice is in effect a small business run by the doctors who have a contract with the Family Practitioner Committee to provide medical services for those people listed as patients. They receive from the NHS an allowance for running the practice, an annual fee for the patients on their lists and extra money if they provide contraception and maternity services – in the case of the former, on an item by item basis. Individual practices can choose how to spend the money they receive and it is this that accounts for the

often disconcerting differences between practices. Some practices take women's health very seriously, organizing well-woman sessions and training for doctors in contraceptive provision. Others try and employ at least one woman GP, even if only on a part-time basis so that their patients have the option of seeing a woman. Other practices do much less.

In July 1975 the NHS was reorganized to allow GPs to enter into a contract with their Family Practitioner Committees to provide free contraception for patients, and for patients not registered with them. A scale of payments was eventually worked out, known as Items of Service fees. At the moment this stands at £11.65 a year for general contraceptive advice (which includes prescribing the pill and fitting diaphragms) and £39.05 for fitting an IUD. This is why when you attend a GP for contraceptives you may be asked to sign a yellow form stating that you have received what you came for. In 1974 GPs had elected not to prescribe condoms. As one letter to the *Lancet* put it, 'It is surely the last straw if the government intends to insult us by filling our surgeries with a lot of louts queuing up for the issue of condoms.'[16] Hopes that this anachronistic attitude will change with the necessity of condoms in the fight against AIDS, and a more positive approach to the role of men in the business of contraception, must be tempered by the knowledge that Family Planning Clinics are closing down in Britain.

By 1982 something like 97 per cent of all GPs had opted to provide a contraceptive service for their patients. This meant some 27,000 individual doctors, which clearly improved the ease of access to family planning services. GPs who provide this service have a C after their names in the list of family doctors available in libraries and post offices. At the same time there are approximately 1,800 family planning clinics up and down the country. These are the progeny of the earliest family planning clinics, set up in the late 1920s and increasing in number until by the 1970s they were almost exclusively responsible for the provision of contraceptive advice. They are currently funded not by the NHS but by District Health Authorities. Sadly today a number are faced with closure. In 1982 there were approximately 3.7 million users of family planning services. Sixty per cent went to GPs and 40 per cent to clinics. In 1983 the number of users had increased to over 4 million, and 55 per cent chose their GPs while 45 per cent opted for clinics.[17] There are a number of good reasons for fighting to keep both these sources of contraceptive provision. As we write this book the new government white paper on the National Health Service threatens to bring about many sweeping changes which may well affect the provision of contraceptive services.

Although on the face of it GPs offer a comprehensive contraceptive service, the fact remains that many of the GPs who have opted to provide contraception for their patients have not received any special training to do so. This means that they are not properly qualified to fit IUDs, diaphragms and caps, or to teach natural family planning (NFP). They are best at writing prescriptions for the pill, which they do over 90 per cent of the time. Certainly over the past decade the training of GPs in this area has improved considerably. In the first place contraception features in undergraduate training courses. In the second, the Joint Committee on Contraception (JCC) was set up in 1972 by the Royal College of Obstetricians and Gynaecologists together with the Royal College of General Practitioners and the National Association of Family Planning Doctors to supervise training in this area and to issue a certificate to doctors who have completed the JCC training course. The course has practical as well as theoretical components and it is fortunately becoming standard practice for young doctors undertaking GP training to obtain the JCC certificate. Unfortunately however, it is by no means mandatory for doctors already offering contraceptive advice. Even for GPs who have undertaken some training, the trend has been to complete the theoretical side but not the practical, which is why some GPs offer such a limited service – the pill or the pill. One of the adverse effects of this situation is that a woman may not be offered a proper choice. She may assume that the doctor prescribes the pill because the pill is the choice for her, not because he has little else on offer. Most women have no idea that their GPs may not be able to offer them a full choice of methods.

Our knowledge of what goes on in GPs surgeries when women ask for advice on contraception has been considerably improved by the studies carried out by the Institute of Population Studies, University of Exeter under Robert Snowden, and published as *Consumer Choices in Family Planning* by the FPA. His team conducted research involving 10,000 women, 1,200 men and medical teams in over 60 clinics and surgeries, over a period of four and a half years. Their aim was to look at the ways in which women 'exercise their choice between the available sources of free contraceptive care currently available, and to document the part played by each major family planning service outlet . . . in the overall pattern of contraceptive provision.' The broadest finding of the study was that clinics offer a much wider choice than GPs and that women do in fact choose to benefit from this. Within the study areas chosen, they found that the pill was prescribed 84 per cent of the time by GPs but only 55 per cent of the time by clinics; IUDs accounted for 23 per cent of the methods in the clinic and 10 per cent from GPs (though this is higher than the national average of IUDs fitted by GPs in 1982 which was only 4.9 per cent of all methods). Vaginal barriers were only prescribed 2 per cent of the time by GPs, and 9 per cent of the time by clinics. The team conducted a postal survey among doctors in the study area and found that 100 per cent of the respondents said that they prescribed the pill, and 98 per cent that they did frequently. This contrasts with the 43 per cent who said they fitted the cap and only 3 per cent who said they did so frequently. There seemed to be evidence that GPs who had attended a training course offered a better service, in that 71 per cent of them undertook IUD fittings compared to only 25 per cent who had not attended a course. Perhaps we should be grateful that that figure is not higher.

In the last few years, as more doctors complete the JCC training, GP surgeries are much more likely to have at least one partner who fits IUDs, diaphragms and caps. DHSS figures show a gradual rise in the number of IUDs being fitted or checked by GPs and a corresponding decline in the number of fittings performed in family planning clinics, though the latter still far outnumber those fitted by GPs. Doctors who themselves do not feel competent to fit barriers and IUDs may be quite happy to refer a patient to a family planning clinic, rather than persuading her to opt for a hormonal form of contraception. In fact there is some evidence that doctors who have completed a JCC training are more likely to refer patients to clinics than those who have not. Clinics themselves have been expanding their services and the range of contraceptives they offer. The methods that were distributed from clinics in 1982 can be broken down into percentages. The pill still came top at 57.2 per cent, followed by the IUD (16.8 per cent), condoms (10.0 per cent), female barriers (7.8 per cent), other (2.3 per cent) and advice only, but no method, in 5.9 per cent of the cases.

Snowden's study found that young women were more likely to start off by going to their GP, and that women spacing children and therefore already seeing their GP with their children were also likely to choose the surgery as their source of contraception. His team found that women transferred from their GP to a clinic for a variety of reasons, including convenience, but more often because they became worried about the side-effects of the method they were using and wanted a second opinion or a change in the contraceptive they used. This accounts for the fact that among pill-users who transfer from general practice to clinics only 58 per cent continue with the same method. But among pill-users transferring from one GP to another 91 per cent continue with the pill. Some women prefer clinics not only because of the wider choice of methods and other services (screening, counselling and so on) but because of their relative anonymity; or because they are less disease-oriented, or because women constitute a relatively high proportion of clinic doctors. But other women find the degree of anonymity off-putting, and the exclusive emphasis on sexuality and contraception embarrassing. They prefer the atmosphere of a GPs waiting room where nobody can guess what they have come for. All in all it seems crucial that these two systems should continue to run side by side.

Trends in contraceptive use since 1970

Accurate statistics on the use of contraceptives are extremely difficult to come by. Surveys carried out in the same year frequently differ and, at best, we are dealing only with very approximate figures. Most surveys question only small samples of people and extrapolate from these. A set of often quoted results from National Surveys is given in Figure 2.4.

Figure 2.4   Ever-married women aged 16–39/40: trends in current use of contraception

Method used	Name and year of survey			
	Family Planning Services E&W 1970 %	Family Planning Services E&W 1975 %	Family Formation GB 1976 %	TNR 1987 %
Pill	19	30	32	23
IUD	4	6	8	7
Condom	28	18	16	16
Cap	4	2	2	n/a
Withdrawal	14	5	5	n/a
Safe period	5	1	1	n/a
Abstinence	3	1	0	n/a
Other	—	3	1	6
Total	71	63	61	n/a
Sterilization – female	n/a	n/a	8	n/a
– male	n/a	n/a	8	n/a
– both	4	13	15	27
Non-users	25	24	23	23
Base = 100%	2,520	2,344	3,378	1,061

NB: The 1970 and 1975 data are for ever-married women aged 16–40 in England and Wales, whereas the 1976 data is for those aged 16–39 in Great Britain. The 1987 survey includes all women aged 16–44.
Source: 'Contraceptive trends in Great Britain', *Fact Sheet* C3, Family Planning Information Service, FPA, Jan. 1989.

Another study of contraceptive usage, using a much bigger sample of 5,866 respondents was carried out in the General Household Survey (GHS) in 1986 at the request of the DHSS and published in 1989. (See Figure 2.5 below.) Women aged sixteen to forty-nine were asked a limited number of questions on their use of contraception. The major trend to emerge was the very high level of contraceptive use. Seventy-one per cent of all respondents used contraception. Among married and cohabiting couples the figure rose to 81 per cent and fell to 48 per cent among single people. Of the 29 per cent not using any form of contraception 6 per cent were already pregnant or intending to have a child, 3 per cent were subfertile, and 3 per cent used natural family planning (the study classified forms of NFP as a non-contraceptive method). Of the remaining non-users some were not involved in a sexual relationship, others were involved in a gay relationship and others were sexually active and risking an unplanned pregnancy. It seems likely however that the number of sexually active couples in Britain not practising contraception must be under 10 per cent – demonstrating beyond doubt the impact of the family planning movement. (Compare this with the picture in the USA, where recent surveys suggest that as many as 45 per cent of the population aged fifteen to forty-four use no method of contraception.) Another trend to emerge from the 1986 GHS survey was a decline in the proportion of women taking the pill – down to 23 per cent from a high of 38 per cent in 1975. This, however, was a selective shift, and the pill today is as popular as ever among young women.

The popularity of the pill seems to wax and wane according to the latest scare, as we will see in the chapter on hormonal contraception. The most significant trend to emerge recently is the rise in the number of sterilizations performed: in 1976, 13 per cent of women (aged 18–44) or their partners were sterilized, compared to 23 per cent by 1986. Sterilization is now the most popular method of contraception amongst married or cohabiting women aged eighteen to forty-four. IUD use peaked in 1979, and subsequently fell, though there is some evidence that a new generation of devices may lead the IUD to stage a comeback. In 1986 there was still no sign of the predicted return of barriers – especially female barriers which remain a minority method. The condom's history has been chequered in recent years, with sales falling off between 1976 and 1982. Not surprisingly condom sales are now rising again, which we will discuss in the chapter on male methods. It has been argued that the last two decades have witnessed two distinct phases in contraception. The decade from the mid-60s to the mid-70s was marked by a decline in mechanical methods and withdrawal, and a swift rise in

Figure 2.5   Percentage of contraceptive use by age of woman: Great Britain 1986

Current use of contraception

	Age								Total
	16–17	18–19	20–24	25–29	30–34	35–39	40–44	45–49	
	%	%	%	%	%	%	%	%	%
Using method(s)									
Non-Surgical*:									
Pill	20	42	55	38	21	8	4	1	23
IUD	1	1	4	9	11	10	7	5	7
Condom	6	6	9	13	15	15	14	16	13
Cap	nil	nil	2	3	4	2	2	2	2
Withdrawal	1	2	3	4	4	4	6	8	4
Safe period	1	1	2	2	2	1	2	1	1
Spermicides	nil	nil	1	1	1	1	1	1	1
Other	nil	ø	ø	ø	ø	nil	nil	nil	ø
At least one	27	50	71	65	54	39	32	31	49
Surgical:									
Sterilization – female	nil	nil	1	3	10	20	28	21	12
– male	nil	nil	ø	4	15	22	20	13	11
(total sterilization)			1	6	25	42	48	35	23
Total – at least one (users)	27	50	72	72	79	80	81	66	71

Not using a method

Sterile after operation	nil	nil	0	1	1	2	6	11	3
Pregnant now	2	6	6	9	5	2	0	nil	4
Going without sex to avoid pregnancy	15	10	4	2	1	1	1	1	3
No sexual relationship	54	32	13	7	6	7	6	9	12
Wants to get pregnant	nil	1	3	5	4	3	1	1	2
Unlikely to conceive because of menopause	nil	nil	nil	nil	nil	nil	1	9	12
Possibly infertile	nil	nil	0	1	1	4	2	2	2
Doesn't like contraception	1	2	1	2	2	1	2	2	2
Just doesn't like contraception	0	nil	0	0	1	0	1	0	0
Breastfeeding	nil	nil	0	0	0	nil	nil	nil	0
Other	nil	nil	0	2	1	0	nil	0	0
Total (non-users)	73	50	28	29	22	21	20	35	29
Base = 100%†	352	317	877	953	893	1023	816	635	5866

ø less than 0.5%

* Abstinence is not included here as a method of contraception. Those who said that 'going without sex to avoid getting pregnant' was their only method of contraception are shown with others not using a method.

† Percentages add to more than 100 because of rounding and because some women used more than one non-surgical method.

Source: *General Household Survey 1986*, Series GHS No. 16, HMSO, 1989.

the level of hormonal contraception. The following decade saw a move away from oral contraceptives (among certain groups) with a substantial rise in the popularity of sterilization.

Kaye Wellings, a former research officer with the FPA from whose work many of these details come, offers an interesting conclusion to her research. She suggests that 'in general, contraceptive usage in this country must be reaching saturation point: we are rapidly approaching near universal, highly effective contraceptive usage . . . Gains in the popularity of any method are therefore most likely to come about at the expense of existing methods.[18] It seems worth pointing out in response to her conclusion that quantity is not the same as quality, and quality in family planning statistics is usually measured only in terms of effectiveness. One of the problems with many studies of contraceptive usage is that they concentrate on how many do what, and miss out on some of the more important and interesting human questions behind the figures. We will look at some of these later in the chapter.

The doctors' view
Doctors who receive training in family planning are likely to be taught to think about the different contraceptive needs of women at different points in their lives. Some find the classification 'delayers', 'spacers' and 'stoppers' helpful, while others opt for a more detailed model, such as that included by the doyen of family planners, John Guillebaud, in his book *Contraception: Your Questions Answered*. He calls his model 'the seven contraceptive ages of woman', and we have reproduced it opposite.

The idea behind these classifications is a simple one. The contraceptive needs of a woman of eighteen and a woman of thirty-five are likely to be different; a woman who wants no more babies will see contraception in a different light to a woman who hopes to conceive in the course of the next year. Guillebaud sees the interplay between three main factors – maximum safety, maximum effectiveness, and separation from intercourse – as varying in their relative importance during a couple's reproductive life span. He rightly points out that this changing pattern of 'reproductive desire' places a considerable responsibility on the doctor or nurse to be well informed about the whole range of methods available. But while these classifications of women into different contraceptive 'ages' may be helpful to doctors and nurses, and in the main Guillebaud's 'suggested methods' are ones we would endorse, there are always problems for women when they walk into predetermined categories.

Quite clearly, a medical practitioner's view of the woman in question will depend on certain things. Some will be the medically determined things like high blood pressure, a history of thrombosis or a disability of

Figure 2.6 The seven contraceptive ages of woman

'Age'	Suggested Method
1. Birth to puberty	No method required. However, responsible matter-of-fact sex education is essential – principally from the parents.
2. Puberty to marriage	Either (a) a barrier method (sheath or cap plus spermicide) or (b) the combined pill, or (c) the best oral contraceptive (i.e. saying no). Choice depends on factors like religious views, the steadiness of the relationship, and frequency of intercourse.
3. Marriage to first child	First choice usually the combined pill, followed by a barrier method for 3 months before 'trying' for the first child. Sponge also usable.
4. During breastfeeding	First choice: barrier method – could be the sponge until periods start. Second choice: (a) IUD (but a small risk to future fertility); (b) Progestogen-only pill (but unknown effect of the minute amount of hormone transferred in the breast milk).
5. Family spacing after breastfeeding	Perhaps shift to combined pill at this time for greater effectiveness and a regular bleeding pattern.
6. After the (probable) last child	First choice: IUD. Other possibilities: barrier methods or the oestrogen-free hormonal methods, according to choice.
7. Family complete, children growing up and other methods unacceptable	Vasectomy: or female sterilization using clips or rings.

Source: John Guillebaud, *Contraception: Your Questions Answered*, Churchill Livingstone, 1985.

some description. Doctors are taught as undergraduates that they should understand medicine in physical, psychological and social terms. But doctors and other medical professionals are not immune to social stereotypes; nor are they immune to popular expectations about sexual behaviour – that sex should be spontaneous, and contraception independent of intercourse (as far as possible). Advertisements for the pill (which only feature in medical magazines) reinforce traditional ideas of femininity: 'The gentle touch/and no lower dose in oral contraception'; 'It's the least you can give a girl' (this advertisement seems to work by making the doctor some kind of ally or participant in the woman's sexuality). The important point however is that allowing doctors to use their medical, psychological and social 'knowledge' to construct a contraceptive profile for individual women may undermine women's ability to choose for themselves, or even to really assess their own needs at any given point. It is symptomatic of the approach of the medical profession to women's fertility that women are not really in a position to evaluate their own needs and make their own requests. True, women are often handicapped by a really appalling lack of information about the workings of their own bodies and about the ways in which fertility can be regulated. Many women on the pill have no idea what brand they are taking, let alone how it works. A woman lacking knowledge and accurate information is powerless to make informed decisions about her own well-being. She may be fortunate if her doctor is following a sympathetic model of changing contraceptive needs at different stages.

For other women however, classifications of their contraceptive needs may run counter to what they want. Women wanting to practise natural family planning may not fit conveniently into their doctor's view of what is appropriate practice. Women wanting to try a cervical cap may be discouraged in favour of a diaphragm. Young women may want to be sterilized, and find that it does not fit in with their doctor's view of appropriate reproductive behaviour. Women who want no children at all may object to their doctor's view of them as potential mothers.

The views of doctors may at times have unfortunate consequences, especially when they become prejudices. Studies have shown that some methods get prescribed to certain groups of women more often than others because they require only a low motivation for their use. Snowden cites a study where in one area proportionately greater numbers of council house tenants attending family planning clinics were fitted with IUDs than were women who were either renting private accommodation or buying their own houses. Jill Rakusen documents cases in Leeds where the injectable contraceptive depo-provera has been given to Asian women at the same time as a routine post-delivery rubella injection. While this package is given to some white women too, it has been mainly offered to Asian women though the evidence that Asian women are more in need of rubella injections has been questioned.[19] The use of the word 'feckless' in medical textbooks to describe a particular 'type' of woman has been documented by Hilary Thomas. She cites a leading article in the *British Medical Journal* in 1972 referring to the need for contraceptive provision to be made available within the NHS before doctors could '. . . feel free to urge feckless, fecund multigravidae to agree to some sort of long-term defence against repeated pregnancy'.[20] The idea of large planned families is rarely mentioned.

Finally, the choice offered to a woman may be in part determined by the provider's own preferences. Potts and Diggory put it like this:

The provider's own confidence in the method being offered is of overriding importance. There is no purpose in recommending a method you yourself don't believe in. If you would not be prepared to use oral contraceptives, or to have a vasectomy, you are unlikely to be successful in advocating these methods to others . . . The person sitting opposite to you needs to know the answer to the question 'Would you use this method yourself?'[21]

In some respects this is obvious. A doctor who has anxieties about the safety of oral contraceptives is not going to push them onto a patient. But in other ways it is a worrying observation. Just because a provider of contraception doesn't like barriers himself should be no reason at all why he should not be objective and sensitive to the needs of the person seeking advice. If a woman feels confident that the method of contraception she is seeking is right for her, and if she is accurately informed, why should it matter a jot what the person sitting on the other side of the table thinks? There is a lack of good information among women, which creates a lack of self-confidence in them and a lack of equality in their relationship with their medical advisors. But how can women take responsibility for their health and their behaviour if their desire to do so is undermined by a professionalism that excludes them? Women should be able to approach the medical profession for information and advice alone, not approval.

A feminist perspective

[The] consistent denial of our ability to make decisions about what we do and when we do it is a crucial part of attitudes to romantic love and the role that women have within it, and is tremendously difficult to fight.

Rose Shapiro, Contraception

We have tried to ensure that the whole of this book is written within a feminist framework. We have asked at each point 'how does this affect the position of women; how far does it improve the options open to them, and how far limit them?' In this short section we want to concentrate specifically on the feminist issues that contraception raises. These are questions of bodily harm and bodily well-being; autonomy and dependency; the construction of a particular type of sexual behaviour; and questions of classism and racism.

Bodily harm and bodily well-being

It will be apparent that understanding and protecting one's fertility is an important theme of this book. Questions of bodily harm and bodily well-being are critical to the whole area of reproductive and contraceptive politics. These questions are far ranging. We are not simply concerned with the long-term cancer risks of using certain oral contraceptives, though these are hardly unimportant and need always to be raised in a feminist context. Bodily well-being and freedom from bodily harm span the whole of our physicality, as 'experiences of one's body', and, since human beings are psychosomatic unities, affect the whole of our lives.

In the context of contraception it is vital to ask feminist questions about all of the available methods. Is a given method enhancing bodily well-being or undermining it? What risks are acceptable for the sake of avoiding an unwanted pregnancy? The answers will vary from woman to woman and time to time, but the response of individual women to their own experiences of a method must be accepted as authentic. It is a documented fact that doctors often label the side-effects of oral contraceptives, for example, as social and psychological in origin, rather than physiological. It may be true that if the pill is taken for long enough the woman's body will eventually 'settle down' and get used to it. Similarly a woman's uterus may finally 'settle down' and get used to an IUD. Or bouts of cystitis following the use of a diaphragm may become more acceptable. But at what cost to the woman? Is the cost one she is happy to put up with for the benefits gained? Or is she compromising herself and her own feelings of well-being? The important point is that a woman should feel she has the right to insist on her own well-being and on her right to be well informed, for if she doesn't then certainly no one else will.

Autonomy and dependency

Bodily well-being is always enhanced by feelings of autonomy, of being in control, but the process of obtaining contraception rarely encourages such feelings. Negotiating family planning facilities is rarely something that people look forward to with any sense of pleasure. Many women (and men) are unable to enter a medical setting without some form of anxiety, however fleeting. Entering a clinic involves entering another world which is controlled by doctors, not 'patients', as users of contraception automatically become. Even surgeries which try very hard to create a relaxed and informal environment cannot wholly succeed in undoing years of conditioning during which doctors were seen as important men with special knowledge who made us better. While many doctors have changed and see themselves as partners in health care with the people who consult them, this is by no means universally true, and the best that many doctors achieve is a friendly paternalism. Entering this world all too easily encourages us to shed our autonomy and believe that the doctor knows best. Women may be particularly vulnerable to this feeling of loss of autonomy. The apparent 'gap' in knowledge between the doctor and his or her patient may be partially responsible, but so, too, is much of the socialization of girls and women and the cult of professionalism.

All this affects the way in which a woman can subsequently think about contraception. A doctor has become involved in a complex triad which would normally only involve the women and her partner. As we saw from the pill advertisement quoted above, the selling technique for different contraceptives plays directly on this ambivalence: 'it's the least you can give a girl'. Contraception becomes a matter between a woman and her doctor, and in many cases her partner is only fleetingly involved. No one has really studied the dynamic of this relationship in the context of contraception. The doctor, or other medical person involved, becomes indirectly responsible for a significant aspect of a woman's sexual life. One of the ways in which women deal with this involvement is to divorce the whole question of obtaining contraception from their understanding of their own sexuality. They cope by playing the game and accepting contraception as a medical matter. The doctor's responsibility thus remains a medical one and not a sexual one, which would be intolerable. The way in which women cope with internal examinations provides a good example of this process. An internal examination involves seeing a part of one's anatomy in an entirely different context, where a new set of rules apply. Instead of a potentially erotic zone, the vagina becomes as asexual as a mouth at the dentist. Except that this switch of contexts is never quite complete. This intimate encounter with professionalism consequently leads to anxiety on the part of many women.

This complicated mixture of health, medical professionalism, sexuality, knowledge, power, and gender is central to the way in which women understand and use contraception. By seeing contraception as primarily a medical matter women are not only increasingly dependent on their doctors but are encouraged to seek medical solutions to problems that may be sexual and social. Unhappiness with any form of contraception may be a sign of unhappiness with a relationship. If a woman is lucky she will get some counselling from her doctor as well as a change in prescription. If she is unlucky she may be told that her body will adjust in time; and because she is afraid to question her doctor's wisdom she continues to see her problem as medical in origin – a matter between her and her doctor (in which he is the wiser) rather than psychosexual and a matter for herself and her partner.

If women are to feel in control of their health in any area of their lives they need to feel that their health is largely their own responsibility and that the medical profession is there in an advisory and technical capacity. Some medical people have gone a long way towards working this out with their patients. Others find the whole idea disturbing. Women always have the option of going elsewhere, though this in itself involves being assertive, and in some places the options are very limited indeed. The closure of clinics obviously reduces choice but women retain the right to go to any G.P., not only their own or another in the same practice.

Sexuality

Little girls and little boys grow up learning about romantic love. While the Sleeping Beauty lies supine for a hundred years, the handsome prince is riding the world and felling a forest in order to get to her; a perfect match of the active and passive, masculinity and femininity. From fairy stories and nursery rhymes children graduate to adolescence and popular culture. Here the subtle and less overtly sexual foundations laid down by nursery education are developed into the ideas about love, sexuality and relationships that shape all the longings and expectations of young adult life. What are these ideas? A flick through any girls' teenage magazine suggests an overwhelming preoccupation with finding love, and keeping it. Everything, from fashion and make-up to 'how to be a more interesting person' is aimed at finding a man, a centre which will order the rest of the difficult priorities of life. The message that our culture stresses over again is that at the centre of the lives of all real women there should be a relationship with a man.

Of course many women value their ability to form and sustain personal relationships and hold it as an important achievement in a world of corporate values. But problems arise when attitudes to romantic love prevent us from acting in our own best interests. Ideas about romantic love may prevent us from being assertive, and getting what we want from a relationship. This may range from being coerced into a sexual relationship sooner than we want to being too embarrassed to ask a partner to wear a condom. Some ideas about romantic love prevent equality in our relationships. Women are encouraged to believe that men have a right to be satisfied, to be spontaneous (not to have to struggle with a condom at the last minute), and that women should be equally spontaneous, always sexually available and responsive to their partners. The belief that men's sexuality is their primary concern extends well beyond early sexual behaviour. Many women are sterilized because they want to protect their partner's feelings of virility, despite the fact that female sterilization is a more complex procedure than vasectomy. In 'perfect' sex it is more often the woman who pays the price.

These popular expectations about sex have considerable importance for the way we see contraception. Rose Shapiro describes some of the consequences in her book *Contraception*. She writes:

The rules we learn about sex and contraception are clear. Sex begins with 'foreplay', which can include a range of activities which get us ready 'to go all the way' with intercourse and intromission. From the moment foreplay begins we lose the power of conscious and deliberate thought, which is why it's best if we contracept well in advance of the tidal wave. The best contraceptive is therefore the one that is least evident at this time, the one that 'does not interfere with making love'. We can be trusted not to become pregnant as long as the decision to use contraception is made well away from sex, so are advised to put in a diaphragm hours before the act occurs, take our pills as part of a nightly routine, or be protected from pregnancy every hour of every day with an IUD. We are promised that as long as we do this, sex can be 'spontaneous' (the word that covers all things sexual in family planning literature) and our minds can be the necessary blank.[22]

In the light of these observations we can return to the question we posed earlier in this chapter. Why is the diaphragm such an unpopular form of contraception, despite being so safe and effective? It is surely because it cuts across all these cultural norms of good sex. It requires forethought on the part of the woman even to have it available, so she has to anticipate that she will have sex. It requires familiarity and ease with one's body in order to put it in properly; it is visible, and is therefore a clear sign that a woman is not being 'natural' and spontaneous; it requires motivation and commitment to use it every time, to keep it in good condition and to ensure that it fits properly. In other words it is too dependent on women being continuously assertive about their needs. But instead of understanding these real reasons, the diaphragm is labelled as 'messy', unspontaneous, requiring more motivation than the average woman can manage and really only suitable for couples who make love occasionally. It is disappointing to find feminist literature reproducing traditional ideas about diaphragms as messy and unspontaneous. Natural methods of family planning are afflicted by many of the same prejudices.

It is tremendously difficult to work against conventional ideas of appropriate sexual behaviour for women. Women internalize the prevailing norms of society, believing that they should be sexually available for their partners and guilty if they are not, and that their ability to make decisions about what they do and when they do it is somehow questionable. The contraceptive culture of the West reinforces this. If experts in the field of family planning write that, among other things, the absolutely ideal contraceptive should be independent of intercourse and not rely on the user's memory, what are women to think other than that their ability to take decisions and act accordingly is being questioned? One of the gains of the woman's movement has been to encourage women to become more assertive in sexual relationships, more assertive about reproductive health and more confident in dealings with those who offer counselling in these areas.

Feminism and sexism, classism and racism

That fertility and contraception are areas in which anti-feminism, racism and classism are rife is all too clear from any reading of family-planning literature. In order to highlight the problem we will give just one example.

In a discussion of the effectiveness of the diaphragm, John Guillebaud cites the Oxford/FPA study, where the failure rate per 100 woman-years of use was an extremely low 1.9 (Pearl Index, see pp. 88–9). In order to explain away this low failure rate he comments that 'the women were basically "middle class" and were probably *unusually* well motivated and careful' (our italics).[23] It is true that the study involved white married women aged between twenty-five and thirty-nine who had already been using the diaphragm for five months at least when they joined the study. Even so, Guillebaud's comment is provocative, particularly when we set it alongside another study of diaphragm use (not cited by Guillebaud) which produced equally good results.[24] This study was carried out in New York and involved over 2,000 women, most below the age of thirty and unmarried – a very different cross-section of women from those in the Oxford FPA study. They had all been taught diaphragm use as simple, safe and effective. During the first year there were only thirty-seven pregnancies, and in twenty-two of these the women admitted to using their diaphragms inconsistently or not at all. (See Chapter 5, pp. 170–1.) Are we to conclude that all these women were also 'unusually well motivated and careful', or middle class, or not really sexually active, or sub-fertile, or any of the other reasons that are given to explain away successful diaphragm use? Why should we accept the prejudice that women are *not* usually well-motivated and careful?

In order to use the diaphragm successfully it is not necessary to be married, over thirty, white, middle class, sub-fertile and sexless. Women who are single, under twenty and have normal sex lives can also use the diaphragm perfectly successfully. So can women with little formal education, no job and no stable relationship. In other words the issue at stake is clearly not the diaphragm but the expectations and prejudices of the medical profession, which are themselves products of inbuilt social attitudes. In order to use the safer forms of contraception effectively, our requirements from the medical profession intensify. After all, it is far easier to write a prescription for the pill than to spend enough time explaining the use of a barrier to a woman so that she has the information and confidence needed to make a genuine choice about what she wants to use.

The starting point must be counselling, support, *good information* and a basic belief in women's ability, volition and motivation. If a woman has no idea about her anatomy or reproductive physiology and is not given appropriate counselling she is unlikely to make a success of a barrier method. But the problem here is with the prejudices of the system, and not with the woman. Guillebaud's comment on the Oxford FPA study, that 'the most fertile and least careful women, along with those with anatomical problems interfering with effectiveness of the method, would not have been available for recruitment – by virtue of already becoming pregnant!' is very disheartening.[25] It derives from precisely the opposite point of view, that the problem is with the woman and not with the system, and is cynical about women's ability, volition and motivation. As a result of such cynicism, good information, counselling and support are not forthcoming. Subsequent failures are blamed on the woman or the method, never on the counselling services. If women are confronted with prejudices like this, little wonder that control over reproductive rights is so hard to achieve.

Conclusion

In this chapter we have covered a wide range of issues relating to the provision of contraception in Britain, from statistics and history to the way in which young people learn about contraception and the way in which the medical profession structures the choices available to us. One of the themes throughout has been the question of access to information and knowledge. Without having information ourselves we remain at the mercy of those who do have access to information and who consequently create the world for us according to their understanding of it. Women with little formal education, and the young, may be particularly disadvantaged here.

It is often said that information is power. It is equally true that information is rarely disinterested and objective, but is subject to all sorts of hidden agendas; it has been one of the achievements of the feminist movement to point out the sexist implications of many of these agendas. One of the things that has become increasingly clear to us as we have researched and written this book is the different perspectives that books written for doctors, books written for women by doctors, and books written for women by other women adopt. Books on women's health written with the aim of demystifying professional information are in another category again, and we hope that this book fits into this category. Writing it is a specific attempt to make material that is inaccessible (medical journals), dull (medical text books), associated with doctors and disease (clinical literature), too technical (pill packet inserts) and unpleasant to look at and read (instructions issued with condoms, diaphragms and spermicides) interesting, usable and appropriate. Throughout the rest of this book we have tried to make as much information as possible available in a readable form. By this we hope to show that good information can act as a tool to empower women in their struggle for reproductive autonomy.

CHAPTER 3

Women and Contraception: Beginning to Take Control

Paternalism is the hallmark of much present-day health care. Professionals have learned a technical language which is not generally accessible to their clients . . . this control of information denies patients' autonomy and their right to self direction, and makes it extremely difficult . . . for them to break down the hierarchical relationships which are a norm of health care . . .

Christine Webb, *Feminist Practice in Women's Health Care*

This chapter is written more as a series of questions, checklists and questionnaires for women, designed to help you work out the nature of your own fertility and contraceptive needs. They need to be read in conjunction with the rest of the book, since there is not room here to do more than list possible difficulties or positive benefits of different methods. The reader is always referred to the fuller and more specific discussions contained in subsequent chapters.

Men, also, will find that Chapter 6 is devoted to their particular problems, Men are, more often than not, left out of the planning of contraception. This is partly because the history of the state provision of free contraception has been geared to mothers, and partly a response – which may well be unjustified – to the supposed lack of interest on the part of many men. None the less it is certainly the case that some men *are* concerned about their fertility and its potential. These matters are discussed in Chapter 6, which also includes special consideration of the two most frequently practised forms of male contraception, condoms and withdrawal.

Evaluating your needs

Evaluating your needs is the first step towards feeling comfortable and at ease with fertility. Doing so involves asking yourself a number of questions which may range from whether you need to use contraception at all to your attitudes to an unplanned pregnancy, and how well your method of contraception protects you from a sexually transmitted disease. Questions such as whether you would like a child, and if so when, whether you want more children, questions about your health and about your acceptance of side-effects are all relevant to deciding which kind of contraception you want to use. And of course you will also be concerned with safety and effectiveness.

Safety and effectiveness
Safety in this context means the relative risk to health from using any form of contraception. Effectiveness means the ability of a contraceptive method to protect you from pregnancy. As things stand at the moment there is an inverse relationship between safety and effectiveness: the safer a method of contraception in terms of your health, the less effective it has been shown to be in large studies. Diaphragms, condoms and NFP are theoretically less effective than pills and IUDs. Every woman needs to make up her mind about the degree of safety she expects from a form of contraception in relation to its effectiveness. But this is a very complicated area, for we are not dealing with clear cut risks or absolute certainties when it comes to effectiveness or safety. At best we have studies of the risks under both headings in the context of large numbers of women. These cohort studies do not necessarily tell us anything about how a particular woman will respond to the contraceptive in question, or how effective it will be in preventing pregnancy in her particular case.

However, certain themes emerge from all discussions of safety and effectiveness. Effectiveness is usually considered in two ways. Firstly there is the theoretical, or method-failure rate, and secondly the actual use-failure rate. The theoretical failure rate assumes that the method is being used exactly as it is supposed to be – no missed pills, no burst condoms, no expelled IUDs. It is the *best* result that can be expected from any form of contraception.

The use-failure rate is what actually happens in practice, including failure to use the method properly. If you only remember to take five pills out of every seven, any resulting pregnancy will be considered a failure of the use-effectiveness of the method. If a method is so unrealistic that a couple abandons it (as has been argued of natural family planning) their decision to abandon it is still measured as an aspect of use-effectiveness. Similarly if a couple don't like using the diaphragm and so leave it out, this is considered to be a problem inherent in the diaphragm and is included in use-effectiveness figures.

The effectiveness of a contraceptive method is often quoted using the Pearl Index. This figure is the number of pregnancies which occur in

100 woman-years of use of a particular method of contraception. It is calculated by multiplying the total number of accidental pregnancies that occur during the study period by 1200 (the number of months in 100 years) and dividing by the total months of use for all those using the method being studied, subtracting 10 months for any pregnancy and 4 months for any abortion), i.e.:

$$\text{failure rate per HWY} = \frac{\text{total accidental pregnancies} \times 1200}{\text{total months of use.}}$$

If this seems complicated there are even more complex ways of working out failure rates, particularly the life-table method of analysis which takes all sorts of other factors into account, such as long-term use and changes in fertility. Fortunately it is not necessary for individual women to work out the effectiveness of methods for themselves. The most often quoted recent survey is the Oxford/FPA study using the Pearl Index (see Figure 3.1, p. 90).

What does this mean in practice? It is not necessarily very helpful to know that if 100 couples use condoms for a year by the end of that year 3.6 of the women will be pregnant. In order to make this a bit more individually relevant it is helpful to work out from these figures the number of years of intercourse which would be *expected* to lead to one conception while using the method in question. In the case of condom use a couple could expect to have something like twenty-seven years of conception-free sex, according to the Oxford survey. Other surveys would argue that this is over-optimistic, and would say that after only seven years there would be an 'evens' chance of one pregnancy. Since stories of pregnancies resulting from burst condoms are not altogether uncommon, it is still important to remember that this theoretical pregnancy occuring once in seven years or once in twenty-seven years could also turn up in the first year of use.

Safety is just as important as effectiveness. A lot of confusing information is handed to women about the safety of contraception. The response to anxieties over the safety of the pill, 'Well, it's much safer than having a baby' is no response at all. In the first place it suggests that the choice is only between the pill and a pregnancy. It ignores the fact that there are a number of other contraceptive methods to choose from about whose long-term safety more is known than about the combined pill. In the second place, the pill is only safer than a pregnancy for a non-smoking women under thirty-five. Women who smoke, and women who are over thirty-five run the same or a higher risk from taking the pill as they would from a pregnancy. Pill scares, IUD scares, spermicide

Figure 3.1   User-failure rates for different methods of contraception per 100 woman-years

Oxford/FPA study (1982 report) – all women married and aged above 25			Range in other reports*
	Overall (any duration)	Age 25–34 ($\leqslant$2 years use)	Age 35+ ($\leqslant$2 years use)	
Sterilization				
Male	0.02	0.08	0.00	0–0.2
Female	0.13	0.45	0.08	0–0.5
Injectable (DMPA)	–	–	–	0–1
Combined pills				
50 μg oestrogen	0.16	0.25	0.17	0.1–1
50 < μg oestrogen	0.27	0.38	0.23	0.2–1
Progestogen-only pill	1.2	2.5	0.5	0.3–5
IUD				
Lippes Loop C	1.4	2.4	1.1	0.3–4
Copper 7	1.5	3.1	0.6	0.3–4
Diaphragm	1.9	5.5	2.8	2–15
Condom	3.6	6.0	2.9	2–15
Coitus interruptus	6.7	–	–	8–17
Spermicides alone	11.9	–	–	4–25
Fertility awareness	15.5	–	–	6–25
Contraceptive sponge	–	–	–	9–25
No method, young women	–	–	–	80–90
No method at age 40	–	–	–	40–50
No method at age 45	–	–	–	c. 10–20
No method at age 50	–	–	–	c. 0–5

* Excludes atypical studies giving particularly poor results, and all extended-use studies.
Source: John Guillebaud, *Contraception: Your Questions Answered*, Churchill Livingstone, 1985.

scares, all inflated by the media, take their toll of women's ability to believe in the quality of the information fed to them by their professional advisers. Rather than considering all these scares here we have tried to look at all the information about safety in each chapter on the different methods, giving particular emphasis to safety in the chapters on hormonal contraception and IUDs. Here we simply want to indicate the relative safety of currently available contraception.

The safest form of contraception is in fact the diaphragm backed up with an early abortion in the event of failure. By safety we are not referring to moral acceptability or anything else, simply the risk of death directly attributable to a method, or the pregnancy that results if the method fails. The most dangerous form of contraception would be the use of the combined pill by a heavy smoker aged over forty-five, though this combination must be rather an unusual one. The pill is only as safe as barriers (backed up with abortions) and IUDs when it is used by non-smokers in the twenty to thirty age-group. After thirty, barriers and IUDs are safer than the pill, and certainly safer than a pregnancy.

Another major problem hampers any attempt to give objective measurements to questions concerning safety. Most available statistics including the ones we have given are based on mortality, or the likelihood of dying from a given method of contraception. They do not measure ill-health, or minor side-effects, or even the long-term consequences of using a method. This is largely because such things are either difficult to measure, or are simply not known. Obviously this limits their usefulness as far as individual women are concerned, since no one expects to die as a result of using a method of contraception. Knowing that a certain, tiny number of women are more likely to die of a circulatory disease because they took the pill tells us nothing about the considerable number of other effects that taking the pill has on the body. We will look at this more fully in the chapter on hormonal contraception. The material given below is only a guide to the most extreme measurement of contraceptive safety – the likelihood of dying because you took it.

Childbearing decisions

Childbearing decisions are often difficult to untangle. They reflect a wide variety of factors, including social background, number of siblings, peer pressure, family pressure, parental background and individual attributes such as a woman's view of her sexual role, her educational aspirations, career expectations, age at marriage and age at first job. Here we take a brief look at some of the physiological aspects of childbearing that may affect contraceptive behaviour.

When is the best time to have a baby? The answer to this is probably when you feel ready to have one, since a pregnancy at thirty-six to a woman who only ever wanted to be a mother may be as traumatic as one to a woman at twenty who wants to have a career as a surgeon. Since physiology does not exist in a social void, social considerations often become as important as physiological ones in determining the outcome of physiological events. Having said this, and accepted that a woman will enjoy pregnancy and childbearing far more if it occurs at the time of her choosing than if it is forced on her, there are nevertheless aspects

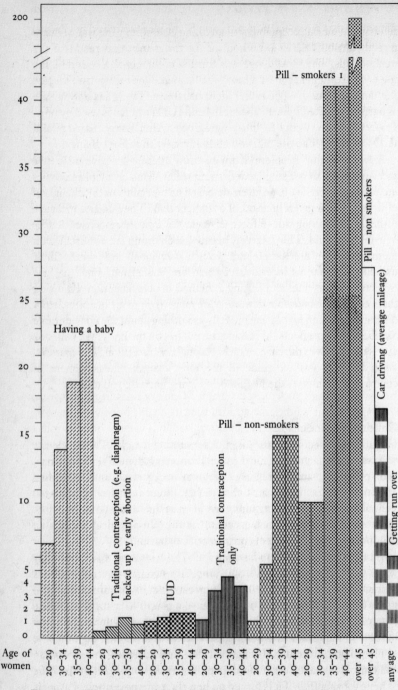

Figure 3.2 The relative safety of various forms of contraception
Annual deaths per 100 000 non-sterile women

Source: Data included from John Guillebaud, *Contraception, Your Questions Answered*, Churchill Livingstone, 1985.

of fertility that are specially significant. Some were reviewed in Chapter 1, and are summarized below.

A fertile couple making love at the most fertile time of the month only have a one in four chance of conceiving that month but within a year 80–90 per cent of women under thirty will have conceived. If these same women tried to conceive again when they were forty, only two out of five, or 40 per cent of them would be successful within a year of trying. A woman's reproductive system functions at its best in the ten years between eighteen and twenty-eight, when ovulation is most regular. After twenty-eight fertility begins to decline, slowly and imperceptibly at first, and certainly not enough to make a significant difference to the length of time it might take to conceive. From thirty-five onwards, however, fertility may be a problem for women trying to conceive their first child, though 75 per cent will still be successful. After forty fertility declines quite dramatically, so that by forty-five only 10–20 per cent of women will still be capable of conceiving and bearing a child. Recent research shows that there may be a penalty for postponing a first birth. The fecundity of a thirty-year-old woman who has had no children may in fact be only as great as that of a thirty-eight-year-old who has had children.

Apart from the ovaries' ability to produce a fertilizable egg, miscarriages take their toll of pregnancies, especially in the first eleven weeks. There is considerable evidence that the likelihood of a miscarriage increases with age. As we saw in Chapter 1, an egg is as old as the woman in whose body it is housed, and with time its quality begins to diminish. A defective egg can sometimes be fertilized, but will not develop into a baby. Miscarriage is nature's way of preventing the birth of babies who will not survive into the next generation as reproducers themselves. Between 10 and 20 per cent of all pregnancies abort naturally in the first eleven weeks. Some recent studies put the figure even higher, at 30 per cent or more, though many of these will be in the first two weeks before the woman even knows she is pregnant. Not all fetuses with abnormalities are aborted however, and women conceiving after the age of thirty-five have a higher risk of conceiving a baby with Down's syndrome than women who have their children while they are younger. There is no sudden jump in risk after the age of thirty-five; rather the risk slowly and steadily increases with maternal age. By thirty-five the risk of conceiving a child with Down's syndrome rises to one in 380, and accounts for 70–80 per cent of spontaneous birth defects detectable by amniocentesis (see Figure 3.3 on page 94). Recently it has been suggested that paternal age also has something to do with the conception of Down's syndrome babies.

Figure 3.3   Risk of Down's syndrome by maternal age at time of delivery

Maternal age	Risk of Down's syndrome in live births
20–24	1 in 1700
25–29	1100
30–34	770
35	380
36	300
37	230
38	180
39	140
40	100
41	90
42	70
43	50
44	40
45	30

Source: Ronald Heinman, ed., *Family Planning Handbook for Doctors*, IPPF, 1988.

There are a number of other factors worth considering in childbearing decisions, especially in the decision to delay children until after thirty-five. Medical, gynaecological and obstetric problems begin to occur with greater frequency, and, though the risks remain relatively small, many gynaecologists will advise that all pregnancies after thirty-five be seen as 'risk' pregnancies. A first baby born to a woman of thirty-five has a higher than average risk of problems during the birth, and first babies born to women over thirty-five have a higher than average perinatal mortality rate. But this is a relative risk, and is still in real terms low. Given good antenatal, obstetric and postnatal care most women who have their first baby after thirty-five will have no more problems than younger women.

The table opposite (Figure 3.4) gives an idea of the safest ages for being pregnant and giving birth, as far as the baby is concerned. In this table, the average risk of perinatal death to a baby born to mothers of different ages and parity is compared to an average risk of 100. 'Perinatal death' includes stillbirths (after twenty-eight weeks gestation) and all deaths in the first week after birth. When looking at the table, bear in mind that the average risk of the baby dying is still less than one in a hundred. It is clear that the 'safest' baby to have is a second baby born while the mother is between twenty-five and twenty-nine; the baby most at risk would be a third child born to a woman still under twenty. At present the perinatal mortality rate in Britain stands at 9.6 per 1000 deliveries (1986 figure). This means that one woman in 100 will face

Figure 3.4 **Average relative risk of perinatal mortality to babies born to mothers at different ages and different parity compared to an average risk of 100**

Age of mother	first baby	second baby	third baby	fourth baby
under 20	106	101	382	
20–24	98	69	77	84
25–29	100	62	91	98
30–34	132	77	102	111
35–39	168	120	108	128
40–44	312	179	220	157

Source: G. Bourne, *Pregnancy*, Pan Books, 1972, © Cassell plc, 1989.

the tragedy of leaving the hospital without taking her baby with her. Many of the babies in this category are premature, others are stillbirths, and others die of a complication in the first week of their lives. Perinatal and infant mortality rates have a social class component. The mortality rates among social classes IV and V is up to *three* times higher than the rate among social class I. This being the case, there is clearly more that can be done to bring down even these relatively low perinatal mortality rates.

The current trend is for women to choose to have their children later: figures from the Office of Population Censuses and Surveys show that the number of women having their first child after thirty-five has risen dramatically, as has the number bearing children between thirty and thirty-four. This being the case, contraception will continue to assume an important role in women's lives although the needs of women at different stages in their reproductive 'history' will differ considerably. Women who have finished childbearing by thirty and women who would like to begin will have very different requirements. For women in the latter category there may be anxiety about the effect of their method of contraception on their ability to conceive quickly once they have stopped using it. In the main there is good news here. Evidence currently available suggests that women using barrier methods and IUDs suffer from no interruption in their fertility. Once an IUD is removed fertility returns immediately. Barriers only affect the outcome of the act of intercourse for which they are used. Among pill-users the picture is a little different. The Oxford/FPA study has produced some important findings which show that taking the pill may delay the speed of conception among some women. We review the evidence in Chapter 8.

Under sixteen: the legal position

Since the Gillick case many young girls, their parents and others in a
position to offer them advice have been in a quandary as to the current
legal position when under-sixteen-year-olds seek contraceptive advice.
In fact the campaign of Mrs Gillick was very useful in that it succeeded
in clarifying the law which until then had been ambiguous. Pre-Gillick,
family planning doctors had only DHSS guidelines to work within. Now
they have the 1985 ruling of the Law Lords which states that as long as
a doctor is convinced that a girl has the 'understanding and intelligence'
to give a legally valid consent he or she can go ahead and provide
contraception and will not be 'committing a criminal offence of aiding
and abetting unlawful intercourse with girls under sixteen'. Doctors
should not use the ruling as a licence to disregard the wishes of parents,
and should try and persuade the girl to inform her parents. The best
interests of the girl however may lead the doctor to give contraceptive
advice without getting parental consent. If a doctor is not convinced
that the girl has the emotional maturity to deal with, for example, a
prescription for the pill, he or she should normally turn to a parent for
consent.[2] In practice, however, the Law Lords' ruling means that most
under-sixteen-year-olds who make a trip to a family planning clinic are
virtually assured of being given the contraceptive advice they need in
complete confidentiality. Neither she nor the doctor needs fear any
criminal law sanctions. This is not to say that most doctors will not
suggest to the girl the advisability of discussing contraception with one
or both parents, but the girl is under no obligation to do so.

The Gillick affair raised many important questions about the relationship between parental rights and the role of doctors in the lives of young
women. While it had some unfortunate aspects – not least in a dropping
off in the number of under-sixteen-year-olds attending clinics – it also
caused many doctors to re-examine their practice and to recognize some
of the issues involved, which, interestingly, were not necessarily the ones
on Gillick's agenda. Some feminist doctors put the dilemma facing them
like this:

... Conflicts arise when adolescents come to us asking for contraception. We
support their 'right to self-determined sexuality' (one of the demands of the
Women's Liberation Movement) but often their sexuality is dictated by outside
forces – the media, the fear of being left out, pressure from boys, and so on.
Sometimes we cannot bring ourselves to ask young women about their sexual
enjoyment – at least two-thirds of them say 'well, he seems to like it'. Not only
are they not enjoying sex, but they seem to have no expectation that they might.
Of course, we are willing to provide contraception, but we also want to find a

way of helping them find out what they want from sex and life. Yet the same forces that push young women into sexual relationships which they may not want also characterize adults as killjoys who want to stop young people having fun. We find our status as powerful adults makes it almost impossible to talk about these issues with young women without being seen as authoritarian, which prevents any two-way discussion. During the time that we were writing this, it became illegal for us to advise anyone under sixteen about contraception without their parents' consent. We welcomed the House of Lords ruling which reversed this change in the law, which had begun to have disastrous effects on the well-being of young women and made it very much harder for us to develop helpful relationships with them.[3]

There is a curious relationship between sexual activity and knowledge about sexual matters, which seems to contradict the conservative belief that information on sex leads to promiscuity. It appears to be the case that when young people are given enough information and counselling about conception, contraception, intercourse and relationships they tend to be more cautious in their approach to sex. This has been borne out by several studies. In one American study questionnaires on sexual activity were given to female college students. Among the sexually active women 25 per cent could not answer any of the questions correctly and only 59 per cent could answer half the questions correctly. No one got the answers 100 per cent correct. Among women who claimed to be much less sexually active 80 per cent answered 50 per cent of the questions correctly and 9 per cent got 100 per cent correct answers. Obviously this could be explained in a number of ways and almost certainly includes class and other social factors. But it does also seem the case that when young men and women are given as much information as they need, they are less likely to take risks with either pregnancy or sexually transmitted disease (STD).

Women under twenty

What is the best form of contraception for teenagers? The answer to this does not lie in statistics on safety or effectiveness, but is frequently the method that the teenager herself wants to use. If a teenager uses the method that she herself most believes in, the chances are that she will use it more effectively than a method she is unhappy with, even if that method is theoretically more effective. The attitude of a young woman to any form of contraception will be determined by a number of factors including her possible ambivalence about sexual relationships. If you are under twenty and new to contraception there is one important point to bear in mind throughout the discussion and that is the high likelihood that you are very fertile, especially if you are already around eighteen. Some doctors refer to the 'super-fertility' of young women. Women embarking on their first sexual relationships are most unlikely to have gynaecological problems that would make conceptions difficult, and the ovaries are producing eggs of top quality. By eighteen a woman's body is mature enough to cope well with a pregnancy. Don't take chances. If you do find yourself in a situation in which you have taken a risk most doctors will give you post-coital contraception. This doesn't only work if you see a doctor the morning after either, though it needs to be within seventy-two hours. See Chapter 10 on 'Post-Coital Contraception' for details.

Contraceptive options

Withdrawal may not be a particularly reliable form of contraception but it is better than nothing. Your partner needs to withdraw before he ejaculates *any* sperm, especially as the first few drops of his ejaculation will contain more than enough to cause a pregnancy.

Natural Family Planning (NFP) is not usually a method that is for very young women because the menstrual cycle takes some time to settle down into a regular pattern. But if you are keen to learn NFP a trained counsellor will be able to help you. You should bear in mind that NFP offers no protection against sexually transmitted diseases (STDs) including AIDS. You also need a co-operative partner. Given good teaching, a fairly regular cycle and a partner who is supportive, there is no reason why you should not practise NFP successfully. Many women enjoy learning about their cycles even if they choose not to use NFP. See Chapter 4 on NFP for more details.

Condoms may rapidly be becoming a girl's best friend. Condoms cut down considerably on the risk of a sexually transmitted disease (including AIDS), with a corresponding reduction in the likelihood of pelvic inflammatory disease (PID) and potentially reduced fertility. There is some evidence that condoms also protect against cervical cancer and they have no side-effects. Women and men can get condoms free from family planning clinics, though not from GPs. Otherwise you have to buy them. Condoms fit in well with the pattern of much teenage sex, which is sporadic, often unplanned and initiated by the boy.

The 'Today' Contraceptive Sponge has lots of advantages. It can be bought over a counter, it can be put in place well before intercourse, it is undetectable and has no side effects. Its only drawbacks are that it has a failure rate up to twenty times higher than the pill and you have to pay for it. On the other hand it is definitely better than nothing.

Spermicides are best used in conjunction with a barrier method such as a diaphragm or condoms. Used on their own they are not very reliable in young, highly fertile women.

Diaphragms have had a bad press but can be used successfully by young women. You have to want to use it, though, and it may take some getting used to. However, it does protect against STDs, possibly including cervical cancer, but not, as far as we know, against AIDS.

IUDs are not often prescribed for young women who have not had a baby. This is because the uterus has a tendency to push out anything that is put into it and is more effective at doing this when it's still small and tense, before a pregnancy. Using an IUD puts you more at risk of developing PID, especially if you have more than one partner. Periods are likely to be more heavy and painful. However, if you do want to use an IUD, having considered the potential risks, you will probably be able to find a doctor willing to fit one for you.

The pill remains the most popular form of contraception among young women, for good reasons. It is highly effective, convenient, makes periods shorter and lighter, and there is evidence that it helps reduce the risk of ovarian and uterine cancer and pelvic inflammatory disease following on from a sexually transmitted disease. According to recent research, if the pill is used for five years among younger women (under twenty-five) the protection against cancer and the prevention of unplanned pregnancies more than outweighs the risk of death due to cardiovascular disease.[4]

Of course the pill is not without its controversies. It has all sorts of other effects on the body, some minor, others more significant. There is a growing body of research that suggests that taking the pill for more than five years before a first pregnancy could make the risk of breast cancer more likely. (See Chapter 8 on hormonal contraception for details.) In some ways the pill is better used in longish stretches. The worst way to use it is to take it for a month or so, then to stop for another month or two before taking it up again. It may be harder for the ovaries to get themselves going again if they are constantly switched on and off. Since early sexual relationships may not be long term it may be tempting to stop and start the pill. There may also be a tendency to stop taking the pill as soon as a relationship finishes. Passionate reconciliations can leave you unprotected. Stopping and starting the pill can lead to periods of amenorrhoea (absence of periods) once you do come off the pill.

Progestogen-only pills can also be used by young women, but they are less effective than the combined pill, and need to be taken at the same time every day, preferably eight to ten hours before you are most likely to have sexual intercourse. Progestogen, or mini-pills, can also make your cycle more unreliable, with mid-cycle bleeding and spotting.

Vaginal examinations
Many young women are put off going to see a doctor because they are afraid of a vaginal examination. In fact a vaginal examination is not a necessary prelude to taking the pill, though once you become sexually active it becomes sensible to have regular cervical smears. Most doctors will be happy to give you your first cervical smear in your own time, but will recommend that you have it within the first two years of becoming sexually active. If you choose a diaphragm or have an IUD fitted a vaginal examination is necessary.

Which doctor?
Some doctors are excellent at making it easy for young women to consult them. You may be lucky and have the kind of GP who checks on whether you need advice on contraception when you visit him or her for something else. You don't have to see your own GP. If you want more anonymity you can see a different doctor in the same practice, or go to a different practice altogether, where you aren't registered. Or you can go to a family planning clinic. They are always listed in the phone book, and you can ring to make an appointment. With some clinics you can just drop in. If you are nervous, take a friend with you. If you suddenly become worried about your method of contraception (for example you develop leg pains while on the pill), you can always telephone your doctor to ask what you should do.

After thirty-five

Older women often feel, and quite rightly so, that their contraceptive needs attract less attention than those of much younger women. While medical journals spawn pages on the counselling of sexually active teenagers, the needs of women who are no longer in the safe age-range for combined contraceptive pills, and pre-menopausal women in particular, are less well considered. The average age of the menopause is currently between forty-nine and fifty-two in most developed societies, but it is quite normal for it to occur as early as forty or as late as fifty-five. Despite this considerable chunk of reproductive life, it can be very difficult for older women to get good information about their changing pattern of fertility, the role of hormonal contraception *vis-à-vis* hormonal replacement therapy, the suitability of IUDs and the reliability of barriers. We have already talked quite a lot about the declining fertility of older women, but the fact remains that unwanted pregnancy remains a very real risk. An unwanted pregnancy after the age of thirty-five when a woman has either decided that she wants no more children or is firm in her decision that she wants none at all, can be a most disorienting experience. There is good evidence to suggest that older women feel more lost and unsettled by unexpected pregnancy than younger women. This could be due to a number of factors. In the first place it may be more unexpected; in the second, women who regard their families as complete develop a new self-image; babies are well behind them. A surprise pregnancy may unsettle a new sense of self. Moreover, choosing an abortion may lead to a strong sense of loss and the passing of fertility. Women who are married with children may anyway find the idea of abortion very difficult to accept, if not absolutely antithetical to the way they have previously seen themselves. On the other hand pregnancy after the age of thirty-five carries more risks both for the woman and for the baby. Good and safe contraception is therefore essential and may make a considerable difference to the way in which a woman is able to experience herself sexually as she begins to approach the menopause. The fact that a significant percentage of abortions in developed countries are for women over the age of thirty-five suggests that at present the standard of contraceptive care offered to older women leaves something to be desired.

How fertile are older women? A study carried out in Hungary recently looked at the cycles of a large number of women between thirty-five and fifty. The investigators found that the incidence of anovulatory cycles (cycles in which the woman did not ovulate) was 32–40 per cent between the ages of thirty-five and forty; 40–61 per cent between the ages of forty-one and forty-five; and 61–87 per cent for women aged forty-six to fifty. The major defect of the cycles was short follicular phases (the first phase of the cycle leading normally to ovulation). The other peculiarity in the cycles of older women is the increased incidence of double ovulations, as if nature is compensating for the anovulatory cycles by super-ovulating in others. What the study showed, however, was that the majority of women between thirty-five and forty-five can still expect to be potentially fertile between four and nine times a year (as opposed to the maximum of thirteen in a highly fertile younger woman).

Another way of considering fertility is to look at the likelihood of sterility at different ages. There are various mathematical models for this. One suggests that at thirty-five the likely incidence of sterility is just under 20 per cent, increasing to 40 per cent at forty and 80 per cent over forty-five. Obviously there is considerable individual and cultural variation in the occurrence of pregnancies among older women. Recent figures from Washington suggest that only one birth in every 4000 is to a woman over forty-five. In Ireland, however, the comparable figure is one in 257.[5] Individual variation seems to depend largely on previous reproductive performance. A woman who conceived at will in her twenties is likely to remain more fertile than a woman for whom conceptions were difficult to achieve even when she was younger (though obviously the fertility of her partner must be taken into account). If 80 per cent of women are fertile for at least two-thirds of their cycles when they are thirty-five, contraception clearly remains an important part of their reproductive health.

The Hungarian study devised an age-specific fertility score which gives an index they now use to predict the fertility of any couple coming to their 'anti-conception' clinic. This has been more effective than working from the assumption that all couples are the same. Basically, a woman and her partner are each given marks out of ten, which are then added to the number of times they make love a month (judged to be between zero and ten; couples who make love more than ten times a month are still given the score of ten). This gives a maximum total of thirty points. On the age-specific fertility index a score of twenty to thirty represents high fertility; in the Hungarian study the group achieving this had a pregnancy rate (without contraception) of 70–100 per cent during the six months of the study. The average fertility group (scoring from ten to twenty) achieved a pregnancy rate of only 10–30 per cent in the six months, while pregnancies in the low fertility group (scoring under ten) were extremely rare with only 0–1 per cent chance of a pregnancy within six months.[6] We have reproduced the system below so that you can work out your own age-specific fertility score. But remember it was designed to be used under clinical supervision – several of the questions are rather technical and you may not know the answer without talking to your doctor or charting your cycle for a few months (see Chapter 4). The scoring system is only included here for interest. We certainly do not suggest that you abandon contraception on the basis of your score, but you may want to talk the matter through with your doctor and use it as a basis for rethinking your contraceptive needs, especially if you are unhappy with your current method.

Contraceptive options
Hormonal contraception is the most controversial of contraceptive methods for older women. It used to be the case that women were advised to stop

Figure 3.5   Age-specific fertility score for men

		score
Age	Under 45	2
	45–55	1
	Over 55	0
Occupation	Not dangerous	2
	Slightly dangerous	1
	Risk group (drivers etc.)	0
Smoking and alcohol	Nil	2
	Occasionally	1
	Heavy drinker, heavy smoker	0
History of fertility	Highly fertile	2
	Fertile following andrology treatment	1
	Fertile following long-term andrology treatment	0
Genital diseases	Nil	2
	Fertile following previous genital disease	1
	Spermatogenetic defects, orchitis, etc.	0

Figure 3.6   Age-specific fertility score for women

		score
Age	Under 40	2
	40–47	1
	Over 47	0
*Regularity of cycles**	Normal, biphasic cycles	2
	Short luteal phase or periodic anovulation	1
	Totally abnormal cycles, permanent anovulation	0
History of pregnancies	Became pregnant easily whenever wanted	2
	Had difficulty achieving pregnancy	1
	Pregnant only after fertility treatment	0
History of contraception	Experienced failures of contraception	2
	Barrier contraception was successful	1
	Coitus interruptus and/or douche successful	0
*Gynaecological findings**	Normal gynaecological findings	2
	Abnormal gynaecological findings, previous PID, endometriosis, etc.	1
	Previous fertility-reducing operations	0

* You may not be able to do more than hazard a guess at the answer to these questions. Women who are used to charting their cycles and are familiar with NFP will know whether they have normal cycles or not. Otherwise you could always try charting your cycle for several months to see if you ovulate normally.

Figure 3.7   The age-specific fertility index

Your index is calculated by adding together your score, your partner's score and the number of times you have intercourse per month on a scale of zero to ten. (If it is more than ten times it is still counted as ten.) This produces a maximum of 30 points, scored as follows:

Score	Category	Pregnancy rate*
20–30	high fertility	70–100%
10–20	average fertility	10–30 %
0–10	low fertility	0–1 %

* The pregnancy rate is based on the rates of couples in the Hungarian study, not using contraception, over a six-month period.

Source for figs 3.5, 3.6 and 3.7: L. Ladyani, 'Premenopausal fertility score as a guide to individual anti-contraception', *Contraceptive Delivery Systems*, Vol. 5, No. 4, 1984. Reproduced by permission of MTP Press Ltd, Lancaster.

taking the combined pill at thirty-five, or earlier if they were heavy smokers (fifteen cigarettes a day or more). Nowadays it is generally considered safe for healthy non-smoking women, with no risk factors (hypertension or a family history of heart disease, for example) to continue taking the combined pill until forty, or even forty-five, provided they have been made aware of the increasing risk of the method and have given their informed consent. The most significant health hazards are a slight but increased risk of cardiovascular disease and of some kinds of thrombosis. Older women should always take the lowest contraceptive dose possible. For smokers however even the very low dose pills become increasingly risky after thirty-five and smoking women are much better off switching to a progestogen-only pill, an IUD or barrier method.

The progestogen-only pill is often a good choice for older women. Clinical trials have shown that it is as effective for women over thirty-five as the combined pill is for much younger women (the Oxford/FPA study puts both at 0.3 pregnancies per 100 women year). In comparison to the combined pill it has fewer major effects on the body's metabolism and therefore is less likely to offer any major health hazards. On the negative side, about one fifth of women using the mini-pill experience breakthrough bleeding or spotting, and 5–10 per cent have episodes of amenorrhoea. This can offer confusing signs to women who are aware they are approaching the menopause. Numerous studies have suggested that, in general, older couples make love less often than younger ones (with plenty of exceptions). If sex is assuming a less important position in your life, remembering to take a pill at the same time every day may become tedious.

One of the ironies in evaluating the safety of contraceptive hormones for older women is that, as the menopause approaches, they may choose hormone replacement therapy (HRT) anyway. They may find themselves taking oestrogens which are unlikely to be any less hazardous to their health than the combined pill, which they gave up earlier as a health risk! Some women taking HRT are given oestrogen preparations in the years leading up to the menopause combined with a progestogen-only pill. The progestogen is given to protect the uterus from the dangers of giving oestrogen on its own (i.e. the increased risk of endometrial cancer) and in some cases this also results in effective contraceptive protection.

IUDs are often considered a good form of contraception for older women since rates of expulsion and infections decrease with age, and are lowest among women over forty. On the other hand, older women may anyway be experiencing heavier periods, and the additional bleeding caused by an IUD may be intolerable. A progestogen-releasing device might be a satisfactory solution to this problem.

Barriers offer safe and effective contraception at any age. Women coming off the pill after many years of use however may find that barriers take a bit of getting used to. Others are surprised at how easy it is to use a diaphragm. The 'Today' contraceptive sponge may be a good option for some older women, particularly after the age of forty-five when its risk of failure appears to be much lower. Using a diaphragm with C-film may provide a very satisfactory method of contraception. Other women find that the gel used with a diaphragm provides useful extra lubrication.

Natural Family planning will probably continue to be a satisfactory option for women who have used it previously and not such a good idea for those who are new to it, particularly in the pre-menopausal years. Most women begin to experience some cycle irregularities as they enter their forties. Anovulation and fluctuating cervical mucus may make it difficult to work out exactly what is going on, and could lead to rather long periods of abstinence. Maybe combining NFP with a barrier at times of increased fertility would be an acceptable option for some couples wanting to use NFP.

Male and female sterilization is the most popular form of contraception in Britain in the late 1980s. More couples aged between eighteen and forty-five rely on it than any other method. Sterilization is a useful solution for couples who are convinced their families are complete, but for others, the psychological importance of fertility outweighs the convenience of a virtually foolproof method of avoiding pregnancy.

Factors for and against sterilization are more fully discussed in Chapter 9.

When to stop using contraception
Different medical sources give different answers to this question, and it is best to discuss it with a doctor who knows you and whose advice you trust. It is best to use a form of contraception until menopause has been reached but not substantially beyond it. IUDs for example should be removed within a year of menopause occurring since they may prove difficult to remove after that. Some forms of contraception obscure the menopause – hormonal contraception for example. Since the menopause can occur at any point after the age of forty, women who experience six months of amenorrhoea associated with any menopausal symptoms (for example hot flushes) should consider stopping contraception. Women over forty who experience amenorrhoea for a year without any of the typical menopausal symptoms should also consider stopping contraception. If there is any doubt about whether or not the menopause has occurred, particularly in younger women, tests can be carried out to detect the level of FSH in the blood. As the ovaries wind down, the pituitary gland pumps out greater and greater levels of FSH to try and stimulate the ovaries to develop egg follicles. If a woman has more than twice the normal upper limit of FSH in her plasma, menopause can be presumed to have occurred.

Some women continue having periods well into their fifties. It is wise to stop any method of contraception that could be obscuring the menopause between fifty and fifty-one. An alternative form of contraception should be used for six months, and if no period occurs contraception can be stopped. If periods return (and some women don't reach the menopause until at least fifty-five), the alternative form of contraception should be used until menopause occurs. The chances of conception over fifty must be very small indeed and some authorities recommend that women stop using contraception at forty-nine (though only if abortion is acceptable to them).[7] On the other hand, according to the *Guinness Book of Records* the oldest recorded mother in history was fifty-seven years and 129 days!

Physically disabled women

Fortunately in the last couple of decades there has been a growing recognition of the sexuality of disabled women and men, and their right to reproductive freedom and fertility control of their own choosing. On one level this may simply mean ensuring that family planning clinics are easily accessible to disabled people; on another, recognizing the appropriateness of otherwise of particular forms of contraception and modifying them accordingly. A blind woman may need to be shown how to orientate her packet of pills if she is using a triphasic variety; a woman with a spinal injury may need to have help from her partner if she is to use a diaphragm comfortably. Many problems of mobility, sexuality and disability until recently considered insurmountable are now seen merely as difficulties needing imaginative solutions and commitment on the part of the contraceptive providers. While the birth-rate in the population as a whole continues to decline, the birth-rate among women suffering from a disability is rising. It is now easier to find doctors trained to give appropriate care to disabled women who wish to conceive and give birth to children. This is vitally important, for only when disabled women and men feel the right to full sexual expression and parenthood will they be fully in control of their contraceptive choices. Public opinion may lag behind the professionals' change of attitude to the disabled. Counselling services offered by organizations such as SPOD (The Association to Aid the Sexual and Personal Relationships of People with a Disability), the Spastic Society and others may help physically disabled women and men to come to terms with public prejudice.

Sadly we don't have space to consider all the forms of contraception and their plusses and drawbacks for women with different kinds of disability. Finding the best form of contraception may take time. If you suffer from a disability of any kind you will certainly need to find a sensitive and caring doctor to talk to, one who understands the nature of your disability and is also well trained in contraceptive methods. As a starting point you can write to SPOD or one of the organizations listed at the back of this book. See also the suggestions for further reading in Appendix 2.

After pregnancy and during breastfeeding

Few women leave hospital after the birth of a baby without having been offered a discussion about contraception. Good contraceptive counselling after childbirth is in a woman's best interests. Despite the physically traumatic events of childbirth, a woman who is not breastfeeding regains her fertility surprisingly quickly. Even if you don't feel interested in sex for a while, your body may be gearing itself up for another pregnancy! Two babies in one year is not unheard of, and women who do not want another pregnancy need to be adequately protected as soon as they become sexually active again. One in two women who do not breastfeed or use contraception would find themselves pregnant again after six or seven months. Waiting for a first period before using contraception is not a good idea, since some women (around 5 per cent) ovulate before their first period after childbirth.

If a baby is breastfed, the woman's body does not register the physiological 'loss' of the baby and so does not begin preparing itself for another pregnancy. The mechanism that supresses ovulation is still not fully understood but it seems that whenever a baby suckles the hormone prolactin is produced. Prolactin may act on the pituitary gland and prevent it from releasing hormones such as FSH, and on the ovaries to inhibit the production of oestrogen. Prolactin may also have an inhibiting effect on the cells in the ovaries that produce progesterone. The effects of prolactin are very short term. Within thirty minutes of release it is broken down by the body and the level begins to fall to within the range of a non-lactating woman. As soon as the baby begins to suckle again prolactin rises dramatically (sometimes twenty-fold within a few minutes of suckling). Obviously women whose babies suckle on and off all day and night maintain very high levels of prolactin while women who feed only six or so times a day have high prolactin levels for only a short period of every day.

It is interesting to look at the evidence of the effectiveness of breastfeeding as a contraceptive in a traditional society – one of the few hunter-gatherer societies that remain. The !Kung bushmen of the Kalahari desert live much as all human populations must have lived many thousands of years ago. Despite the fact that the women try to have as many children as possible, and there are no sexual restrictions during lactation, on average each woman has less than five children. The reason for this is the prolonged, continual suckling that the baby and child are offered. Anthropologists who have studied the !Kung have found that the children under the age of two never leave their mother's breasts for more than fifteen minutes at a time, but continually return to the breast as a source of nourishment and comfort, by night as well as by day. The result is a dramatic decline in fertility. The ovaries switch off for the duration of breastfeeding, and the average !Kung woman has a space of three to four years between births. Instead of 400 or so periods in a lifetime, the !Kung woman may experience as few as twelve. On a global scale this physiological trick has a very significant effect on the number of conceptions prevented. In the 1970s it was estimated that in developing countries breastfeeding offered 38 million couple-years of fertility protection per annum compared with 24 million couple-years per annum for all family planning programmes combined.[8]

In non-traditional societies the speed with which fertility returns seems to depend on how often the baby is fed, with women feeding more than eight times a day remaining amenorrheic (without periods) for longer than women who suckle less frequently. But even in fully breastfeeding women, menstruation occurs within six weeks in 1–2 per cent of women. The point at which food supplements are introduced, and whether or not night feeding continues, also seem to play a part in determining when fertility returns. Night nursing in particular seems to play a significant role in delaying the return of fertility. Even when supplements are added, a woman who still breastfeeds her baby during the night (for around an hour in total) can expect to remain amenorrhoeic for six to ten months longer than women whose babies give up night feeds earlier. Although there is a significant interest in breastfeeding again in the West, few mothers have the opportunity or the support that they need to feed their babies as intensively or as long as is required to make breastfeeding a reliable form of fertility control. An earlier recommendation that a woman needs to suckle her baby at least five times a day with a total duration of more than sixty-five minutes to maintain infertility has recently been shown to be inadequate. This being the case, lactating women need to use some form of contraception which does not interfere with breastfeeding.

Contraceptive options

Condoms are often an ideal method of contraception after a pregnancy though they may need to be used with some additional form of lubrication if you are feeling sore and have had stitches. They have the advantage of being safe and easy to get hold of, and many men like to feel that they are making life easier for their partners in the weeks after a birth. They do not interfere in any way with lactation.

Diaphragms need to be refitted after a baby because a different size may be needed. Some women find they need a slightly smaller size, others a larger one. Most doctors will suggest that you wait at least until you have had a six week postnatal check before having a new diaphragm fitted. Even if you have a new diaphragm fitted then, you may need another size within the following year. If you find your diaphragm becoming uncomfortable, or your partner can feel it, it may be that your muscle tone has improved and you need a smaller size. If you tore badly or had an episiotomy that has taken a while to heal, the idea of a diaphragm may not appeal very much. Certainly the months following a new baby may not seem the best for trying out a diaphragm for the first time, when there is already so much to cope with. The spermicide used with a diaphragm may provide welcome lubrication. Diaphragms do not interfere in any way with lactation.

Other caps present the same advantages and problems as diaphragms. If you used one before you were pregnant, you may be happy to go on using it. Check the size with your doctor at the six week postnatal check up.

The 'Today' contraceptive sponge may represent a good option for women who are breastfeeding and have not resumed menstruation. It is easy and pleasant to use, and easy to get hold of. Since a number of studies have suggested a high failure rate, and few women want to risk another pregnancy after they've had a new baby, it is less suitable for non-breastfeeding women.

IUDs are sometimes fitted immediately following the expulsion of the placenta, though more often a doctor will prefer to wait until six weeks or longer after the birth. IUDs fitted immediately or shortly after a birth do tend to be expelled more frequently than those fitted at other times, so is important to check the threads regularly. IUDs seem to be used more comfortably in women who have had at least one child, so even if you have not considered one before, an IUD may be a good choice now. It does not interfere with lactation, though the heavy bleeding that sometimes occurs in the first few periods may seem like the last straw if you are already tired from feeding a demanding baby.

The combined pill is often a good choice for non-breastfeeding mothers since it is simple to use and highly effective. You will usually be advised to start taking the pill early in the fourth week after the baby is born. The combined pill is definitely not recommended for women who are breastfeeding. The oestrogen in the pill has the effect of reducing both the volume and quality of the milk. In addition the baby receives a certain amount of both oestrogen and progestogen through the milk, and very little is known about the long-term effects, if any, that this might cause.

The progestogen-only pill is a good choice for women who want to use oral contraception and are breastfeeding, since there is no evidence that it reduces the milk supply or the duration of lactation. There is some evidence in fact that it may marginally increase both. A minute quanity of the hormone does get into the milk, and hence is fed to the baby, but it has been estimated that this would still not amount to more than one tablet if the baby is breast fed for two years. To date there is no evidence that the progestogen does any harm to the baby. Studies of the blood of babies whose mother takes the progestogen-only pill have not been able to demonstrate any hormone present since the levels are below the sensitivity measurable by current equipment. However, if you are worried about even a tiny amount of hormone being passed on to your baby, you will probably prefer to use non-hormonal contraception. The POP has the advantage of being nearly 100 per cent effective in breastfeeding women.

If you are breastfeeding and want to use the POP, you should start taking it sometime after the seventh day, when lactation is fully established. If you are not breastfeeding you can start taking the POP at any time before the fourth week.

Natural Family Planning in relation to breastfeeding is discussed further at the end of Chapter 4. NFP during lactation requires considerable skill and dedication. If you are experienced then you may have no problems in continuing the method. It is not recommended that you take up NFP for the first time during breastfeeding.

Among non-breastfeeding women, the cycle quickly reverts to normal and NFP can be used successfully as a method of fertility control. One disadvantage is that getting up even once in the night to feed a baby – whether with a bottle or by breast – can have a disruptive effect on the temperature chart, making the shift in temperature difficult to read. Cervical mucus will not be affected at all in a non-breastfeeding mother.

Sterilization is an increasingly popular option among women who consider their families are complete. Most doctors nowadays will counsel against sterilization in close proximity to a birth, since it has been found that some women regret their decision at a later date. However, if you really feel strongly that you would not want another pregnancy under any circumstances, it is usually possible to have the operation within a couple of months of having a baby. Quite apart from any psychological considerations, sterilizations carried out in the days immediately follow-ing birth have been shown to be associated with a higher failure rate and an increased risk of post-operative complications such as bleeding and thrombosis, so most doctors prefer to wait for a while before performing the operation.

Injectable contraception always uses a form of progestogen, thereby avoiding the problems associated with oestrogen. Since 1984 Depo Provera has been available in Britain for contraception and more recently another drug, NET EN has been added, though officially only for short-term use. An estimated 1 per cent of women in Britain using any form of family planning are using an injectable, though the proportion is higher than this in other parts of the world, including European countries. If you think this may be a useful contraceptive for you, we recommend that you read the relevant section in Chapter 8 on hormonal contraception. You should not receive the injection until five or six

weeks after you have had your baby, or you could experience heavy
bleeding. As with the POP your baby will receive tiny amounts of the
hormone through your milk, but this is estimated to be less than 0.5 per
cent of the maternal dose. Again, nobody really knows what effect, if
any, this has on the baby, but if this worries you, you will not be
happy with an injectable contraception. One advantage of injectable
contraception is that it is extremely effective and does not require a daily
dose. Injections are normally given every twelve weeks in the case of
Depo Provera and eight weeks in the case of NET EN.

Getting enough information

Information about fertility and contraception *is* available, but it is not
always very easy to find or in a 'user-friendly' form. It is also not always
available very quickly. When the major pill scare, linking certain types
of the combined pill with breast cancer, broke in 1983 the majority of
GPs up and down the country had no more specific information available
than the women who had read the newspaper articles. They had to wait
for a full report to appear in the *Lancet* the next day before they too knew
what the scare was all about. The scale of this lack of information was a
fairly unusual occurrence.

We have already seen that some GPs are not happy about fitting IUDs
or caps. Many know very little about natural family planning. Some
doctors may not be very up to date about issues such as the effectiveness
of the 'Today' sponge, or the new Femshield. However, family planning
doctors should have easy access to the information you require. Obviously doctors will vary in the extent to which they will have both the time
and the inclination to share information with you; but it is not unknown
for GPs to make photocopies of relevant articles for their patients.

Doctors are not the only source of information. There are a number
of different bodies which exist almost exclusively to provide information,
such as the FPA and the International Planned Parenthood Federation.
Most have good libraries and are willing to give any information. We
have included an address list at the back of this book.

The options

As a conclusion to this chapter we have included a chart which you can
use to think through your various fertility and contraceptive options.
Once you have worked your way through the maze, the rest of the book
is designed to provide you with further information about each method
of contraception currently available.

Figure 3.8 Choosing contraception

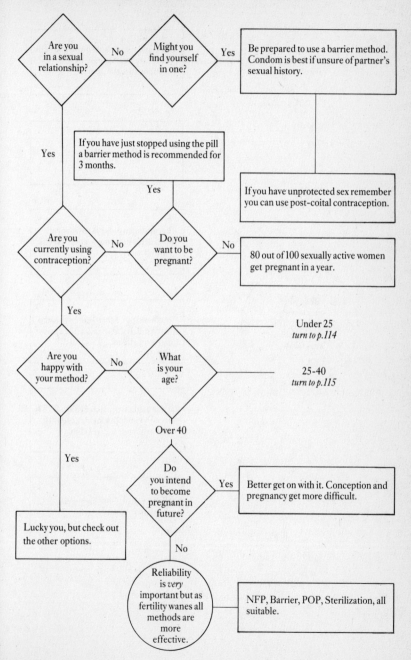

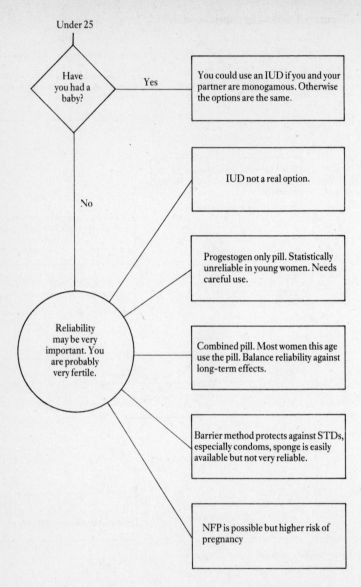

Under 25

Have you had a baby?

Yes — You could use an IUD if you and your partner are monogamous. Otherwise the options are the same.

No

Reliability may be very important. You are probably very fertile.

IUD not a real option.

Progestogen only pill. Statistically unreliable in young women. Needs careful use.

Combined pill. Most women this age use the pill. Balance reliability against long-term effects.

Barrier method protects against STDs, especially condoms, sponge is easily available but not very reliable.

NFP is possible but higher risk of pregnancy

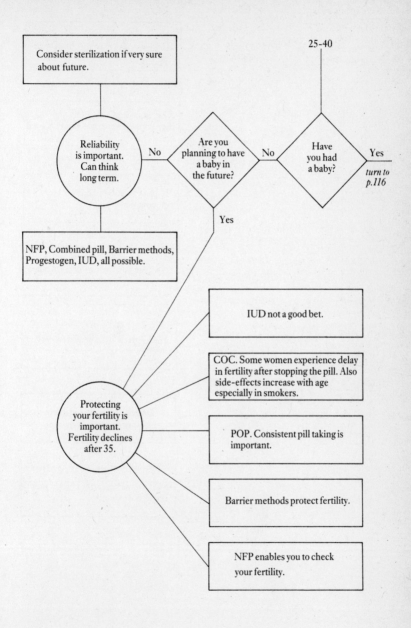

Consider sterilization if very sure about future.

Reliability is important. Can think long term.

No

Are you planning to have a baby in the future?

No

25-40

Have you had a baby?

Yes

turn to p.116

Yes

NFP, Combined pill, Barrier methods, Progestogen, IUD, all possible.

Protecting your fertility is important. Fertility declines after 35.

IUD not a good bet.

COC. Some women experience delay in fertility after stopping the pill. Also side-effects increase with age especially in smokers.

POP. Consistent pill taking is important.

Barrier methods protect fertility.

NFP enables you to check your fertility.

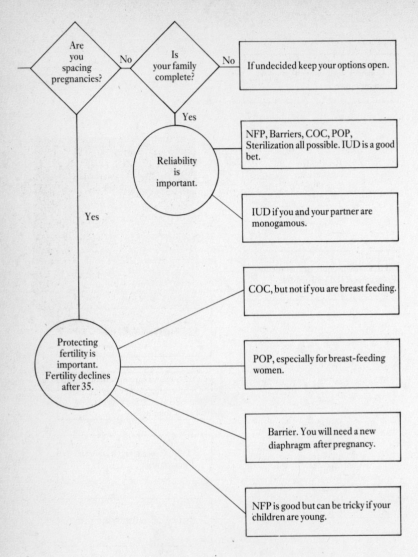

PART TWO   CONTRACEPTION

CHAPTER 4

Fertility Awareness and Natural Family Planning

It is the medical man's business to tame and control the stork.

Marie Stopes, *Contraception*

To live with our bodies, and not in spite of them, is a discovery our 'civilized' world is just now making... We need to understand the natural laws of our bodies in order to achieve optimal enjoyment as well as new depths of communication...

Ingrid Trobisch in Preface to *Natural Sex* by Mary Shivanandas

The most non-interventionist way of living with fertility is to discover the body's own pattern of fertility and infertility. If you do not want a baby, you abstain from sexual intercourse or other close genital contact when your body tells you that it is fertile; if you do want to become pregnant you time intercourse to coincide with the days of maximum fertility during your cycle. This, in a nutshell, is natural family planning. These chapters on contraception start with NFP (as it has come to be known) because it is at the very bottom of the interventionist tree. An understanding of the physiology of the fertile body (fundamental to NFP) is the root and trunk on which all other contraceptives systems are based. One of its attractions for those who practise it is the autonomy it offers from the medical establishment; those who use it are directly or indirectly making a clear statement that normal fertility is not a medical matter and does not therefore need doctors to control it. It does not require trips to the family planning clinic or GP to stock up on supplies, it does not interfere with health or well-being and its enthusiasts claim that it brings with it a whole range of *positive* side-effects.

It is very important to point out at the beginning of this chapter that NFP is not recommended for a woman who is unsure of her partner's previous sexual history. Making love without a condom even when you know you can't get pregnant is simply not worth the risk of the sexually transmitted diseases (including AIDS) which this exposes you to.

The foundation of NFP is *fertility awareness*. Fertility awareness is the process of reading the signs that the female body offers month by month to indicate its rising, peaking and declining fertility. These signs are not arbitrary but a direct response to levels of circulating hormones in the body. A women practising fertility awareness learns, often with remarkable accuracy, to read her body. Once she has the knowledge, it is hers to use as she likes, to conceive, to abstain, to contracept. The terms NFP and 'fertility awareness' have recently come to take on rather specific meanings. NFP refers to using a variety of indicators to work out the most fertile time of the month and abstaining from sexual intercourse at that time. Fertility awareness seems now to mean using exactly the same methods to work out when you are fertile, but using a barrier, or withdrawal rather than abstinence at this time. In this chapter however we will use 'fertility awareness' to refer to the whole process of learning the signs that the body offers a woman. When we are referring to fertility awareness as a system which involves using a barrier during the fertile time, we will capitalize it – Fertility Awareness.

A short history

It seems extraordinary that as recently as 1926 professional family planners such as Marie Stopes could be making wild generalizations about the pattern of infertility and fertility in a woman's cycle. She wrote that 'the length of the supposed "safe period" varies in individual women; in some it lasts over a fortnight; in some it lasts three or four days; in many it does not exist at all . . . so far as observations and experience confided to me go, *the ordinary working-class healthy woman has no safe period at all* [her italics] . . .'[1] Marie Stopes's opinion has more to do with class prejudices and eugenic arguments than with any scientific theory, but the fact remains that it was not until the late twenties and early thirties that there *was* any definite understanding of when ovulation occurred in a woman's cycle. This is not to say however that there were not plenty of learned pronouncements on the subject before this. For centuries medical men assumed that women were like bitches; menstrual bleeding was a sign of fertility, like being on heat, and conception was more likely during or just after a period. It is curious that it took quite so long to pinpoint the mid-cycle nature of ovulation since a number of discoveries pointed in this direction long before the two scientists, Kyusaku Ogino of Japan and Herman Knaus of Austria, working quite independently of each other, 'discovered' the timing of ovulation in the 1930s.

As early as 1843 a French scientist called Raciborski had noticed that women who married shortly after their period had finished usually conceived in the first menstrual cycle of marriage, but if they married late in the cycle another period seemed to pass before pregnancy occurred. The fact that a woman's temperature is higher in the second half of a cycle was noted as early as 1868, but it was not until 1904 that the Dutch gynaecologist Van de Velde noted a possible relationship between this and ovulation. Ogino and Knaus's revolutionary discovery was that the number of days between ovulation and the next period tends to be fairly constant. Ogino put it at twelve to sixteen days and Knaus at fifteen. From this both men established systems for working out when intercourse was safe, systems which were rapidly taken up by Catholic doctors. One book that appeared in 1932 was called *The Rhythm of Sterility and Fertility in Women* by a Dr Latz, and the new method of family planning quickly took on the name 'rhythm method' or 'calendar rhythm'. The trouble with the calculations, as we will see, is that they make no allowances for months in which the cycle deviates dramatically from its normal length, and this leads to a certain amount of unreliability.

Meanwhile other developments were taking place. Throughout the 1930s and 1940s advances were made in detecting the effects of sex hormones present in a woman's body at different times in the cycle. In 1933 two scientists, Sequy and Vimeux, began to study cervical mucus and relate it to what was known about the timing of ovulation. Changes in the cervical mucus, in particularly the shift from being thick and whitish to liquid and profuse had been noticed as early as 1840, though the significance of the changes was not understood. It was not until the 1960s that Dr John Billings, an Australian Catholic gynaecologist, began to work out rules for using the changes in cervical mucus as a means of family planning. This became known as the Billings or ovulation method of NFP. Since the 1960s natural family planning has come of age. New systems that combine cervical mucus, temperature taking, elements of rhythm, cervical examination and a more general body awareness have been shown to be more effective than relying on cervical mucus alone. These 'multi-index' or 'sympto-thermal' methods have made fertility awareness and NFP a far more attractive method of fertility control than the original rhythm method. What is more, when used by well-taught, highly motivated couples the level of unintended pregnancies is, as we shall see, extremely low.

The search is now on for still more accurate ways of pinpointing the time of ovulation – if possible far enough in advance to allow for sperm survival of around five days. A number of devices, such as First Response and Ovustick, are already on the market for use in detecting the most fertile time. These work by measuring the LH surge in the blood which happens only twelve to thirty-six hours before ovulation, far too late to be effective in indicating the need for contraception. The time is certainly coming when there will be NFP test kits readily available from chemists which can also measure the rising tide of oestrogen or other body chemicals in time to prevent conception. But women who are well versed in the signs their bodies offer them may not need such kits, since, as we will see in the next section, hormonal assays (measurements) have not so far proved to be any more accurate than women's own subjective impressions.

Natural signs of fertility and infertility

I would definitely consider natural family planning if I was married or in a relationship that was secure enough to take children . . . but I have no idea about the timing of ovulation. I wish I did. It is very important to me that I menstruate.

This comment from someone who wrote to us sums up well the attitude of many women to the idea of natural family planning. It seems attractive, but risky and only really suitable for a woman who is ready to have children. And the reason that it is considered risky? Because fertility seems such a dangerous thing. Many women have protected themselves against it for years, and the idea of going to bed 'unprotected' is more than a little scary. The vast majority of women have very little idea of the recurring pattern of fertility and infertility that characterizes an ordinary menstrual cycle. But World Health Organization trials suggest that almost 90 per cent of women can learn to detect the signs of impending ovulation after just one cycle of observation,[2] and women experienced in reading the signs can be as accurate in pinpointing the most fertile time of a cycle as the scientists who check the levels of hormones in their blood and urine and scan their ovaries with ultrasound. If a woman can pinpoint her fertile time accurately it follows that she can work out the times when contraception is quite superfluous since there is no egg to fertilize anyway.

One of the problems with natural family planning is that it is usually presented in terms of a method that you 'follow'; first there was the calendar rhythm method, then the temperature method; then came the Billings or ovulation method, otherwise known as the cervical mucus method, from which evolved the sympto-thermic method; finally we have FAM – the fertility awareness method. Unfortunately some of the promoters of different 'methods' are quite militant about the efficacy of their system, and hate to see its purity diluted with other ideas. On the other hand, a growing number of people are simply interested to understand what their body can offer them in terms of fertility awareness, and who wish to use this understanding for their own purposes, whether for conceiving or cutting down the use of contraception to a minimum, or any other reason. This section is largely addressed to such people. We want to present as full an account as possible of the state of the art in fertility awareness. The following section looks at how the findings of recent research have been systematized into methods, and stresses that to use NFP for successfully avoiding conceptions it is best to work with a trained counsellor for a couple of cycles at least.

A review of the hormonal cycle

We suggest that you begin by rereading the section in Chapter 1, 'A perfect conception'. The important thing as far as fertility awareness is concerned, is the interplay between the two hormones produced by the pituitary gland in response to signals from the hypothalamus, FSH and LH, and the two produced in the ovaries, oestrogen and progesterone. The complex mechanism of their ebb and flow is also shown in Figure 4.1 below which charts an ideal twenty-eight day cycle with ovulation occurring on the fourteenth day and menstruation fourteen days later.

An ideal cycle works like this. The FSH (follicle stimulating hormone produced by the pituitary gland) stimulates a group of follicles to begin to develop, which in turn produce oestrogen. Oestrogen rises in the blood stream, affecting the cervical mucus and endometrium. As one egg becomes dominant it pumps out more and more oestrogen which operates a positive feedback mechanism stimulating a massive surge of LH (luteinizing hormone, again produced by the pituitary gland). The LH peak follows on shortly from the oestrogen peak (certainly within twenty-four hours and sometimes much less) and persists for about forty-eight hours during which time the egg becomes fully mature and leaves the ovary. It is thought that ovulation occurs somewhere between sixteen to twenty-four hours after the LH peak and thus anything up to three days after the oestrogen peak. Once ovulation has occurred, the level of progesterone begins to rise rapidly in the blood stream produced by the corpus luteum left behind in the ovary when the egg erupted. It is this that causes the basal bodily temperature to rise a little and the cervical mucus to alter its consistency back to the thicker mucus of the infertile period. It is the body's manifestation of this internal drama that is the basis for fertility awareness; oestrogen and progesterone produce tangible signs which can be felt, seen and measured. It is to these we now turn. Figure 4.2 shows the complex feedback mechanism of the hormonal pathways in more detail.

Figure 4.1 The complex and finely tuned menstrual cycle

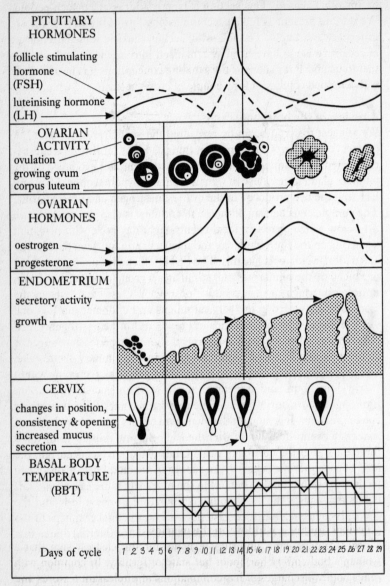

Source: Nancy Loudon, *Handbook of Family Planning*, Churchill Livingstone, 1985.

Figure 4.2 The complex feedback mechanism of hormonal pathways

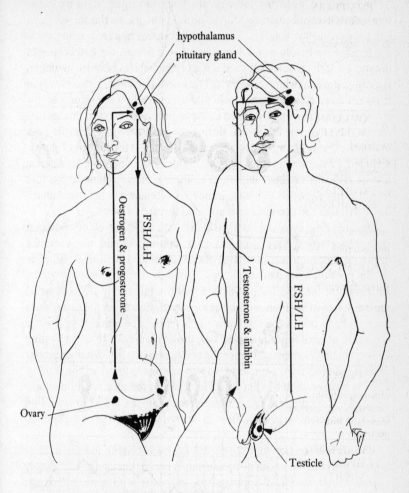

Cervical mucus: a window on the ovaries

Cervical mucus is an unfortunate name for the clearest sign that a woman's body offers her about her state of fertility. In common with other bodily discharges, it has connotations of unpleasant textures and lack of hygiene. But cervical mucus is the best indicator of the level of circulating oestrogen in the body, and the level of oestrogen is directly correlated to the growth, in the ovary, of the egg (known as the Graafian follicle) which is going to be released that month. By learning to read the fluids that the cervix creates in response to oestrogen, a woman can tell accurately when the level of oestrogen first begins to rise (created by the group of immature follicles which start to ripen) right up to the time when the one mature follicle pumps out its maximum surge of oestrogen prior to ovulation. The cervix produces mucus in response to the level of oestrogen in the blood because it acts as the gatekeeper of the uterus; if the ovaries are producing oestrogen it is because ovulation is getting close, in which case the cervix needs to change its gatekeeping function from a no-entrance policy to a positively welcoming one for any sperm that may be deposited in the vagina. The cervical mucus that blocks the arrival of the sperm during the pre-ovulatory infertile days makes the cervix like an impassable muddy track. At the time of ovulation it is as if a four lane motorway opened up for the sperm. The cervical mucus radically changes its structure from a dense cellular mass to a free-flowing network in which hundreds of channels help the sperm move through the cervical canal and into the uterus.

Day one of the cycle begins with menstruation. The levels of oestrogen and progesterone have dropped to a minimum, and the carefully prepared endometrium, burgeoning with sugars and extra blood supplies for the possible arrival of an embryo, is sloughed off through the cervix. At this point (or possibly just before – at the tail end of the last cycle) the low levels of hormones in the blood cause the FSH to begin its work once more in the ovaries. Initially the level of production is below the threshold needed to stimulate the new group of follicles to start ripening and producing oestrogen. Hence the cervix remains dry. After a number of days (varying from woman to woman and cycle to cycle) the level of FSH is high enough to stimulate the group of follicles into action and within five days they are secreting oestrogen into the blood stream. The cervix, ever sensitive to such shifts in hormone levels, begins to produce mucus.

The correlation between the onset of cervical mucus and the level of oestrogen in the blood can be measured. Women practising NFP simply note that their mucus has appeared and know that with oestrogen rising, ovulation cannot be far away. In a well-designed experiment to test the accuracy of such perceptions it was found that the forty-three women who charted an ovulatory cycle were almost all spot on when their own assessments of the beginning of their fertile period were checked with oestrogen levels in their blood.[3] In a study of twenty-two menstrual cycles also carried out by Billings and his team, it was found that the average time for the beginning of the first sign of oestrogen in the blood was around six days (6.2) before the time of ovulation (the time of ovulation being defined as the day following the peak of LH in the blood stream). In a similar study, by Anna Flynn, of twenty-nine cycles from nine women the first mucus sign was identified 5.2 days before the LH peak – a finding identical to that of Billings (who defined ovulation as the day *after* this LH peak).[4] In both studies, however, there was quite a wide range in the timing of the onset of mucus signs in relation to the LH peak or ovulation: ten days before to just three days in the Billings study and from twelve days to three days in the Flynn study.

So what are these mucus signs that herald the rising tide of oestrogen in the blood, and the onset of fertility? Following menstruation the vulva and vagina tend to feel very dry. Towards the end of a period taking out a tampon may feel uncomfortable. This is a sign that no fertile cervical mucus is being produced. The professional NF planners refer to this as 'a positive sensation or feeling of dryness in the genital area'. The number of dry days varies from women to woman and from cycle to cycle. A long cycle will have more dry days; a short cycle may have no dry days at all. In the next stage there may be some mucus present variously described as thick, tacky, opaque, sticky, pasty, or crumbly. It is usually a whitish-yellow in colour. The important point is that it should still leave the vagina and vulva feeling dry. If it does it is still considered to be the basic kind of infertile mucus.

The main purpose of the infertile mucus is probably to act as a barrier for the uterus against both sperm and any infections that might be present in the vagina. It contains many leukocytes – white blood cells responsible for 'eating up' any kind of microbe that strays into the vagina (including sperm). Despite on-going research its full purpose is not yet fully understood, but it is clearly a useful indication to a woman that the growth of follicles in her ovaries has not yet advanced enough to produce oestrogen.

As the follicles in the ovary ripen, the cervix crypts begin production of the first fertile mucus. It is important to remember that in some women these fertile signs follow on directly from menstruation – they have no dry days at all; other women may go for a week or longer after menstruation before seeing the first fertile mucus. This first fertile mucus is often creamy and white or it may be slightly sticky and cloudy. The main point is that it produces a feeling of moistness in the vagina and vulva. The wetter the mucus becomes the closer a woman is moving towards ovulation. When held between finger and thumb the mucus stretches a little before breaking. Over the next few days – anything from twelve to as few as three – the mucus will gradually become more and more 'fertile'.

The most fertile mucus, produced when the levels of oestrogen in the blood stream are at their highest, is very clear, stretchy (sometimes stretching ten centimeters or so before breaking) and resembles a thin eggwhite. Its technical name is Spinnbarkeit, which is German for spider's web, and this is a good description for the thin stretchy threads which can be drawn out of it. Some women can easily see this fertile mucus, others are only aware of a feeling of moistness or wetness around their vagina (this mucus is 98 per cent water). Scientists studying this fertile mucus have called it type E mucus (E meaning oestrogenic). This mid-cycle mucus contains a high proportion of salt. If a sample is spread on a glass slide to dry and looked at under a microscope, it produces a pattern known as ferning, since it looks like fern leaves. This is the result of the mucus drying in distinctive channels, each edged with salt. The more salt, the more ferning, and the more ferning the more likely is ovulation. If you taste this fertile mucus it has a definitely salty flavour.

While the effect of the infertile mucus is to keep the sperm out, fertile mucus helps the sperm reach the all-important egg. It does this in a number of ways. The fertile or E type mucus has two components; if you look at this mucus closely you will often see that the clear stretchy mucus coexists with another type of mucus which is slightly lumpy and

Figure 4.3 Fertile mucus showing ferning

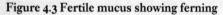

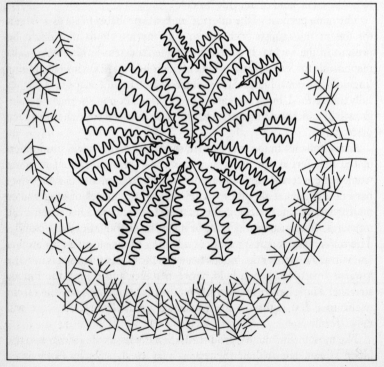

Figure 4.4 Fertile mucus letting sperm pass through

Infertile mucus blocking the path of sperm

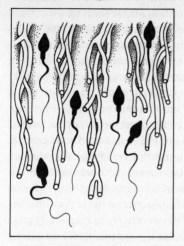
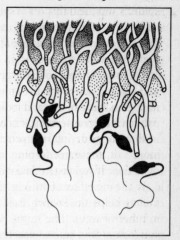

may be whitish in colour. This seems to have a role in catching any malformed or unsuitable sperm that might try swimming into the uterus. It also seems to act as some sort of a support structure for the clearer, stretchy mucus. For maximum fertility both types of mucus need to exist together.

Basically the vagina is a very hostile place for sperm. Not only does it contain armies of leukocytes which directly threaten the sperm (by eating them up), but it is uncomfortably acidic. If left in the vagina sperm lose their motility within four to six hours, and are consumed by the leukocytes within the next twelve to twenty-four hours. This seems to be what happens when the impenetrable cervical mucus blocks their way to the uterus. During the fertile phase of the cycle however the special cervical mucus protects the sperm from the worst effects of the vaginal environment, and transports them through it as soon as possible. Semen is very alkaline and seems to act as a buffer against the acidity of the vagina until the sperm can make it into the cervical mucus. At mid-cycle this mucus is also comparatively alkaline, has minimal numbers of leukocytes, and plenty of dissolved sugars and amino acids which feed and sustain the sperm. In addition to this the sperm are probably 'washed' by the high level of water in the mucus, so getting rid of the seminal fluid which surprisingly appears to be too alkaline for their long-term survival.

The thin slippery mucus has a quite different cellular structure to the dense thick mucus of infertile period. Instead of an impassable forest as many as 400 channels open up within it for the sperm to swim up. Some of these channels lead straight into the uterus, while others lead into the crypts of the endocervix. There has been a considerable amount of research into the transport of sperm and it has been suggested that there are three discernable phases: a 'rapid phase', a 'storage phase' and a 'slow release phase'. The rapid phase which lasts for two to ten minutes, sees the very quick transport of sperm from the cervix into the fallopian tubes – sperm have been found there as soon as five minutes after ejaculation. These are the sperm which have found their way into a channel in the mucus leading directly into the uterine cavity. (They may have been helped on their way by the contractions of the uterus, caused either by orgasm or by the prostaglandins in the semen which stimulate the uterus to contract – both as yet unproven hypotheses.) Unless an egg is already waiting in the fallopian tube however, these sperm are not likely to be very successful in fertilization. Sperm with a better chance of survival are those which, guided by the channels in the cervical mucus, find their way into the crypts of the cervix where, during the storage phase, they feed off the carbohydrates in the mucus before launching forth in flotillas. This is the slow release phase. Since it is the case that a successful conception occurs most often if intercourse takes place one or two days *before* ovulation, the forming of reservoirs of sperm and their nourishment and protection is one of the most important functions of the cervical mucus.

In NFP jargon the most important day of fertile mucus production is called *peak mucus day*. This is not necessarily the day when the most mucus is produced. Rather it is the *last* day when the fertile stretchy mucus is present. It is called the peak day because it corresponds very closely to the peak secretion of oestrogen in the blood stream. Once the oestrogen has peaked the symptoms of fertile mucus rapidly disappear, so that the last day on which they are present is a very significant sign of impending ovulation. The peak of oestrogen occurs either on the same day as the peak in LH, or one or two days before. It is the peaking of the LH that determines when ovulation will occur, and the literature on how soon after the oestrogen peak ovulation occurs differs. Some studies seem to suggest that ovulation nearly always occurs within thirty-six hours of the oestrogen peak. Others claim that the ovulation follows the peak mucus day by 'not more than three days'. Since sperm nourished by fertile mucus can live for anything up to five days (and some studies have found living sperm seven days after ejaculation), whether ovulation follows the peak mucus day by thirty-six hours or three days may not be so important. Intercourse on the peak mucus day will always maximize the chances of conception.

Obviously there is one drawback with the concept of the peak mucus day. It can only be identified retrospectively. Experienced users of NFP claim that the shift from fertile to non-fertile mucus occurs from one day to the next and that identifying it, even retrospectively, does not present any problems. But women may have other problems with detecting their cervical mucus. Some women simply do not produce very much of it – and therefore have to rely on sensation rather than on the sight of the mucus. Similarly in other women the wet stretchy fertile mucus may be hidden in a denser-looking mucus; but there may still be enough there to enable sperm to enter the cervix and uterus. In other women the production of fertile mucus fluctuates from month to month; in one month it may be easy to see what is happening, and in another much more difficult. It does seem to be the case however that practice is the key to reading the mucus signs. Only in a very small percentage of women with normal ovulatory cycles is it almost impossible to follow the progression of the fertile mucus.

Once the peak mucus day has come and gone the cycle comes under the sway of progesterone, secreted by the corpus luteum. Progesterone acts against the effects of oestrogen; the mucus rapidly reverts to the thick, sticky infertile mucus characteristic of the first days of the cycle which remains until the onset of the next menstruation, though in some women menstruation is preceded by a wetter type of mucus. This however is *not* fertile mucus.

These then are the changes in the cervical mucus that characterize a cycle of fertility. By studying the changes women can know when it is safe to have unprotected intercourse.

Observing your mucus

Observing mucus becomes considerably easier with practice. Some mucus collects at the outside of your vagina and you can observe it simply by feeling it with your fingers or looking at it on a piece of loo paper. In order to have a sense of its texture however you should feel it. If you hold it between two fingers you can draw your fingers apart and see how stretchy it is. You will quickly learn to tell the differences between pasty, crumbly mucus and the thin, stretchy mucus which occurs at mid-cycle. The most efficient way of observing mucus is to look at it and feel it every time you go to the lavatory. If you have difficulty in observing any mucus at all, it may be that you produce very little. Don't be discouraged; persistent observation may bring results. Some women find that it is easier to detect their mucus after they have been to the loo, since this helps to push mucus currently higher in the vagina downwards. Talking to a NFP counsellor may be helpful.

Temperature shift

One of the easiest measurable indications of progesterone is body temperature. Temperatures go up and down depending on what time of the day it is. Even under conditions of constant rest the basal temperature varies from a minimum between 3 and 6 a.m. to a maximum between 3 and 7 p.m. With the formation of the corpus luteum, the progesterone secreted into the blood stream causes a woman's basal temperature to rise by about 0.2°C or 0.35°F. The shift in temperature occurs *after* ovulation has taken place, and remains until one or two days before the next period, when the drop in progesterone is indicated by a drop in temperature. Some women find this a useful way of telling when their period is about to start. The attraction of taking temperatures is that it offers an objective measurement; it can be plotted on paper and studied in a way that many find reassuring. Cervical mucus comes and goes. Some cycles may have intermittent patches of mucus as the body tries to ovulate but for some reason (out of practice because of the pill, influence of prolactin in breastfeeding, approach of the menopause) doesn't quite make it. The mucus signs may be confusing. With a clear-cut temperature curve a woman, her partner, and her NFP counsellor can see clearly whether or not ovulation has taken place. Women who are trying to conceive may be reassured by a good temperature curve that they are ovulating. We know of one woman who felt that a hysterectomy had threatened her sense of her own femininity. She was helped by taking her temperature and seeing that her ovaries were still working well and that her hormonal cycle continued despite the operation. A good temperature chart can become, for many women, a positive indication of their own well-being.

By taking your temperature every morning (or at least for around ten days mid cycle) and marking it on a chart specially designed for the purpose you can gain a very clear indication of when your temperature rises, and therefore when ovulation can be presumed to have taken place. Unfortunately temperature shift is a retrospective sign and gives no indication at all of when ovulation might be due. A typical chart showing a clear temperature curve from a cycle in which ovulation has taken place is seen in Figure 4.5.

Some temperature curves are clear cut and easy to define; others move up very slowly. Others need a professional eye to make sense of them. The chart of a woman who gets up and down to a baby during the night may be very hard to read accurately. Even one nightly disturbance may have an effect on basal body temperature (BBT) and may make a chart difficult to read. People who have studied temperature charts in great detail have come up with a number of useful techniques for

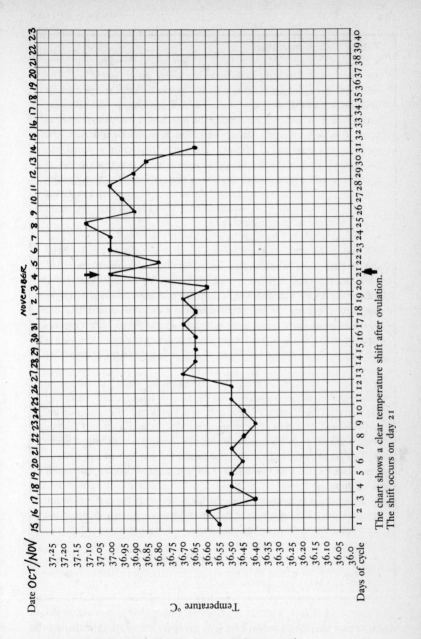

Figure 4.5 Temperature changes in an ovulatory cycle

Taking your temperature

• Your temperature should be taken at more or less the same time every day – preferably first thing in the morning before getting out of bed. The point is to get a comparative temperature graph, and this seems the best time for getting this on a day-to-day basis. Some women find this quite impossible, and may be interested in the results of a study carried out in 1974 in which nineteen women recorded their temperatures in the morning, at 5 p.m. and at bedtime. The 5 p.m. temperature was always the highest, but it was still quite possible to detect a temperature shift at whatever time the temperature was taken. The early morning temperature shift remained the easiest to interpret, however, and if a woman is relying on the temperature method alone for her fertility control it may be better to stick to early morning temperatures.

• Temperatures can be taken orally, vaginally or rectally. Most women will choose to put a thermometer under their tongue, but it has been shown that some women who had difficulty interpreting their oral temperature found a more noticeable rise with a vaginal or rectal temperature. One woman who had difficulty with early morning temperature taking because of her small daughter's noisy eruptions into her bedroom at 6.30 a.m. found that she could successfully take her temperature vaginally. She kept her thermometer under her pillow and took her temperature without her daughter noticing and trying to pull it out of her mouth.

• Specially designed fertility thermometers are easier to read than ordinary clinical thermometers. But the kind of temperature charts that are sold with these fertility thermometers in Boots and other chemists are not very well designed. The temperature shift is sometimes difficult to read. Natural family planning teachers can supply you with better charts.

• Temperature taking via the mouth takes about five minutes, while temperatures taken via the vagina or rectum seem to become stable after three minutes.

• Shake the thermometer down the night before so that early morning temperature taking involves the minimum of hassle. Read and record the temperature when you are up and about – it's not necessary to make an instant record if you're half asleep.

• It is best to use the same thermometer throughout a cycle – different thermometers have been known to give different temperatures and minute accuracy is all-important.

interpreting them and we will look at these in the section 'Putting it all together'.

The length of the cycle

So far we have looked at the signs given by cervical mucus and the effects of progesterone on temperature as key indicators of fertility. Another, but cruder, indication can be worked out from the length of the cycle itself. As we saw in the section on history, it was not until the 1930s that Knaus and Ogino worked out that ovulation preceeded menstruation by a relatively fixed number of days. Knaus put it at fifteen, while Ogino considered it was between twelve and sixteen days, which is now considered to be largely correct. On the basis of their discoveries both men worked out ways of calculating the 'safe' period in a cycle, taking into account the survival time of sperm and ovum which they put at three days and one day respectively. Since Ogino's calculation built in a flexible number of days between ovulation and menstruation his method offered more reliability.

To calculate the beginning of the fertile period using Ogino's method it is necessary to have lengths of the last six consecutive cycles (e.g., thirty-two, thirty-three, thirty-one, thirty, thirty-five and thirty-two days). To calculate the earliest infertile part of the cycle you take the shortest cycle and substract nineteen to find the number of infertile days (i.e. $30 - 19 = 11$). Day twelve would see the start of the fertile period. The figure nineteen is made up of sixteen (longest number of days from ovulation to menstruation) plus three days for sperm survival. Ogino's calculation is considered by some to allow too little time for sperm survival, which has now been put at five days rather than three. To make the calculation safer, it is now suggested that you take your shortest cycle and subtract twenty-one. In this case, day nine would be the last infertile day available for unprotected intercourse.

The calendar method for calculating the *end* of the fertile period is very rarely recommended since temperature taking offers a far more objective and reliable method. However, for interest, Ogino calculated that to work out the end of the fertile period you take the longest cycle and subtract ten (i.e. $35 - 10 = 25$). The number ten comes from the shortest period of days between ovulation and menstruation minus survival time for the egg (i.e. $12 - 2 = 10$). In this case day twenty-six would see the start of the infertile period after ovulation. It must be stressed that the calendar calculation is much less effective than studying the other signs of fertility. Its main use is as a double check against them.

The main problem with using a calculated method, rather than observing what is actually happening in *this* cycle, is that very few women have absolutely regular cycles. In one study of an average of thirteen cycles in 30,000 women almost two-thirds of women had cycles that varied by more than eight days. Ovulation can be accelerated or it can be delayed. There is some evidence that great excitement or fear can accelerate ovulation, while illness, tension, bereavement, stress or weight loss can delay ovulation. A woman relying on calendar calculations alone has no indication of the time of ovulation which probably accounts for the high rate of pregnancies that occur with this method.

Other effects of oestrogen and progesterone

The cervix

Oestrogen is a potent hormone and as the growing follicles pump it out into the blood stream it produces various other effects some of which are observable, others invisible. Its effect on the cervix itself is particularly useful for women who want to detect when they are ovulating. Some women find the idea of feeling their cervix unpleasant; others find it no problem. The attitude of medical professionals towards women becoming acquainted with the changes in their cervices is, as one might expect, mixed. In one recent book on women's health the authors write: 'The ascertaining of the viscosity of cervical mucus is not too practical, and might be of doubtful significance when contaminated with uterine and vaginal fluid, and *the manipulations involved come close to being dangerously infectious*.' [Our italics.][5] Dr Billings of the Billings method is also negative but for a very curious reason, '. . . digital exploration of the vagina, cervical palpation . . . make it impossible for the behaviour of the mucus during the fertile phase and the peak symptom to be recognized with certainty.'[6] It is difficult to see how feeling the cervix with a clean finger could do anything other than enhance the detection of fertile mucus. As far as the risk of infection is concerned it seems unlikely that a freshly washed finger could pose any more threat of infection than the average penis, which is hardly sterilized before use.

The changes that take place in the cervix are relative and probably need to be learnt over a couple of months. In the first part of the cycle the cervix is firm, with the os cervix (the opening) closed. The uterus lies low in the pelvis and the cervix is usually easy to feel with a finger. It often seems to be tilted to one side or the other. For women who have not had a baby (or not delivered vaginally) the cervix feels like a small firm bump, some say like the tip of the nose while the cervical os feels like an indentation in the centre. One woman said that she thought of her cervix as being a bit like a *glacé* cherry with the stone removed. In women who have delivered babies vaginally the cervix usually feels different afterwards since the os in the centre never completely closes.

Under the influence of oestrogen the cervix begins to change its texture and shape. Its texture becomes softer, until it feels spongy rather than rubbery, rather like the texture of the lips. The os becomes wider until it is possible to put the tip of a finger into it. At the same time the cervix rises up in the pelvis, straightening itself out as it does so. It becomes much more difficult to reach with a finger during the fertile time since it is so high in the vagina. It is not fully understood why this is so, but it may be to ensure the best possible position to receive the maximum number of sperm.

The changes in the cervix usually begin four or five days before ovulation so, together with the cervical mucus, they can provide a good indication that a woman is fertile. Almost immediately after ovulation and under the influence of progesterone the cervix sinks back down low in the vagina, becoming firm and closed once again. Recognizing this is useful for women who want to avoid using contraception in the second half of their cycle, especially if this sign is seen in the context of the other

Figure 4.6 The changes in the cervix in relation to ovulation

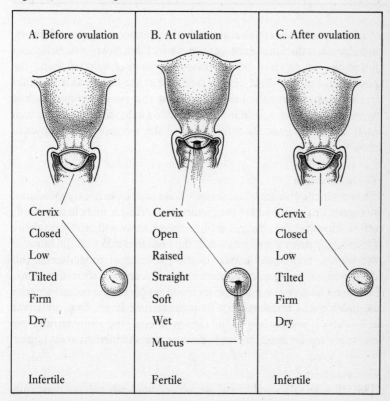

A. Before ovulation	B. At ovulation	C. After ovulation
Cervix	Cervix	Cervix
Closed	Open	Closed
Low	Raised	Low
Tilted	Straight	Tilted
Firm	Soft	Firm
Dry	Wet	Dry
	Mucus	
Infertile	Fertile	Infertile

Source: E. Clubb and J. Knight. *Fertility: A Comprehensive Guide to Natural Family Planning*, David and Charles, 1987.

non-fertile signs. Occasionally women who have had babies may find that the rising and lowering of the cervix is less obvious. As the uterus has become more relaxed it may be less able to move the cervix.

Feeling your cervix
In order to feel your cervix you will need to get into a comfortable position where you can reach it easily. Some women find squatting helpful, others that standing with one leg on a bed or something similar is easier. You should gently slide your forefinger into your vagina, as high as it will go until you reach your cervix. If you examine your cervix every day you will quickly get used to the different phases that it passes through. Once you have come to know what changes to expect, feeling it for a week or so mid-cycle will be enough. Some women have particularly long vaginas, and find that it is very difficult to reach their cervix. Examining the changes in the cervix is not essential to NFP and if you find it difficult or unpleasant you can still rely on the other signs.

Interestingly the cervix has attracted the attention of feminist thinkers, in particularly the nineteenth-century writer Olive Schreiner. Schreiner found the os cervix a potent image of the way women shape the possibilities of the whole human race, just as the cervix, as it stretches in childbirth, shapes the head of the baby that passes through it. She wrote that it 'forms . . . an intranscendable circle, circumscribing with each successive generation the limits of the expansion of the human race.'[7]

The endometrium
Changes in the endometrium are only detectable by surgical procedures, so cannot be used to add to the picture of pending fertility that the body offers. However the changes are interesting so we will briefly list them. Oestrogen causes a proliferation in the cells that make up the lining of the uterus, vagina and cervix. In the presence of progesterone this development stops, and the endometrium enters a secretory phase, becoming thicker as it builds up its blood supply to become as receptive as possible to a fertilized egg. As progesterone levels drop under the self-destruct mechanism of the corpus luteum, the endometrium can no longer sustain itself, begins to disintegrate and menstruation begins.

Fallopian tubes
The fallopian tubes and uterus are never completely still but constantly contracting and moving. Once ovulation has taken place however, activity of the uterus decreases considerably. The kind of smooth muscle tissue

which makes up the uterus and the fallopian tubes is much more active in the presence of oestrogen, and this activity is suppressed by the influence of progesterone. It seems that one of the effects of oestrogen is to cause muscular contractions that draw the fallopian tubes down over the surface of the ovary to maximize the chances of the fimbria catching the ovum as it pops out of the ovary. Another, as yet unproved function of oestrogen-caused contractions may be to help draw the sperm through the cervical canal and into the uterus.

Breasts

Some breasts are very sensitive to hormone fluxes, and high levels of both oestrogen and progesterone can make them feel tender. However, because the effects of the two hormones are different, the feeling in the breasts may also differ at different times. Many women are more familiar with breast tenderness before menstruation than at ovulation. During the premenstrual phase and under the influence of progesterone, the blood flow in the breasts increases (just as it does in the endometrium), which causes the connective tissue in the breast to swell, leading to the feeling of fullness and tenderness. In the same way that progesterone prepares the lining of the uterus for pregnancy, the milk ducts in the breast begin to develop – a process that would accelerate rapidly if a pregnancy were to occur. This continues for the first couple of days of menstruation, but five to seven days after the start of a period the breasts return to their smallest size, which is why this is the time that women are recommended to check their breasts for lumps. As the oestrogen level rises again another breast cycle starts, and breasts under the influence of oestrogen may feel tingling and painful as a miniature re-run of the original growth of the breasts (which occurred under the first surges of oestrogen during puberty) begins to occur again.

The type of tenderness that occurs with the rise in the progesterone level in the blood can be a very useful confirmatory sign to a woman that ovulation is over and intercourse will not result in a pregnancy. Cycles in which there is no breast tenderness at all, and no premenstrual tension, cramps or pain may well have been anovulatory.

Ovulation pain

Ovulation pain, or Mittelschmerz (German for 'middle pain') can be a useful sign for some women that ovulation is about to occur, is occurring or has occurred. Such pain can be sharp or dull, on either side or throughout the lower abdomen, lasting from a few hours to several days. Unfortunately it is very difficult to decide exactly what the pain is caused by, and therefore which point in the process of ovulation it indicates.

R. F. Vollman who studied thousands of cycles found that approximately
45 per cent of women had abdominal pain accompanying ovulation in
some cycles, but that this pain occurred anywhere from nine days before
the BBT (temperature) shift to two days afterwards.[8] It used to be
thought that this pain was caused by the release of blood and fluid into
the peritoneal cavity as the follicle burst at ovulation. More recently it
has been found that some women experience the pain at the height of
the LH surge in the blood. In this case it seems likely that the pain may
be related to the pressure built up as the follicle bulges against the
surface of the ovary, just before ovulation. In some women the pain at
mid-cycle is considerable, and disturbing if not understood for what it
is. One woman we know of was told that she had salpingitis (inflammation
and infection in the fallopian tubes) and had to submit to a long drug
therapy and ultrasound examinations before she finally worked out for
herself that her pain was cyclical and corresponded to the time of
ovulation. Once she had made this discovery and began to relax when
the pain occurred the problem rapidly sorted itself out.

Mid-cycle bleeding
In a very few women the peak of ovulation is marked with spotting, or
mid-cycle bleeding. It may take the form of spots of blood, or it may
tinge the mid-cycle mucus pink, red or brown. It seems to be caused by
the fluctuations in oestrogen levels that occur at the very height of
fertility, just before ovulation. For the women who have this fertility
signal it can be very useful.

It is important that unexpected and unexplainable bleeding at any
stage of the cycle should be checked up. A mid-cycle bleed due to
ovulation is obviously harmless but if mid-cycle bleeding is not common
to your body it may be best to discuss it with a doctor.

Moods and libido
In nearly all female mammals oestrogen has a definite effect on libido.
Many female animals will not tolerate mating except at times of high
oestrogen. Human beings are an exception in that women may be
interested in sex at any time in their cycles. None the less many women
experience a definite tide of desire that correlates closely with the phases
of the menstrual cycle. One of the peaks of sexual interest seems, not
surprisingly, to occur at ovulation. We asked a number of women to
write about the ebbs and flows of sexual feelings that occurred during
their cycles. One woman wrote: 'I have a dream that recurs with a
surprisingly cyclical regularity. It is a dream about a man who never
became a lover though I always wished he had. At some point in my

cycle he always turns up again in a dream, and I find myself saying, "Ah well, time for ovulation again" – and I'm always right.'

Other women find that desire peaks just before or during menstruation. It is harder to account for this physiologically since progesterone tends to have the effect of decreasing libido, as some women on the pill have noticed. It may be the engorgement of the tissues in the uterus and cervix that makes them specially sensitive to sexual arousal at this time. Some women like to think that this pattern of arousal is nature's way of compensating them by giving them a maximum chance of arousal when they are least likely to conceive – the basis of natural contraception.

There is another idea about libido and the ovarian cycle. Some recent research on the levels of steroids in the blood such as cortisol, progesterone, oestrogen and testosterone found that there was in fact no direct relationship between the level of oestrogen and arousal, frequency of intercourse and sexual gratification. On the other hand there was a definite relationship between arousal and gratification and women's testosterone levels. The study found that the level of testosterone in the blood stream increased around the time of ovulation and that the frequency of intercourse was related to this. It would be surprising if nature had not provided some extra stimulation to sex at the time of ovulation, though it is also true that changes in libido are largely submerged or reinterpreted by human beings in psychological and social terms.

Using the signs to control fertility

Once you have come to understand the signs of fertility and infertility that your body offers you, how you use the information is entirely up to you. Some women simply *like* to find out what is going on in their bodies by looking at their mucus. They happily use a barrier method of contraception in the first part of their cycles until they are sure ovulation has come and gone, enjoying sex without any contraception on the remaining days. Others prefer to go the whole way, abstaining from intercourse when they are fertile, looking at all the different signs to try and pinpoint as accurately as possible the changes that take place in their bodies. In this section we will outline the systems that have been developed for using NFP. We will work chronologically through the cycle, showing how the picture of fertility/infertility can be built up. Our aim is to maximize the number of days in a cycle available for sexual intercourse without using contraception. Obviously sex does not need to involve intercourse and fertile days could be used for sex which does not involve genital contact.

Figure 4.7A Blank fertility chart

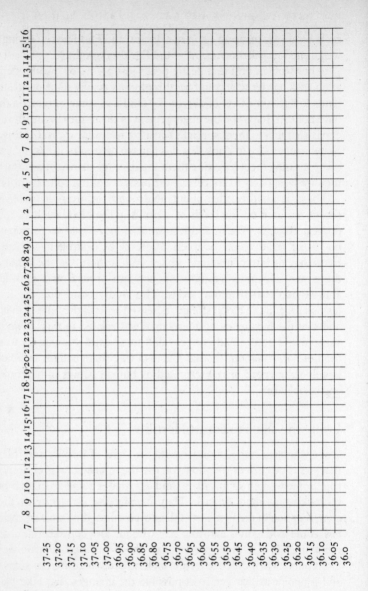

Date

Temperature °C

Days of cycle	1	2	3	4	5	6	7	8	9	10	11	12	13	14	15	16	17	18	19	20	21	22	23	24	25	26	27	28	29	30	31	32	33	34	35	36	37	38	39	40
Period/mucus																																								
Mucus (description)																																								
Cervix																																								
Breast tenderness																																								
Fertile/ Safe days																																								
Intercourse																																								
Ovulation pain																																								

last day of menstrual bleeding

shortest cycle minus 21

day of onset of mucus

day of onset of fertile mucus

peak mucus day

peak mucus day plus 4

third day of temperature rise above coverline

length of cycle

shortest cycle length in last 6 – 12 months

longest cycle length in last 6 – 12 months

KEY

P = period

D = dry day (no mucus dry vaginal sensation)

M = mucus (non-wet, non-fertile mucus)

F = fertile mucus

(F) = peak mucus day

Fertile/safe day symbols

S = safe for intercourse

F = potentially fertile/highly fertile

* = last day of calendar calculated infertile phase

Cervical symbols

→ • = evening of third day from post ovulatory closed cervix

• = low and closed

○ = higher and opening

O = high and fully open

Figure 4.7B Completed fertility chart

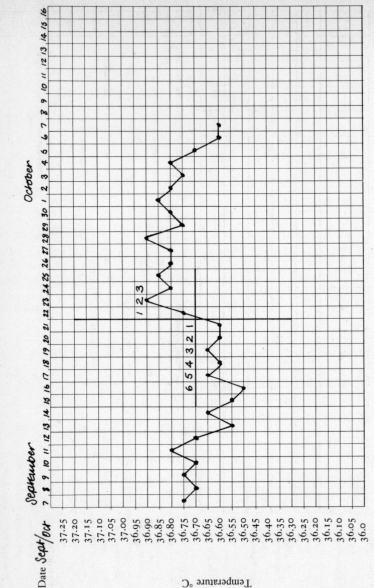

Date Sept/Oct

Temperature °C

Period/mucus	P	P	P	P	D	D	M	M	M	M	F	F	F	Ⓕ	M	M	M	D	D	D	D	D	D	D	D	M	M	M	P
Mucus (description)				BROWN SLUDGE		OPAQUE WHITE	OPAQUE WHITE CRUMBLY	OPAQUE WHITE MILKY	STRINGY STRETCHY	OPAQUE STRETCHY	WET CLEAR STRETCHY	CLEAR SLIPPERY WET STRETCHY	WET CLEAR	OPAQUE TACKY	OPAQUE TACKY	THICK SCANTY										MILKY	MILKY	MILKY	
Cervix					•	•	•	•	○	○	○	○	○	○				→•											
Breast tenderness																													
Fertile/ Safe days	S	S	S	S	F	F	F*	F	F	F	F	F	F	F	F	F	S	S	S	S	S	S	S	S	S	S	S	S	
Intercourse		✓	✗	✓	✗					✓	✓		✓	✓			✓	✓	✓		✓	✓	✓	✓	✓	✓	✓	✓	✓
Ovulation pain											✓	✓	✓																

last day of menstrual bleeding	5
shortest cycle minus 21	9
day of onset of mucus	8
day of onset of fertile mucus	12
peak mucus day	15
peak mucus day plus 4	19
third day of temperature rise above coverline	18
length of cycle	30
shortest cycle length in last 6 – 12 months	30
longest cycle length in last 6 – 12 months	35

KEY

P = period

D = dry day (no mucus dry vaginal sensation)

M = mucus (non-wet, non-fertile mucus)

F = fertile mucus

Ⓕ = peak mucus day

Fertile/safe day symbols

S = safe for intercourse

F = potentially fertile/highly fertile

* = last day of calendar calculated infertile phase

Cervical symbols

→• = evening of third day from post ovulatory closed cervix

• = low and closed

○ = higher and opening

◯ = high and fully open

As we have already pointed out, NFP includes various systems – the calendar rhythm, temperature, ovulation and sympto-thermal methods and Fertility Awareness. Many books on NFP organize their material according to which system they are teaching. Since all the research to date suggests that the sympto-thermal is by far the most reliable, our approach, in describing NFP techniques in detail, is basically a sympto-thermal one. If, however, you are keen to use another system – temperature, for example, to indicate when the safe period begins – it should be easy to extract the relevant information. One of the most useful tools for learning NFP or fertility awareness is a chart that covers all the days of a given cycle. We've included two, one filled out and another blank that can be used for photocopying. However, we want to stress again that working with a trained counsellor is still the best way of learning any system of NFP.

The ovarian/menstrual cycle can be divided into three phases for the purposes of discussing NFP.

1. The early infertile days
2. The most fertile period
3. The absolutely infertile days at the end of the cycle.

We will look at the ways of working out each of these.

The early infertile days

Menstruation
How safe is it to make love during menstruation without contraception? In the vast majority of cases the first *four* days of the cycle (in other words menstruation) are infertile, with a 99 per cent chance of avoiding pregnancy. There has to be a certain number of days for the FSH level to rise in the blood stream and for the follicle to ripen, though no one is sure of the least number of days in which this is possible. In a twenty-eight-day cycle it is around fourteen, in a twenty-five-day cycle around eleven. The safety or otherwise of this time has been formulated as the 'true menses rule'.[9] This states that in order to use the first four days of the cycle for unprotected intercourse, two conditions have to be met. Firstly the woman must have experienced a thermal shift in the last cycle (proving that ovulation occurred, and that this is therefore a true period), and secondly the last six cycles need to have lasted twenty-five days or longer. In filling out our model chart we've indicated clearly the first four days as absolutely safe for sex – the first markings we put down – because we have assumed that the previous cycle met these two conditions.

Figure 4.8 The true menses rule

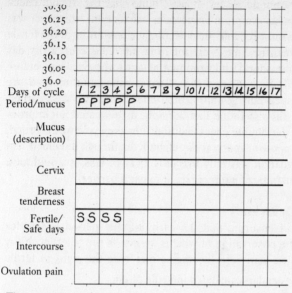

The true menses rule
Days one to four of the cycle are assumed to be safe for sex

Calendar calculation

The second indicator we have put down on our model is the *calendar calculated* infertile phase (see p. 148). If, for example, the last six cycles were thirty-two, thirty-three, thirty, thirty-five and thirty-two days long, then the calculated infertile days are thirty (the shortest cycle) minus twenty-one, making nine. In other words, for this cycle, day nine is the last available for safe intercourse. But few of the most recently developed methods of NFP simply leave it at that. It has been claimed that, calculated this way, these days are 95–99 per cent infertile. While this may be true, it is still safer to double check by observing the state of the mucus. The rule is then that a woman must assume potential fertility at the sight of the first mucus symptom *or* on the first calculated fertile day, *whichever is soonest*. In other words, if a woman has signs of fertile mucus on day seven or eight of her cycle, she should assume that she is fertile, even if the calendar calculation suggests that she will be infertile up to day nine. Similarly, a woman who is still dry on day nine should assume she is potentially fertile, even though she has not seen any fertile mucus.

This rule was born out by a study in 1984 by Dr Anna Flynn, in which eight fertile, healthy women who were experienced in fertility awareness were asked to deduce their fertile time from sympto-thermal indicators.

These subjective findings were then tested against ultrasound scans of the ovary and hormone assays. It was found that the double check method (first mucus symptom *or* calendar calculation, whichever was soonest) was the most reliable for detecting the beginning of the fertile phase. One woman became pregnant from intercourse on a dry day (calculated by ultrasound and hormone assays to be five days before ovulation), but if she had used the calendar calculation method she would have stopped having unprotected intercourse two days earlier. Interestingly, it was also found that hormone assays could not improve on reliability of the double check method.[10] In the cycle we recorded, mucus began to appear as early as day eight. Even though it seemed very unlikely that ovulation was only five days away or less, it would have been vital to abstain from intercourse, or to use a barrier.

The alternative dry day rule

A further way of ensuring that the early infertile period is safe for intercourse is the observation of what is known as the 'alternative dry day rule'. Because semen in the vagina may hide the signs of fertile

Figure 4.9 The calendar-calculated infertile phase

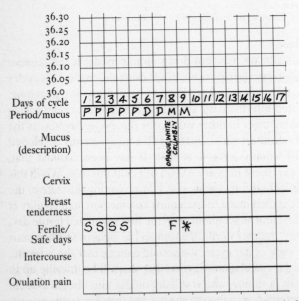

The calendar-calculated infertile phase: * indicates the calculated end of the infertile phase (shortest cycle minus 21) but note that the mucus appeared on day 8 so fertility must be assumed from day 8.

mucus, a woman may assume that she is dry when in fact her cervix has already begun to produce fertile mucus. The rule therefore suggests that a woman has intercourse only on *alternate days* during the early dry days so that she can be absolutely sure to detect the first mucus signs. Other people think this is unnecessarily belt-and-braces, if a woman is using a calculated method and studying her mucus. From our own experience we find that women who are very familiar with their cervical mucus can easily detect fertile mucus in the presence of semen and even contraceptive creams and gels. The alternative dry day rule may be useful for women who are learning NFP – certainly many instructors will insist on it, and we have marked the alternative dry day rule indicators on our chart.

Early changes in the cervix

Some women like to add information offered by the cervix to confirm the infertility of the early days. As long as the cervix remains firm, low,

Figure 4.10 The alternative dry day rule

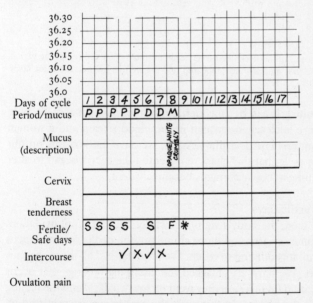

Days following intercourse (v) are marked (x) to show that they are not safe, though see discussion in text.

The alternative dry day rule: the day following intercourse is assumed *not* to be safe during the first dry days of the cycle. Intercourse on the evening of day 4 means that day 5 is not considered safe for intercourse in case the presence of semen disguises the onset of mucus.

Figure 4.11 Changes in the cervix

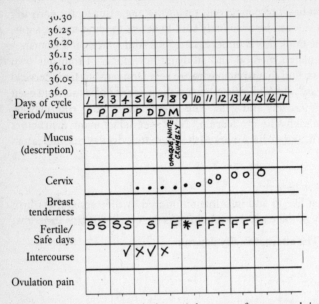

Changes in the cervix: in this cycle the cervix began to soften open and rise in the vagina shortly after the first mucus signal appeared and reached its highest and most open position on day 15.

closed and tilted, it can be considered infertile. As soon as it alters in any way, there is clearly oestrogen in the blood stream and a woman should assume potential fertility. Again, we have marked this on our chart. In the cycle that this chart represented the cervix began to alter at the same time as cervical mucus became evident.

The most fertile days

As we have seen, the body's signs of fertility build up until ovulation. Mucus becomes clearer and more abundant, the cervix softens, opens and rises until it is difficult to reach. We have marked all these changes on our chart. We have also marked the cramping feelings that occur around ovulation (in this case they went on for two days) and the feeling of fullness in the breasts. In this cycle the *peak mucus day* occurred on day fifteen. This was the last day on which the thin stretchy mucus was present and the vagina felt wet. It represented the peak of oestrogen levels in the blood stream. Together with the Mittelschmerz, open, high and soft cervix and full breasts it was very apparent that fertility was at its highest. We have marked all these very fertile days with an 'F'. The

Figure 4.12 The most fertile days of a cycle

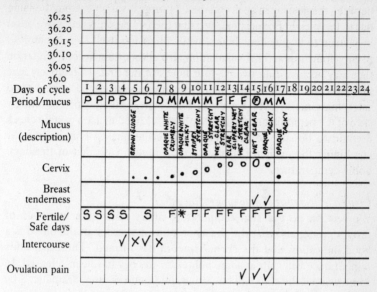

The most fertile day of a cycle: highly fertile mucus began on day 12 and continued until day 15. Day 15 is identified as the peak mucus day Ⓕ as it was the last day on which thin, stretchy mucus was present. Ovulation pain and breast tenderness are shown.

last day that the cervical mucus was present we have marked with an 'Ⓕ'. The vagina felt wet from day twelve but on day sixteen it felt quite a lot drier. This was how day fifteen was identified as the peak mucus day. Intercourse on days fourteen, fifteen and sixteen would have offered the best chance of pregnancy in the whole cycle.

The absolutely infertile days at the end of the cycle

Three indicators can tell us the point in the cycle at which ovulation has occurred and the ovum's life span is over. They are: the peak mucus day, the shift in basal bodily temperature, and a closed cervix.

The peak mucus day

How soon after the peak mucus day is it safe to resume intercourse without contraception? You can assume that you are infertile on the *evening of the fourth consecutive day of dryish sensation in the vagina after the peak mucus day.* In our chart (see Figure 4.14), days sixteen, seventeen and eighteen (marked 1, 2, 3) were still considered potentially fertile, but by the evening of day nineteen (marked 4) it was assumed that ovulation must have taken place and that the ovum was no longer capable of being fertilized. This calculation is based on the fact that the space between the oestrogen peak and the LH surge is variable (from the same day to forty-eight hours later), and that the LH peak precedes ovulation by sixteen to twenty-four hours, while the ovum itself lives for around twenty-four hours. This calculation also allows for a second ovulation that may occur within twenty-four hours of the first – a relatively rare phenomenon resulting in twins. Four days is considered to be a good safety margin. But just as we used a double check method to be absolutely sure of the beginning of the fertile phase, we need to use a double check method to be sure of the end of the fertile phase. This is done by combining the evidence of the cervical mucus with that of the basal bodily temperature.

Using a temperature shift to confirm the mucus

We saw on p. 132 that temperature alters under the influence of progesterone, and that the presence of progesterone in the blood is a good indication that the corpus luteum has formed. The basal body temperature will shift at some point *after* the egg has been released. In some women the shift will be minor and in others more dramatic. The rule here is that once *three high temperatures* are recorded the absolutely infertile phase has begun.

The best way of interpreting a temperature shift is by using what is known as a 'coverline'. This is a line drawn over the six temperatures immediately before the first rise in temperature. In order to confirm a true rise in temperature the three following temperatures *must* be above this coverline. If one falls back beneath it it is a clear sign that ovulation has not taken place and it is important to wait for another three temperatures above the line before assuming that the infertile phase has begun. This rule is known as the 'three over six' rule. The shift need only be as little as 0.1°C but one of the three temperatures should be at least 0.2°C over the coverline.

The pattern of temperature rise varies from woman to woman and cycle to cycle. In some cycles it is abrupt and easy to interpret. In others it rises slowly, or in steps, or in what is called a 'saw tooth rise'. The coverline and three over six rule will help interpret most charts accurately, and once the shift has been truly identified intercourse can take place on the evening of the third day of higher temperature without any risk of pregnancy.

Sometimes a spike occurs in a chart – a higher temperature that occurs for any reason whatsoever. Over-sleeping, a cold, a bad night, a lot of alcohol or any other departure from routine can produce unexpected spikes in a chart and should be indicated. When used in conjunction

Figure 4.13 The temperature rise following ovulation

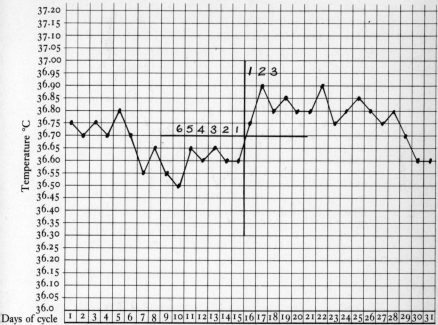

The temperature rise following ovulation: the coverline is the line drawn over the six temperatures immediately before the first rise in temperature. According to the evidence of temperature alone it would be safe to resume sexual intercourse on the evening of the third day of the temperature rise, i.e. the evening of day 18.

with mucus observation it is usually easy to identify spikes as aberrations in the true basal temperature pattern. As we mentioned earlier, it has also been the experience of some women that charting is more difficult if they have to get up even once in the night to see to a child. Their BBT tends to fluctuate more dramatically, and if, in addition to this, it is difficult to record a BBT regularly at the same time each day because of babies who start shouting at 6.00 a.m., the charts may be difficult to interpret. A skilled NFP tutor may be able to help out; or maybe exclusive reliance on NFP is not such a good idea at such times.

In our chart the temperature rise occured on day sixteen, the day after the peak mucus day, which meant that intercourse could take place on the evening of the third day of the temperature rise – i.e. the evening of day eighteen. However, using the double check method, and adding the evidence of the cervical mucus, we get a slightly different story. The

Figure 4.14 The end of the fertile period

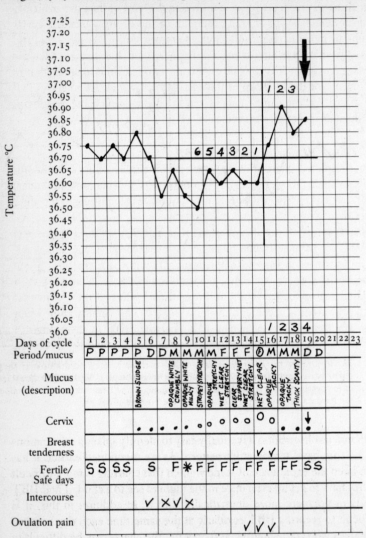

The absolutely infertile phase at the end of the cycle. The evidence of the cervical mucus shows that intercourse can be resumed on the evening of day 19

cervical mucus tells us that intercourse can only be resumed on the evening of the fourth day after the peak mucus day. This means the infertile period should be considered as starting from the evening of day nineteen, since we use the latest indicator of the end of the fertile period as the safest way of avoiding pregnancy.

A closed cervix

The third way of detecting or confirming the start of the post-ovulatory infertile phase lies in charting the path of the cervix. Once the cervix begins to move from its soft, high, open position to its firm, low and closed position it is almost certain that oestrogen has peaked. Like the peak mucus rule, it is necessary to leave enough time for ovulation to occur and for the life span of the egg. The closed cervix rule says that the infertile phase can be considered to have begun on the evening of the third day from this change.

Other information on the chart

The completed chart (Figure 4.7b) also includes information about ovulation pain, about the feeling of full breasts at ovulation and tender, heavy ones just before menstruation. (There was no spotting or bleeding other than at menstruation in this cycle.)

Building up detailed information on a chart may seem a complicated activity. We have described more or less every fertility change that can be recorded, as a way of demonstrating how to be extra safe. Some women who are very experienced in fertility awareness do not need such detailed records. They come to know their bodies to the extent that fertility awareness becomes almost instinctive. They simply know when they are fertile. It is also true that charting is for many women a fascinating exercise, in the initial stages at least. Watching a cycle unfold itself is an intriguing process, and as we will see in our concluding discussion of fertility awareness, can be a step towards self-awareness for many of the women who practise it.

Natural family planning: does it work?

It seems very risky. I might consider it but I think my nerves would suffer too much . . .

When I got married my husband and I decided to use contraception as little as possible. We used the rhythm method combined with a sheath during the fertile period except when we wanted children. We planned three children that way . . . Recently however I became pregnant by mistake. I think our method of family planning failed because I was ill and forgot the timing of the safe period.

I started with the pill, moved on to the diaphragm and finally abandoned them all for NFP. I used it successfully for six years and in the second cycle after consciously setting out to conceive became pregnant. Since having my daughter it has been harder to do it properly, and we use a diaphragm until I can really feel my period coming. But once she's a bit older I'll definitely go back to it.

The women who wrote to us had a variety of opinions about how well

NFP prevents unwanted pregnancy. The majority (who had in fact never used NFP) considered that it would be the least effective form of contraception, while others who had used it were mostly positive about its effectiveness. The women who practised limited NFP (only using a barrier in the fertile period) felt enthusiastic about the method and considered it safe. But in the main it seemed that the old jokes about 'Vatican roulette' have stuck in the minds of many people: 'What do you call people who practise the rhythm method? Parents!'

Like all other methods of contraception NFP has been subjected to a number of well-designed trials, often involving thousands of couples for a number of years. It is important to remember that we have included a number of different 'methods' under the heading NFP. Different trials have tested different methods. So when we talk about the failure rates of NFP we have to know what methods were being practised in the trials. A further point is that NFP, more than any other method of fertility control, relies on motivation and good teaching. While highly motivated couples can achieve a very low pregnancy rate with NFP (particularly sympto-thermal methods), it does not take much imagination to understand why a couple who are not too anxious when the next child arrives will have a higher failure rate. A woman with an IUD who decides to become pregnant needs to make a specific visit to the doctor to have her device removed. For her, the decision to try to make a baby cannot be a spur of the moment one. But in some clinical trials some couples using NFP did make sudden decisions.

In order to understand 'failures' (though NFP professionals quite rightly refuse to see a pregnancy as any kind of 'failure') most systems for judging the effectiveness of a family planning methods consider two measurements, the 'method failure', or 'theoretical failure' (which assumes that the couple used the method perfectly and the fault was inherent in the method itself) and 'use –failure' (which assumes that the couple did not use the method properly). The question of 'failure' in NFP has been much discussed. Is failure to abstain during the fertile period an inherent failure of the method or the couple using it? John Billings, founder of the Billings method, has this to say:

It is extraordinary that we should still have to insist that husbands and wives have complete freedom to depart from the use of any method of fertility regulation at any moment they choose, and that the pregnancy which results from a conscious departure from the rules of a method is not a failure of the method. It is not a failure of anybody or anything. . . . If (a couple) engages in intercourse when the woman recognizes that she is within the phase of her fertility, by what logic and semantics can the pregnancy be called 'unplanned' . . .[11]

In other words if you have been taught to use NFP and know what you are doing, if you choose to sail a little too close to the wind, a resulting pregnancy (according to Billings) cannot be called 'unplanned'. Many other family planners would not accept this. However, the best designed studies to test method- and user-failure have asked the participating couples each month to indicate whether or not they intend to try to conceive that month and have excluded from the study at that point those who answered affirmatively.

As we saw in Chapter 3, contraceptive failure rates are worked out according to 100 woman-years – the Pearl Index – or (more recently) life-table analysis. The most important point to emerge from all the clinical trials carried out is that the sympto-thermal method is the most successful, calendar rhythm the least, and the ovulation or mucus methods somewhere in the middle. Since we would not recommend any method of NFP that does not take into account as many signs of fertility as possible, we have confined ourselves to looking only at the failure rates of the sympto-thermal and Fertility Awareness methods.

Sympto-thermal methods

Most of the recent trials suggest that well-motivated, well-taught couples can achieve a remarkable degree of success using this method. One international study, covering Canada, Colombia, France, Mauritius and the USA is worth describing in detail. Known as the Fairfield Trial (1977) this well-designed study involved 1022 couples who contributed charts for 21,736 cycles over a two-year period. In all, 128 unplanned pregnancies resulted, an overall rate of 7.47 conceptions per 100 woman-years. Interestingly there was a significant difference between the success rate of those attempting to prevent pregnancies altogether and those who were spacing their families. Among the data recorded from Canada, ninety-nine couples attempting to have no more children had only two unplanned pregnancies or a failure rate of 1.09 per 100 woman-years, while sixty-two couples spacing their families had sixteen unplanned pregnancies, or a failure rate of 16.09 per 100 woman-years. The overall figure of 7.47 per 100 woman-years reflects this mixture of motivation.

The study looked at a number of specific things – the effectiveness rate when a couple used a barrier method during the fertile period, the method-failure rate as opposed to the user-failure rate (a number of couples contributed information about dates of sexual intercourse on their charts so that this could be more easily calculated), the average length of the cycles and so on.

The couples who were using sympto-thermal methods had a lower failure rate even than those who used a barrier method during the fertile period: 6.24 per cent as opposed to 10.33 per cent. The average cycle length was 28.43 days and only about a third of the women had cycles that varied by eight days or less over the period of two years. Finally the research found that the method-failure rate was extremely low; out of all the cases when the couple were following the method strictly there were only sixteen pregnancies, or 0.93 per 100 woman-years – comparable to the pill or IUD.[12]

It is only fair to point out that other studies have produced less successful results (for example a study in Oxford in 1982 where the use-failure rate was 15.5 per 100 woman-years). But it remains true that well-taught, well-motivated couples can make this method work for them very well indeed and, as we shall see in the next section, more is at stake for some women, than merely avoiding pregnancy.

The Fertility Awareness Method
Not many trials have tested Fertility Awareness. One recent study in America gave women the choice of using either barrier methods, withdrawal or abstinence in the fertile period. Eighty-six per cent chose to use barrier methods, withdrawal or both, and only 14 per cent abstinence. After one year the pregnancy rate for everyone stood at 10 per cent (life-table analysis). So it seems the sympto-thermal method with abstinence may lead to a lower pregnancy rate than using the method with a barrier or withdrawal.[13]

Natural family planning: who uses it?

Ironically the great high point of NFP popularity in Britain came well before the more reliable, more sophisticated sympto-thermal methods were developed. In 1959 an estimated 16 per cent of couples were using the calendar rhythm method. By 1970 this had fallen to 6.7 per cent, while by 1980 surveys suggested that only 200,000 women were using NFP in this country. Only 200 women were taught NFP in family planning clinics in that year. In other words NFP is in no way comparable in terms of numbers with the major methods of birth control practised in Britain. At the same time, those involved with the method profession-ally do report a small but steady increase in the number of doctors and other medical people coming forward for training in teaching NFP. The teaching courses run in Birmingham are all over-subscribed; there is now a newsletter published by the National Association of Natural Family Planning Teachers and a widespread network of teachers is growing up. While many of the people involved are Roman Catholics, there is increasing secular following for NFP as more women become interested for personal, health reasons rather than religious ones.

Worldwide use of NFP is also slight in relation to sterilizations and pill use. Between 1 and 13 per cent of married women of reproductive age are said to rely on it, or some 10–15 million users, compared to 100 million sterilizations and 50–60 million pill and IUD users. Those using NFP tend to use calendar rhythm – the least effective method. However, as in Britain, there is a growing, secular following for NFP. In India, for example, well-designed trials are introducing a modified sympto-thermal method to poor village women with a certain amount of success.

Natural family planning: for and against

It seems a middle-class idea, and Catholic. Perhaps when you are older and only want it about twice a month, then it may be all right.

I know when I ovulate by my mucus, but it is only academically interesting. I feel angry that I was twenty-eight before I learnt about fertile mucus – I was aware of its presence from the age of fourteen but had no idea of its significance. Every girl should be told when she learns about menstruation.

I used to think that the only times I would ever be able to make love without contraception would be when I wanted a baby. Now most of the time that I make love I don't have to use anything. It's brilliant. No more rubbery smells, or at least only a few times a month!

Given the ready availability of low-dose hormonal pills, better and safer IUDs and a variety of barrier methods, why should anyone consciously trying to avoid conceptions go without? Why do women use natural methods? Why, when almost 100 per cent effective birth control is only as far away as the doctor's surgery, choose a method that is time consuming, requires commitment, co-operation and may (for at least seven out of 100 women) let you down before the year is up?

Some women use natural methods because their consciences dictate that they should. Catholic women may choose NFP in response to Catholic teaching on the subject. Pope John Paul II has written and spoken strongly against contraception, arguing that people who use it 'manipulate ... human sexuality – and with it themselves and their married partner – by altering its value as "total" self giving.' On the other hand, Catholic teaching has strongly endorsed natural methods. In his *Apostolic Exhortation on the Family* John Paul wrote that 'the necessary conditions [for marriage] also include knowledge of the bodily aspect and the body's rhythm of fertility ... every effort must be made to render such knowledge accessible to all married people and also to young adults before marriage ...'. John Paul issued a 'universal and unrestricted call' for all men and women to learn NFP, thereby understanding the nature of their own fertility. However, the fact remains that many Catholic women do use 'artificial' as opposed to 'natural' family planning, though as NFP has become more sophisticated in its approach, natural methods may again become a more serious option for them.[14]

For non-Catholics, what is the attraction of NFP? A clue lies in the use of the word 'natural'. Rose Shapiro writes (a bit cynically) that NFP is ' "natural" family planning, with natural used in its modern (advertising based?) sense to mean *good*. The obvious implication is that mechanical contraception is unnatural, and therefore *bad*.'[15] While it is true that some promoters of NFP (perhaps especially Catholic ones) are positively puritanical about the method and strongly hostile to mechanical or chemical methods of contraception, this is not universally so. At one extreme Mary Shivanandas in *Natural Sex* claims that nobody who prescribes or fits artifical methods of family planning should even be allowed to teach NFP since the two approaches are 'diametrically opposed. Natural methods work with the natural fertility cycle, artifical family planning manipulates or interferes with natural processes.'[16] Other people see fertility awareness as a tool that a woman can use as she likes. Rather than opting for a method that, as in Mary Shivanandas's book turns into a complete way of life, fertility awareness can be an enhancement and a broadening of bodily horizons. Many women are attracted to fertility awareness because it teaches them more about their bodies, and puts their fertility within their own grasp. In this sense it is natural – meaning working with the uninterrupted processes of the cycle of fertility.

This is one half of the attraction. The other half is the pleasure of making love without contraception.

Abstinence or barriers?

It seems rather important to make a distinction here. There are a number of women to whom natural methods mean abstinence during the fertile period. The rhythm of coming together and moving apart during each cycle is important to them. On the other hand there are probably equal numbers of women who are drawn to natural methods because they don't like using contraception. This dislike is not ethical in nature but practical. They don't like being on the pill, are uncomfortable at the thought of an IUD, don't like the feel of condoms and find diaphragms even worse. Keeping contraception to a minimum is an enhancement of their sex life, not an absolute rule.

Couples who practise abstinence stop any close genital contact that could lead to conception as soon as a woman's fertile period starts, and begin making love again when it is clear that ovulation has come and gone. One woman described the sense of respite she had when she switched from the pill to NFP: 'I felt I was always available, and if I didn't want sex I had to explain why not. Sex has become a luxury now, not an automatic reflex on getting into bed.' Mary Shivanandas's book is full of stories of couples whose relationships have blossomed since they started building abstinence into their lives. Passive women become more interested in sex, busy men become more tolerant and interested in their partner's lives. Couples start talking to each other again. In fact the couples that we spoke to had mixed feelings. Some of the men said that they did not have as much sex as they wanted, and some of the women found that it was difficult to abstain from sex at the one point in the month when they felt most interested. Almost everyone said that abstinence made getting back together again a special experience, and several women commented that days that were out as far as intercourse was concerned were still good for other forms of bodily contact. One woman said that 'it's been good for me to see that my husband is prepared to touch and massage me for my own sake, and not for what he might get out of it.'

Almost all NFP teachers will teach the sympto-thermal method using abstinence in the fertile days. The major reason given for this (aside from the psycho-sexual ones) is that in the presence of semen and spermicides it becomes difficult to detect cervical mucus. Is the moisture the result of semen or cervical mucus? This is still a rather untested area. In one US study, for example, the mucus charts of women using a barrier during the fertile period were similar to the charts of women who abstained.[17] Other people have suggested making love with an unlubricated condom since this cuts out both semen and spermicide. But it is also true that making love with only a condom at the most fertile time of the month would offer a rather high chance of failure if something unexpected happened to the condom. As we have already pointed out above, many NFP enthusiasts think that using a barrier is somehow totally inimical to the whole point of natural methods – cheating the system. Other women who do combine fertility awareness with a barrier argue that there is no system to cheat, and that the whole point of learning fertility awareness is to become autonomous, not to buy into another set of rules and regulations.

Criticisms of NFP and fertility awareness
You can usually spot a negative approach to natural methods when an author calls it 'periodic abstinence' rather than its usual designation,

NFP. NFP has come in for some criticism and it is as well to examine this here. The best-known criticism is that couples using NFP have a higher chance of conceiving a handicapped child. There are several arguments advanced. Couples using the traditional calendar rhythm technique are likely to run into difficulties if the menstrual cycle becomes unexpectedly irregular, which happens at either end of reproductive life. A baby conceived towards the end of a reproductive life span would have a higher chance of having some handicap – Down's syndrome for example – because of his or her mother's age. So a woman in her forties using calendar rhythm exposes herself on both counts – the method is more likely to fail and the baby has a higher chance of having a handicap. A couple using a more reliable form of contraception would not run this risk. This is a fair criticism but no one now would recommend calendar rhythm anyway, and certainly not to a woman in her forties for whom pregnancy would represent all sorts of risks.

The second criticism of NFP is that couples using it avoid unprotected intercourse during the most fertile time. This means that any accidental pregnancy would be the result of a fertilization taking place at one or other extreme of the fertile phase, either with an ageing sperm or an ageing egg. In rabbits there is some evidence that when fertilization takes place with aged gametes the rate of abnormal offspring is raised considerably. However, since rabbits ovulate on coitus whereas women ovulate spontaneously, and since these experiments involved the deliberate ageing of rabbit gametes prior to fertilization, the relevance of this evidence can be called into question. Furthermore a recent trial conducted by the WHO looked at couples using the ovulation method who became pregnant at the extreme limits of the fertile phase. They found no evidence of an increased level of congenital abnormality among their babies.[18]

Anna Flynn, author of *The Manual of Natural Family Planning*, draws the conclusion that 'all the scientific evidence to date gives no reason to suspect that modern natural family planning methods lead to an increased risk of congenital abnormalities.' Other authors are more cautious. Potts and Diggory, whose section on 'periodic abstinence' is generally negative, argue only that there is 'insufficient evidence to force a broad policy condemnation' of NFP.[19] Put in perspective it would seem that couples who use NFP carefully (and we have seen that conscientious couples can achieve very high success rates) face no greater risk than the rest of the population, and that when they come consciously to conceive their children, their ability to pinpoint ovulation leads to the greatest chance of sperm and egg being in peak condition.

NFP and men

Most of the books about NFP gush about your man taking your temperature for you and filling in the chart so that he can feel really involved. I found that idea faintly nauseating. This is something I do myself, for myself.

When we started this business, I wasn't convinced. Now I feel quite proud of the fact that I know exactly where my wife's cycle has got to each month. Most of the other men I know haven't a clue about their wives' and girlfriends' bodies.

A basic condition for the success for NFP is that both partners think it's a good idea. Trying to keep track of the cycle of fertility when a partner will not co-operate may lead to dropping out of the method pretty quickly. Certainly if the choice is NFP with abstinence, both halves of the couple have to be convinced that there is something in it for each of them. In one of the couples we spoke to the man felt that he was putting up with something for the sake of his wife, who was 'a puritan and wanted to go the whole way'. He did not like abstinence and could not really understand why his wife would not let him use a condom in the fertile time since neither of them is a Catholic. But being a gentle and tolerant person, he was prepared to put up with it.

Some women find it discouraging when their partners are not as interested in their fertility as they themselves are. Others prefer to do it all themselves anyway. Obviously there are no rules as to which way is best, but it is true that NFP has a higher drop-out rate than many other methods of fertility control, and that one of the reasons behind this, worldwide, may be that men do not like abstinence, and women do not like to insist on it even if they are prepared to try it themselves. Most of the men who wrote to us had no experience of using NFP, though several indicated that they would like to try it. One letter is worth quoting more fully:

What do I think of natural family planning? I think my reactions have changed over the time that we've been doing it. At first it was quite exciting, discovering about fertility and so on, and we were really 'in' to the times of abstinence – massage, long talks, all that sort of thing. Then I began to get a bit fed up with it – always having to look at the chart, like consulting an oracle. The crunch came on a day when I heard that I'd got a new job. I wanted to go out and celebrate, which we did. Fine. But when I wanted to make love afterwards, to celebrate privately as it were, no such luck. We had a furious argument – really one of the worst, and ended up making love at the end of it all. It was a bit ironic really. Anyway we agreed to compromise, to use a barrier sometimes in the fertile time, and abstain if she really wanted to. Since then, it's been working much better. I don't feel as if I've joined a religious order any more. There is more flexibility in the arrangement.

NFP during breastfeeding and the menopause

If you are interested in using natural family planning during breastfeeding, we recommend that you refer again to the section on breastfeeding in Chapter 3. It seems fair to conclude that outside a traditional breastfeeding context the complete supression of fertility is rarely obtained. The diminished fertility that most breastfeeding women do experience is not enough to rely on, and to practise NFP while breastfeeding requires considerable dedication. Most mothers with a small baby are too tired even to consider it, added to which is the difficulty of getting a good basal bodily temperature chart if you are getting up several times a night. Mucus production and cervical changes have to be the main tools, and these may be risky since the body may make several attempts to ovulate before it succeeds. However, some women have practised it successfully. We certainly would not recommend anyone who was not already very skilled at reading the signs of her own impending fertility to use NFP during breastfeeding, particularly without the support of a good NFP teacher. If you do decide to try it, we would refer you to some of the specialist books available and an NFP counsellor.

Keeping track of fertility in the years leading up to the menopause requires patience and dedication. Again, this is probably not a good time to begin using NFP for the first time, but women who are skilled in fertility awareness find it perfectly possible to continue as they get older. A number of books on NFP have special sections on the pre-menopausal years and we recommend these, and the support and counselling of a good NFP teacher.

Where to go from here

If you have found this chapter interesting and would like to take NFP and fertility awareness further there are several options available. The first is to begin to study your own cycle and record your observations for a month or two. A second option is to write to the National Association of Natural Family Planning Teachers at one of the addresses listed at the back of this book. These addresses are those of the area co-ordinators who will be able to give you information about local NFP. A further alternative is read some more about it. The reading list at the back of the book gives the titles that we found most helpful in preparing this chapter.

CHAPTER 5

Barrier Methods of Contraception for Women

Diaphragms and caps were to family planning what the steam locomotive was to transportation: they were the first in the field, brought emancipation to millions and for a long time had no rivals. Ultimately they were overtaken by a new technology, in this case oral contraceptives.

Potts and Diggory, *Textbook of Contraceptive Practice*

I do wish to emphasize that on safety grounds the diaphragm is clearly the best contraceptive.

Carl Djerassi (one of the developers of the contraceptive pill),
The Politics of Contraception

Preventing pregnancy by blocking the path of the sperm into the uterus is the most intuitively understandable form of contraception; for this reason it is one of the oldest. Long before men considered condoms, women blocked the track of sperm with a wide variety of materials. Evidence from ancient Egyptian, Hebrew, Roman, Greek, Indian, Chinese and Japanese cultures testifies to the extraordinary diversity of the substances women used. But while vaginal barriers seem the most obvious and somehow 'natural' means of preventing conception, it is almost as if nature herself anticipated human attempts to close the entrance to the cervix and designed the vagina to thwart such interference in the natural course of a conception.

The inherent characteristics of the vagina make it a very unpredictable place; it changes its shape with different emotions, blossoming and expanding with sexual excitement. A diaphragm that fitted when the vagina was quiescent and relaxed may be in quite the wrong place when it is most needed. The upper vagina may lengthen and enlarge by up to 5 cm during sexual intercourse. The cervix rises and dips, opens and closes in a rhythm all its own. And the vaginal fluids, uniquely designed to protect the sperm that enter the vagina in the fertile period, are notoriously difficult to predict. A spermicide which performs like magic in vitro may be quite unable to catch and immobilize all the sperm which reach the safety of a stream of cervical mucus within seconds of ejaculation. As the space around the cervix balloons out the spermicide may be inadequate to cover the suddenly enlarged surface area. In short, ovulation prepares the vagina to catch, hold and convey sperm into the fallopian tubes against enormous odds.

The more research that is done on the vagina the more remarkable it appears to be. No less than twenty-six pheromones have been isolated from the vagina, and while no one is clear what role, if any, these have in human reproductive physiology, it is interesting that their quantity and character are influenced by the production of oestrogen and progesterone, and they are always most abundant at the time of ovulation. Recent research has shown that the vaginal secretions, which increase enormously during sexual excitement, facilitate the spread of fertile cervical mucus throughout the vagina. In other words it is not necessary for sperm to be deposited near the uterus, since long strings of cervical mucus may reach right down to the entrance to the vagina. Moreover, during sexual excitement the labia open and retract making it much easier for any sperm deposited outside the vagina to find a way into the protective shelter of cervical mucus. Once orgasm is over, the vagina collapses back against itself to prevent sperm from leaking out again. This creates a reservoir to keep sperm in contact with the cervix for as long as possible.[1]

Given this extraordinarily well-adapted organ, it is not very surprising that efforts to dam it with rubber, spermicide, gold and grass have sometimes failed. Perhaps what is more surprising is the fact that modern barrier methods can be used with a very high degree of success. Vaginal methods of contraception are also among the safest ways of living with fertility. And even though classified with steam transport and considered slightly archaic and anachronistic in a modern world, for many women caps, diaphragms and sponges have an enormous amount to recommend them.

A short history

Vaginal barriers have a 4,000–year-old history. The Petrie Papyrus, written around 1850 BC, and the Ebers Papyrus dating from 1550 BC contain contraceptive recipes which were essentially barriers to be placed in the vagina. One suggests that honey, natron (sodium carbonate) and crocodile dung were to be mixed into a paste and inserted into the vagina. It is quite likely that this paste would have been reasonably effective, since it would have had spermicidal properties, and may well have been a reasonably good physical barrier. During the middle ages rock salt and alum were used as barriers, while vaginal sponges have an even longer history. They are mentioned in early Hebrew literature, and approvingly in the Talmud.

Caps and diaphragms

The modern history of vaginal barriers begins in the 1830s and 40s with the vulcanization of rubber and the invention of the cervical cap. One of the earliest mentions comes from a Dr F. A. Wilde writing at this time who describes the cervical cap as 'comfortable and effective'. It is likely that the earliest cervical caps were custom built, with an impression of the cervix being made in wax and a rubber cap created from the impression. Another mention of the cervical cap comes in an advertisement placed in Allbutt's famous *Wife's Handbook* of 1886, for which he was banned from the medical profession. The check pessary described is clearly a cervical cap '. . . a simply devised instrument of pure soft medicated rubber . . . strictly in accordance with the female organisation . . . Post free with directions for use, 2s 3d each.'

In the 1880s a German physician, Hasse, using the pseudonym Mensinga, developed the diaphragm. It was much like contemporary diaphragms, and used a watch spring in the brim. The diaphragm was quickly adopted by Dr Aletta Jacobs who opened the world's first birth control clinics in Holland in 1882. For this reason it became known as the Dutch cap, a name that lingers to this day. The use of the word 'cap' has caused considerable confusion over the years. In general, at the turn of the century it referred to small cervical caps that were designed to fit snugly over the cervix. They remained popular throughout the 1920s and 30s. Marie Stopes, who opened her first birth control clinic in 1921, prescribed the cervical cap with a spermicide for most of her clients. However, her rivals the National Birth Control Association (later the FPA) preferred to use diaphragms in their clinics and a certain amount of competition ensued. Gradually the diaphragm gained ascendancy, though not without a fierce struggle from Stopes. Both sides made absurdly exaggerated claims for the efficacy of their method. Stopes claimed a 99.4 per cent success rate for her cervical cap and imputed an 85.5 per cent failure rate to the diaphragm which she said caused distension of the vaginal muscles. In reply Dr Norman Haine claimed that Stopes's cervical caps failed 88 per cent of the time and produced erosion of the cervix. Neither side had any concrete evidence to go on!

Over the years the cervical cap more or less faded from memory, though Lambert and Son continued to manufacture them for a tiny minority of women. Their patience has been rewarded. In 1988 the

FDA of America, having earlier banned cervical caps for general use, licensed them once again. Demand is expected to be very high, and the suppliers are still Messrs Lambert and Son. The most popular cervical cap is the Prentif cavity-rim cervical cap, frequently referred to as *the* cervical cap. There are two other related caps, the Vimule and the Dumas or vault cap. If the cervical cap catches on in America it is possible it may have a revival in the UK. Over the years the diaphragm has been standardized in three types: the flat spring diaphragm, which is most often used in the UK, the coil spring and the arcing diaphragm. Diaphragms are made by Ortho and Durex, and come in sizes 55 mm to 105 mm.

Spermicides

Although Leeuwenhoek, a scientist in Holland, first observed sperm under a microscope in 1677 it was not until the nineteenth century that scientists began to experiment with ways of immobilizing them with spermicidal agents. By 1885 Rendell, a London chemist, had developed the Rendell pessary, made from soluble cocoa butter and quinine sulphate. Interestingly Rendell's company, like Lambert's, was destined to continue until the present. One woman who wrote to us had used an early type of Rendell pessary.

I married in February 1934. My mother, not wanting people to think I *had* to get married, asked a friend who owned a chemist shop what was available, and he offered 'Rendells', a pessary made from cocoa butter. This had to be inserted at least five minutes before 'love making'. They were very *smelly* and greasy, very off-putting, but I used them for two years.

In the 1920s and 30s many new spermicides were developed, including ones made from mercury and weak acids. The real breakthrough came in the 1940s with the development of surface acting agents, known as surfactants, which work by affecting the cell structure of the sperm. One of the most widely used spermicides today is nonoxynol 9 and it comes as a surprise to discover it was invented in the 1940s. Since then there have been virtually no new developments in spermicides as research interests were directed towards the development of synthetic hormones. By the mid-1970s spermicides were once again considered an interesting research option, and there are currently a number of new formulations being developed, as well as new research taking place on the older spermicides.

The sponge

When the sponge was launched in the USA in 1983 there were plenty of headlines about the 'new' contraceptive. The 'Today' sponge as currently marketed is certainly a new product, but, as we have seen, the idea of sponges is an old one. Natural sea sponges, or other bundles of natural fibres (such as cotton waste in India) have been dipped in spermicidal agents and used to block the cervix for centuries. It was said in the eighteenth century that no aristocratic French lady went out for dinner without first being 'prepared' with a sponge. Francis Place (1771–1854), one of the first proponents of birth control in the UK, suggested the sponge as an alternative to late marriage to reduce the birth rate. Jeremy Bentham, the philosopher, recommended the sponge to the poor as a means of reducing the tax burden on the rich at the end of the eighteenth century, and by the nineteenth century natural sea sponges, moistened with water or soaked in a quinine sulphate solution, were widely recommended to the working classes. Annie Besant, famous for her challenge to the laws prohibiting the distribution of contraceptive information, recommended this method.

In the 1970s, as research interest returned to barrier methods after several decades of eclipse, the idea of the sponge once again became attractive and caught on very quickly after its launch in the USA in 1983. Over a million women there have used it, and worldwide figures suggest a reasonable success rate.

Recent developments

The history of the development of barrier methods for use by women is by no means complete. Femshield, the so-called female condom, invented by a Danish nurse, was launched in spring 1988 by the manufacturers Medicor, though at the time of writing it is still not available over the counter. Meanwhile a number of new devices are currently being tested and undergoing development. A series of vaginal rings, some releasing spermicide, others releasing progestogen only or a mixture of progestogen and oestrogen, are a definite possibility for the future. Custom-built cervical caps are another option, though initial tests with these have been disappointing. Disposable diaphragms, impregnated with spermicide and worn for a period of up to forty-eight hours, are another strong possibility for the future.

Diaphragms

Diaphragms: do they work?

The diaphragm has a popular reputation for being one of the unreliable methods of contraception. But is this true? The two studies of diaphragm use discussed in Chapter 2 suggest that it may be far more effective than is popularly thought, particularly since the two studies involved women from different backgrounds. The UK study was part of the Oxford/FPA study, involving over 17,000 women who were recruited to the study between 1968 and 1974 and followed up since. Over 4,000 of the women were diaphragm users and had been for at least five months before the beginning of the trial. Most of the women were between twenty-five and thirty-nine, married and white. The overall failure rate was 1.9 per 100 woman-years (compared with 0.2 for the pill and 3.6 for condoms). The most effective users were those who were over thirty-five, had used a diaphragm for four or more years and had completed their family. They achieved extremely low failure rates (0.7 per 100 woman-years). At the other end of the spectrum were younger women whose families weren't complete and who had used the diaphragm for less than two years, whose failure rate was 5.3 per 100 woman-years.

There have been attempts to explain away this result, by pointing out that the women were unusually well-motivated and careful, middle-class and so on. In fact it is true that effectiveness improved as women became older and used the diaphragm for longer. Another study however suggests that the key to successful use is not age or parity or length of use, but motivation, good teaching and good follow-up. This was the largest contemporary study of diaphragm use in the USA, carried out by the New York-based Margaret Sanger Research Bureau. It involved 2,168 women, mostly under thirty and mostly unmarried. Sixty-one per cent were under twenty-five and only 29 per cent were married. The study, which was carried out between 1971 and 1976, involved promoting the diaphragm as a simple and safe method of contraception. The Bureau provided counselling, follow-up and good fitting. At the end of the first twelve months the rate of pregnancies was calculated at 1.9 per 100 woman-years for the youngest women, aged fifteen to seventeen, rising to 3.00 per 100 woman-years for women aged between thirty and thirty-four. At least twenty-two of the thirty-seven women who became pregnant in the first year of the study admitted they had used their diaphragms inconsistently, or not at all. At the end of the first year 84 per cent of the women chose to go on using the diaphragm – a particularly high continuation rate. The research team commented on the fact that once a woman had chosen the method for herself, it was used successfully regardless of age, ethnic background, parity, marital status or educational level.[2]

It seems difficult to reconcile these success stories with other studies in which failure rates of up to 29 per cent have been recorded. It is likely that the discrepancy may partially be accounted for by differences not in the women themselves but in the quality of teaching, back-up and fitting they received. If a diaphragm is presented to a woman as messy, inefficient, difficult to use and unlikely to work she is less likely to use it successfully than if she is given positive messages about its efficiency and convenience. Guillebaud cites the example of women who are introduced to the diaphragm after the age of thirty-five. They frequently express surprise at its simplicity and convenience, and complain that doctors and nurses had earlier damned the method with exceedingly faint praise. Among women who like using diaphragms and therefore use them consistently pregnancy rates can approach those expected with an IUD.[3]

Diaphragms: who uses them?

It seems likely that the number of women relying on a diaphragm increased slowly and steadily throughout the first half of the twentieth century, with numbers peaking at the end of the 1950s. By the 1940s the 'diaphragm-and-chemical method' was *the* clinic method. Norman Himes, who was a leading authority on contraception, wrote that it was 'undoubtedly the contraceptive method that has received the most general approval from doctors having the widest experience in this field in clinics and in private practice. It is the "best" method in the sense that it is the most widely recommended by the clinic doctors for the majority of cases.'[4] A diaphragm in the 1940s cost between 5s and 7s 6d.

How successful was the 'clinic method' in the 40s and 50s? From reports based upon follow-up studies of thousands of women it was estimated that diaphragms were successful 85–95 per cent of the time. A major study conducted by Hannah Stone found the diaphragm was 94 per cent effective.[5] Promoted by doctors therefore as the most effective contraceptive then available, it is not surprising that in 1959, when the Population Investigation Committee reported on its use, they found that 12 per cent of couples using contraception were using the diaphragm. A study of women attending 315 FPA clinics in the 1960s found that 95 per cent were offered the diaphragm. The history of the diaphragm thereafter is one of declining popularity. In the 1960s the introduction of the pill and IUD spelt the demise of diaphragms-and-chemicals. In 1973 only 5 per cent of new attenders at clinics chose the diaphragm, though by the end of the 1970s the trend away from barriers was slightly reversed. UK and US clinics reported that the diaphragm was becoming a little more popular again. At one UK clinic serving 11,000 first-visit clients per year the proportion of women choosing the diaphragm rose from 5 per cent to 8 per cent in 1978. Among more than a million young women receiving first time advice at the PPFA clinics in the USA 12.9 per cent chose the diaphragm in 1980 as opposed to 5.7 per cent in 1975.

The trend of diaphragm use in Britain in the 1980s has yet to become clear. The General Household Survey, carried out in 1986 and published in late 1989, suggested that only 2 per cent of contraceptive users rely on the diaphragm or cap. The figure rises to 3 per cent among married or cohabiting women. In fact these low figures are probably inaccurate. According to FPA statistics the number of women in England and Wales who attended family planning clinics and were fitted with diaphragms in 1986 was 137,307. This figure does not include women already using a diaphragm who did not have it renewed that year, or women fitted for diaphragms by their GPs. DHSS statistics for primary birth control method at the first visit of the year to family planning clinics in England show a very slow but steady increase in the percentage of women using a diaphragm or cap. From 6.8 per cent in 1974 the figure had risen to 9.2 per cent in 1986.[6] John Guillebaud's estimate of 4 per cent of all contraceptive users may be nearer the mark.[7]

Diaphragms: for and against

The diaphragm . . . is a rubber dinghy for spermicide . . . Why [it] and all that sails within it should be so gross is unimaginable . . .

Germaine Greer, *Sex and Destiny*

When I first saw a diaphragm I was terribly surprised. It looked enormous. I think I said to the doctor, 'You'll never get that inside me'. But he did and I've used a diaphragm ever since. I don't know why people make such a fuss about the supposed mess and the loss of spontaneity. If I feel like having sex, whether it's at bedtime or in the middle of the afternoon, I put my diaphragm in and have a good wash. There is no interruption, you can't see, taste or smell the spermicide, and I know I'm not going to get pregnant – so I enjoy sex. What could be easier? I take it out the next morning.

I think diaphragms simply take a bit of getting used to. Then you either like them or you don't. I combine a diaphragm with NFP and think it is an ideal solution to the problem of contraception. It also seems to work, because both the times we've decided to make babies, I've conceived in the first cycle.

I thought it was a pretty crude way of avoiding pregnancy. I also had cystitis on and off the whole time I used it. I think it was the diaphragm that finally persuaded me to be sterilized.

I know a woman who has diaphragms 'planted' everywhere, from her bedside table to the sitting room to the document wallet of the car. She says she just pops one in should the need arise . . .

Why do only two or three out of every 100 women using contraception use a diaphragm? Germaine Greer, in *Sex and Destiny*, offers her explanation. Diaphragms are disgusting and antithetical to good sex. 'The loaded diaphragm is quite likely to shoot out of the inserter's tentative grasp and to fly through the air, splattering glob in all directions.' The use of spermicide with a diaphragm is the final insult:

The spermicide is usually cold and dense, with a slithery consistency; it is meant to coat the cervix, but succeeds in coating everything else as well with chilly sludge. If intercourse continues so long that this sludge is dissipated, it is a sign that a fresh injection is required, so that a night of love becomes a kind of spermicidal bath.[8]

To women who like using a diaphragm this will seem an unfair caricature; if using a diaphragm were so awful, nobody would bother. Other writers have suggested that successful users need to be a bit 'obsessive' (though why any more obsessive than a woman taking a contraceptive pill every day is never explained). Diaphragms are seen as suitable for couples who only make love 'occasionally'. At best the diaphragm is damned with faint praise as being 'entirely harmless . . . and reasonably effective',[9] though only those with 'low sex drives are likely to continue using the cap for a long period of time.'[10] The messages that comments like these give about women's sexuality, about the sex act, and about 'normal' expectations of sexual behaviour are worth examining.

Of course, one of the reasons that more women do not use diaphragms is simply that they are not encouraged even to try them. Walli Bounds, the research officer to the Margaret Pyke Centre, has pointed out that GPs often fail to mention barrier contraception such as diaphragms when talking to patients. 'There is a great deal of ignorance about barrier methods among doctors . . . Most of them are inexperienced in fitting caps.'[11] While this applies particularly to the cervical cap, it also applies to diaphragms. Yet several studies have shown that when diaphragms are well presented women will use them happily and with a remarkably high continuity rate. The study in New York cited earlier put the continuity rate at over 80 per cent after one year.

This being the case, why are diaphragms seen as essentially for the middle-aged and middle class? With the advent of the pill and IUD, the current contraceptive culture puts anything that interferes with total and immediate access of a man to a woman in the category of 'unspontaneous'. Any form of contraception that requires a *woman* to make a decision about whether or not she wants sex, which moreover means that she needs a demystified view of her genital organs, of fertility, and of responsibility in sexual behaviour, goes against the code of free, easy, and 'natural' sexual play. In order to cope with the inherent tension thus imposed on successful (read obsessional) diaphragm users it is necessary to label them as either middle-class (read repressed, over-educated, over-cautious, no fun) or middle-aged (only once a fortnight on a specified night). That a woman can be interested in sex, like it, want it often and still use a diaphragm, is stretching the definitions too far. Many medical writers reveal a very clear image of what sex should be like as soon as they start discussing diaphragms. Here is what Potts and Diggory have to say:

Every woman has to decide her 'strategy' in using her contraceptive. If she decides to insert it only when sex has already been suggested or the first overtures played, she runs the risk of either being swept along on the tide of sexual passion and failing to insert it at all or else calling a halt to the proceedings whilst she finds and fits her cap only to find that sexual ardour on one side or the other has cooled so that in fact the device is no longer needed. If she plans to insert her cap at bedtime whenever she feels it will be needed, she may overestimate her partner's desires and when no overtures are made may then feel frustrated and foolish. When sex is frequent, most women prefer to put the cap in every night as a routine action like brushing their teeth; in this way a woman is prepared for sex, but if it does not occur, she is not frustrated.[12]

Another writer puts it even more bluntly: '. . . the wise wife should adopt the motto of the Boy Scouts and insert the diaphragm routinely before going to bed.'[13]

In these writers we have another clue as to why diaphragm use is considered middle aged. It is on a par with cleaning teeth, with the Boy Scouts, with regular nightly habits in which sex is routine (takes place in bed, at night only); the woman sets out to please her husband; she never makes sexual overtures herself and is foolish and frustrated when her husband rolls over and goes to sleep. While the pill is associated with exciting sex that can occur anywhere, anytime, the woman who uses a diaphragm is confined to making love only within ten yards of her bathroom cabinet. With advocates like this in the medical profession, it is surprising that anyone can bring themselves to use the diaphragm at all.

Just as the condom needed a new image, so too does the diaphragm.

We asked women who use diaphragms to list some of the advantages and to tell us how they overcome the 'bathroom cabinet' syndrome. Here are some of the responses:

- It is small, neat and entirely the woman's responsibility.
- If it is fitted properly, it is quite undetectable.
- If used with an unscented spermicide, or C-film, the spermicide itself is no problem.
- With a bit of practice, inserting it is very simple – why shouldn't women be manually dextrous and skilful in handling their genitals?
- A well-fitted diaphragm is perfectly comfortable, and very safe.
- In a good relationship putting a diaphragm in even half-way through needn't represent any 'break' in the mood. It can even increase desire, since if you are already aroused, having to wait for a minute before intercourse can start can heighten sexual tension. There is nothing at all to stop a partner from helping to insert a diaphragm, checking it is properly in position, or simply carrying on making love to you while you put it in yourself.
- Using a diaphragm needn't mean that you can't have oral sex. Obviously if you insert it, get spermicide everywhere and then think about oral sex it will not be a very attractive option. On the other hand, either put it in after you have finished the oral part of your love-making, or use C-film with your diaphragm, or use spermicide sparingly, on the side that goes next to your cervix only, and have a good wash afterwards. If you are worried that you have not used enough spermicide, you can always use an inserter to put in a little more just before intercourse or use a pessary.
- Most women use too much spermicide, to try and be extra safe. In fact too much spermicide can make the diaphragm fit less snugly, as well as making it less pleasant to use.
- A diaphragm can be inserted well in advance if you want to act more 'spontaneously'. If for any reason you do not want your partner to know that you are using a diaphragm, inserting it at the beginning of an evening together (for example) means that it will be safely in place if you decide to make love later. A diaphragm offers a way of living with fertility that does not interrupt the natural rhythms of your body, that helps to protect your fertility by creating a physical barrier to viral and bacterial infections, that protects your cervix in the same way, and that works very effectively at preventing pregnancy, particularly if you find a way of using it every time you make love.

Being positive about the diaphragm as a form of fertility control does not mean that there is nothing more to be said. The next sections look at some of the questions you may have if you are thinking of trying a diaphragm as your method of contraception.

Diaphragms in practice

How a diaphragm works

Diaphragms work by lying diagonally across the cervix, the vault and most of the anterior vaginal wall. One side of the rim is tucked behind the cervix and the other fits snugly up against the pubic symphysis. The spring keeps the diaphragm taut and in place, pressing up against the walls of the vagina. It is this that keeps the diaphragm from falling out, rather than an exact fit. Because the fit is not exact the diaphragm is not sealed around the edges and spermicide is used. This is inserted so that it is held against the cervix. During intercourse, the diaphragm forms a barrier between the penis and the cervix, and on ejaculation, most of the semen is held away from any possible contact. If any sperm do manage to swim around the edges of the diaphragm, they should be promptly inactivated by the spermicide.

The use of spermicide with diaphragms

Perhaps more women would be tempted to use diaphragms if spermicide wasn't a part of the package. The accusation of messiness is certainly one that needs to be answered. It is true that most spermicides leave much to be desired though the recent introduction of an unscented spermicide (Gynol II) is a definite step in the right direction. As suggested above, some women use more spermicide than is necessary, or effective. Greer's 'spermicidal bath' suggests she was using too much spermicide. One recent study has suggested that putting gel or cream around the rim of the diaphragm actually contributes to the loss of the correct placement of the diaphragm.[14] Traditional teaching suggests that about

Figure 5.1 How a diaphragm fits into the vagina

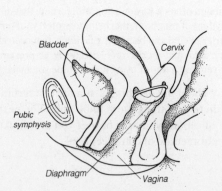

Bladder

Cervix

Pubic
symphysis

Diaphragm

Vagina

one inch of spermicide should be squeezed on to each side of the diaphragm and a little around the edges. More recently, however, practice has begun to shift. In America women are taught to put only about a teaspoonful on the side of the diaphragm that will be next to the cervix. This makes insertion easier and less messy. Another recent development is the use of C-film with diaphragms. C-film is a form of spermicide. It comes as 5-cm square sheets of a wafer-thin water-soluble film impregnated with nonoxynol 9, which dissolves when inserted into the vagina. This represents a less messy way of using a spermicide but its effectiveness is unclear. In 1988 in a pilot trial involving twenty women at an Edinburgh family planning clinic, the C-film/diaphragm combination was tried for a period of six months with no pregnancies (eight or nine of the women might have been expected to conceive in this time with no contraception). Seventeen of the women much preferred the C-film to the gels or creams they had used before. The C-film is placed on the side of the diaphragm that will cover the cervix and is held in place by the diaphragm. A much larger trial is currently under way and the results should be available by 1990. Since C-film is available free from family planning clinics, there is nothing to stop women who want to try the combination for themselves from doing so, though as yet there have been no large-scale studies of its effectiveness.[15]

It has recently been suggested that diaphragms make for adequate contraception without any spermicide at all. This idea has been followed up in Australia where a research team came to the conclusion that there was little or no scientific evidence to support many of the instructions given to users of barrier contraception as far as the use of spermicides is concerned. Because of this the instructions issued in different countries tend to be quite different. A gynaecologist in New York fitted women with small diaphragms (60–65 mm) and told them not to use spermicide at all. He followed up 997 women between 1974 and 1978 and reported only ten pregnancies. However when the Marie Stopes Centre also attempted to study the 'non-spermicide free-fit diaphragm' technique they found that the pregnancy rate was so unacceptably high that they were forced to abandon the trial.[16] The best current advice is to use not much more than a teaspoonful of spermicide on the side that sits against the cervix, and a little more around the edge that will be put in first, to help with insertion.

There is also quite a lot of contradictory discussion about how far in advance of intercourse a diaphragm can be inserted and how much additional spermicide is needed if intercourse is repeated. Current wisdom in the UK is that if intercourse is delayed by three hours or more, additional spermicide needs to be applied, either with an applicator, or in the form of a pessary (though not an oil-based one – see Figure 5.2 for spermicides that can be used with diaphragms). Another applicator full of spermicide needs to be used each time intercourse is repeated. The diaphragm should be left in place for at least six hours after the last act of intercourse. A number of research papers have questioned these rules but, at the time of writing, there have been no large-scale studies of them. (Spermicidal pessaries are likely to be less messy than cream or gel and can be inserted more discreetly if you wish.)

Figure 5.2 Spermicides for use in conjunction with barrier methods

Name	Active ingredients	
Jellies		
Duragel	Nonoxynol 11	2%
Gynol 11	Nonoxynol 9	2%
Ortho Gynol Gel	Diisobutylphenoxypolyethoxyethanol	1%
Staycept jelly	Octoxynol	1%
Creams		
Delfen	Nonoxynol 9	5%
Duracreme	Nonoxynol 11	2%
Ortho-Creme	Nonoxynol 9	2%
Pessaries		
Double Check	Nonoxynol 9	6%
Orthoforms	Nonoxynol 9	5%
Staycept pessary	Nonoxynol 9	6%
Foams		
Delfen foam	Nonoxynol 9	12.5%
Film		
C-Film	Nonoxynol 9	28%

A further objection to spermicides comes from one or two studies that suggest that spermicide absorbed from the vagina into the bloodstream may be unhealthy and that women who conceive while using spermicides may have a higher risk of a handicapped child. More recent studies have not substantiated this fear, but we will look at both sides of the picture in our discussion of spermicides on pp. 190–1.

Diaphragms, PID and cervical neoplasia
Diaphragms and spermicides help protect you from most sexually transmitted diseases, and consequently against PID with its attendant risk of damage to the reproductive organs. Diaphragms protect you from

STDs partly because they are used with spermicides, which extend their destructive role from sperm to viruses and bacteria, and partly because they form a mechanical barrier to organisms and prevent them from passing through the cervix. A recent American study concluded that the combination of a barrier plus a chemical – most commonly a diaphragm and spermicide – offers the best protection against tubal damage, more so than condoms, or spermicides on their own.[17] Other studies have suggested that it may be less the diaphragm that protects than the behaviour of diaphragm users (by nature of the socio-economic background from which they are supposed to come), since they tend to have fewer sexual partners and to begin sexual relationships at a later date than other women and that this itself may be a major factor in preventing PID. While this may be true it is certainly not the whole story. A study of 2,000 women attending a family planning clinic found that women who used diaphragms, or who had partners who used condoms, had cervical gonorrhoea only one fifth as often as IUD and pill users, which again suggests a substantial protective effect against PID. At the time of writing it is not known if diaphragms offer any protection against AIDS. It is certainly safest to assume that they do not.

The diaphragm has also been shown to offer significant protection against cervical cancer. While it is not fully understood what causes cervical cancer, two British studies have shown that using a barrier method for at least five years reduces the risk of developing cervical neoplasia or the pre-cancerous changes of the cervix. The Oxford/FPA study found the following rates of cervical neoplasia per 1,000–women years: all women, 0.73, pill users, 0.95, IUD users, 0.87, and diaphragm users 0.17. Taking into account factors such as number of sexual partners, age at first coitus, smoking habits, etc., the figure for diaphragm users rose to 0.23 – still substantially less than the rates for non-diaphragm users. In another study it was found that the relative risk of developing cervial neoplasia rose among oral contraceptive users but dropped among diaphragm and condom users with length of usage.[18]

Diaphragms and urinary tract infection

Unfortunately for some women the diaphragm does have a major drawback in that it predisposes them to urinary tract infections. The connection has been suspected for some time, but it has only recently been widely discussed in medical journals. One of the most important studies to date was based on an examination of the data from all 17,000 women who had taken part in the Oxford/FPA research to see how many had been referred to hospital for urinary tract infections. The most significant predisposing factor seemed to be current diaphragm use, particularly if the woman had not used the diaphragm for more than two years. In this period, rates of referral were two to three times higher than referrals for non-diaphragm users. The women were referred because of kidney infections, bladder or urinary tract infections. (The study did not take into account the minor episodes of cystitis treated by GPs so we do not yet know whether one-off cystitis attacks are more frequent among diaphragm users.)

The research team, led by Professor Vessey, suggested two possible explanations. In the first place there is the consistent finding that the bacteria E coli is found in the vagina of women who use diaphragms in greater quantities and more often than in women who don't. Secondly there appears to be evidence that the flow of urine is altered in some way among diaphragm users. A study in California found that diaphragms caused an alteration in the urine flow and the angle of the bladder neck. It might be that the diaphragm prevents urine from leaving the body at its normal rate. Quite why these two factors should predispose women to more urinary tract infections has not been clearly explained. Vessey and his team suggest that women who are already predisposed to urinary tract infections should not use diaphragms. They also recommend that all diaphragms should be carefully fitted, since it may be that over-large diaphragms cause the problems. To quote Professor Vessey, 'the UTI message came out of the data very strongly – women who have any history of UTI really shouldn't use the diaphragm for birth control.'[19]

If you are very keen on using a vaginal barrier method of contraception and have a history of UTI you do have other options. There are three types of diaphragm available, and it may be that one of the others could help. Secondly, you could try using a cervical cap, since at the time of writing there is no evidence suggesting that cervical caps also predispose to urinary tract infections. Equally, if your problem with a diaphragm seems to be bouts of cystitis, you could try ensuring that your bladder is emptied both before and after intercourse, and drinking more fluids than normal. If you really cannot solve the problem, then a switch to a different form of contraception may be the best solution.

Choosing a diaphragm: where to go and what to expect
If you decide that a diaphragm may be the contraceptive for you, either your GP or your local family planning clinic will be able to fit it for you. Fitting in this context simply means finding the right size of diaphragm for your particular anatomy. Family planning clinics sometimes have more time; you will have the fitting with the clinic doctor and also see a nurse who will show you how the diaphragm works, what to expect, and answer any questions you may have. GPs vary in the amount of time

they have available, and some will refer you to the practice nurse for extra discussion. Fitting a diaphragm involves no pain but it helps if you feel comfortable about a doctor examining your vagina. All diaphragm fittings start with a pelvic examination to check that there is no reason why you shouldn't use a diaphragm. If you wish to be examined and fitted by a woman doctor, say so at the outset. Most clinics and practices can arrange for this.

The doctor or nurse will work out from her examination the size of diaphragm that may be best for you, and will insert a practice ring. If it is too big or too small, she will try rings of different sizes until she finds the one that offers the best fit. Most women need a diaphragm of between 70 and 80 mm. When you first see the size of a diaphragm it may look surprisingly large. Once you understand how it sits inside you the size makes more sense. When the doctor has decided on the best size, she will ask you to feel its positioning yourself, and explain how you should insert it. First time users are given the opportunity of putting a practice diaphragm in and taking it in and out a few times. Sensitive practitioners will leave you on your own while you experiment with the easiest way for you. Squatting on the floor, lying on your back with your legs bent, or standing with one leg raised on something are all good positions to adopt. The only important rule is that you cover your cervix with the diaphragm every time. You check this by feeling for your cervix with your index finger. If it is on the other side of the rubber, you've got your diaphragm in correctly; if you can feel it uncovered, something has gone wrong, and you should start again. When you feel confident about the procedure you will probably be given a practice diaphragm to take away for a week, so you can get used to 'living' with it, and see how you get on while you make love, go to the loo, ride a bicycle and so on. You should not be able to feel your diaphragm at all. If you can, it is probably the wrong size. You should of course use an alternative form of contraception for this week. At the end of a week you should return to the clinic or GP with your diaphragm in place; you'll get a final check for size, and a prescription for your own diaphragm and spermicide.

It is worth reiterating here that a correct fit and type of diaphragm can make *all* the difference to whether or not you will decide to continue using this form of contraception. A diaphragm that is even 5 mm too big can be uncomfortable to use, felt by your partner, lead to cystitis and be generally a miserable experience. One of the women who wrote to us had this to say:

After my baby I carried on using a diaphragm. The doctor checked the size and said that it still seemed to be OK. But it never felt right. It was difficult to insert,

Which diaphragm?
Different doctors have their own quirks when it comes to prescribing diaphragms and spermicide. Some will prescribe Ortho diaphragms which are cream coloured and have a coil spring; others offer Durex diaphragms which are a transparent brown colour and have a flat spring. Less frequently you'll be offered an arcing spring diaphragm. The type of diaphragm which is best for you may be a matter of trial and error. Each of the three types of diaphragm has a slightly different feel to it as the tension of the spring around the perimeter is slightly different. The flat spring variety is often tried first and is usually the easiest and least slippery to insert. The coil spring is softer and may be a better option for women who find the pressure exerted by the flat spring diaphragms uncomfortable. The arcing diaphragm forms a bow shape when compressed and combines features of both the other two diaphragms. It is meant to be especially helpful when the muscle tone is less good since it exerts firm pressure on the walls of the vagina. If you find it difficult to place the back of your diaphragm behind your cervix, the arcing spring variety may solve the problem. If you aren't happy with the one your doctor has selected for you, ask to try another. The same is true of spermicide. Some doctors prescribe gel, others cream. Only trial and error will help you work out which you prefer. If you want an unscented, colourless and stainless jelly, ask for Gynol II. We have found from experience that women doctors who are diaphragm users themselves are much more clued up about the choices available.

seemed to be slipping out and was uncomfortable during intercourse. I went back to the doctor determined to switch to the mini-pill. She suggested a different size of diaphragm and gave me one 5 mm smaller. The difference was astonishing. Whereas the other one had always felt wrong, this one felt absolutely right from the start. I carried on using it until we decided to conceive our second child.

Gaining or losing weight
You will probably be advised to return to the clinic if you have any problems, if you gain or lose half a stone, or after a pregnancy. In fact how often refitting is needed is not clear. In one recent study of nineteen women who gained 10 lbs or more, 37 per cent required different sized diaphragms. Yet among the control group whose weight was unchanged 59 per cent also required a different size. Pregnancy may make a difference, though the changes in the vagina and cervix may mean that several different sizes are needed in the course of a year. It is best to wait for the six-week postnatal check-up before beginning to use a diaphragm again.[20]

Diaphragms need replacing every year or so, depending on how often they are used, the climate and how well they are looked after. It is always a good idea to check for tiny pinpricks where the rubber has worn through. Some diaphragms get a bit discoloured after a time, and you may wish to replace it on purely aesthetic grounds. It is always a good idea to wear your diaphragm when you go back to the clinic or GP for a new prescription so that the size can be checked again.

Cervical caps

Cervical caps: do they work?

It is very difficult to know how many women in this country use cervical caps, since in most major studies figures for diaphragms and caps are not separated. If the diaphragm is a minority interest, the cervical cap was until recently regarded as little more than a historical curiosity, and there were very few well designed and executed trials of its efficiency. However considerably more information has come to light since the American Food and Drug Administration (FDA) decided in 1980, some 100 years after their invention, to categorize cervical caps as 'investigational devices' and to list them as among 'probably harmful contraceptives'. This meant that anyone wishing to prescribe or use a cervical cap had to do so in the context of a study of its effectiveness and safety. Over the years a number of such studies took place and we now have a much clearer idea of the kind of device the cervical cap is. In 1988, after eight years of campaigning and in the absence of any evidence to suggest its harmfulness, the FDA approved the cap for routine use.

A major randomized, comparative study of the cervical cap and diaphragm, costing $2 million, conducted by Dr Gerald Bernstein for the FDA, was completed in March 1986. At the same time, nearly 100 other individual practitioners and clinics were given permission to try out the cap. A total of 30,000 women were involved. Bernstein's study showed a 93.6 per cent effectiveness for the cap and 95.4 per cent for the diaphragm. This was the theoretical effectiveness. In practice rates of 88.3 per cent were achieved for the cap and 87.4 per cent for the diaphragm. There was a wide variety in the results drawn from the other research projects carried out, with the best cap use-effectiveness rate being 97 per cent and the worst about 81 per cent.[21]

If you decide to try a cervical cap you can expect a level of effectiveness probably a little lower than that provided by a diaphragm, though much will depend on how good a fit your practitioner is able to provide you with, and on using the cap absolutely consistently. The role that spermicides play with cervical caps, and whether they become more effective if spermicide is always used is still not fully understood. Similarly, no one knows certainly what bearing the length of time a cervical cap is worn at any one time has on its effectiveness.

Caps: for and against

If we had known that there was a small, discreet little cap which could stay in for days or weeks at a time, which a man could not detect (as he often definitely can the diaphragm and its wallow) which needed no spermicide – or at most a dab – which could be made of gold, which would last a lifetime, neither Gregory Pincus nor Jove himself could have got us to give it up.

Germaine Greer, *Sex and Destiny*

A cervical cap looks like a small diaphragm, but fits securely over the cervix rather than against the vaginal walls. It is much more difficult to use than a diaphragm, and much more likely to result in contraceptive failure due to slippage during intercourse. While it was once very popular, it is rarely used today.

Howard I. Shapiro, *The Birth Control Book*

Germaine Greer's celebration of the cervical cap as the banished and forgotten princess of family planning must have come as a surprise to many women who had never even heard of it. That such an ideal form of fertility control could have been lost and replaced with the diaphragm clearly represents, for Greer, a blow to women's reproductive freedom. Her championship of the cervical cap must have added grist to the mill for those campaigning in the USA for FDA approval of the cap. What is it about the cervical cap that is so attractive to a new generation of contraceptive users? How can it have disappeared for so long? Why are doctors so unwilling to mention it, let alone fit it for us? While it is not the ultimate answer to every woman's contraceptive needs, it has not deserved its almost complete eclipse. In this section we will try and present a fair case for the cervical cap as a very good form of contraception for some women, and one that should definitely be brought back into the consulting rooms of GPs and family planning clinics.

Advantages
The cervical cap shares many health advantages with the diaphragm. Users are less likely to develop an STD and subsequent PID (see last section). It is controlled by the woman, has no systemic effects and, once fitted, leaves a woman relatively free of the medical profession. The cervical cap also brings with it a number of additional advantages which lead some women to greatly prefer it to a diaphragm. Firstly it can be inserted well in advance and left in place for up to forty-eight hours

before removal. Some authorities suggest that the cap can be left for three days, though many women complain of odour after forty-eight hours. Moreover, the cap needs only one small application of spermicide with each insertion. Most studies of cap efficacy recommend that the cap should be filled approximately one-third full of spermicide. Too much spermicide interferes with the suction of the device. Once inserted you can forget about additional spermicide for the next forty-eight hours, no matter how many times you make love. This makes the cap both easier to use and more aesthetically pleasing than a diaphragm. As one woman commented, 'I can put my cap in on a Friday night and forget about contraception for the whole weekend. It's ideal.'

A recent study showed, interestingly, that Gynol II jelly and Ortho creme kept their spermicidal action for longer with the cervical cap than with the diaphragm; Ortho creme plus cervical cap were the best combination, with spermicidal activity still present after two days.

The smaller size of the cap means that it is more discreet than a diaphragm and less likely to be felt. The fact that it is held in place with an airtight seal means that the smell, taste and feel of spermicide is almost entirely absent. In a number of recent surveys carried out in the USA, women commented on how much they liked the cap, its ease of use, the absence of health risks and side effects, the ability to leave it in place for long enough to permit sexual spontaneity and its small size and comfort in use. In one study 80.53 per cent of the participants continued to use the cervical cap after one year – a very high continuation rate.[22] The most common comment that the researchers received was one of satisfaction at being able to use a cervical cap.

Disadvantages

The cervical cap, like all forms of contraception, has its disadvantages. In the first place, not all the women who want to have a cervical cap fitted are able to use one. In order to work properly, the cervical cap needs to fit firmly and snugly over the cervix, but not every cervix will accommodate a cervical cap. If your cervix is very long, or very short, or irregularly shaped, or has been damaged in childbirth or some other gynaecological procedure, or enters your vagina at an angle, a cap is far more likely to be displaced. Some women have very long vaginas and find inserting and removing a cap more trouble than it's worth. In various surveys in the USA between 10 per cent and 25 per cent of women keen to use a cap were unable to be fitted. It is possible that a Vimule cap or vault cap might have served the purpose better but they are not commonly available.

Assuming that a cap can be fitted, there are a number of other factors that might discourage some women. In some of the US studies, odour was a significant problem for some women, though only, it seems, if they kept their caps in for longish periods of time. One study that gave women the option of keeping their caps in place for up to a week found that odour was such a problem that by the end of the study the researchers had revised the guidelines and recommended removing a cap after forty-eight hours. Other researchers have suggested that washing the cap with lemon juice or vinegar might help, though this might also lead to the speedier deterioration of the rubber. Yet other researchers have suggested that using different spermicides might reduce odour problems. It seems however that the simple expedient of removing the cap and washing it with water every twenty-four to forty-eight hours will solve the problem just as well.

A third problem is that some women find that even well-fitting caps get dislodged during intercourse. Most practitioners will recommend that you use a condom for the first month in case this happens. Quite often it has something to do with particular love-making positions. If you discover that making love in a particular way always dislodges the cap it makes sense to use a different form of contraception for such occasions. If your cap is continually being dislodged it suggests that the fit is not what it should be, and you should either change the size of cap, or think about another form of contraception, perhaps one of the other caps.

But perhaps the most significant disadvantage of the cervical cap is unwanted pregnancy. Non-use and dislodgement only account for about 50 per cent of the pregnancies that do occur. Some women use their caps carefully, with spermicide, without experiencing dislodgement, and still become pregnant. It is not understood quite how a pregnancy can still occur with careful use, but it is probably due to anatomical changes in the vagina and cervix during sexual excitement. As we saw in the opening of this chapter, the behaviour of the vagina and cervix during intercourse, particularly in the fertile period, are designed to thwart even the most carefully fitted barrier.

Caps in practice

Caps available in the UK

In the UK the term cervical cap applies to two devices only, the Prentif cavity-rim cervical cap and the check pessary. The cavity rim cap is small and thimble shaped, made in a firm, natural rubber, coloured pink. The check pessary is made of a slightly softer rubber, and is brown coloured.

Figure 5.3 Different kinds of cervical cap

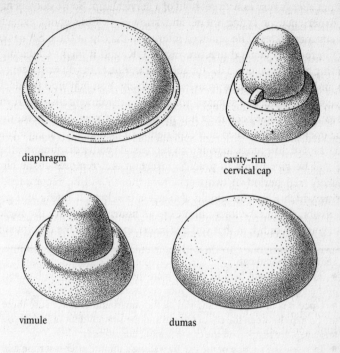

diaphragm

cavity-rim
cervical cap

vimule

dumas

Both are designed to fit snugly over the cervix – the fit is very important. Unlike the diaphragm, the cap is held on by suction and should be very difficult to dislodge. Cervical caps come in four sizes, ranging from 22–31 mm in 3 mm stages. This measurement comes from the internal diameter of the upper ring. Interestingly, 85 per cent of women successfully fitted with a cervical cap need one of the two smallest sizes, and maybe more women could be successfully fitted with caps if even smaller sizes were available.

There are two other caps available in the UK, though not usually called cervical caps. The first is the Vimule cap which is bell shaped and is held in place by a combination of suction and tension. It comes in three sizes, 45, 48 and 51 mm. The other is the Dumas or vault cap which is bowl shaped and works a little bit like a diaphragm. It has a thinner dome through which the cervix can be felt, comes in five sizes from 55 mm to 75 mm, and does not cover the cervix closely.

In the vast majority of recent studies the Prentif cavity-rim cap has been used; unfortunately there is simply not enough documented evidence about the way in which the other varieties of cap work.

Obtaining and using a cervical cap

It is not always very easy to get hold of a cervical cap. Some doctors have no experience of fitting them, and know very little about expected effectiveness rates. The renewed interest in the cap in the USA has not yet filtered into general practice in the UK, and it might take a bit of hunting before you find a doctor able and willing to fit you with a cervical cap and to teach you how to use it effectively. You may find the doctor bypasses the issue and suggests you try out a diaphragm instead. If your doctor is really not keen then it is probably best to go elsewhere, since your doctor's enthusiasm and experience in fitting cervical caps could make a lot of difference to your own success. As with a diaphragm fitting, you will be given time to practise insertion and removal at the clinic itself. A trial period of two weeks to a month will be recommended during which time you should also use a condom. A fitting and good discussion might take forty minutes to an hour. Don't leave the surgery until you are confident that you can insert and remove the cap yourself.

Using a cervical cap

• The cap should be $\frac{1}{3}$ to $\frac{1}{2}$ filled with spermicide, folded in half and pushed gently in the direction of your cervix until it will go no further.

• Once it is in place, feel the rim all the way round to make sure there are no gaps between the top of the cap and the surrounding vagina. If you feel a gap, try tugging on the cap to see if it comes away.

• Increase the suction of the cap by waiting a minute after insertion and then pinching the excess rubber at the top of the dome, and pulling it gently downwards.

• Try and dislodge the cap by pulling it with one or two fingers. If it dislodges easily, intercourse will probably dislodge it too. Take it out and try again. A well-fitting cap should be quite tricky to move.

• The string that comes with a new cap is to help you remove it. Once you have developed your own system for breaking the suction the string isn't needed. The person who fits your cap for you will explain the best way of breaking the suction and removing the cap.

• Use your cap for only forty-eight hours at a time, but ensure that it stays in place for at least six hours after the last intercourse, even if this means keeping your cap in place for a bit longer than forty-eight hours.

The cervical cap deserves far more attention than it has currently received, given its effectiveness, safety and ease of use. In America, by dint of being banned and reintroduced, the cap has received more publicity than in the UK. Articles in women's magazines and in journals such as *Time* have introduced the cervical cap as if it were a newly invented device to many women who would never have considered it before. As the link between diaphragms and urinary tract infections persuades women with a history of cystitis not to use the diaphragm, the cervical cap should be readily available as an alternative. Given the large scale studies now completed in the USA there is no excuse for the failure of some professionals here even to mention the cap as an available method of contraception.

Spermicides

Spermicides: do they work?

In the UK spermicides are rarely recommended for use on their own and for this reason studies of their effectiveness are difficult to come by. The Oxford/FPA study reported a failure rate of 11.9 for spermicides used alone which was the highest figure recorded for any form of contraception except natural family planning. Other studies have put the first year failure figure closer to 31 per cent. On the other hand these high figures have not been confirmed by other researchers. In 1976 a French study of fifty-one women using either a spermicidal gel or cream found a failure rate of only 2.3 per 100 woman-years. Japanese women using foaming spermicidal tablets have had failure rates of only 3.2 per 100 woman-years over a fifteen-month period, while the Patanex Oval foaming suppository marketed in West Germany and used in a trial by 652 women had a failure rate of only 0.3 per 100 woman-years.

A study of the spermicidal C-film shows just how contradictory the evidence on effectiveness can be. A study sponsored by the FPA in London found a failure rate of 62 per 100 woman-years when women used C-film and nothing else. Yet another similar study of C-film reported a failure rate of only 9 per 100 women-years. There are no really satisfactory explanations for this wide discrepancy. It may be the product or the users. As we saw in the introduction to this chapter, *in vitro* tests cannot offer reliable evidence as to the likely success rates of a spermicide *in vivo*.[23]

By all the available evidence, using a spermicide on its own is not a good idea if you really need to avoid a pregnancy. On the other hand, spermicides certainly have a role to play. Even on the worst estimates, spermicides will prevent two-thirds of the pregnancies that would occur in otherwise unprotected intercourse.

How many women rely just on spermicides? Since spermicides alone are not recommended by clinics or prescribed by doctors there are few 'official' statistics. Like condoms, spermicides can be bought over the counter, and it is clearly difficult to estimate from sales how many couples rely on spermicides. In the General Household Survey of 1986 however about 1 per cent of users claimed that their current method of contraception was spermicides alone.

Spermicides: for and against

Two issues in particular need discussion in relation to the use of spermicides. One is the evidence of possible connection between spermicides and fetal abnormality, and the second is the role of spermicides in preventing STDs.

Spermicides and congenital abnormality

In 1981 and 1982 research papers were published that suggested that women who became pregnant while using spermicides, either alone, or with a barrier, were more likely to have babies with a congenital abnormality, including Down's syndrome and neural tube defects (such as spina bifida). In 1986 a woman was awarded $4.7 million in an American court because her disabled child was considered to have been exposed to spermicides *in utero*. Subsequently the research has been questioned. The original studies were very small and not necessarily reliable. More recently two larger, well-conducted studies have found no additional risk of carrying a handicapped baby when using spermicides. One study was specifically designed to examine the link between genetic conditions such as Down's syndrome, while the other looked at a wider range of birth defects.

In the first study the previous contraceptive history of women carrying fetuses with genetic abnormalities were compared with carefully selected controls. Eleven per cent of the women whose fetus had a genetic abnormality had used spermicides either in the month before or after their last period, or at the estimated time of conception, compared with 12 per cent of the controls. Twenty-five per cent had used spermicides in the previous year compared with 23 per cent of the controls. The researchers concluded that there was no statistically significant link between spermicide use and trisomy (the kind of genetic defect that causes Down's syndrome).

In the second study the mothers of 4,594 children born with birth defects were interviewed and asked about their lifetime contraceptive history. The researchers found no significant association between any of the birth defects examined and the use, or duration of use, of spermicides. The researchers concluded that 'the risk of five specific birth defects – Down's syndrome, hypospadias, limb reduction defects, neoplasms and neural tube defects – are not increased by exposure to spermicide contraceptives in the first four months of pregnancy, at the time of conception, or at any time before conception.'[24]

These results are good news for women anxious about the use of spermicide. After the first studies were published some women had been upset by their doctors' warnings about spermicide. One woman who wrote to us commented: 'I told my doctor that I'd used a diaphragm and spermicide in the cycle in which we'd conceived my baby and she started talking about amniocentesis and spermicides damaging babies. I was very upset. No one had ever mentioned the possibility of such a thing before.' Another wrote: 'I'd often wondered if it was something that I'd exposed myself to that led to my son being a Down's baby. I was using C-film when he was conceived. I often feel guilty about it.' While clearly no one can say absolutely for certain that spermicides could never in any circumstances contribute to a birth abnormality, on the evidence so far it is not a problem that women should worry too much about.

Spermicides and sexually transmitted diseases

A number of *in vitro* studies have demonstrated that organisms that cause gonorrhoea, genital herpes, trichomoniasm, and AIDS are damaged or killed by spermicides. The bacteria that cause gonorrhoea are killed by twenty different spermicides even when they are diluted to half their original strength. Some spermicides are more lethal than others, depending on the concentration of spermicidal agent in the cream, jelly, foam or pessary. Nonoxynol 9, one of the most commonly used spermicides, has a strong protective role against STDs. A 'Today' contraceptive sponge (which contains Nonoxynol 9) was injected with cultures of Neisseria gonorrhoea and Herpes Simplex II. The gonorrhoea microorganisms were dead within five minutes and the herpes within ten. Experiments with Nonoxynol 9 and the AIDS virus have demonstrated that this spermicide inactivates the virus. A recent *in vitro* study by R. Elgin looked at the effect of both Nonoxynol 9 and Nonoxynol 11 at concentrations lower than those expected in the vagina of a woman using spermicide. Both types inactivated the virus and virus infected cells after three minutes' exposure. The author concluded that spermicides should help prevent transmission of the AIDS virus.[25]

Unfortunately *in vitro* experiments do not necessarily predict how effective a spermicide will be against sperm or against other microorganisms *in vivo*. Substances that are highly effective in the laboratory may behave differently when diluted by the fluids produced by the cervix and vagina. However, as we have seen, there is mounting evidence to suggest that spermicides can play a significant role in fighting STDs. In one US study of eighty-seven STD patients, all of whom were using oral contraceptives or IUDs, or had been sterilized, thirty-seven were provided with Nonoxynol cream and asked to use it on every occasion they made love. After six months only 3 per cent had become reinfected with an STD, compared to 22 per cent of the controls.[26]

Other female barrier methods

The 'Today' contraceptive sponge

The 'Today' sponge was developed by a biomedical engineer in the late 1970s. It is made of polyurethane and impregnated with Nonoxynol 9. The manufacturers made a number of attempts before settling on the current version, a white, mushroom-shaped disposable sponge measuring about 5 cm × 2.5 cm with a tab to help removal. 'Today' sponges come in packets of three, and each can be worn continuously for twenty-four hours. It is difficult to estimate how many women have adopted the sponge as their main method of contraception, but we do know that between its launch in 1983, and January 1985, about 1.25 million women in the USA had used it.

As far as its effectiveness is concerned, there is more material available. A study was carried out at the Margaret Pyke Centre in London as part of a much larger trial in ten family planning clinics worldwide. Two hundred and forty-nine volunteers were randomly allocated either the sponge or a diaphragm, and were followed up for the next twelve months. A hundred and twenty-six received sponges, and a hundred and twenty-three arcing spring diaphragms. By the end of the year, twenty-five of the sponge-users had become pregnant and ten of the diaphragm-using group, despite the fact that each woman was well counselled and followed up. These figures represent failure rates of 24.5 per cent and 10.9 per cent respectively. Among the diaphragm users 50 per cent of the failures were estimated to be use-failures in that the women concerned did not use their diaphragms for every act of intercourse in the cycle in which conception occurred. Among sponge users – despite the higher pregnancy rate – only 32 per cent of the women felt that their pregnancies could have been due to a failure in their use of the method. In view of this disappointingly high failure rate the research team came to the conclusion that the 'Today' sponge was an ideal method for women wishing to space children and not too anxious if they became pregnant, and for women with lowered fertility, either breastfeeding or pre-menopausal, but they could not recommend it for women who needed to avoid pregnancy at all costs. Interestingly, however, they also felt that since so many women found the sponge so pleasing in all other aspects

Figure 5.4 The 'Today' sponge

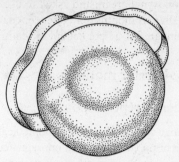

– freedom from health hazards, simplicity, spontaneity – the moderate effectiveness might be a risk they were prepared to take.[27]

In America the experience of failure has been a little different. The 'Today' sponge has been available for longer – since 1983 – and evidence collected in a major study involving thirteen centers over two years put the success rate in the first year at 89.9 per cent and in the second year 96.7 per cent. Among inexperienced users in the first year about ten in every 100 became pregnant, while among those who continued using their sponges into the second year only five out of 100 had unexpected pregnancies.[28] Interestingly there is some evidence that the sponge is less effective for women who have already had children. Perhaps a larger sponge is needed.

Femshield

The world's first female condom has been described variously as looking like an elephant's contraceptive, a vacuum cleaner bag and a sock. . . . I marvelled at how natural it felt, as though there was nothing there at all. Not surprising, since our condom had split . . .
James Castle in the *Observer*, 6 November 1988

At the time of writing the bulk of the information available about Femshield was that put out by Medicor Ltd, the manufacturers, and the very limited material from a pilot study at the Margaret Pyke Centre in London, plus a few newspaper articles. It had not been released for general use and so we were not in a position to try it for ourselves or talk to other women who had. What follows is therefore necessarily limited.

As we have seen, the Femshield is a soft, loose and strong polyurethane tube, about 15 cm long and 7 cm in diameter, with a ring at the top and the bottom. The upper ring is designed to cover the cervix in much the same way as a diaphragm, while the lower ring sits outside the vagina. The polyurethane used is up to 40 per cent stronger than the latex used

Figure 5.5 Femshield, 'the female condom'

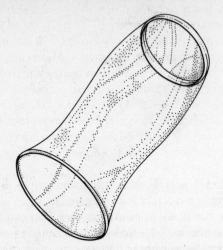

in condoms, so there is less chance of the Femshield bursting or tearing. At the same time, the material is softer than latex and is supposed to give a more natural feel. The manufacturers say that it is as easy to insert as a tampon, that it follows the natural inner contours of the vagina and is highly unlikely to tear. Other advantages are that it can be inserted several hours in advance of intercourse, will be available over the counter without prescription and is therefore, like spermicides and the sponge, a form of contraception effective against STDs that women can control entirely themselves.

Unfortunately little is known about Femshield's effectiveness as a contraceptive at present. Most of the interest lies in its ability to prevent the transmission of STDs, particularly AIDS. The Femshield is being marketed as an alternative to condoms for safer sex, and though there are no published accounts of its effectiveness it seems likely that it will be much like a diaphragm/condom combination as far as preventing pregnancy is concerned.

Looking at pictures of the Femshield, one may perhaps be forgiven for pondering on what it might be like to use. Of the twenty-four couples using it at the Margaret Pyke Centre, 50 per cent of the women thought that it was preferable to a male condom, 79 per cent thought that the effect on sexual pleasure was better and only 21 per cent that it was worse. The men were less keen. Only 37 per cent thought that it was better than a condom, though 63 per cent thought it no different to, or better than the conventional condom from the point of view of sexual pleasure. As far as sexual pleasure goes, the Femshield seems to come out quite well. Sixty-two per cent of couples produced orgasms up to the usual standard, 9 per cent had better ones, and only 29 per cent found their orgasms rather below par.[29]

The manufacturers are currently improving the device in the light of some of the observations made by the couples. Meanwhile a number of other studies are under way. The WHO is conducting trials in various developing countries, and technical trials are underway in the USA, Denmark, Germany and Sweden. In the UK 200 volunteer couples are testing the Femshield for the Margaret Pyke Centre. John Guillebaud, director of the Centre, has described the Femshield as a major advance. In a press release put out by Medicor he was quoted as saying:

I have found in my work . . . that a number of patients and their partners prefer a method of contraception which is non-systemic – without dangers of side effects. There was already, even before the anxieties about sexually transmitted diseases, a large body of opinion that was worried about any method that might harmfully affect the whole body. Compared to the sheath, I think there are two overriding advantages. According to preliminary information we have received, men often state that they find the sensations of intercourse more normal when using Femshield with a good lubricant than when using a male condom. Secondly, the method is under a woman's control. I believe the problem with the normal condom is that many women, even if they would prefer them to be used, feel over-dependent on their partner. But a woman can elect to purchase Femshield herself and can fit it in advance of intercourse and *she* is in control.[30]

Recent developments

The Contracap

The Contracap is a spermicide-free, valved, custom-fitted cervical cap. It is part of a long tradition of caps made specially for the woman concerned. A recent experiment involved forty women using Contracaps for periods of up to a year. An impression was made of each of their cervices and a cap made from a special rubber material. The caps had a one-way valve, letting out cervical fluids and menstrual blood, and were designed to be worn all the time. The women in fact wore their caps for periods ranging from two days to seven months. Twenty-three women wore caps for more than three months and three for six months. Unfortunately there were nine pregnancies in this time, eight of which occurred in the first three months of use, and seven of which could not be accounted for by a displaced cap. Despite the very high pregnancy rate, the women liked their caps. It is therefore to be hoped that work on them will continue until one is developed that is really effective in preventing pregnancy, as well as being highly acceptable.[31]

Vaginal rings

A vaginal ring releasing either spermicide or hormones (either proges-togen alone, or a combined oestrogen/progestogen formula) has con-siderable appeal. Rings can be made of soft, silicone rubber, impregnated with the spermicide or hormone and left in place for varying lengths of time. Spermicide-releasing rings would probably need replacing each cycle, while some hormone-releasing rings could stay in place for two or three months. So far both types of ring have only been used on a trial basis, but both have proved popular with the women who have tried them out. In one trial of a progestogen-releasing ring, all but two of the twenty-seven volunteers felt that it was the best form of contraceptive they had ever used. Previously most had preferred the pill.

Tests for a variety of different vaginal rings are currently underway, and it is to be hoped that this option will become a realistic one in the next few years. The advantage of the hormone-releasing rings is in the relatively small quantities of hormone delivered to the body. Many of the effects produced are local, rather than systemic. The progestogen-releasing rings, for example, work largely by changing the quality of cervical mucus, though there is some evidence of cycle disruption as well. Some people believe that within a few years much hormonal contraception will be of this sort.

CHAPTER 6

Men and Contraception

Any preventative means, to be satisfactory, must be used by the woman, as it spoils the passion and impulsiveness of the venereal act if the man has to think of them . . .
George Drysdale, 1854, quoted in *The Sexual Politics of Reproduction*

It's the responsibility of both men and women, but because women are more directly affected if something goes wrong I suppose it is not surprising that most of them take the responsibility most of the time.
Hilary Thomas in *The Sexual Politics of Reproduction*

I'm fed up with the idea that men screw and women get pregnant. As far as the men I know are concerned, they spend their whole time being careful and neurotic about risking a pregnancy.

We often forget that in the history of contraception men have played a considerable role. Long before the nature of a woman's cycle was understood, the role of sperm in procreation had been recognized and coitus interruptus was practised to avoid unwanted offspring. Though it is almost impossible to quantify, the condom and coitus interruptus between them have probably played a more substantial role in the demographic shifts that have occurred throughout Western Europe than female methods. Even before rudimentary barriers were playing their part in female contraception in the eighteenth and nineteenth centuries, there is good evidence that the birth-rate was beginning to fall; the best explanation is that coitus interruptus was becoming widespread.

Despite this history, and the fact that throughout the nineteenth and twentieth centuries the wider availability of condoms has given men even greater involvement, and despite the fact that among couples relying on sterilization it is now more likely to be the man who has been sterilized, the role of men in fertility control is not well recognized or understood. It is often said that men are irresponsible, reluctant to get involved, out to get one thing. Even if this were true in some cases, it is equally true that the providers of contraception, the media, and the whole socialization process of men *and* women have reinforced and perpetuated this situation. Why was it for example that GPs chose not to include condoms in the family planning services they provide? One GP has gone on record as writing 'It is surely the last straw if the government intends to insult us by filling our surgeries with a lot of louts queuing up for the issue of condoms.'[1] If women have suffered from the medicalization and specialization of contraception it is equally true that men have lost out too, through their exclusion; it is only now, as condoms return to fashion, that the significance of men in fertility control is being re-evaluated.

Perhaps the problem has been that, apart from vasectomy, male methods of fertility control have simply not lent themselves to a medical takeover, with the result that they have been denigrated. It is obviously impossible to 'fit' a condom, and with coitus interruptus you either get out in time or you don't. There is not much your GP can do to make either more effective. There is something embarrassingly sexual about a condom; its proper function cannot be hidden under complicated medical terminology like the pill. The very fact that the condom cannot be divorced from sex – in fact is useless without an erect penis to disport itself on – and the long association between condoms and sexually transmitted diseases have led to a situation in which 'male methods' have been seen as something less serious and more seedy than the nice clean clinical methods available for women.

Ironically, it is only with the return of an uncontrollable sexually transmitted disease to the arena of human relationships (syphilis played much the same role in the eighteenth century) that the condom is once again taken seriously. In an attempt to make condom use widespread it is proving necessary to glamorize it and represent it as a rather erotic addition to sex. But this too has its limitations. If the condom is not second rate and seedy, neither is it the final answer to the spread of AIDS or the traumas of teenage sexuality. The condom certainly has a part to play, and even if 'real men come in a jiffy', they can also play a major role in co-operating and supporting their partners in the management of fertility, whether or not they choose to rely on condoms. It would be a great pity if the role of a man in fertility control were to be reduced to a question of whether or not he carries a condom.

There are at least three major impediments to the full involvement of men in contraception. The first is tied up with our current sexual ideology. It has been said that you can't argue with a teenage erection. In other words, young men have to do what young men have to do and young women presumably have to take precautions or take the consequences. The idea that men have irresistible biological urges and damage their health if they abstain reinforces the current idea that contraception is women's business. Women are socialized to accept this. Many women, young women in particular, are prepared to risk an unwanted pregnancy because they subscribe to the belief that it is not fair on the man to expect him to take responsibility for the outcome of their sexual act. Only if women are able to say what they want and to determine the way in which their relationships run will they be able to share responsibility with men more equally.

The second main impediment is the way in which the provision of contraception is structured. The provision of birth-control is still linked to maternal and child health services. Women with small children frequently combine visiting the doctor on behalf of their children with obtaining contraception. 'Well Woman' clinics are for women and not men. Family planning clinics are designed to cater for women and are often uncomfortable places for men on their own. It is not really surprising if few men use these clinics, except to accompany partners, and even this is not particularly common. Most condoms supplied through clinics are distributed to women. A recent attempt to start a men-only clinic in North Manchester drew only forty men in ten weeks, despite the fact that the clinic was advertised in newspapers and on the radio, and that the adverts pointed out that the clinic was staffed by men and distributed free condoms.[2]

At present only 8 per cent of the world contraceptive budget is spent on the development of male methods of fertility control. This is the third impediment to the full involvement of men in contraception. As long as a situation continues in which it is only women's fertility that is considered 'controllable', and where the delicately balanced cycles of women are considered more interruptable than the more robust, linear reproductive systems of men, women will continue to bear the responsibility for avoiding pregnancy, and men will continue to regard contraception as women's business. This is not in any sense to wish dangerous health hazards on men. On the contrary, the experience with high dose oestrogens should make us doubly sceptical about any new systemic methods of birth control, whether for women or men. It is to say, however, that for too long it has been the assumption that contraception is a woman's issue. We would argue on the contrary, that living with fertility in a harmonious and safe way can be an enhancement of personal life, and of relationships, and that this is as true for men as for women.

Condoms

A short history of condoms

The condom has a long and interesting history. With an ancestry dating back to early Egyptian civilization – though the exact purpose of the elaborate, tasselled condom-like exotica shown in wall paintings is not fully understood – condoms are now used by around 40 million couples throughout the world. Around 400 years ago the condom was used primarily as a protection against syphilis and other sexually transmitted diseases but by the beginning of the eighteenth century the role of condoms in preventing pregnancy was becoming clear. Nowadays the condom retains its double function, as a barrier against disease and a protection against pregnancy. One of the first written descriptions of condoms comes from Fallopius, the Italian doctor who gave his name to the fallopian tubes and coined the word 'vagina' (which means sheath, as in sword sheath or scabbard). He described a linen condom which was put over the tip of the penis, lubricated with lotion, and seems to have had startling success in preventing syphilis.

By 1705 the first references to Quondams or condums were appearing in English, mainly in bawdy verses. One verse dated 1708 referred to the possibly mythical Dr Condom who 'invented' the condom. It praised 'matchless Condom' whose invention had 'Quenched the heat of Venus's fire/ And yet preserved the Flame of Love's Desire'. By 1717 condoms were well known enough for one English physician, Daniel Turner, to describe them as 'the best, if not the only Preservative our Libertines have found out at present; and yet by reason of its blunting the sensation, I have heard some of them acknowledge that they had often chose to risque a Clap, rather than engage *cum Hastis sic clypeatis* [with spears thus sheathed].'[3] Some things don't change!

The condoms that the libertines were wearing were made from lamb or sheep's caeca or appendix. They were probably of reasonably good quality, were painstakingly made and were very fine (0.038 mm; a standard 1989 condom is 0.05 mm thick). It is only recently that modern condoms have approached the same 'gossamer' quality. What is more, animal-skin condoms behave more like human skin than latex in that they conduct heat rather better, so they probably had a less dulling effect on sensation than modern latex condoms. Certainly numbers of Americans still think so, and lambskin condoms account for one in every twenty condoms sold in the USA. Other couples find the appeal of an animal-skin condom rather questionable. That master of all sexual matters, Casanova would have agreed with them. Although he used the little 'preventive bags invented by the English to save the fair sex from anxiety', and himself from an STD, he was also reluctant 'to be enclosed in a piece of dead skin to prove that I am perfectly alive'.

In the eighteenth century, London had the curious distinction of being the condom capital of the world. In the nineteenth century it was again an invention of two British men that took condom manufacture into its next phase. In 1843–4 Goodyear and Hancock vulcanized rubber for the first time, which made it a far more durable product. From the 1870s condoms moved into a new era of mass production, interestingly more or less at the same time at which the birth-rate began its systematic fall. These early rubber condoms left rather a lot to be desired by today's standards. They were considerably thicker and had a seam running along their entire length. A woman of seventy-three who wrote to us described one: 'My mother showed me a "sheath" my father used. It was a big, washable, rubber one. She told me that he put it on like a sock and when he left her it used to stay behind, and they had to fish for it.' Marie Stopes, who had an opinion on most aspects of human sexuality, disliked condoms intensely. Part of the problem was her own faulty understanding of physiology. She believed that at moments of great passion the glans somehow became interlocked with the cervix; a condom would obviously affect this interlocking, especially if the couple were using one of the first teat-ended condoms, marketed under the uncompromising name of Dreadnought in 1901. Stopes would not tolerate any device that did not allow the 'entry, mingling, and mutual exchange of reactions between the man's uncovered organ and the woman's', *except* during the first few weeks of marriage. In this exceptionally delicate time the condom came into its own, protecting the new bride from the sight, feel or smell of semen, which Stopes thought might have a profound (presumably negative) impact on the relationship. By the 1930s crêpe rubber gave way to latex and condoms as we know them came of age. The best latex comes from Malaysia and Thailand, and is the sap of the rubber tree suspended in water and stabilized with ammonia and antioxidants.

Modern condoms
Latex condoms appeared in the 1930s. The Japanese, always ahead in condom design and packaging, introduced coloured condoms in 1949. In the 1960s lubricated condoms were introduced, while the first spermicidally lubricated condoms appeared on the British market in 1975. Modern condoms are made in large, fully automated factories and turned out by the million. Glass formers of the desired shape are dipped into liquid latex rubber, passed through an infra-red oven and

then through a bath of dyed rubber. The thickness of the condom depends on how slowly the former is withdrawn from the latex. A series of brushes turn down the top of the condom to make the familiar ring and the condom is passed through another furnace (at 55°C) which fuses all the layers together. The condoms are removed from the former by water jets, transferred into linen bags, washed in de-ionized water and rinsed again in water that includes a bactericide, starch and silicone. Then all condoms are tested electronically for holes, while samples go through water, air and tension tests for strength. Once tested the condoms are packed mechanically, boxed and are ready for distribution.

Condoms sold in the UK are not generally sized so men buying condoms have at least one less embarrassing hurdle to overcome. In a recent survey of over 100 different condoms available in Britain, some complying with the British Standard and some not, all were between 170 mm and 200 mm long and around 50 mm wide. In fact, the British Standards Institute insists on a minimum of 160 mm length and 49–56 mm width. Thickness ranges from 0.21 mm to 0.03 mm. Very thin or very thick condoms tend to be more expensive. At least with thicker condoms you are more likely to get your money's worth, because they are stronger. Condoms come in a variety of styles — teat-ended, smooth-ended, straight-sided, contoured and ribbed, though the teat end is a peculiarly British addition. Most Europeans and Americans prefer their condoms plain.

Condoms: do they work?

After coming off the pill my boyfriend and I decided to use condoms, but at least one or two out of the three condoms we used burst. I had to use the morning-after pill on at least three occasions.

Everybody seems to have a story about a burst condom to tell, except me. I'm beginning to wonder if my husband and I have a very sedate style.

Bursting condoms are more often due to a lack of lubrication or a snag from long fingernails than to a design or structural fault in the condom itself. Modern condoms are surprisingly strong, and although no system has yet been devised to guarantee that every single condom is absolutely perfect, the British Standard that came into force in 1979 (and is currently under revision) goes a long way to ensuring that this is in fact the case. The BSI allows for faults such as pinholes in five out of every 1000 condoms in continuous production. Standards in other countries such as Sweden are even higher. Most well-known brands of condoms are tested electronically. Electronic screening works on the principle that rubber cannot conduct electricity, which means that an electric current cannot pass through an unflawed condom. Condoms are rolled on to tube-shaped electrodes and given a mild electric 'shock' using either a wet or a dry method. Either way, if the rubber allows a current to pass through it, it probably has a pinhole in it and is automatically rejected as faulty.

Quite apart from the electronic testing, the BSI insists on its own tests for all condoms that bear the kite symbol. The primary test for holes is the water leakage test, in which 300 ml of water is poured into a condom. The condom is then sealed and rolled on absorbent paper. Other countries specify an air test in which the condom is inflated. British condoms are also tested for strength; a small section is cut from the middle of the condom and mechanically stretched until it breaks. New condoms are expected to perform better than condoms that have been artificially aged but any condom is expected to stretch to at least six times it original length before breaking.

Most of the literature on condoms says that they are unlikely to let you down if you use them properly. The London Rubber Company says that it only gets one complaint for every million condoms it manufactures, while other well-informed estimates have suggested that with good quality condoms only one in 1,000 is likely to burst. Given this reassurance, we were surprised by the number of letters we received from women who had experienced a number of burst condoms – certainly suggesting an accident rate much higher than one in 1,000.

Condoms are a safe and reliable way of living with fertility. A number of excellent studies have shown just how effective they can be when used consistently and before any genital contact has taken place. Putting a condom on just before ejaculation occurs increases the risk of pregnancy. One of the earliest studies of condom use took place in Oxford between 1935 and 1950. The failure rate per 100 woman-years was 7.5. More recently the Oxford/FPA study has produced some extremely interesting material. Between 1968 and 1974 they recruited 17,000 married women aged between twenty-five and thirty-five, using different forms of contraception. The study first reported back on condom use-effectiveness in 1974, then again in 1982 when it was put at 3.6 per 100 woman-years as an overall estimate, with women between twenty-five and thirty-four having a failure rate of 6.0, and women aged over thirty-five a rate of 2.9 (both per 100 woman-years). More recently the AIDS epidemic led them to carry out a re-examination of the failure rates among condom-users which showed that duration of use, the age of the woman, parity and cigarette smoking habits were all determining factors. Social class and future family intentions had no particular effect on the success or otherwise with which a couple used condoms. Once the team had fed all the information available into a computer they were able to come up with a way of 'predicting' which women would be most successful at condom use.

The lowest predicted rate was for non-smoking women with a maximum of two children, aged forty to forty-four who had used the condom for four or more years. Unexpected pregnancies were extremely unlikely in this group, with a rate of 0.6 per 100 woman-years. In contrast to this they found that women most likely to experience condom failures were those who already had four or more children, were between twenty-five and thirty-four, currently smoked and had been using condoms for less than two years. These had a predicted failure rate of 14.7 per 100 woman-years. Unfortunately the study reveals nothing about the likely failure rate for women under twenty-five, neither was it able to make a distinction between method-failure and use-failure. We have reproduced the results below.[4]

Condoms lubricated with spermicide, available in the UK since 1975, should, theoretically, be more effective. At least if a drop of semen leaks from the condom it has the chance of being 'neutralized' by the spermicide. Unfortunately, however, it is almost impossible to test this hypothesis. Condom failure can be attributable to so many things that to design a trial which would solely test the difference that the spermicide makes when all the other variables are taken into account would need an enormous number of volunteer couples. As far as we know this kind of trial has not yet taken place.

The use of spermicidal pessaries, cream, gel or foam by the woman has also been presumed to make a difference in condom effectiveness. As with spermicidally lubricated condoms, the additional spermicide might be very useful in the case of a drop or two of semen, but less effective in the case of a major spill such as a burst condom or one that falls off completely. Additionally, the use of spermicides makes the whole procedure of condom use less straightforward. Some women do not like the feel of melted pessaries and find that this *plus* the condom is just too much interference. Condom use is probably better if it is as simple as possible; the FPA now endorses this opinion and suggests that spermicide should be presented as an optional extra.

It is worth noting, however, that one of the commonly used spermicides, Nonoxynol 9 (found in Delfen cream and foam, Ortho creme, Gynol 11, Ortho-Gynol gel, Double Check and Staycept pessaries) has been found to inactivate the AIDS virus under laboratory conditions; more research is taking place, but it is possible that if it is not just an

Figure 6.1 Predicted condom failure rates (per 100 woman-years) by age, parity, smoking habits and duration of use

Age	Parity	Smoking	Duration of Use (months)		
			−24	25–48	49+
25–34	0–2	Never	4.5	3.1	2.0
		Ex	5.9	4.0	2.6
		Current	6.5	4.4	2.8
	3	Never	6.1	4.1	2.7
		Ex	7.9	5.4	3.5
		Current	8.6	5.9	3.8
	4−	Never	10.6	7.3	4.7
		Ex	13.6	9.4	6.2
		Current	14.6	10.2	6.7
35–39	0–2	Never	2.9	1.9	1.2
		Ex	3.8	2.6	1.6
		Current	4.2	2.8	1.8
	3	Never	3.9	2.6	1.7
		Ex	5.1	3.5	2.2
		Current	5.6	3.8	2.4
	4−	Never	6.9	4.7	3.0
		Ex	9.0	6.1	4.0
		Current	9.8	6.7	4.3
40–44	0–2	Never	1.3	0.9	0.6
		Ex	1.8	1.2	0.8
		Current	1.9	1.3	0.8
	3	Never	1.8	1.2	0.8
		Ex	2.4	1.6	1.0
		Current	2.6	1.8	1.1
	4−	Never	3.3	2.2	1.4
		Ex	4.3	2.9	1.9
		Current	4.7	3.2	2.0

Source: Martin Vessey et al., 'Factors Influencing Use-effectiveness of the Condom', *British Journal of Family Planning*, Vol. 14, No. 2, July 1988.

unexpected pregnancy you are worrying about, a good dose of spermicide containing Nonoxynol 9 could give you further reassurance.

Condoms: who uses them?

Surveys about contraceptive usage are not new, and because people's sexual habits have always interested researchers, we have information about condom use over many decades. In 1922 Marie Stopes sent out

questionnaires to doctors about their own practices and received 128
replies. Condoms proved to be the second most popular method of
contraception with forty-four doctors relying on them at some point.
Ironically, considering the condemnation heaped on the practice of
withdrawal by the medical profession (and Marie Stopes), almost half
of the respondents – sixty-three – used withdrawal themselves. Another
survey, carried out by Dr Hannah M. Stone and published in 1933, was
one of the largest that had been carried out until then. It involved 1,987
women who had been seen at the Newark Maternal Health Centre.
Surprisingly only 8.5 per cent of her sample had never used any form
of birth control, while withdrawal was practised by 64 per cent and
condoms used by 48.3 per cent of couples at some point. During the
1940s and 50s condom use gradually increased – probably as more
women attended clinics for advice and were discouraged from relying
on withdrawal or douching. By the 1960s the condom was the most
widely used contraceptive device in Britain. Among 1,340 couples
married in the period 1930–49 who were interviewed in the course of
the Population Investigation Committee study in 1959, 48 per cent had
used condoms during their married life and 36 per cent were currently
doing so. But the 1960s saw the introduction of the pill and IUD – and
condom use has fallen off ever since. In 1970 28 per cent of married
women between sixteen and forty were estimated to rely on condoms,
but by 1975 this figure had fallen to 18 per cent. In 1983 the General
Household Survey (published in 1985) provided a useful glimpse of
contraceptive trends in the early 1980s though unfortunately only women
were questioned about their contraceptive practices. Among those aged
sixteen to forty-nine, regardless of marital status, 13 per cent reported
that they relied on condoms, at that time roughly 1,300,000 women in
the UK. This still makes condoms the third most popular method of
family planning, after sterilization and the pill.[5]

It is difficult to predict what will happen to the level of use now that
condoms are being marketed as fashion accessories. Certainly the
number of brands available has increased dramatically, but, up until
1987, the sales of most condoms had not increased quite as rapidly as
the share prices of their manufacturers. The price of shares in the
London International Group (which includes the London Rubber
Company) rose by 150 per cent between 1985 and 1987. The company,
which has almost 96 per cent of the condom market in the UK, considers
that the fear of AIDS may have reversed the long-term decline in
condom sales. Likewise, importers to Britain of rather more trendy
condoms – teatless condoms from France, Jiffi condoms from West
Germany or American condoms such as Lifestyles – have noticed an

enormous increase in demand in the UK. Clearly marketing is having an effect – if condoms are trendy, the trendier they come, the better.[6]

Condoms in Practice

Buying condoms

Could I ever become unselfconscious enough about sex to buy condoms myself?

I get condoms from Family Planning Sales, because I once saw an ad. And yes, I still get them from there because I am embarrassed buying them in shops. I once went to an NHS clinic but found the atmosphere so off-putting I'd never go again.

I haven't bought condoms for a couple of years and I don't remember any 'brand loyalty', but the thickness of condoms does *make a difference.*

When I was a student it was embarrassing buying condoms because they were 'under the counter'. But now it's no problem since they are on display. Plus everybody accepts that they can be talked about in the open these days.

My husband and I were half trying for a baby so we weren't really bothered about using contraceptives, but when some of the new condoms came on the market we thought we'd try them for a laugh . . . when we tried to put it on, it didn't fit. It was too tight and quite painful, though at the time we thought it was funny . . . Sheaths could be sized in a similar way to women's tights, i.e. small, medium and large. I think sales of eight inches and bigger would quadruple due to male pride.

Condoms are unique among contraceptive methods in their considerable capacity to cause embarrassment. The processes of buying condoms, storing them, putting them on, explaining why they burst or fell off, and getting rid of them afterwards, are all potential trip-wires of embarrassment for the unwary. With familiarity and confidence in a relationship it becomes possible to negotiate these hazards without any difficulty. Most people who have come into contact with a condom at some point in their lives however (which is the majority of us) will probably remember one or two embarrassing moments. Buying condoms is one process that has become infinitely easier in recent years, as supermarket chains add them to their lines and chemists move them from directly under the beady eye of a cashier. For some men buying condoms was never a problem; the 'Anything else, Sir?' at the barber's needed only a 'yes' and a number and the whole process was complete. Nowadays, when women are just as likely to buy condoms as men, the more retail outlets the better. Some people still find embarrassment a problem, and for them the solution could be mail order. Most newspapers carry advertisements in the personal columns and if this seems almost as bad, remember that lots of other people do it. Of course it is not

necessary to buy condoms at all. Your local family planning clinic will
supply them to you free of charge. Many clinics can now offer you a
choice of condom, but vary in the number that they hand out at one
time. A recent survey found a range of between three and twenty-four
a week.

The question of which sort of condom to buy is more tricky, since
there are now over 100 different condoms available in the UK. Not all
of these are readily available, and in fact there is probably little to choose
between the condoms sold in leading retail outlets as far as doing the
job they are designed to do is concerned. Undoubtedly, however, some
do it with more style. Not all condoms have been passed by the British
Standards Institute. Most countries have their own internal system of
testing, which may be as vigorous, or even more so, than the BSI tests.
Unfortunately it is not always possible to tell from the package which
standard the condoms comply with. Swedish condoms are tested
thoroughly and are generally very reliable. Sweden imports many of its
condoms from Japan, and condoms are tested there and then again in
Sweden. This is relevant since Swedish condoms are now available in
the UK. Look out for them under the names Okeido (super-strong),
Birds 'n' Bees (green and ribbed) and Black Jack (lubricated, shaped
and black). It is not possible for us to include a list of all the different
condoms available, and their particular merits. But it is worth pointing
out that in a major piece of market research carried out by the magazine
Self Health in September 1987 and April 1989 some of the condoms
tested failed to come up to standard. These included condoms specifically marketed as protecting against STDs. Aegis Anti-VD, Blausiegel
Koralle, Duet Supersafe Ribbed and Duet Supersafe Studded were all
found to have an unacceptable number of holes in them.

Using condoms

*Are condoms a good form of contraception? Yes, because they seem to be 100 per cent
safe. No, because they are 'sex killers'. Either you are permanently prepared (somewhat
presumptuous) or else always having to find and fix when your mind is on other matters.*

*I enjoy using condoms and my girlfriend enjoys them as well (except when I withdraw,
and she's always a little anxious). The only drawback is the loss of spontaneous
intercourse, but then on the other hand that leads to more attention to foreplay which is
better for my partner.*

*Sheaths invariably make for bad experiences. The process is laborious, kills ardour,
makes the fingers greasy, drastically reduces 'sensitivity' and makes the act seem
unnatural. Equally importantly, a sheathed penis looks repulsive (especially with little
bubble located on tip) and reduces sex to the level of high farce.*

How to choose a condom
___

Appearance
- Colour; usually beige or pink, but many others available
- Shape; straight sided or contoured with or without a teat-end
- Surface; smooth, or ribbed etc

What you choose is up to personal preference. It is not clear whether the teat-ended type makes any difference to the risk of bursting but which ever you choose it is important to remember to leave half an inch for the ejaculation when it is put on.
___

Dressing
- Spermicidal lubricant
- Powder
- Scented and flavoured

Lubrication is important in reducing the risk of a burst condom. Spermicide may make condoms more reliable and may help in reducing the risk of AIDS. Ready treated condoms may be convenient but both spermicides and lubricants are easy to obtain and use separately (be careful not to use oil-based products).
___

Thickness
Condoms range from 0.03–0.09 mm in thickness. There is anecdotal evidence to say that the thinner the greater sensitivity for the man. Condoms tend to tear because of weak spots rather than the overall thickness, but the new British Standard will not allow less than 0.04 mm.
___

Safety
Some condoms carry the British Standard Kitemark. This means that they conform to BS 3704, and that the manufacturers are regularly monitored to ensure standards are upheld

Some brands simply claim to comply with BS 3704, but carry no Kitemark. They may once have passed the BS tests but they do not undergo regular quality checks.

Some imported condoms have passed quality testing in their country of origin and may be just as good as a kitemarked condom. Others may be of very low quality.

There is no international standard yet and so claims in relation to this are premature and misleading.

Electronic testing is done as part of the manufacturing process and means very little in terms of safety.

It is probably best to buy a condom with the kitemark, although even these fail sometimes. It is important to buy a brand which has an expiry date and not to use out-of-date condoms.

I like using condoms because they are simple and comparatively unmessy, don't involve doctors, don't involve taking a pill, which I don't trust, and don't involve too much pre-planning for sex. I use spermicidal pessaries with them.

I quite like the sheath because it avoids the necessity to wash after intercourse and the wetness of semen when you get up in the morning.

The people who filled in our questionnaire or wrote to us almost invariably had an opinion about condoms, and sometimes felt very strongly. Many men felt that the main advantage of condoms was that it gave them the responsibility for a change. The most common disadvantage mentioned was the *feeling* of making love with a condom on. We once heard it described as a little like 'eating a Mars bar with the paper still on'. Other people described it as 'slightly squelchy', 'a wrinkly feeling', 'lacking that nice warm skin-to-skin feeling'. It is this alteration in sensation that leads some couples to delay putting the condom on until they get towards the end of making love, and it may be this, as much as bursting condoms or condoms that fall off during withdrawal, that accounts for some accidental pregnancies.

In fact the small amount of seminal fluid that leaks from the penis during love-making but before ejaculation contains only a minute amount of sperm and is highly unlikely to cause a pregnancy. But in the heat of the moment, do men always withdraw in time and put on a rather tedious condom? If you think you might be risking a sexually transmitted disease it could be dangerous to you to have intercourse before putting a condom on. If you are a woman, the leaking seminal fluid may not have enough sperm to make you pregnant, but it could contain enough viral or bacterial agents to give you an infection. Equally the risk to men of exposing an unprotected penis in an unknown environment may well not be worth the slightly improved sensation. We will look more fully at the role of the condoms in STDs in the next section.

Other than putting the condom on at the right point it is important to make sure that there is enough lubrication around to prevent a condom from bursting. In two British studies bursting condoms were given the responsibility for causing pregnancy in 1.4 cases per 100 couple-years, and other studies have put the rate still lower (0.4–0.83). Lubrication minimizes the likelihood of accidents and if there doesn't seem to be enough of it, add some more, either in the form of saliva, KY gel or a spermicidal gel such as Gynol II which has the advantage of not being scented and contains Nonoxynol 9.

After ejaculation and *before* the man completely loses his erection is the best time to withdraw, though a spokesman for IPPF calls the recommendation for immediate withdrawal 'quite unnecessary and cruel'. One woman wrote to us: 'After his ejaculation when he pulls out, it feels like being a chicken and having the plastic bag of giblets pulled out.' According to our research, more accidents seem to happen at this juncture than at any other: 'On several occasions the condom has been lost on withdrawal and created moments of blind panic . . .'. In our questionnaire we asked people to describe their worst moments with contraception. More than one said that it was discovery that the condom had disappeared on withdrawal. Holding the condom on firmly is the best policy so that no semen leaks into the vagina. The penis is still likely to be covered with semen, so close genital contact at this point could still lead to a pregnancy. Disposing of condoms ecologically may present a problem. The bulk of the condom degrades relatively swiftly, but the ring at the end seems to be more resistant. Apparently the marine laboratory of the Department of Agriculture and Fisheries for Scotland has reported large numbers of fish ringed with rubber bands 3.6 cm in diameter . . . The best advice available favours putting well-wrapped condoms in the dustbin.

Condoms and sexually transmitted diseases

There are at least twenty-five different infections that can be spread sexually. AIDS is the most recent and most serious to come to light, while others such as gonorrhoea or chlamydia can have a harmful effect on subsequent fertility as well as being painful and unpleasant. Some STDs such as thrush are irritating but as far as we know not dangerous. STDs seem to go in waves. During the Second World War they were a major public health problem, but the war was followed by a marked decrease in incidence. Since then, however, the number of diseases spread sexually and the number of people affected each year has risen steadily. In the years 1970–85 the number of cases rose three-fold and now more than half a million are reported each year, though the actual figure could be higher still. In fact this apparent increase in STDs has been slightly accelerated by a change in the classification system which in 1971 added six new infections which had formerly fallen outside the category of STD. Thrush, which is now officially an STD, can be caused by all sorts of things such as a course of antibiotics, or the bodily changes associated with pregnancy, and is not therefore necessarily sexually transmitted, though once it has developed it may be passed from a woman to her partner (and back again). Other people have argued that what the figures show is less a real increase in the number of STDs than an improvement in diagnostic techniques, contact tracing and the loss of stigma associated with STDs, which means people are much more willing to ask for treatment.

Even given these provisos, the fact remains that in 1984 there were over 53,000 cases of gonorrhoea reported, and though this is less than the number of cases recorded annually in the 1970s, it still represents a nasty hazard to women's delicate reproductive organs. At the time of writing the cumulative total of HIV positive cases recorded in England, Wales and Northern Ireland was 7,697; there were 1,794 cases of AIDS in the UK as a whole and 965 deaths (at 30 September 1988). The AIDS epidemic is doubling in size every eleven or so months and while at the moment it is largely confined to homosexual and bisexual men, the heterosexual spread of the disease has almost certainly started.[7] The incidence of herpes simplex continues to rise and there are nearly five times as many cases now as there were in 1972. Given these infections, and the large number of non-specific genital infections circulating in British society, the current advice to use condoms if you are not absolutely sure of your partner makes a lot of sense. Let's look at the case for the condom.

Figure 6.2 The condom barrier
The wall of a standard latex condom is 38,000nm thick. Tested, the condom holds water. A water molecule is 20nm; virus, other organisms, and sperm are all much larger.

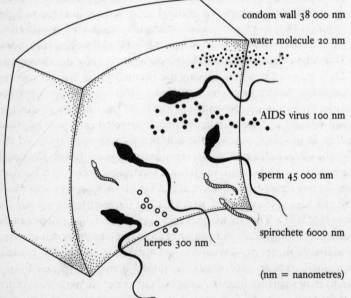

condom wall 38 000 nm

water molecule 20 nm

AIDS virus 100 nm

sperm 45 000 nm

spirochete 6000 nm

herpes 300 nm

(nm = nanometres)

Source: Nancy E. Dirubbo, 'The condom barrier', *American Journal of Nursing*, October 1987.

Figures 6.2 and 6.3 are designed to give some indication of the relative sizes of sperm, the herpes virus, AIDS virus, air and water molecules, and a condom wall. The picture of the man, the dog and the train, representing an AIDS virus, an air or water molecule and a sperm respectively, shows even more clearly the relative sizes of things. The argument goes that if a condom is well enough made to hold in water molecules it should be equally effective against the AIDS virus which is five times as large. The Herpes Simplex virus which is three times as big as the AIDS virus is the next largest but is still eight times smaller than Neisseria gonorrhoeae (the gonorrhoea-causing bacteria). Relatively speaking, the microscopic sperm looks enormous – about 450 times larger than the AIDS virus.

The limited research that has so far been carried out suggests that this argument (i.e. that if a condom can keep in a water molecule it can also keep in a disease-causing microbe) can be verified in a laboratory. In one experiment that was carried out in California the researchers put herpes viruses into a condom and then put the plunger from a hypodermic syringe inside the rubber. The condom and the plunger were then inserted into the syringe and the plunger moved up and down fifty times. The condom was surrounded by a special fluid designed to encourage the growth of any virus that escaped. The research team found no virus in the growing medium, despite the fairly vigorous treatment of the condom. There have also been studies among prostitutes whose clients do or do not wear condoms. In a study of 376 prostitutes in Zaïre where HIV is prevalent, only eight of the women were uninfected; these were the only eight who said that at least half their clients wore condoms. There is good evidence from Sweden that condoms can prevent the transmission of gonorrhoea. In 1971, worried about the high incidence of the disease, the Swedish FPA began a campaign to promote condoms. A year later the number of cases had fallen by 7,000 to 31,000, and nine years later the number of cases reported had halved.[8]

It is important to point out that the role of condoms in preventing the spread of an STD between partners does depend on its being used properly. If one of the partners knows that he or she could pass on an STD they should consider non-penetrative sex anyway, since there is always the slight risk of the condom coming off, or bursting. At best condoms can only offer safer sex, not 100 per cent safe sex. Some of the thicker condoms on the market do the job better than the thinner ones. The condom 'HT Special' proved to be at least twice as strong as other brands when tested by *Self Health* magazine.[9]

Figure 6.3 Relative sizes of sperm, AIDS virus and water molecule

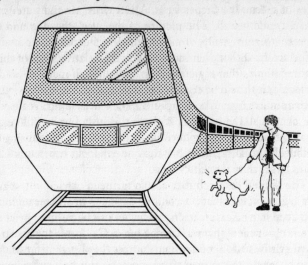

On a mammoth scale the dog is the size of an air or water molecule,
the man of an AIDS virus, and the train is the size of a sperm.

Source: Ibid.

Condoms and pre-cancerous changes of the cervix

There is growing evidence that condoms can play a part in preventing
cervical cancer. While the exact cause of cervical cancer is not fully
understood, it seems very likely that it is initiated, or promoted by a
sexually transmitted agent – possibly the herpes virus, or the virus
responsible for genital warts. All barrier methods appear to offer
protection against the pre-cancerous changes of the cervix which could
lead to the full-blown condition. In a well-conducted study in Britain
the relative risk of developing cervical abnormalities was found to
decrease with condom or diaphragm use, but increase with the length
of oral contraception use. Women who have used a barrier method, such
as condoms, for at least five years seem to have a lower risk of developing
these abnormal cells in the cervix. Another recent study showed just
how significant condoms might be in preventing cervical cancer. A
hundred and thirty-nine women whose cervical cells showed some
degree of abnormality were asked to use condoms for sex and given no
other treatment at all. In 136 of them the condition began to reverse,
and around three years later, 125 women had had no recurrence of the
condition. While more work needs to be done in this area, it seems clear
that protecting the cervix from direct contact with the penis may offer
women safer sex than would otherwise be the case.[10]

Condoms and PID

We have already noted that around 53,000 cases of gonorrhoea are treated each year in Britain. The potential effect of gonorrhoea on a woman's fertility is one of the tragedies of this particular form of STD. The fact that at least half of the cases of gonorrhoea in Britain occur in under-twenty-four-year-olds suggests that the toll taken of future fertility must cause considerable suffering. Chlamydia is an infection with a similar potential for causing PID which, in turn, causes about 20 per cent of all the fertility problems that afflict women. What happens when a woman comes into contact with a bacteria such as gonorrhoea is that she risks exposing her delicate fallopian tubes to inflammation and subsequent damage. If the infection passes through her cervix (which is more likely to happen if she already has an infection such as genital warts, thrush, or herpes, or during the highly fertile days of her cycle when the cervix is open and the mucus plug thins out) it can attack her reproductive organs. The body's defence system does its best to ward off the attack, but in the process, scar tissue is formed. It is this scar tissue that can cause the damage by blocking the tiny opening in the fallopian tube down which the fertilized egg would travel. Sadly, even one case of gonorrhoea can cause damage leading to reduced fertility or infertility in one in eight women who become infected. Chlamydia, which is sometimes symptomless, can have an equally devastating effect.

Estimates from America suggest that any new partner brings a 15–20 per cent risk of a subsequent episode of PID. Evidence suggests that damaging bacteria fix themselves on to the sperm and travel up into the woman's reproductive organs with the rest of the ejaculate. A condom would ensure that such bacteria got no further than its teat-end. The fertility problems of PID are largely confined to women. In men, gonorrhoea seldom gets past the urethra and since it usually produces very obvious symptoms such as a discharge and considerable pain it is unlikely to go unnoticed. In only about 2 per cent of cases do bacteria get as far as the epididymis, in which sperm are transported, and cause infertility. However, no man should ever assume that any symptoms of an STD are innocuous, but should always seek medical help.

When things go wrong

Even the most careful people sometimes have accidents. Condoms do burst, or fall off and get lost. If you ever find yourself with a condom accident, in which either a little or a lot of semen has escaped, the inevitable conclusion is not a baby nine months later. There are several things you can do. Some books recommend that if you have a spermicide to hand you should use it rapidly, and that if you have any choice, foam may be the quickest and most effective. But unfortunately sperm are fast movers, and have been found on the other side of the cervix within ninety seconds of an ejaculation. Even the fastest application of spermicide is unlikely to be 100 per cent effective. It is only really worth using a spermicide if post-coital contraception is for some reason unavailable. Given that this is a much more reliable option, the obvious thing to consider is the point that has been reached in the woman's cycle. If a period is due in a week, or less, the chances of an accidental conception are very low since it is unlikely there will be a viable egg to fertilize. An accident in the middle of the cycle, or shortly after a period has finished, is a different matter, since this is the most fertile time of the cycle. In this case post-coital contraception is a very good idea. It needs to be started within three days of the mishap (if you use a hormonal method) or five days if an IUD is inserted. Many GPs are willing to prescribe post-coital contraception and we have covered the options available in Chapter 10.

Coitus interruptus, or withdrawal

I practised withdrawal very early on in my first few relationships. It is not very satisfactory. When I was first having sex I was a lot less controlled than I am now so how I didn't get girls pregnant I don't know. I guess I was lucky. You feel more (than with a condom) but the risks aren't worth it and the girl is on edge.

Risky and unsatisfying, but beats the condom any day.

A bonkers form of contraception.

Withdrawal is certainly better than no sex at all, and when we've had nothing else available we've used it. But I can't imagine wanting to rely on it as my only method of contraception. It is so – how shall I put it – vacuous. First there is something, then there is nothing. Very incomplete.

Once I was in a relationship and we used withdrawal all the time. I liked it. No messing with contraception. I felt very earthy and natural – as if this was a time-honoured method of having pleasure without any consequences. Maybe that was part of the way we constructed our relationship anyway.

Coitus interruptus, or withdrawal as it is more commonly called, is indeed a time-honoured method of enjoying a sexual relationship without too much risk of a pregnancy. One of the earliest historical references comes in the book of Genesis in the Bible:

Then Judah said to Er's brother Onan, 'Go and sleep with your brother's widow. Fulfil your obligation to her as her husband's brother, so that your brother may have descendants.' But Onan knew that the children would not belong to him, so whenever he had intercourse with his brother's widow he let the semen spill on the ground, so that there would be no children for his brother.

The fact that Onan received a divine punishment does not seem to have done much to halt the spread of withdrawal, however, though it may have started the tradition in which coitus interruptus has always been faintly (or volubly) disapproved of. Men throughout history have practised withdrawal, and as long as there has been a medical profession, it has been decried as psychologically and physiologically damaging, as ineffective and irresponsible. But is it? Like natural family planning and like condom use, withdrawal cannot be professionalized or medicalized. You either do it successfully or you don't. Its very autonomy is its attraction.

Withdrawal: does it work?

Because it is a home-made form of contraception, withdrawal has had little scientific scrutiny. There have been few well-designed studies of its effectiveness. The research material on hormonal contraception, IUDs and barriers is literally a thousand times more extensive than that on withdrawal. Consequently it is rather difficult to say much about it. From the studies that have been carried out, withdrawal compares well with other methods of contraception. A study in Indianapolis showed a failure rate of 10 per 100 woman-years, as compared to an average of 12 for all other methods. Among high income groups this failure rate fell to 3, precisely the same as for the diaphragm. In 1949 (before the pill and IUD were available) the Royal Commission on Population reported that 'no difference has been found between users of appliances and users of non-appliance methods as regards the average number of children'. Appliances would have been condoms, diaphragms and caps.[11] While, over a large population of users, it is unlikely that coitus interruptus could approach the effectiveness rates of consistent pill taking, or IUD use, for individual couples who are experienced and good communicators there is no reason why they should not practise it with the same degree of success that they might expect from a barrier.

Withdrawal: who does it?

Withdrawal is still widely practised around the world; in some countries, such as Italy, Turkey and Kenya, it is still the most popular method of birth-control. Surveys may have difficulty in gauging the real extent of the practice because of the number of euphemisms under which it is known. A question such as 'Do you practise a form of contraception?' may elicit a negative answer, whereas the question 'Are you being careful?' receives a positive one. Being 'careful', being 'considerate', 'taking responsibility', 'practising self-control', 'looking after it', are all ways of describing withdrawal. Over 4,000 years ago one Jewish writer described it as 'threshing inside and winnowing outside', and the euphemisms have never stopped.

In Britain, according to the General Household Survey of 1986, 4 per cent of respondents were using withdrawal, twice as many as used the cap and four times as many as practised any form of natural family planning. According to earlier surveys, however, this represents a substantial falling off. In a 1970 survey no less than 14 per cent of respondents claimed to be using withdrawal, making it the third most commonly used method of birth-control after condoms and the pill. This decline in popularity may be due to a number of things: young women are more likely to seek professional advice about contraception than they were twenty years ago, and are most unlikely to have withdrawal recommended to them; condoms are much more readily available; withdrawal has had an almost universally bad press (with the notable exception of Germaine Greer's crusade in *Sex and Destiny*). There is now a widespread belief that withdrawal is risky, unsatisfactory and not worth bothering about. This swing is unfortunate, particularly if it discourages a young and inexperienced couple from trying it when they have nothing else to hand. As we have seen, withdrawal can have a very respectable success rate.

Withdrawal: for and against

Withdrawal tends to work best if a man is comfortable with his own body and sexuality. Sexual anxiety can lie at the root of premature ejaculation, and men who suffer from the latter will probably not make very good candidates for coitus interruptus. Adolescent males who are still developing control over ejaculation may also be less effective than men who understand and are well able to control their build-up to orgasm. For these reasons coitus interruptus may well be a more satisfactory method in well-adjusted sexual relationships than in those that are just starting out. The irony is that its usage tends to be the other way round, with couples new to sex or to each other adopting it and moving on to 'something more reliable' after their relationship is established. It is couples who have stuck with coitus interruptus and built it into their relationship as an integral part of sex who speak most highly of it. The women who inspired Germaine Greer with their accounts of coitus interruptus grew up with it, as it were, in their sexual relationships and recognize the sexual potential inherent in the self-control that a man is able to develop. Germaine Greer is excellent in her explanation of how thoroughly we may have misunderstood the proper practice of coitus interruptus:

Clearly if coitus interruptus is practised as an unsatisfactory substitute for 'normal sex' and masquerades as 'normal sex' until the last minute or so, it will be a cause of anxiety and disappointment. If a man brings his partner to orgasm and then sets about achieving his own outside the vagina, this unsatisfactory scenario will not be acted out. What the tendency of modern sexologists to denigrate coitus interruptus really indicates is their own lack of sexual imagination, or as some might prefer, their own lack of creativity and tenderness . . . Coitus interruptus can be as bad as bad sex always can be . . . but if it has been resorted to out of consideration for the woman in the first place, it is not likely to take such a barbarous form. Most intelligent sex contains an element of coitus reservatus in that the male attempts to prolong his erection by avoiding orgasm, thereby enhancing his own and his partner's pleasure.[12]

Greer's point is that coitus interruptus, when practised properly, may serve as an enhancement of sexuality, particularly from the point of view of the woman, by developing the couple's sexual skills. Its effectiveness as a contraceptive may be an added bonus. In our current contraceptive climate, however, it seems that few couples are willing to take the time to delve into its potential, and in the main it is still only used as a stop-gap measure before getting on with the real business of contraception. At least in the current generation of medical books on contraception, coitus interruptus is being given a tolerant, if patronizing, hearing. Potts and Diggory claim that it is like 'a type of primary education from which many individuals in the West have graduated'.[13] As far as Greer's argument is concerned, this would seem to miss the point entirely. Guillebaud, taking on from Potts and Diggory, endorses their view that if a couple is happily practising coitus interruptus, they should be left well alone, but suggests that the addition of a spermicide might 'cope satisfactorily with any small deposit of sperm before withdrawal.'[14]

Conclusion

Because contraception is seen as a 'woman's issue', and women are conditioned to put up with unsatisfactory situations, we are still waiting for a safe, user-friendly method – but men can walk on the moon.

New methods of contraception for men do not appear to be developing very quickly. The idea of a male pill has been around for several decades, but it is far from becoming a widely used contraceptive method. We appear to be stuck with the idea that reversible contraception is primarily a woman's concern, and, with the development of quicker, safer sterilizations for women, even 'irreversible' contraception in the form of a vasectomy is no longer the obvious choice for couples who want no more children. There have been efforts to change attitudes, and in 1984 the FPA launched 'Men Too'. This campaign aimed to make men aware of their responsibilities for contraception, personal relationships and childrearing. It also aimed to encourage the providers of relevant services to support men in these responsibilities and to bring these issues into public discussion. A few men-only clinics also opened around this time in an effort to involve men more. However we suspect that only when (or if) the subject of fertility and sexual responsibility becomes an integral part of the education of all young people will the situation alter in any significant sense.

CHAPTER 7

Intrauterine Devices

I am fifty-two and have had a Lippes loop for about twenty-four years. After my son was born in 1965 I decided I didn't want more children and so had it fitted by the Marie Stopes clinic. It cost £5 as far as I remember – the best £5 I ever spent. No trouble at all . . .

I was advised by a nurse friend to have a coil fitted. I did, but have regretted it ever since. I was fitted in June, almost four years ago, and because of an infection that went into my fallopian tubes, had to have it removed in October of that year. I was treated with eleven weeks of double dosage antibiotics but two years later, I'm still suffering lower abdominal pain.

Two quotations from women who wrote to us sum up the considerable range of experience among women who use the IUD. That it can affect women so differently makes writing about it problematic and the material in this chapter can only, sadly, reflect part of this width of experience.

'IUD' has become the internationally recognized abbreviation for 'intrauterine contraceptive device', though it is sometimes referred to as the IUCD. More popularly the IUD is known as 'the coil', since the earliest devices were made of wire in the form of a coil. Local names have developed around the world, such as 'al amalia saghirah' in Morocco which means the 'small operation' as opposed to the 'big operation' which describes sterilization. This example offers a clue to the way in which IUDs are often regarded. An IUD may be almost as effective as a sterilization but it is not such a major step, either psychologically or physically. The 'operation' is a relatively minor procedure, but once in place the IUD provides excellent protection against pregnancy for as long as it remains *in situ*.

The IUD was the first form of contraception with a reliably low failure rate. At first glance it comes remarkably close to being the so-called 'ideal contraceptive'; it takes only one initiative to use, is intercourse independent, is very reliable, cheap, reversible and has few side effects. But the very fact that we are not all users makes one look again.

Women who do not like the thought of an IUD can offer a number of reasons: squeamishness and a fear of large metal helixes placed in delicate, sensitive tissues; confusion over how it works; fear of infections; and alarm at implications of the mass control of women's fertility were just some of the reasons mentioned to us. Not all of these fears are groundless. The introduction in the 1970s in the USA of an IUD known as the Dalkon Shield resulted in a rash of adverse publicity about its apparent connection with septic late abortions, septicaemia and even death. This had the dual effect of stimulating a new wave of studies to find whether these problems were common to all types of IUD, and unsettling the faith of many women in their safety. The litigation which followed the Dalkon Shield affair had a major effect on other companies manufacturing IUDs. They watched A. H. Robins, the makers of the shield, pay out nearly $100 million dollars to 4,000 women. During 1985 and 1986 several manufacturers stopped producing IUDs, citing financial rather than safety issues for pulling out. For a time, no IUDs at all were available in the USA. The recent introduction of the TCu-380A and the Progestasert have restored IUDs as a choice for American women, who no longer have to travel abroad to obtain one. However, despite hundreds of research papers on all aspects of IUD use, the facts about them are still not really clear.

A short history

The history of the IUD is notable for its length rather than its innovations. From earliest times it was known that an object placed in the uterus prevented pregnancy more often than not, and apart from some refinements, things have changed remarkably little. The stones placed in the uteruses of camels during long desert journeys are as well-cited an example as Casanova's little gold balls, though whether he placed these in the vaginas or the uteruses of his women is not so clear. During the nineteenth century the use of intra-vaginal/intra-cervical devices for the correction of various 'malpositions' of the uterus is often referred to and it seems very hard to believe that the contraceptive nature of these was not quickly noticed. These 'stem pessaries', as they were called, were very fashionable during the second half of the last century, and the address of Dr C. H. F. Routh to the British Medical Association in 1878 in which he condemned his colleagues for their involvement in 'teaching a way to sin without detection' was probably a reference to their use.[1]

By 1909 a Dr Richard Richter, from what is now Poland, had published a paper describing the use of a flexible silkworm gut ring with a diameter of 25 mm and two threads – one of the earliest IUDs. His work was largely ignored but in 1929 a doctor called Grafenberg reported on the use of a pliable ring of coiled silver wire. He was at great pains to point out the importance of choosing the right women to wear the rings, but his advice was not heeded and in the context of a general rise in pelvic infections in Europe his Grafenberg ring was discredited and it took another thirty years before the IUD was once again publicly reassessed. In 1959 two papers were published which revived the fortunes of the IUD: one by Ishihama in Japan, and the other by Oppenheimer in America who described the use of the IUD over the previous twenty years and independently produced evidence of low pregnancy rates. In Britain, Dr Margaret Jackson, one of Britain's earliest family planning doctors, had long since been using the Grafenberg ring IUD in her practice in England.

In 1962 the first international conference on the IUD was held in New York. Among the suitable materials for IUD construction that were discussed the new biologically inert plastics attracted most attention. It presented new possibilities since almost any shape of device could be made. These plastics were 'deformable' and had a memory so that a device could be fitted in a narrow tube for easy insertion through the cervical canal. Once in place it would spring back to its original shape. The first device of this nature was the Margulies spiral, followed rapidly by the Lippes loop, named after its inventor Jack Lippes and still occasionally used today.

The next stage in the evolution of the IUD was led by a Chilean, Jaime Zipper, and an American, Howard Tatum. They found that the addition of copper wire to a device made it effective even when the size of the device was decreased. The smaller the IUD the fewer the problems associated with it. More recently IUDs which release progestogens into the uterus have been developed.

IUDs: do they work and who uses them?

It is thought that there are about 60 million women using IUDs in the world, and that 40 million of these are in China. It is also a popular choice in Scandanavia, where as many as one in four use the method. Seven per cent of women aged between eighteen and forty-four in Britain currently use the IUD (compared to 23 per cent who use the pill), a total of around 600,000 women.[2] IUD use is not evenly spread over different age groups, but shows a clear increase with age. Only 1 per cent of women aged eighteen or nineteen have an IUD, but this rises to 10 per cent in the over-thirty age-group. Its use, since first introduced in the 1960s, has crept up slowly and it appears to have gained from the relative fall from favour of oral contraceptives among older women.

In the last two decades women have come to expect a very high degree of protection from pregnancy with the pill, establishing new norms for effectiveness. The IUD, particularly the latest generation, shares this near zero rate of pregnancies. The failure rate is usually quoted as a range of 0.3–6.0 pregnancies per 100 woman-years. The Oxford/FPA study quotes the failure rates of different devices, citing an overall failure rate for the Lippes Loop C of 1.4, and for the Copper 7 of 1.5. Figures relating to IUD failures are interesting for two reasons. Firstly there is no use-failure rate to take account of – i.e. no failures due to incorrect use or memory lapses. Any pregnancies that result are entirely due to a failure in the method. Secondly the range that is usually given for failure rates is not due to inaccuracies in working out failure rates but to the fact that failure rates change with length of use and the age of the wearer. IUDs seem to be particularly effective at the latter end of reproductive life and problems usually diminish with time. This is good news for some women, less good for others. As one woman put it, 'Does this mean that the uterus simply gets worn down, and "tamed" by the IUD? Does it simply give up fighting?'

In fact there is good evidence that there is no relationship between duration of IUD use and the length of time it takes to become pregnant following its removal. Cynics who claim that the increasing efficacy with length of use is due to increasing rates of IUD related sub-fertility should perhaps look again. The declining incidence of complications experienced by women wearing IUDs could of course be due to a self-screening process. Women who eventually get fed up with the bleeding will simply have the device removed. It is true that, as far as failure rates go, among the traditional plastic devices the larger the device the lower the pregnancy rate – but the higher the incidence of side-effects. While smaller devices are relatively trouble free, they may result in more pregnancies. The introduction of copper bearing devices has certainly helped to get around these problems, as has the introduction of progestogens. All in all, the IUD ranks second only to the combined pill in terms of performance and some of the newer devices even improve on it in practice (these include TCu-380A, TCu-220, Multiload-375 and the Nova T).[3]

The relative unpopularity of the IUD, then, must be explained largely by the real or perceived complications encountered by the users of the method. Perhaps the first complication encountered lies in simply getting hold of one. We have already seen the bias among GPs towards the pill

for women of all ages. If you want to try an IUD for yourself, overcoming
this is the first hurdle.

Getting an IUD in Britain today

IUDs are rarely at the top of any doctor's list of possible contraceptive
methods. This may partly be because doctors do not expect women to
be very enthusiastic, and partly because it means making a separate
appointment and is a time-consuming procedure. We looked at some
of the prejudices against IUDs among GPs in Chapter 2 and would
simply reiterate here that if your GP is very off-putting about an IUD it
could be that he or she is not very happy with his or her ability as a
'fitter'. Not all GPs will automatically refer you elsewhere. If you are not
happy with your doctor's attitude, go to a family planning clinic where
you are much less likely to encounter a problem.

Once you have made a decision to have an IUD inserted and found
a doctor to fit it you will be asked to give a brief medical history to make
sure that there are no reasons for not going ahead. There are only a few
absolute counter-indications for an IUD: pelvic infection, pregnancy,
undiagnosed bleeding, copper-allergy (if a copper bearing device is to
be fitted) and valvular heart disease. Other things in your previous
medical history may cause problems, such as previous uterine surgery,
an unusually shaped uterus, heavy or painful periods and diseases like
diabetes. The most significant and serious problem associated with the
IUD is that of pelvic infection. Complete frankness with your doctor
about previous pelvic and venereal diseases is in your own best interests.
You will also be asked about your sex life; again this is not prurient
interest on the part of the doctor but to make sure that you are not going
to put yourself at risk of an infection and possible sub-fertility by having
an IUD inserted inappropriately. The age at which you first had sex and
the number of partners you have or have had affects your risk of PID
and other IUD problems. If after discussion the IUD still seems a good
choice you will probably be asked to make another appointment at a
future date to have the IUD inserted. This is to give you a chance to
think about any new information you have been given, and to think over
your decision. Some places will give you leaflets to read; others are less
helpful. Booking another appointment also means that you stand a better
chance of having the fitting done by someone experienced. It is often
the case that in GP practices one partner specializes in fitting IUDs and
it is obviously in your own best interests to see someone with plenty of
experience. Some doctors prefer to fit IUDs at certain points in the
menstrual cycle, so you may be asked to come back on a particular date.

Having your IUD inserted

The atmosphere at an IUD 'insertion', as doctors usually refer to it, should be relaxed and reassuring. The procedure should be fully explained to you before starting, and you should have an opportunity to ask any questions you may have. If you have any views on the type of device you want to try, now is the time to say so. In fact, if you feel very strongly about the IUD you would like to use it may be better to discuss it at the initial consultation since not all surgeries and clinics have all devices available at a given time.

The first stage of the insertion will be an internal examination. This is done to assess the exact position of the uterus so that the IUD will be placed safely within the cavity. If you have not had a recent cervical smear it can be done at the same time. The insertion of an IUD needs to be done in as sterile a way as possible which means there will be a certain amount of fussing reminiscent of an operating theatre. You may find this off-putting, but it doesn't mean that someone is about to wield a scalpel! The next stage will require the insertion of a speculum into the vagina so as to get a good view of the cervix. The speculum (the same type as used for taking a smear) is a metal device like the bill of a duck. Its insertion into the vagina should not be painful, but can be uncomfortable, particularly if the doctor has not warmed it up first. At this point you will be asked to relax – an almost impossible thing to do – but if you can just let your legs flop apart and keep as loose as possible the procedure will be less uncomfortable, easier to do and over more quickly. Deep breathing of the sort practised in yoga or pregnancy classes is a good way of keeping yourself relaxed.

Once the speculum is in the vagina it is opened up and the vaginal walls part to reveal the cervix with its os, the opening which leads via the cervical canal to the uterine cavity. The doctor can check it for any abnormalities. If all is well she will clean it with a piece of gauze soaked in antispetic, held with long forceps. The cervix is then held steady with an instrument called a tenaculum. This may cause a slight pinching sensation but should not hurt. With the cervix held steady by the tenaculum, a 'sound' is passed through the os. This knitting-needle-like probe is used to find out the exact size and direction of the cavity of the uterus, important since no two women have exactly the same shaped uteruses. Once the doctor has worked out the size of your uterus, she or he notes the depth to which the inserter holding the IUD should be placed. These precautions are vital and help to prevent badly placed IUDs, or even worse, a perforation in your uterus.

An IUD comes in a sterile package. Before being inserted it needs to be squeezed into the inserter, which is a fiddly job and can make even experienced doctors look unreassuringly ham-fisted. Once it is in place the inserter is passed through the cervical os, and the IUD is deposited high up in your uterus. The inserter is removed and the strings of the IUD which pass through the cervix cut to about 2.5 cm from the os. The speculum and tenaculum are removed and the fitting is complete. This description makes the procedure sound rather lengthy, but it should take only about five minutes.

It is often said that the whole procedure is painless. Many women would disagree. While one woman commented, 'I expected it to be painful, but I relaxed completely and breathed deeply. I didn't feel a thing when it went in', another wrote, 'I was basically just too tense and screwed myself up with nerves. I'm not really very surprised that it hurt.' If you find that having a cervical smear carried out is uncomfortable, it is likely that you won't find having an IUD inserted any better. Most women get some period pain-like cramps when the inserter is passed through their cervical os, and in some women these are quite severe though short lived. Very rarely the whole procedure makes some women feel faint and dizzy. You should say at once if you feel at all unwell and the fitting will be slowed down or stopped. If you are really anxious it is quite possible to have a local anaesthetic, which will be in the form of several injections around your cervix.

Afterwards
Before you leave the clinic you should be told what to expect in the weeks and months to come. If the information you receive is not adequate, ask for clarification. You will probably have a light bleed for a few days and may have period pains. Your next period may be considerably heavier than normal, and more painful than usual. Ordinary painkillers should do the trick, but if they do not you should talk to your doctor to check that all is well. You will be told about checking the threads to make sure that your IUD is still in place. This is particularly important at the end of your first period since more IUDs are expelled at this point than any other. If you find you connot feel the threads you'll need to go back to your doctor. It is possible that you will have expelled the IUD or that something more serious, such as a perforation has taken place. A follow-up appointment should be made to check that all is well, usually a month or two later, and thereafter on a six monthly or annual basis. You will also be told the danger signs to look out for, which we will discuss in more detail later. A missed period could still mean a pregnancy so you will need to be alert to the possibility. Disappearing threads could also be a sign of a pregnancy since the threads get drawn upwards as the uterus enlarges.

Timing the fitting

The best times to have an IUD fitted or removed are a matter of controversy within the medical profession. Traditionally IUDs were fitted during menstruation, since if a woman is menstruating she can't be pregnant and it is dangerous as well as illegal to try to insert a coil into a pregnant uterus. The cervix is also slightly softer and the os a little less tightly closed during menstruation. More recently there has been a move away from this orthodoxy. One argument says that if you have to wait for three weeks before you have an IUD fitted you have three extra weeks for a conception to occur. More significantly, IUDs are more often expelled in menstruation and it seems pointless to insert a device at the very time it is most likely to be expelled. A study in the USA showed a doubling of expulsions of Copper T devices fitted on days one to five of the cycle compared to those fitted on days eleven to seventeen. Doctors increasingly feel that fitting an IUD can be done safely at any point in the cycle, as long as there is no question of a pregnancy.[4]

Removing an IUD is ideally timed with reference to the last time you made love. If one of the ways in which an IUD works is by preventing a fertilized ovum from implanting it would be quite possible for it to be removed after a conception but before it had prevented an implantation. Having your device removed during a period, or after seven days' abstinence, or seven days of using a barrier should solve the problem. If an IUD is being removed as a matter of urgency because of a pelvic infection it might be worth considering hormonal post-coital contraception, though the risk of conceiving under these circumstances is probably very small.

There is also still no fixed policy on when to fit an IUD after a birth or an abortion. The dilation of the cervix at delivery, and to a smaller extent during an abortion, makes the chances of expulsion very high if the device is fitted immediately. Some studies have put it as high as 31–41 per cent.[5] Since the uterus is very soft just after delivery there is a greater chance of perforation, while the possibility of tiny amounts of blood, placenta and amniotic fluid left behind after both delivery and abortion could also be dangerous, since they make an ideal environment for growing organisms. The risk of infection, which we know is greatest at the time of insertion anyway, may be increased. On balance it seems that an IUD should not be inserted immediately after birth, or even in the first six weeks post-partum unless there are very special reasons for doing so. In the case of abortion, the convenience may outweigh the risks. Since fertility can return within ten days of an abortion, it is clear that protection against an immediate subsequent pregnancy is important. An abortion or miscarriage after twelve weeks of pregnancy should be considered as similar to a delivery in terms of risks, so again, a six-week wait, during which condoms are the safest protection, is probably the best strategy.

IUDs can be left in place until they 'run out', assuming you are happy with the method. The inert plastic devices which are rarely used nowadays can stay in indefinitely as long as no new problems occur. Some long-term users of IUDs develop bleeding problems after many trouble free years. One explanation offered is that salt deposits build up on the device. If all is well, an IUD can be kept in place until the menopause. The more commonly used copper bearing devices need replacing as and when the copper runs out. Most have an officially approved lifespan of three years, though some of the newer devices can last for five years. Among women nearing the end of their fertile years there may be a case for less frequent changing of IUDs than is officially recommended. Since many of the problems seen with IUD use have the highest incidence immediately after fitting and the procedure itself has its risks and discomforts, there is great appeal in a device that lasts as long as possible. This is one of the problems with the hormone releasing IUDs which only last for a year.

Types of IUD available in Britain

What type of IUD might you have fitted if you choose this as your method of contraception? By and large any new IUD fitted will be a copper releasing one, though some women prefer to continue using the inert plastic devices. Progestogen releasing devices are not available yet in Britain. Whichever one you have fitted its principal features will be the same as all other IUDs. All are made of inert plastic which springs back into shape once inserted in your uterus. All contain some substance which shows up on an X-ray, usually barium sulphate, in case the IUD gets 'lost'. All are flat, measure between 2 and 4 cm in length and have a similar width. Most have a vaguely uterine shape with a wider upper pole and a narrow lower pole to which the threads are attached. The development of this T-shape did not occur until 1968, despite the fact that doctors had been aware of the T-shape of the uterus since at least 1858. The uterus is a dynamic rather than static organ. It is always moving with gentle contractions. A T-shaped IUD seems to be the most suitable to adapt to this constant motion, and also has relatively little bulk, which means less chance of being expelled.

Copper releasing devices differ from the inert IUDs in that they have a much smaller surface area. The copper, usually in the form of copper wire, is wound around the plastic, most often along the vertical component of the T. Copper was added to IUDs when it was discovered

Figure 7.1 The IUD fits the uterus as if in a pear

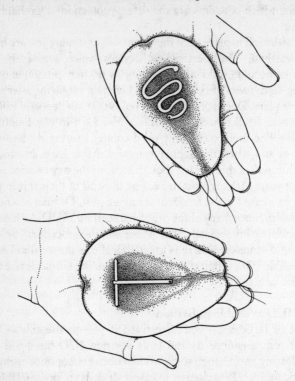

Source: PIACT de Mexico, A.C. Shakespeare 27, Col. Anzures, Del. M. Hidalgo, C.P. 11590

that copper wire in the uterus of rabbits dramatically reduced the number of places in which a fertilized egg could implant. Its main impact, as we have seen, is to make IUDs smaller, less easily expelled, and better at preventing pregnancy. A plain plastic T without any copper could lead to a pregnancy rate as high as 18 per 100 woman-years. With copper added the rate falls to around 1 per 100 woman-years. Unfortunately copper tends to disintegrate and it is this which determines the life expectancy of a device. Recently the life of some IUDs has been extended by using a silver core to the copper wire, which slows down the rate of decay. Nova T and TCu-380 Ag are two such devices. Other copper bearing devices are the Copper-7, and TCu-220c. The numbers included in the names refer to the surface area of the copper (in square millimetres) on the device.

The hormone releasing devices also resemble a T with the hormone in a reservoir in the vertical component. The hormone is in a specially prepared base to produce a constant release over a year or so. The development of sophisticated membranes which would allow a slow release of hormone over a longer period of time is the next important step.

The basic design of the IUD has altered very little since the 1960s. The Dalkon Shield was the only real innovation and this departure led to its downfall. At present there is work in progress which might lead to a very different sort of IUD, for example, a surgical nylon thread with copper wire coiled round it. It would be easy to insert and might produce fewer side-effects. Work on reliability and safety is of course paramount in the introduction of any new IUD.

How IUDs work

A lot of women who might have considered using an IUD have been put off by the fact that it has been said to work by offering a monthly abortion. Germaine Greer in *Sex and Destiny* describes it with character-istic bluntness as an 'abortionist's tool'. In fact the truth is that no one knows exactly how an IUD works. Much attention has been given to two observations: firstly that an IUD will prevent pregnancy if fitted post-coitally, and secondly that if the IUD is removed, and contraception used afterwards, conception may still occur. This certainly seems to imply that the IUD works after fertilization has taken place. This possibility has been grasped with both hands by the anti-abortion lobby who echo Greer in seeing IUDs as abortifacients. Present understanding of the IUD however suggests that this is a considerable over-simplifi-cation. A number of good recent studies suggest that the picture is more complex.

One recent study (1987) has shown that the IUD generally works by preventing fertilization.[6] Ova were collected from different parts of the genital tract from women with and without IUDs. Those recovered from IUD users showed no clear evidence of fertilization, whereas of the ova collected from non-IUD users 50 per cent had been fertilized. What is more, there were virtually no ova recoverable from the uterine cavities of the women using IUDs. Analysis of blood samples from IUD users backs up this evidence. Very sensitive testing for hCG (human chorionic gonadotrophin), produced by the embryo, can detect fertilization before implantation, or less than seven days after ovulation. It seems that fertilization had occured in less than 1 per cent of menstrual cycles of IUD wearers. While this evidence does not give any information about the way in which the IUD *does* work, at least it suggests that IUDs are not offering an early abortion every month. It seems much more likely

Figure 7.2 The IUDS most commonly available in Britain today

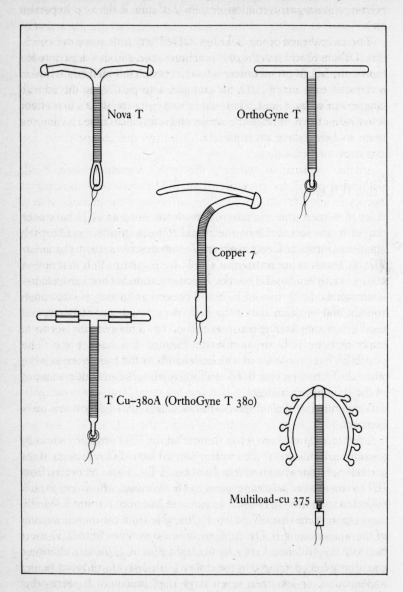

Nova T

OrthoGyne T

Copper 7

T Cu–380A (OrthoGyne T 380)

Multiload-cu 375

that they work by exerting some kind of anti-fertility effect before sperm and egg have a chance to meet.[7]

Many ingenious experiments have shown that the presence of a foreign body placed in the uterus, such as an IUD, results in the production of particular chemicals and cell types. These may well be exerting a major anti-fertility effect. To look at the range of possibilities we will start at the 'top' of the genital tract and consider the action of traditional (inert and copper bearing) IUDs. To date there is no evidence that IUDs have any effect on the function of the ovaries – which would explain the lack of any metabolic side-effects with this method. An ovum is released each month as usual and seems to pass along the uterine tube, maturing as it goes. Some sources suggest the IUD's first effect is to disrupt the normal gentle action of the fallopian tube causing the ovum to hurry along the tube and drop into the uterine cavity too immature for fertilization.

Another explanation concerns the body's immune system itself. Within the uterus the presence of an IUD causes an outpouring of leucocytes into the cavity. Leucocytes are cells of the immune system which the blood produces in large numbers whenever a foreign substance is sighted or detected. They attack and kill the invader by engulfing the smaller particles and releasing noxious chemicals against the larger ones. IUDs seem to provoke this aggressive response. This description of large white blood cells invading the uterus sounds most unpleasant – as though the IUD were acting like an infection. In fact, this so-called 'foreign body inflammatory response' is not related to infections and can occur in completely germ-free settings. The intensity of the leucocyte response seems to be proportional to the size of the device and to be increased in the presence of copper ions. This would neatly explain the observation that the size of the IUD may be reduced with no loss of efficacy if copper is added.[8]

What is the anti-fertility effect of all these leucocytes since they clearly have no effect on their preliminary target, the IUD itself? They are thought to stop conception in several ways. Firstly these cells may actually engulf sperm as they swarm into the uterus, destroying a large number before they have a chance to reach the ovum. They may also act on sperm by poisoning them with the products of their own breakdown, causing decreased mobility and eventual death. Secondly the ovum itself may also be disabled by these noxious substances making it unreceptive to sperm and unable to be fertilized. Thirdly, if a blastocyst (the ball of cells formed after fertilization) does succeed in developing it may be attacked in the same way. The last step in the chain of events leading to a successful pregnancy is the implantation of the blastocyst in the endometrial lining of the womb. This also seems to be affected by an IUD. The inflammatory response makes the endometrium less receptive to the blastocyst and when, in addition to this, there are copper ions present, the local production of chemicals known as prostaglandins actively prevents implantation. Finally there may be some effect on cervical mucus when a copper bearing IUD is used, making it impenetrable by sperm.[9]

The significance of each of the different stages for the way an IUD works is not known, but it does seem probable that in the majority of cases, it prevents fertilization, and that the other mechanisms only rarely come into play. Thus the IUD operates its own belt-and-braces system of contraception which makes it a highly effective form of birth control.

The new progestogen laden IUD offers all the additional anti-fertility effects associated with progestogen (see pp. 283–4 for a full explanation). When an IUD is used post-coitally it must work by preventing the implantation of the fertilized ovum. To work effectively it needs to be placed in the uterus within five days of unprotected intercourse, and can remain in place as long as the woman chooses. IUDs used post-coitally are discussed on pp. 327–8.

Where, then, should IUDs be placed in the spectrum of contraceptive methods? Some would argue that they should be compared to barrier methods with the barrier erected a little further up the genital tract. The passage of sperm is basically prevented, and if some should slip by there is a block to implantation. They have the advantage of not being related to intercourse (important for some women) and almost compete with the pill in terms of efficacy but without upsetting the delicate hormonal balance of the body. Unlike sterilization, which is also a single decision affair, the IUD can be 'reversed' within ten minutes.

The question of whether the IUD causes repeat abortions needs to be considered by anyone thinking of using one. We have seen that its mechanism is not fully understood, and that the evidence to date suggests that it only rarely acts by stopping a fertilized egg from implanting. But if this is ever the way in which it works, the IUD as a contraceptive method will have different implications for different women. If a blastocyst is taken to be a human life then normally fertile women must face the fact that they lose many an unborn 'child' throughout their reproductive lives as blastocysts are naturally and unknowingly lost. Using an IUD may occasionally add to this toll of loss. Many women using IUDs accept this and have no problems with it, particularly if they are well informed as to all the other anti-fertility affects of the IUD. Other women may be less sanguine and they should work out any misgivings before having an IUD inserted. A woman who feels subconsciously guilty about her IUD will never be happy with it, since guilt is a powerful emotion which can't be reasoned away. Women who have deep-seated objections to abortion should be wary of using the IUD as, if there is in their minds the slightest doubt that these devices ever work to cause an abortion they will regret and resent the decision for a long time to come.

Progestogen releasing IUDs

The idea of a progestogen releasing device is not new. As early as 1968 animal work was carried out which produced hopeful signs, but twenty years later there is still no such device available in the UK. The Progestasert is available in the USA but in 1988 it was withdrawn from Britain by the manufacturers largely for financial reasons. There is still a lack of written material available about its safety and effectiveness. Progestasert combines the effects of a traditional IUD with those of hormonal contraception. Its great advantage is that the progestogen it releases has a largely local effect and so many of the unwanted effects of oral contraceptives are avoided. Moreover, being an IUD, one of its big plus points is that you can't forget to take it at the right time.

The Progestasert releases 65 micrograms of progestogen per day over the course of a year. Different countries have developed different recommendations as to the length of time the Progestasert should be left in place. In France for example eighteen months is considered to be a safe life span for the device. Since the problems associated with any IUD peak in the first three months it is obviously desirable to use devices which last as long as possible. Both the WHO and the Population Council have also developed longer lasting systems.

Like all IUDs the way in which the Progestasert works is not fully understood. Shaped like a plastic T, it presumably works like the others and its fitting and removal follow the same principles. The progestogen is thought to have two main effects. Firstly it makes the endometrium lining hostile to the fertilized ovum, so reducing the chances of implantation, and secondly it makes the mucus in the cervical canal thick and relatively impenetrable by sperm. It may also produce more systemic effects since some women develop disturbances in their periods a bit like those seen with the progestogen-only pill.

On the whole, however, the addition of progestogen to the IUD seems to solve some of the major problems associated with traditional IUDs. The changes in cervical mucus seem to make the passage of harmful organisms into the uterus much less easy which considerably reduces the likelihood of a pelvic infection. Blood loss and the accompanying pain experienced by wearers of conventional IUDs is dramatically reduced – making this form of IUD much more tolerable. The main disadvantage is the possibility of the development of an erratic cycle with some inter-menstrual bleeding (see p. 288). There may also be some interference with the tubal transport of the fertilized ovum leading to an increased risk of ectopic pregnancy, though this is by no means certain. Finally there is always a long-term possibility of side-effects caused by hormones which have not yet been recognized. This is a very poorly documented field, but most of the evidence to date suggests that progestogen releasing IUDs are a very positive development.[10]

Side-effects of IUDs

Most women who have an IUD fitted will have no problems at all except for slightly heavier periods, and will be able to wear it comfortably until it either has to be changed or the need for contraception ceases. IUD continuation rates are higher than for any other form of reversible contraception with 80 per cent or more of women still using their devices one year after insertion.[11] This positive statistic cannot be entirely explained by the fact that an effort is needed to have an IUD removed but must also reflect a certain level of satisfaction with the method. Nevertheless, some women do experience some side-effects with IUDs. These can be divided into immediate and longer-term or continuing problems.

Immediate problems

These are the problems encountered during and immediately after an IUD fitting. The frequency with which they occur is difficult to determine since they depend considerably on where and by whom the device is fitted. A well-counselled women with an experienced practitioner is far less likely to have problems than a frightened woman in the hands of an inexperienced doctor.

Perforation

IUDs do not perforate. For this to happen we need a practitioner.

Jack Lippes[12]

When an IUD is fitted it is very important that it is placed in the right part of the uterus at the top of the cavity. Failure to do so is the most frequent cause of problems.

Perforation is a dramatic-sounding term for a relatively rare occurrence – it is thought that about one in 1,000 fittings go wrong in this way. The IUD gets either pushed into or right through the uterus wall. This is much more likely to happen if the uterus is an unusual shape. A careful examination prior to the fitting should cut down the risks considerably. Unfortunately and surprisingly a perforation may go unnoticed by either the doctor or the woman at the time and only show

Figure 7.3 Side-effects of IUDs

Expulsion	Approximately 1.2 to 13 per cent of IUD users See table for details	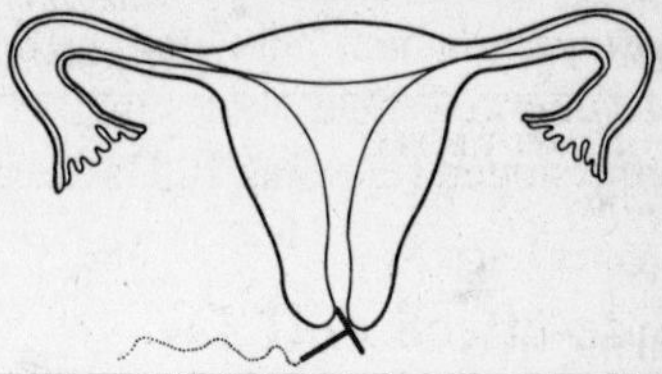
Perforation	Approximately 0.06 to 1.2 per cent of IUD users See table for details	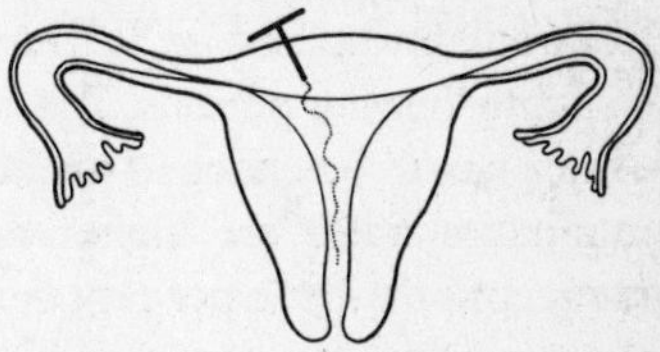
Bleeding and pain	5 to 20 per cent of women discontinue IUD use because of this	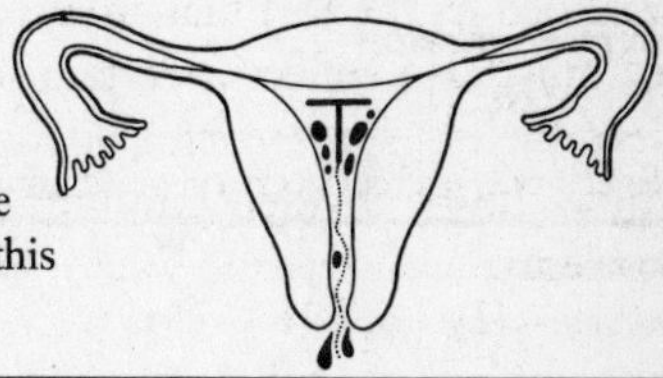
Infection	Twice as likely as in women not using any contraception	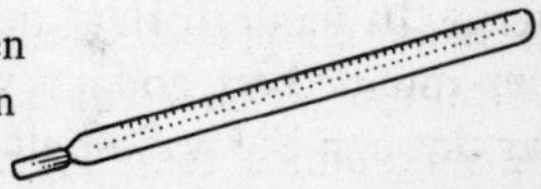
Pregnancy	the majority are intra-uterine and in about one third the IUD will have been expelled —2 per cent of IUD users— 3 to 9 per cent of these are ectopic pregnancies	

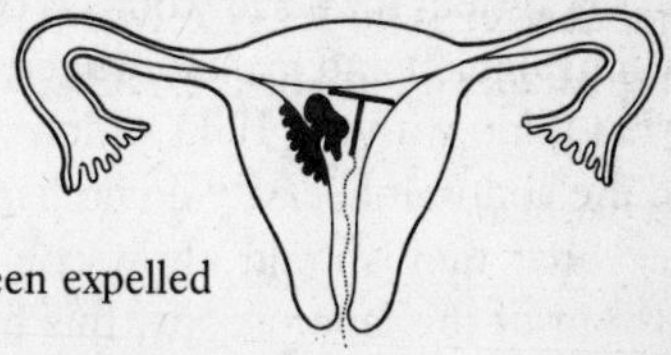

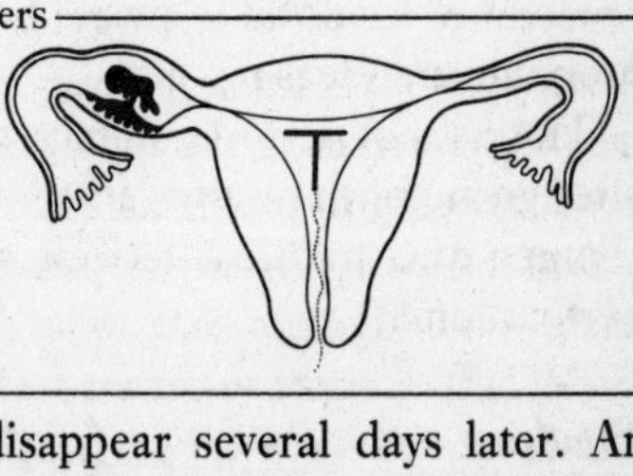

up when the threads of the IUD disappear several days later. An ultrasound scan may show the IUD outside the uterus. Occasionally during the fitting itself the woman feels an unusual amount of pain and begins bleeding – fairly obvious signs that the IUD has perforated the

Figure 7.4   Reported uterine perforation rates for IUDs

Device type	Number of perforations	Number of insertions	Rate per 1,000 insertions
NON-MEDICATED			
Plastic			
Lippes Loop	89	76 631	1.2
MEDICATED			
Copper-bearing			
Copper-7	14	22 914	0.6
TCu-200	7[a]	9 838	0.7
TCu-380A	2[a]	3 536	0.6
Nova T	2	3 181	0.6
MLCu-250	0	2 553	–
MLCu-375	0	1 772	–
Hormone-releasing			
Progestasert	13	11 356	1.1

[a] Specifically excludes cervical perforations.

Source: Technical Report Series 753, *Mechanism of Action, Safety and Efficacy of Intrauterine Devices*, WHO, 1987.

uterus. In modern IUD designs all the potentially sharp points have been rounded off, and it is thought that they cannot possibly work their way through the wall unaided. The vast majority of perforations must occur at insertion.

Treatment for perforations is controversial. A small hole in the uterus will heal itself and probably needs no further attention. The question is what to do with the IUD which remains. Some doctors feel that IUDs in the abdominal cavity do no harm and are best left well alone. Others feel that they should always be removed particularly since, with the advent of the laparoscope, this has become a relatively minor surgical procedure. Removal is always best if the device is a copper bearing or progestogen releasing one.

The risks of perforation increase if insertion is done in the six weeks after giving birth or after an abortion (after twelve weeks of gestation). Women who are breastfeeding also seem to carry an increased risk of perforation.[13]

Expulsion

IUDs can be expelled; this can occur at any time, particularly if they are placed too low, though most expulsions are in the three months following a fitting and particularly during periods. The IUD passes through the cervix and is often lost down the loo without the woman being aware that anything has happened. Estimates as to how often this happens vary from one in 100 to fifteen in 100. Apart from the position in which the IUD was put there are a number of other factors that make expulsion far more likely. Young women, women who have never been pregnant and those using the larger inert IUDs all have a higher chance of expulsion. An IUD inserted immediately after delivery or an abortion also carries a higher chance of being expelled. The uterus has a natural tendency to push anything placed inside out again and the firm tense muscles of young nulliparous women are better at this than the softer muscles of a woman who has had a child. Feeling the threads regularly, and particularly after a period, should alert you if the IUD has been pushed out.

Figure 7.5   Expulsion rates at one year of use in selected comparative trials

Device	Range of reported expulsion rates per 100 women
NON-MEDICATED	
Lippes Loop D	7.8–13.10
MEDICATED	
Copper-bearing	
Copper-7	5.3–15.5
TCu-200	1.4– 8.8
TCu-380A/Ag	3.3– 7.1
Nova T	2.5– 9.2
ML Cu-250	2.4–11.4
ML Cu-375	4.1– 9.4
Hormone-releasing	
Progestasert (progesterone 65 μg)	1.2– 4.2
* ML = multiload	

Source: Technical Report Series 753, *Mechanism of Action, Safety and Efficacy of Intrauterine Devices*, WHO, 1987.

Continuing problems

Bleeding and pain

I had an IUD for a year: terrible period pains for four to five days a month. I noticed the days I wasn't bleeding each month. It was honestly like being in labour for one day a month and was an enormous relief when it was removed.

I'd recommend the IUD to other women if they don't mind their periods getting heavier.

Mine did but not unduly, and as far as I remember they weren't any more painful after the first couple of times.

If you have an IUD fitted you will almost certainly notice an increase in the amount and length of your bleeding during periods. Unfortunately this heavier bleeding is often associated with increased dysmenorrhoea (period pains). If you decide to continue with your IUD you may well find that your periods return to a more normal pattern after a while. Heavier bleeding and painful periods are the most common problem of IUD use and yet the exact reasons for their occurrence are not fully understood. As they are considered neither to threaten the quality of life (many women would disagree) nor future fertility they have been rather ignored by researchers. It is currently thought that IUDs may have a direct physical effect on the delicate endometrial lining and that the local increase in various hormones thought to be caused by the IUD may lead to a decrease in the blood's ability to clot.

The severity of the bleeding and the extent to which it occurs seems to depend on the type of device fitted and on your age and number of children that you have. Generally the larger the device, the greater the amount of blood loss. Inert plastic devices are the worst offenders in this respect and some studies have shown them to be responsible for a doubling of blood loss.[14] Smaller copper bearing IUDs appear to increase blood loss only by half as much again but the copper seems to increase the length of the period. The pain associated with the increased bleeding is probably due to the uterine contractions which are stimulated by the presence of anything, be it blood or an IUD. Estimating the amount of blood lost is always a tricky business, but the fact that in some women using IUDs the body's iron stores do in fact get depleted points to the fact that excess bleeding is a very real problem. Fortunately anaemia related to IUDs is very rare.

IUDs which release progestogen act in the opposite way and decrease bleeding, though they have the disadvantage that they make periods relatively unpredictable with frequent bleeding between periods. In about 10 per cent of women using progestogen IUDs periods disappear altogether.[15]

Interestingly older women and those with more than one child request the removal of their IUDs for pain and bleeding less often than other groups. This probably reflects a smaller incidence of problems, but may also mean that women with completed families are prepared to raise their tolerance level for the sake of avoiding another pregnancy.

The treatment for menstrual problems experienced by IUD wearers is controversial. A number of drugs, including aspirin, seem to be effective in decreasing blood loss and pain. They are anti-inflammatory drugs and seem to work by reducing the inflammatory action of the IUD. Ironically there is at least a theoretical risk that by using an anti-inflammatory drug you may risk decreasing the efficacy of your IUD. In practice this has not been proved to be the case and it seems reasonable to take aspirin if this helps.[16] Some doctors prescribe drugs which increase the clotting ability of the blood to help control the bleeding, and others recommend progestogens to be taken by mouth. This is peculiarly perverse for the many IUD wearers who specifically want to avoid hormonal contraception. Apparently however some women are prepared to adopt this extreme measure.

Infection

In the minds of many women serious pelvic infection and IUD use are inextricably linked. Reports of infection with resulting infertility and even deaths from septicaemia in IUD wearers makes depressing reading. The Dalkon Shield affair massively undermined many women's belief in the safety of IUDs. The high incidence of infections in women who had had the Shield fitted and the appalling complications they developed if they became pregnant with the device in place are a truly black spot in the history of contraception. The reasons for these disturbing happenings are difficult to explain. A number of research projects were set up in the wake of the affair to see if the problems were common to all IUDs, and the data to emerge so far suggests they are not. The most recent work is relatively reassuring, but individual women will still want to know what sort of risks they run if they do opt for an IUD.

A general overview of pelvic infections may be helpful to put the problems associated with IUD use in perspective. Pelvic infections are generally caused by ascending organisms, i.e. the germs that come from the vagina and spread upwards through the cervix and into the uterus and fallopian tubes. Unfortunately there may be no indication that an infection is present until a fairly late stage has been reached and the fallopian tubes have become involved. The significance of tubal involvement is that salpingitis (as an infection in the fallopian tubes is called) can cause irreversible damage. It can effectively block off the passage which leads from the ovary to the uterus. If the tubes are blocked the ovum cannot get through, cannot be fertilized and cannot implant in the endometrium. A blockage in both tubes can rule out any possibility of pregnancy by normal means. An attack of salpingitis results in infertility in approximately one in eight affected women.[17]

One of the difficulties of any pelvic inflammatory disease (or PID as it is known) is that it is notoriously difficult to diagnose. The symptoms are low abdominal pain, an unpleasant smelling discharge, fever, general malaise and possibly bleeding irregularities. But many women rarely have such classic symptoms and some of these symptoms can be caused by quite different problems. The only way of making an accurate diagnosis is by having a look at the tubes by means of a laparoscope, a procedure not without its hazards and impractical for every day use. A woman who arrives at her doctor's surgery with pain in her lower abdomen and a fever can't afford to wait for an appointment for a laparoscopy. If she does have PID she needs antibiotics right away to save her fallopian tubes. The tendency therefore is to over-diagnose the condition and to treat all possible cases with broad spectrum antibiotics.

The belief that IUDs themselves cause infection is simply wrong. Harmful organisms are required to cause an infection in the first place, and as all IUDs fitted in the UK are pre-packed in sterile conditions the organisms must come from elsewhere. One of the major problems of the IUD is that it has to be inserted into the uterus by way of the vagina which is bacteriologically rather 'dirty'. The vaginas of all women have colonies of organisms which do not usually cause infections, but these same bugs, if pushed into the uterus, may lead to an infection. In most women most of the time, such infections are rapidly dealt with by the body's immune system and cause no problems. Occasionally, though, an IUD insertion can trigger off an active infection. It has been shown that the bacteria count in the uterus is very high immediately following an IUD insertion, but in the vast majority of women within thirty days the uterine cavity and the IUD are sterile again.[18] The immune system has warded off any dangers. But if there is already an established vaginal or cervical infection (which may be present without the woman being aware of it), the fitting of an IUD will simply push these disease-causing organisms into the uterus and a serious infection may result. This is why it is important not to fit an IUD if there is any suspicion of an infection. Unfortunately it is difficult to ensure this is always the case. The second route of infection occurs when a woman with an IUD becomes infected with an STD which she has caught from her partner. The presence of the IUD may make the likelihood of the infection spreading upwards more likely.

In the West about 1–2 per cent of all women of reproductive age develop PID in any one year.[19] In the 1970s when the link between IUDs and PID was thought to be indisputable, the risk for an IUD wearer was thought to be as high as ten times the risk for other women. The data supporting this was flawed in several ways. IUD wearers were compared with women using other forms of contraception but it has now been realized that these other methods actually *protect* women from

PID. Diaphragms act as a physical barrier, and hormonal methods probably produce a mucus barrier, both resulting in a physical block to ascending organisms. Compared with women not using any contraceptive method, IUD wearers had the same or a somewhat greater risk of PID; the risks for women using other contraceptive methods were much smaller than either. Studies carried out since 1980 have reassessed these risks.[20]

Overall, women using IUDs are about twice as likely to develop PID as women using no contraception but this risk is concentrated in the first months after insertion and thereafter to women exposed to STDs. For women in mutually faithful monogamous relationships, once the first months are over, there is no additional risk of an infection caused by an IUD. It has been found that in the first month after insertion the risk of PID for IUD users is four times the risk of those using no contraception. Two to four months after insertion the risk is down to 1.7 – three times the risk for non-users. Thereafter the risk is similar to those who use no contraceptive method. Since the problems are associated with the earliest months after a fitting, women who have been appropriately counselled will be in a good position to get immediate

Figure 7.6 Percentage of IUD users among women hospitalized with PID

Out of 267,000 women hospitalised with PID . . .

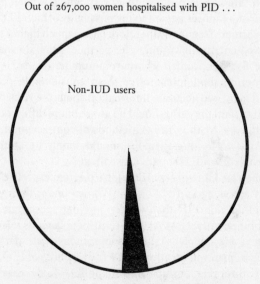

Non-IUD users

. . . 8560 were IUD users

Source: B. J. Struthers, 'Effects of using IUDs: a review of some epidemiological and vital statistical data', *British Journal of Family Planning*, Vol. 13, No. 4, 1988.

treatment for any suspected infection brewing.[21] Figure 7.6 above helps to put the role of the IUD in PID in context.

Another defect of some of the earliest studies was that they did not take into account the type of IUD fitted. The data on PID includes statistics from the Dalkon Shield which has now been removed from the market. Its problems are not relevant to today's devices, except as a salutory tale. One of the main differences between the Dalkon Shield and all other IUDs lies in the threads attached to the lower pole. The Shield had a 'multi-filament' thread and it is thought that this acted as a wick, drawing up harmful organisms from the vagina. The mono-filament threads of all other devices probably do not share this property and therefore should not carry quite the same risk.[22] The risk of PID among women wearing Dalkon shields was five times higher than that of other IUD wearers, and the risk did not decline but remained the same as long as the device was *in situ*. Differences in PID rates between the users of the various current models of device are still being studied, but are likely to be minimal. The exception to this is the progestogen releasing models which, by their action on cervical mucus, protect against infection.[23]

It is now becoming clear that when any work on contraceptive methods is done the differences in the lifestyles of women should be taken into consideration. Studies have shown that every time a woman has a new sexual partner she exposes herself to the possibility of an STD. Women who change partners frequently therefore have a much higher risk of an STD than women who have only one partner. An IUD may create unacceptable risks for women who have a number of sexual partners while a barrier method might offer them considerable protection. Women need good and accurate information about the risks of STDs, including AIDS, and they also should be aware of the differences in the protection afforded by the various methods of contraception. Women who choose not to be monogamous should simply be aware of the additional problems an IUD might cause them.

Some women are more likely to develop PID from exposure to STDs whether they are using an IUD or not. Women under twenty-five are more likely to develop PID than women in older age-groups, though this is probably due to the fact that long-term monogamous relationships are rarer in young people. A non-monogamous male partner of a monogamous woman will greatly increase her chances of PID. Women in mutually faithful relationships are very unlikely to develop PID and the risk of doing so is barely altered by wearing an IUD.

As we have already pointed out, the peak incidence for PID in IUD wearers is the first month and thereafter the risk decreases. It is ironic therefore that very occasionally a severe infection should develop after an IUD has been *in situ* for a considerable length of time. Such an infection may be caused by a yeast-like organism called actinomyces. This is usually quite harmless but there is some evidence that it can produce severe PID in a few long-term IUD users. Actinomyces can be detected on a cervical smear. If there are clinical signs of an infection developing, treatment with penicillin and the removal of your IUD will usually be effective.[24]

A small study, still under way, is suggesting that another yeast infection, thrush, may be more common in IUD users than in those using other contraceptive methods. This is very different to actinomyces, in that it leads to an uncomfortable vaginal infection. Fortunately it has not so far been implicated in a pelvic infection, though repeated attacks of thrush may be a quite sufficient reason for a woman to want to have an IUD removed.

IUDs and cancer
There is no evidence after hundreds and thousands of woman-years of use, and after painstaking research, that there are any cancers associated with the IUD. Unfortunately the IUD offers no protection against any cancer either, unlike barrier methods which protect against cervical cancer and hormonal methods which reduce the risk of endometrial and ovarian cancer.

IUDs: pregnancy and fertility

This section looks at the problems encountered when pregnancy occurs with an IUD *in situ* and at the effect of IUD use on fertility. Pregnancies do occur in a few unlucky IUD wearers. This may be following an unrecognized expulsion but pregnancy also occurs with the IUD in place. As with a normal pregnancy the embryo usually nestles in the uterus but occasionally the implantation occurs outside the womb, this is then referred to as an ectopic pregnancy.

The rather sad image of a baby being born clutching its mother's IUD is the stuff of old wives' tales. Of the 2 per cent of women who conceive with an IUD in place, some choose to continue with the pregnancy and have a healthy baby. The IUD lies outside the amniotic sac where the baby cannot possibly get its hands on it and therefore can never arrive with this scrap of plastic to taunt its mother! A missed period in an IUD user should always be followed up with a pregnancy test. If it is positive then it is important to try to find out where the IUD has got to. Quite often the threads can still be easily felt, indicating that the IUD is either in the uterus or in the cervical canal. If it's impossible to feel the threads, it may have been expelled already or else is still in place but the threads have been drawn up into the enlarging uterus. If your doctor can feel the threads easily, he may try to gently remove your IUD. If the pregnancy is the result of your IUD lying in the lower half of the uterus (having been partly expelled) then it will come out easily and the pregnancy can remain undisturbed.

If it is not possible to remove the IUD this way an ultrasound scan will show you what is going on. In about 30 per cent of cases the IUD is not seen on the scan. If this happens you have to decide whether to continue with the pregnancy on the assumption that the device has been expelled. If the scan shows your IUD still in your uterus then you need careful counselling to help you decide what to do. There are a number of risks involved in continuing the pregnancy. The risk of a miscarriage following early gentle removal is approximately 20–30 per cent whereas the chance of a miscarriage with the device in place is about 55 per cent – three times the rate seen in a 'normal' pregnancy. The majority of miscarriages are early in the pregnancy, but with an IUD in place the incidence of so-called 'mid-trimester spontaneous abortions' (miscarriage after the third month) is high – reckoned to be twenty-five times that in 'normal' pregnancies. The particularly worrying, but rare, septic miscarriage which can carry grave risk for the mother due to the infection accompanying the loss of the fetus, was seen unusually often in women with Dalkon Shields. The risk of this occurring in women using other IUDs is much lower and may not be greater than for the rest of the population.

There is some evidence to suggest that prematurity is more common in pregnancies with an IUD in place and if you carry on with the pregnancy you should be aware of this. Despite this rather gloomy data many women have produced perfectly normal healthy babies with an IUD still in place. The chance of producing an abnormal baby is no greater with an IUD, and congenital abnormalities seem, in fact, to be slightly less common in these babies. The reason for this may be that only the fittest fetus will survive the first few months of intra-uterine life in the presence of an IUD, so even a minor defect becomes fatal and a miscarriage results. Pregnancy with an IUD can succeed, though the majority of women who conceive with an IUD in place, or following its expulsion, choose to have an early abortion.[25]

Ectopic pregnancy

Early diagnosis of a pregnancy is very important in IUD wearers for reasons outlined above and because of the risk of ectopic pregnancy. If a pregnancy becomes established in a site outside the uterine cavity then the life of the woman is put at risk. A developing placenta can 'burrow' its way into any body tissue causing a great increase in the blood supply to that area. The wall of the fallopian tube, the commonest site of ectopics, cannot cope with these changes and the chance of rupture is very high. If this happens the resulting blood loss is dramatic and the rapid surgical removal of the doomed pregnancy is life saving. Unfortunately the diagnosis of an ectopic pregnancy is difficult, and made more so by the need not to delay. The earlier the diagnosis, the less the risk to the mother. If there is anything in your medical history which might increase the likelihood of an ectopic pregnancy it is very important to let the doctor know. For example, the risks of ectopic pregnancy are greater in those who have had PID, a previous ectopic pregnancy, tubal surgery and possibly in those using the progestogen-only pill.

It used to be believed that IUD wearers were at greater risk of an ectopic pregnancy than the rest of the population. Recently a great deal of research has shown that this is not strictly true. The risk in an IUD wearer is 50 per cent less than the risk in a woman using no form of contraception. However, if conception does occur in an IUD user, then there is a greater chance of the pregnancy being ectopic. The IUD, in other words, is less good at preventing ectopic pregnancies than at preventing a normal pregnancy. The minor differences in effectiveness in preventing conception between the various IUDs are therefore reflected in their corresponding risk of causing an ectopic pregnancy. Progestogen releasing devices are the exception to this and may carry a real – if slightly – increased risk of ectopic pregnancy.

To put this in perspective, IUD users have only a very small chance of becoming pregnant. If they do, 3–9 per cent of the pregnancies will be ectopic. Among women who are not using the IUD the chance of an ectopic pregnancy is only 0.8 per cent. This rather confusing idea is further complicated by the fact that barrier methods of contraception and the pill both have a protective effect against ectopics. The general advice offered is that the IUD is fine if you have no other risk factors that could cause an ectopic pregnancy. But if you do then it would make sense to use another form of contraception.[26]

Symptoms of an ectopic pregnancy
A woman with an ectopic pregnancy may start to get symptoms before her period is due, but more usually she will have missed a period, or rarely two periods, before getting symptoms. She may well have the

normal nausea, breast tenderness, etc. of early pregnancy. In addition she may develop the following:

• Sharp, low abdominal pain, often one-sided
• Vaginal bleeding which may be slight, brownish and characteristically starts after the pain.
• Feeling of faintness or actual fainting (fainting is a worrying sign and should be taken seriously).
• Sharp pain on the tips of both shoulders.

These symptoms individually can be caused by a variety of conditions and this is not intended to be a complete guide to self-diagnosis, but merely some pointers to bear in mind, particularly if you have any reason to think that you are in a high risk group for ectopic pregnancy. If you think that it is possible that you have an ectopic pregnancy it is essential to get medical advice immediately.

Fertility and the IUD
Does using an IUD have any effect on long-term fertility? The great majority of women who have used an IUD will conceive just as rapidly as women who have used no contraception. Since the hormonal ebb and flow of the body is not affected, the only consideration as far as fertility is concerned is the state in which the IUD leaves the reproductive organs. As we have seen, there is a small group of women who become infertile as a result of PID which they developed with an IUD in place. The risk of this kind of infertility varies with the number of partners a woman has, and in studies where all the subjects are older married women the IUD seems to have no effect on their future ability to conceive. Nor does the duration of IUD use seem to affect fertility, which is no great surprise if we bear in mind the fact that the first three months of use are the most likely time for PID to develop, and that the risk of infection diminishes thereafter.

There is no evidence that the endometrial lining is altered in any long-term way so as to prevent implantation, and the chances of miscarriage are no greater following IUD use than in the rest of the population. The loss of fertility is a tragedy and any threat to long-term fertility must be taken very seriously. This is why careful consideration of lifestyle, age and future plans of any woman considering an IUD is absolutely essential. Careful counselling before a decision is made would reduce the incalculable misery of infertility to a minimum.

Conclusion

The IUD is not a very popular form of contraception in Britain now. The bad press following the Dalkon Shield affair has certainly given all IUDs a bad name, rather unjustly. The rapidity with which IUD manufacturers withdrew from the field following this denied many women the choice of an IUD in America. The fact that some American women were prepared to travel to Canada to get other IUDs suggests that, for some women at least, they make a very good form of contraception. Unfortunately it is the stories of those with bad experiences which have passed into the folk wisdom of the day.

As we have seen throughout this book, the way in which a woman sees herself will always be one of the key factors in her choice of contraceptive method. Women who are 'aware' of their bodies, their sexuality and their fertility also have clear ideas about fertility control. The way in which an IUD simply sits as an unresponsive object inside them, quite unaffected by the body's waxing and waning fertility, may be anathema. The IUD appears to be so unsubtle, to provide such 'overkill', that it seems out of place in such a finely tuned engine as the female body. Other women see the IUD in a very different light. They are surprised at how small and delicate an IUD looks. The very fact that it does not tamper materially with the rhythm of their fertility is a positive attribute; it does not interfere with love-making, nor can it be felt by either party. It requires no repeated premeditation, is discreet and invisible and very effective.

Ironically, it may be the Dalkon Shield affair that saved the IUD from an untimely grave. The large volumes of research data it led to, the clarification of who is most at risk of infection, and the better quality of information about IUDs that can now be offered, are very much in women's best interests. By the same token, these large amounts of data mean that the IUD will probably never become a widely used method. We know too much about it. As long as it is ever implicated in a bout of fertility-reducing PID, or causes heavy and painful bleeding, there will be plenty of women who are simply not prepared to risk it.

CHAPTER 8

Hormonal Contraception

Two years ago I seemed to be at the surgery every few months with a series of ailments ... recurring migraines, painful joints, pronounced physical fatigue and lethargy and the appearance of a number of strange lumps under the skin on my arms ... The most serious medical problem was recurring attacks of severe abdominal pain, which when investigated turned out to be caused by a gallstone – something which is apparently unusual in someone of my age ... Recently I read a self-help book on women's health issues. I was both interested and angered to find that long-term use of the pill can lead to all the health difficulties I had experienced. My anger is directed largely at my GP who failed to make the connection herself despite the fact that I had repeatedly expressed my desire to stop taking the pill ...

I've been very satisfied with my contraception. My GP always weighed me and took my blood pressure. I was never given a repeat prescription. Of course I read of the various scares and medical reports that appeared from time to time between 1973 and 1980 but I didn't smoke, didn't put on weight, didn't suffer headaches or depression so I reckoned the small risk was worth the convenience of spontaneous sex and freedom from unwanted pregnancy.

The first day I took the pill I lay awake half the night thinking I was going to die. Was I just misinformed?

I went on the pill, I found it exceedingly easy to adapt to, with minimum effort. The good points for me were its effectiveness, its peace of mind and its ease to use. I found the reliability of my periods spot on, and the knowledge of being able to plan ahead for events – e.g. swimming and squash – improved my life.

Hormonal contraception has become the touchstone of contraceptive practice in the developed world and is regarded by many as the nearest thing to perfect contraception developed so far. Others regard the use of hormones on such a massive scale as potentially dangerous and irresponsible. To cover all aspects of hormonal contraception in one chapter, including the polarity of views that have developed on the subject, is clearly an impossible task. We hope to indicate the lines of the debate, discuss the most significant research findings and explain how such small and innocuous looking pills prevent you from becoming pregnant.

Hormones are naturally occurring chemicals in animals and plants which act as messengers. They are released from a site of production in one of the body's glands and drift along in the bloodstream until they reach a cell that recognizes them. They then produce some sort of change in the cell's activity. Progestogens and oestrogens are two groups of sex hormones which have the specific function of determining sexual characteristics and controlling reproduction. As we saw in Chapter 1, left uninterrupted they control the cyclical pattern of ovulation and menstruation, pregnancy and the return to fertility. These hormones are sometimes called sex steroids as they share a ring-shaped basic structure with all other steroids. The progestogens all share similar properties. Progesterone is the name of the most important of the progestogens produced in the human body, and the only one found in blood. In the same way oestrogens all have similar properties, but although oestradiol is the commonest of the oestrogens produced in the body, the word oestrogen tends to be used to refer to the mix of such hormones found in blood.

For many people, knowledge of hormonal contraception begins and ends with 'the pill'. The very fact that, although hundreds of drugs are in tablet form, 'the pill' has come to have only one meaning, is a tribute to its huge social impact. At least 150 million women around the world have used the pill at some time, and for many it is synonymous with contraception. The combined oral contraceptive pill (COC as it is officially known), is the most commonly used form of hormonal contraception. It is made up of two types of hormones, oestrogen and progestogen. The strength and mix of these hormones vary from brand to brand, but both are always present. The mini-pill, or progestogen-only pill (POP), which is gaining in popularity in the UK, leaves out the oestrogen component. We will look at the action of both in a later section. Other hormonal methods are the progestogen releasing IUD and the injectable contraceptive Depo Provera, a three-monthly injection of a slow-release progestogen first used in the 1960s and now licensed for long-term contraceptive purposes in Britain. Much of the new work in the field of fertility control involves finding new ways of 'delivering' hormones into the body. The development of new plastics and other materials is opening up new possibilities, and it seems likely that in the not-too-distant future the pill will no longer enjoy a place of such pre-eminence among hormonal contraception.

A short history

The idea of oral preparations which prevent pregnancy is certainly not new. In ancient China a drink containing twenty-four live tadpoles was supposed to offer five years of contraceptive protection, and there are many other references to concoctions – some quite revolting – which have been swallowed down the ages. Generations of Rajasthani villagers in India have chewed carrot seeds to avoid pregnancy.

A rational approach to oral contraception depends on an understanding of the physiology of reproduction, and as we have seen, this came remarkably recently. Progesterone was not identified until 1928 and oestrogen not until 1929. A decade later these hormones were being used in America to inhibit ovulation in women by a Dr Rock and a Dr Kurzrok. Natural progesterone and oestrogens had to be administered by injection as they are destroyed by the digestive system, and moreover they were taken from animal sources, which was more than a little impractical. Eighty thousand sows' ovaries were required to make twelve milligrams of the oestrogen known as oestradiol! The first major breakthrough in synthesizing sex hormones came in the early 1940s when Russell Marker succeeded in extracting progesterone from Mexican yams. Plants remained the source of raw material until the 1960s when the first completely synthetic steroids came into production.

The first clinical trials of hormones as a means of preventing pregnancy were started in 1956 in Puerto Rico. The drugs used were norethynodrel, a progestogen mixed with an oestrogen called mestranol. The combination was found to be very effective in preventing pregnancy and the combined oral contraceptive pill was born.

In 1960 the first pill, Enovid, was licensed by the US Food and Drug Administration. In the same year in England the first clinical trials of the pill were held in Birmingham and in 1961 oral contraceptives were approved by the Medical Advisory Council of the FPA. Since that time millions of women have used them and there have been hundreds of hours devoted to understanding their use. With the discovery that side-effects are related to the amount of hormone in each pill the doses have been cut down. The oestrogen component of the pill was the first to be labelled as the 'baddie' and efforts were concentrated on reducing it to a minimum. More recently progestogens have also been implicated and new work is aiming to reduce these too.[1]

The oestrogens used in the pill are ethinyloestradiol and mestranol (in fact converted in the body to ethinyloestradiol). There are several different progestogens of varying potency used in the pill and POP, but the most commonly used ones are levonorgestrel, norethisterone, ethynodiol diacetate, and recently gestodene and desogestrel. When first introduced in the 1960s, the pill contained 150 μg (micrograms) of oestrogen plus a progestogen. By 1969 the move toward a lower-dose pill had begun and the standard pill, or so-called low-dose pill, came to contain 50 μg of oestrogen. More recently these pills have been superseded by ultra-low-dose pills. These contain only 20–35 μg of oestrogen. Developers of hormonal contraception are constantly on the lookout for new ways of reducing the amount of hormone in contraceptive pills and biphasic and triphasic oral contraceptives were developed specifically with this intention. Each pill contains oestrogen but different pills contain different amounts of progestogen. The first pills to be taken in each cycle contain the smallest amount of progestogen and the level increases in either two or three steps before the end of the packet.

The pill first became available, then, during the 1960s, a time of considerable social change. It offered a promise of and indeed contributed very significantly to the sexual liberation of the age. The slow emergence of unwanted side-effects has raised many questions about the price we are prepared to pay for control of our fertility, and this, too, is an important part of the history of the pill. 'Carefree' contraception has its price; in the 1960s the price paid by some women included strokes, heart attacks and other types of thrombosis. It was not until 1969, however, that the Committee on Safety of Medicines announced that there was an increase in the risk of thromboembolism among pill users. Thousands of women became pregnant as they stopped taking their pills and the first pill 'scare' took its toll. This pattern of a scare followed by a panic reaction and an acceptance phase has been repeated again and again over the years.

In 1983 there was a particularly notable episode. On 21 October, front-page news in almost all the daily papers announced that the pill caused both cancer of the breast and cervix. The studies on which these claims were based had not even been published at this point and GPs were as much in the dark as the women who phoned them in panic. The research on which the media scare stories were based was published the next day in the *Lancet* and, with the publication of other studies, this particular pill scare has moved into perspective. But pill scares have certainly not ceased – the most recent occurring in April 1989. We look at the evidence on the pill and cancer in a separate section.

Aside from the effects of scares, it is interesting to see how use of the pill in Britain has altered in the twenty-eight years since it was introduced. When it first appeared it was used largely by married, middle-class women who could afford to buy it. It was not until 1967 that it was officially available to unmarried women and not until 1974 that it was available without charge. Since then the pill has become the choice predominantly of the young and single, and it is in this group that its popularity has continued to increase. In 1976 33 per cent of single women used the pill, rising to 46 per cent in 1983. Married and cohabiting women have moved in the opposite direction, with only 24 per cent of this group using the pill in 1983 compared to 28 per cent in 1976. Perhaps most significant of all is the change in the age profile of pill users. In the UK between 1976 and 1983 pill use increased for women under thirty and decreased for women aged thirty to forty-five.

The pill in Britain today

Patterns of use

It has been estimated that there are about 50 million women using the pill worldwide at any one time, of which approximately 3 million live in Britain. Accumulating statistics about the use of hormonal contraceptive methods is easier than with other methods. Prescriptions handed out by clinics and GPs can be counted, and while this does not mean that all the pills that are handed out are used, it is subject to less error than inquiries about, for example, condom use. DHSS statistics show that in 1986 about 52.6 per cent of women who attended family planning clinics for the first time that year were using the pill. Another study, carried out by Taylor Nelson Research in 1987, which studied the contraceptive habits of 1,061 women aged sixteen to forty-four, found that only 23 per cent were using the pill, though among young, single women aged eighteen to twenty-nine 41 per cent were using the pill.[2] The General Household Survey in 1986 found that about 23 per cent of women aged sixteen to forty-nine who were using contraception were using the pill.[3] Figures are not usually separated to show what proportion of women use the combined pill and which the progestogen-only pill.

Young people often choose the pill in preference to any other method. The Brook Advisory Clinics see predominantly young clients, the majority are under twenty. Interestingly, 80 per cent of these young women choose the pill as their method of birth-control. Brook Clinics pride themselves on the quality of the advice and information they offer – which should mean that these young women are making a real choice.

Safety

Doctors often tell women who go on the pill that to do so is safer than to become pregnant and have a baby. Somewhere in the region of ten women will die because they became pregnant, out of the 100,000 women who conceive in a year. Of the same number of under-thirty-six-year-old women who take the pill only five will die each year because of it. Women who are over thirty-five and women who smoke are in a slightly different category. For them a pregnancy would actually be safer than taking the pill. Ironically the risk of illness from smoking is much greater than the risks from the pill and yet many women are more afraid of their pills than their cigarettes. Deaths among pill-users are almost all due to cardiovascular diseases and smoking makes pill taking considerably more dangerous. It has been calculated that instead of five deaths per 100,000 women only 0.7 would die each year if no pill-user smoked and all were under thirty-five years old.[4] If you are interested in comparing the safety of the pill with other forms of contraception, see p. 92.

Reliability

The pill is the most reliable reversible method of contraception with a failure rate in the range of 0.2–1 pregnancy per 100 woman-years of use. As with any method of contraception this figure is accounted for by a combination of method-failures and use-failures. Method failures, where the pill lets you down despite taking it properly, are thought to be very rare. The ultra-low dose preparations with less than 30 μg of oestrogen are possibly slightly less reliable and a few studies have found that phasic pill preparations are also marginally more likely to fail. A recent study in the Netherlands suggested a significant increase in the risk of pregnancy in those using phasic pills, but many other studies have found pregnancy rates comparable to the 'ordinary' pill.[5] There is some evidence that very thin women are also at increased risk of pregnancy whilst using the pill because they tend to have lower blood levels of hormones while on the pill than women of average weight. The reason for this is unclear. Since ultra-low dose pills have been introduced, the margin of error in pill taking has been substantially decreased. This means that pregnancies are more likely in the case of forgotten pills, or after attacks of vomiting or diarrhoea, than they might have been with the higher-dose variety. Similarly there has been recent publicity about women who have become pregnant while taking the pill after having taken antibiotics prescribed by their GP. It is always a good idea to remind your doctor, if she gives you any prescription, that you are on the pill and ask if there is any possibility of an interaction which might affect the pill's reliability. Antibiotics, for example, reduce the pill's effectiveness by acting on the normal bacteria in the bowel which in turn reduces the pill's absorption. Appendix 1 gives a list of the most commonly used drugs and how they affect pill reliability. The section on how to take the pill has advice on what to do if you are taking a course of drugs.

The combined oral contraceptive pill

How it works

As we have already seen (p. 251), the pill is made up from a combination of hormones, oestrogens and progestogens, 'messenger' chemicals that occur naturally in plants and animals. Hormonal contraception works by fooling the body into reacting to hormones introduced from the outside, known technically as exogenous hormones. These exogenous hormones have to be very similar to the real thing so that they can trick the right organs into behaving in a way that inhibits fertility.

The way in which progestogens and oestrogens work to prevent pregnancy is relatively well understood, compared to the amount which is known about their actions on the rest of the body. Natural hormones have an influence all over the body, with minute amounts of the chemicals changing the functions of cells in many different parts of the body. Unfortunately the same is true of the exogenous hormones used in the pill and they do not restrict their actions only to the reproductive organs. It is no wonder that the addition of relatively large amounts of hormones to an otherwise finely balanced system leads to many alterations in the body's state and causes many side-effects.

The pill works by preventing ovulation. If your body does not ovulate then pregnancy is prevented 'at source'. Even if an egg did succeed in escaping the chances of a successful conception are greatly reduced due to various other changes that the pill causes in the reproductive organs. In Chapter 1 we saw how the normal ebb and flow of hormones involved in the menstrual cycle make ovulation happen. The FSH and LH released from the pituitary gland act on the ovary. The production of FSH and LH is directly affected by oestrogen and progesterone. In a woman taking the pill the blood levels of oestrogen and progestogen are high due to the extra hormones she is taking. These act on the pituitary gland, telling it to reduce the production of FSH to a minimum and preventing the surge of LH so that no ovarian follicles ripen and there is no release of an egg. Ovulation cannot take place. The hormonal state in pill takers is often said to be similar to that seen in pregnancy, because following fertilization oestrogen and progesterone are also produced in high levels, initially by the ovary and then by the placenta. This has the

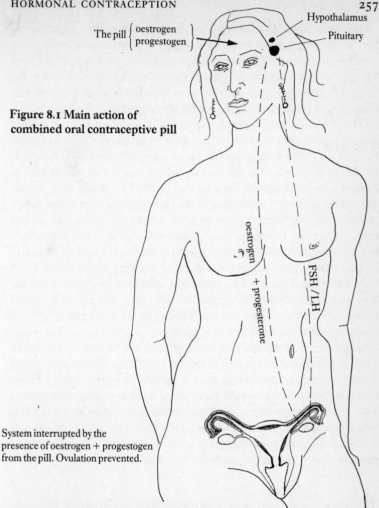

The pill { oestrogen progestogen

Hypothalamus

Pituitary

oestrogen + progesterone

FSH /LH

Figure 8.1 Main action of combined oral contraceptive pill

System interrupted by the presence of oestrogen + progestogen from the pill. Ovulation prevented.

same effect on the pituitary gland, telling it not to produce any of the hormones that might stimulate ovulation again.

Sometimes in women on the pill the level of extra hormones in the blood falls. If this happens the pituitary gland may step up the production of FSH sufficiently to produce a ripened follicle and even the release of an egg if the hormone levels remain low enough to allow a surge of LH. This is one explanation for pill failures. If you do not take your pill daily, or something interferes with its absorption, the levels of oestrogen and progestogen in your blood could fall. The exception to this is the seven-day break normally following the twenty-one days of pill taking. During these seven days the exogenous hormone levels fall and the levels of endogenous (natural) oestrogens (oestradiol) start to rise, but activity of the pituitary gland has been so dampened down by the preceeding twenty-one days of pill taking that it is unable to reach the critical level before the next packet of pills has been started. The level of hormones in the blood creeps back up to the protective levels needed to suppress the pituitary hormones. Figure 8.2 shows this pattern clearly.

The bleeding that occurs during the pill-free interval is not really a proper period since there have been no cyclical hormonal changes in the previous twenty-one days. When no more pills are taken, however, the fall in the levels of exogenous hormones mimics the fall in natural hormones seen at the end of a normal cycle. The imposed hormonal state of the first twenty-one days of the cycle produces a thin and rather different endometrium to that produced during a normal menstrual cycle. When the hormones fall off this lining is shed but produces a period which is less heavy and darker in colour than a normal period.

The effect of the pill on other parts of the reproductive tract is not fully understood but it seems likely that inhibiting ovulation is not the only way in which the pill works. We have seen that the endometrial lining of the womb is thin and less welcoming for the implantation of a developing embryo than that produced in a normal cycle. The progestogen element in the pill is thought to have two further contraceptive actions. Firstly it causes cervical cells to produce a thick mucus which is hostile to sperm, preventing them from swimming through the cervix and into the uterus. Secondly progestogens, and possibly oestrogen as well, may have some effect on the way in which the fallopian tubes work, upsetting the timing of the cycle so that even if an egg were released it would not be at the correct point of maturity when it reaches the part of the tube in which it would normally be fertilized.[6]

Types of combined oral contraceptives available in Britain

Monophasic pills
This type of COC is the most commonly used pill. They are produced in blister packs, each containing twenty-one tablets, and each tablet contains the same amount of oestrogen and progestogen.

Oestrogens used: ethinyloestradiol or mestranol (which is converted to
    ethinyloestradiol in the body)
Dose: 20, 30, 35 or 50 μg
Pills with 20 μg have a slightly increased risk of failure but the least
    likelihood of side-effects. Pills containing 50 μg are rarely used now

Figure 8.2 The pill-free week

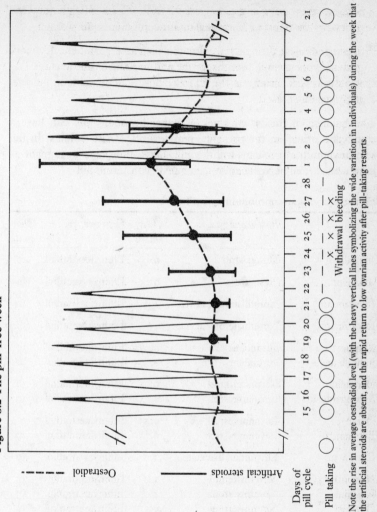

Days of
pill cycle

Pill taking

15 16 17 18 19 20 21 22 23 24 25 26 27 28 1 2 3 4 5 6 7 21

Withdrawal bleeding

Oestradiol

Artificial steroids

Note the rise in average oestradiol level (with the heavy vertical lines symbolizing the wide variation in individuals) during the week that the artificial steroids are absent, and the rapid return to low ovarian activity after pill-taking restarts.

Source: John Guillebaud, *Contraception: Your Questions Answered*, Churchill Livingstone, 1985.

because they carry a greater risk of side-effects though they are necessary for effective hormonal contraception in some women.

Progestogens used: desogestrel, ethnodiol diacetate, gestodene, levonorgestrol, lynoestrenol, norethisterone and norethisterone acetate.

Dose: this is very variable as the effective dose is dependent on the type of progestogen used.

The balance of these two types of hormone in the pill can have a significant effect on the presence and severity of side-effects. In the section on minor problems with the pill, suggestions have been made as to how these can be reduced by a change to a different pill.

Figure 8.3 Types of monophasic pill

	Progestogen type	Dose in mg	Oestrogen type	Dose in µg
Mercilon	Desogestrel	0.15	Ethinyloestradiol	20
Marvelon	Desogestrel	0.15	Ethinyloestradiol	30
Loestrin 20	Norethisterone acetate	1.0	Ethinyloestradiol	20
Loestrin 30	Norethisterone acetate	1.5	Ethinyloestradiol	30
Minulet	Gestodene	0.075	Ethinyloestradiol	30
Femodene	Gestodene	0.075	Ethinyloestradiol	30
Ovranette	Levonorgestrel	0.15	Ethinyloestradiol	30
Microgynon 30	Levonorgestrel	0.15	Ethinyloestradiol	30
Ovran 30	Levonorgestrel	0.25	Ethinyloestradiol	30
Eugynon 30	Levonorgestrel	0.25	Ethinyloestradiol	30
Conova 30	Ethynodiol diacetate	2.0	Ethinyloestradiol	30
Neocon 1/35	Norethisterone	1.0	Ethinyloestradiol	35
Norimin	Norethisterone	1.0	Ethinyloestradiol	35
Ovysmen	Norethisterone	0.5	Ethinyloestradiol	35
Brevinor	Norethisterone	0.5	Ethinyloestradiol	35
Ovran	Levonorgestrel	0.25	Ethinyloestradiol	50
Minilyn	Lynoestrenol	2.5	Ethinyloestradiol	50
Ortho-Novin 1/50	Norethisterone	1.0	Mestranol	50
Norinyl-1	Norethisterone	1.0	Mestranol	50

How to take monophasic pills

Starting pill taking
- Take first pill on day one of menstrual cycle

  or • Take first pill on day five of menstrual cycle

- Complete contraceptive protection immediately

  • Contraceptive protection not immediate, extra precautions are needed for the first seven days of pill taking

- Expect less than twenty-eight days from this period to your first pill withdrawal bleed

  • Expect a withdrawal bleed about when your next period was due

With either system some bleeding while taking the tablets from the first packet is quite common, but you should continue to the end of the pack anyway. Day 1 of the menstrual cycle is the first day of a period.

Day by day and month by month routine
- Take one tablet daily at about the same time each day
- Finish all twenty-one tablets
- Have seven pill-free days; sometime during this week you will have a withdrawal bleed
- Take the first pill from the next pack on the same day of the week as you took the first pill of the first pack. You must take the pill on this day without fail even if you still have some bleeding
- And so on, and so on . . .

The pill-free week
The number of days in the break is *critical* and anything which lengthens this leaves you at risk of pregnancy.
It is very important to:

- be careful to take the last few pills of each pack properly
- start the new pack on the correct day and take the early pills reliably

This is not meant to imply that erratic pill-taking for the rest of the pack is safe, but to emphasize the importance of pills which are often forgotten.

Missed pills

Less than twelve hours late:
- take missed pill as soon as you remember
- continue as normal

More than twelve hours late:
- take missed pill as well as your normal pill
- continue regular pill taking
- use a barrier method or abstain for seven days
- if the seven days include any of the pill-free week start a new pack of pills immediately with no gap at all (this will mean that your 'period' will be delayed until the end of the second pack)

Other problems

If you have vomiting or very severe diarrhoea the pill may not work, so carry on with the pill but use a barrier method as well for the duration of the illness, for seven days after that and then follow the advice on missed pills.

Certain drugs reduce the pill's effectiveness, including some common drugs like antibiotics. If your doctor gives you these remind her that you are on the pill. The general rule is to carry on with the pills but use extra precautions for the duration of the course of tablets, for seven days after this and then follow the missed pill rules. Appendix 1 has a list of some common drugs and how they interact with the pill.

Delaying the pill-free week

If you want to delay your 'period' then you can simply start a new pack immediately you finish the last, leaving no pill-free gap. You then have the choice of whether to take some, or all, of the second pack. The only thing to be careful of is that you have at least twenty-one days of pill taking before having your pill-free week (so don't use half packs). The pill-free week allows your body to recover from the changes imposed on it by the pill, and the twenty-one days on and seven days off the pill mean you take as little hormone as possible for daily protection. It is therefore important not to miss the pill-free week too often.

Triphasic pills

These contain the same hormones as the monophasic pills. The difference lies in the dose of hormone in each tablet. There are pills of three different formulas in the same pack which are usually made in different colours for the sake of clarity.

In some triphasic pills the oestrogen dose is the same in each tablet, while in others there are two different oestrogen strengths. The amount of progestogen in the tablets of each pack increases in three steps.

The advantage of this type of pill is that the total progestogen dose is lower than with a conventional pill, which may help to reduce side-effects. They were developed to mimic more closely the hormonal profile of a normal menstrual cycle. The extent to which this has been achieved is debatable, but triphasics do offer low-dose, reliable contraception with little break-through bleeding. There is also some evidence that there are fewer metabolic disturbances with this type of pill which could be significant for long-term side-effects. (Biphasic pills are rarely used. They are very similar to the triphasics except that there are only two different formulations of pill in each pack.)

Figure 8.4   Types of biphasic and triphasic pills

	Progestogen type	Dose in mg	Oestrogen type	Dose in µg	Number of tablets
Binovum	Norethisterone	0.5	Ethinyloestradiol	35	7
	Norethisterone	1.0	Ethinyloestradiol	35	14
Trinovum	Norethisterone	0.5	Ethinyloestradiol	35	7
	Norethisterone	0.75	Ethinyloestradiol	35	7
	Norethisterone	1.0	Ethinyloestradiol	35	7
Synaphase	Norethisterone	0.5	Ethinyloestradiol	35	7
	Norethisterone	1.0	Ethinyloestradiol	35	9
	Norethisterone	0.5	Ethinyloestradiol	35	5
Logynon	Levonorgestrel	0.05	Ethinyloestradiol	30	6
	Levonorgestrel	0.075	Ethinyloestradiol	40	5
	Levonorgestrel	0.125	Ethinyloestradiol	30	10
Logynon ED.	As Logynon with 7 inactive tablets				
Trinordiol	Levonorgestrel	0.05	Ethinyloestradiol	30	6
	Levonorgestrel	0.075	Ethinyloestradiol	40	5
	Levonorgestrel	0.125	Ethinyloestradiol	30	10

How to take triphasic pills

> Refer to the instructions for monophasics for most advice; in addition:
> Starting pill taking
> - start the pack on day one of your menstrual cycle
> - no extra precautions needed
>
> Day by day month by month routine
> - see monophasics *but*
> - you will need to remember to take the three groups of different dose pills in the right order
>
> Missed pills
> - see monophasic pill
>
> Delaying the pill-free week
> - you can delay this by seven to ten days by taking the last group of tablets from a new pack of pills (discard the rest)
> - you could ask your doctor for a packet of monophasic pills which are at a dose equivalent to the pills in the last group of tablets in your triphasic pack. This way you can delay your period for up to twenty-one days

Every day (ED) pills

These are identical to the other combined pills but they are packaged with seven dummy pills. The seven inactive tablets are taken after the twenty-one active tablets and are instead of the pill-free week. The advantage is that there is no need to remember to restart pill-taking; however, the pills must be taken in the right sequence or there will be a loss of effectiveness. Follow the manufacturer's instructions carefully for details on taking these pills.

> REMEMBER: there is still a slight risk of pregnancy while taking the pill, especially if the hormones in the blood drop below a critical level. This level is not reached in the pill-free week so long as it is preceded by twenty-one days of consistent pill taking. Changing types of pill could leave you vulnerable if the second type of pill is of a lower dose (including triphasics) than the type you were on. In these circumstances the new pills should be started with no seven-day gap between packets.
>
> Finally, lif you think you have taken a risk then you can take the 'morning after pill' as long as it is within seventy-two hours of the risky episode.

Side-effects of the combined pill

In order to prevent a pregnancy successfully the hormones in the pill have to be absorbed into the bloodstream. Unfortunately once in the blood stream they do not just travel to the pituitary gland and reproductive organs where they do their main work, but all over the body where they affect many different cells. Quite how is difficult to predict, especially as the actions of even the natural hormones that they imitate are not fully understood. Moreover, the exogenous hormones upset the production of the natural ones. It should come as no surprise, then, that these relatively powerful drugs have all sorts of effects which are unrelated to their contraceptive role. By no means all of these are bad, though publicity about the pill tends to emphasize the negative rather than the positive ones.

It is extraordinary that much of what is written about the human body implies that, despite the infinite variations of people's outsides, their inner workings are all pretty identical. The fact is of course that we are just as individual inside as out. The differences are important when we realize that the effects of any drug, treatment or disease will be subtly different from person to person. It has been found, for example, that the levels of active hormone in the blood after taking the same combined pill can vary as much as ten-fold between individual women. This is due in part to differences in absorption from the stomach and in the time taken to eliminate the drug from the system. It follows that while using the same drug some women may be taking an unnecessarily high dose while others may be running the risk of a pill failure. Luckily most of us probably fall somewhere in the middle. The measurement of blood levels still only offers a crude estimation of the hormones' inpact, and tells us nothing about its effect on different cells.

Long-term studies which record all the ill-health of women using the pill and compare it with that of similar non-pill users are one of the most satisfactory ways of analysing the pill's effects on women's general health. There are three major 'prospective' studies of this sort. In 1968 the Royal College of General Practitioners (RCGP) set up a study of 23,000 pill-users and a similar number of non-users. In the same year Martin Vessey set up a study in Oxford in collaboration with the Family Planning Association (the Oxford/FPA study) to look at a whole range of methods of contraception. In the USA a similar project began in 1968 which is known as the Walnut Creek Study. All the groups involved with this type of study publish their findings intermittently. The really long-term effects of the pill (if there are any) are still waiting to be analysed in the future. Unfortunately in Britain financial problems are putting the existing trials at risk.

Major side-effects

The vast majority of women who 'go on the pill' experience no more than a few minor and annoying side-effects. We have included this section on major side-effects, however, because we feel women should be well informed about any risks they run, even if these risks are small. We were surprised by the number of letters that we received from women who *had* experienced significant side-effects such as venous thrombosis and pulmonary embolism. The majority of these women commented on the fact that they had not realized that it was their pill-taking that had exacerbated the risk.

Cardiovascular disease

The risk of some diseases of both heart and blood vessels seem to be increased in women who are on the pill, and the development of a thrombosis is important in most of these problems. A thrombosis is the formation of a blood clot within a blood vessel which can lead to the blockage of the vein or artery. The blood contains substances which both help it to clot when necessary and prevent it from clotting at other times. Any change in the body's chemicals such as those caused by taking the pill can upset this finely held balance and lead to unwanted clot formation.

Venous thrombosis (clots in the veins)   One of the most significant types of thrombosis occurs in the deep veins of the lower leg and is known as a deep vein thrombosis or venous thrombosis. It causes pain and swelling:

In 1971 I decided to take the pill which I took until Easter 1972. At that time we were on holiday and I thought despite my precautions one leg had been badly sunburnt; it was hot, swollen and painful. It wasn't until I returned to our doctor to tell him I'd decided to stop taking the pill and try for another baby that he told me I'd had a thrombosis in my leg . . .

Thrombosis can be treated with drugs that decrease blood clotting. The danger of such a clot is that a small part of it may break off and become lodged in the lung, causing chest pain, shortness of breath and bloody sputum. This condition is known as pulmonary embolism, and can be fatal. Venous thrombosis is more common in overweight people, those who are bed-bound and those with leg injuries. Pill takers are also at a greater risk of venous thrombosis, and it is the oestrogen that seems to be responsible. Oestrogen increases the blood factors which lead to clot formation and decreases those which dissolve clots. It also has an effect on the platelets which are responsible for initiating clot formation. Moreover it is thought that oestrogen may have an effect on the structure of vein walls, on blood flow and on immune factors.

Most of the material on venous thrombosis available to date is based on women who developed thrombosis while taking the old-style pills, with between 50 and 150 μg of oestrogen. Most results from those studies estimated the risk as about two to six times higher than among non-users, beginning about a month after starting the pill and stopping about one month after finishing taking the pill. Among women taking the newer ultra-low-dose pills the risk is almost certainly considerably lower. Different women seem to have different predispositions to venous thrombosis. Women whose mothers or sisters have had the condition are at increased risk, as are women who have had the condition before going on the pill. Women with group A blood appear to have a greater likelihood of developing a thrombosis than women with blood groups B and O. Being blood group O seems actually to offer some protection from the disease.[7]

Disease of the arteries   If a clot develops in an artery it is known as arterial thrombosis. One of the main causes is the process of atherosclerosis, which is the hardening and encrustation of the inside surface of the artery. This condition is believed to be related to the amount and type of fat circulating in the blood. Fat in the blood stream is transported in many different forms, but two of the most important are high density lipoproteins (HDLs) and low density lipoproteins (LDLs). Both are partly fat and partly protein, but they differ from each other in that the LDLs have a higher fat content and tend to lay down fat in the arteries, leading to atherosclerosis, while the HDLs act as scavengers, collecting fat as it circulates in the blood, and protecting the arteries. The significance of the pill in all this is that it affects the levels of these circulating blood fats. Oestrogens seem to increase the level of HDLs whereas progestogens decrease them. The combined activity of these two hormones may alter the ratio of the two lipoproteins which could result in the accelerated formation of atherosclerosis seen in some pill users.[8]

Several factors might further predispose a woman to arterial disease if she were also on the pill. Raised blood pressure, untreated diabetes, obesity and several rare diseases which have an effect on the liproproteins of the blood could do this. The risks may also be increased by heavy cigarette smoking. Considerable research has been done on smoking, arterial disease and the pill and though the results are not conclusive, several studies suggest that smoking and being on the pill have a synergistic action, that is, they create a greater risk of atherosclerosis than would have been the case if the risks of the two on their own were simply added together.[9] The health risks of smoking are well publicized in the West, and it is probably partly for this reason that more emphasis is given to the most pessimistic of the studies done. It is useful to bear in mind that with increasing age atherosclerosis is present in most adults. This is one reason why women over thirty-five are not often prescribed the combined pill. It has been estimated that heavy smoking adds five to ten years to a woman's age in terms of her risk of arterial disease – a sobering thought.

Pill manufacturers are trying hard to develop a balance in the hormones of the combined pill which would minimize the risk of developing atherosclerosis. Some studies show that the triphasic formulations of the pill do not upset the lipoprotein balance. The manufacturers of three recently developed progestogens, desogestrel, gestodene and norgestinate, claim that these have little or no effect on the lipid profile in the blood. Ken Fotherby's work shows that different progestogens do have varying effects on HDL levels. This may offer hope for a safer pill in the future.[10]

Heart attacks   These can be caused by thrombosis in the coronary arteries which supply the heart which leads to the death of part of the heart muscle. The pill may increase the risk of a heart attack in a pill-user by the processes of clot formation and atherosclerosis described above. Heart attacks are extremely rare in young women, pill takers or not, but it has been estimated that the risk for a pill-user is two to four times the risk for a non-user. Studies have calculated the absolute risk and produced results of 0.05–0.57 per 1,000 pill-users per year. An increased risk of heart attack seems to be present only while you actually take the pill. It is also not very clear whether or not the chance of having a heart attack increases with the length of time that the pill is used.[11]

Strokes   Strokes are usually associated with the elderly and classically manifest themselves as an inability to move on one side of the body and an inability to speak. A stroke is the result of the death of a part of the brain, and can be caused by a number of factors, one of them being an arterial thrombosis. It is currently estimated that the risk of this kind of stroke is increased by a factor of about seven in pill-users.[12] Haemorrhagic strokes, caused by bleeding into the brain tissue, are about twice as common in pill-users as women of the same age who do not use the pill. The combined effect of smoking and taking the pill is less clear, but it seems likely that smoking increases the chance of a haemorrhagic stroke but not of the thrombotic type of stroke.[13]

Blood pressure   The combined pill increases the blood pressure of most of the women who use it. In the majority of the women who take the pill this is no particular cause for concern since the blood pressure remains well within healthy limits, but there are other women who seem to be particularly sensitive to the effects of the pill and develop a significant increase in their blood pressure. Stopping the pill almost always results in a return to the previous level. Unfortunately, raised BP does not usually give any symptoms but the risk of developing almost all the diseases of the heart and blood vessels mentioned above is increased by raised blood pressure. The reason for the increase is not fully understood. The best treatment is preventative, and regular blood pressure testing is essential for any woman on the pill.

The combined contraceptive pill and cancer

Cancer has become one of the most feared words in the English language and any indication that a certain drug or environmental pollutant could increase the risk of cancer is followed by a flurry of studies and debate. There is certainly no shortage of publications on the link between the pill and various cancers. Between 1977 and 1980, 3,735 papers were published about oral contraceptives and cancer and the flow of data continues unabated. Unfortunately the poor understanding which we have of the causes of cancer makes any work in this field difficult to carry out. Moreover the length of time that may elapse between exposure to a carcinogen and the detection of the disease adds to the research problems. None the less certain trends have emerged from the data to date and this section will look at them briefly. Since oestrogen and progestogen apparently have their greatest effects on the cells of the breast and of the reproductive tract, it is on these organs that most attention has been focused.

Cancer of the breast   Breast cancer is the commonest cancer among women in the West. Each year 24,500 women in the UK develop a tumour and 15,000 die of the disease. The causes of breast cancer are complex and it seems probable that there is more than one form of the disease. A number of risk factors have been established, such as another family member who has had the disease, an early onset of menstruation, late menopause and late first pregnancy. The risk of breast cancer also seems to increase among women who have had 'benign breast disease', where lumps and cysts develop in the breast which are not themselves cancerous. Hormones are thought to play a part in at least one form of breast cancer, though their exact role is still unclear. Progestogens, for example, reduce the risk of benign breast disease which would logically appear to lower the risk of breast cancer. Trying to draw conclusions from the complex tangle of hormones, breast cancer and benign breast disease is not at all easy.

Some of the earliest work on the pill and breast cancer was done using beagle dogs and monkeys; both developed higher rates of breast cancer than animals not taking hormones.[14] However, extrapolating from animal work to humans needs considerable caution. Beagle bitches are anyway extremely prone to developing breast tumours and many laboratory monkeys are caught in the wild and their age and past life make it difficult to draw sound conclusions. However it was this animal work that led to a heightened awareness of a possible risk to women taking the pill and various studies were initiated. One of the first important studies published in 1972 (Vessey, Doll and Sutton) showed that there was no increase in breast cancer and that in fact the pill protected against benign breast disease.[15]

In 1979 a study in the USA (Paffenburger) found an increased risk of breast cancer in women who had taken the pill for two years or more, particularly if this use was before their first pregnancy. Paffenburger's results were questioned and more studies carried out with generally reassuring results.[16] In 1981, however, another pill scare broke. This was the result of an American study by Pike which implicated the pill in breast cancer in women who had used the pill for more than four years or before a first pregnancy. Further results published in 1983 emphasized the increased risk run by women who used the pill before the age of twenty-five.[17] This was the big pill scare of 1983 when the story was published as front page headlines in most British newspapers but not published in the *Lancet* until the following day. The handling of the whole affair was unfortunate though it served the purpose of giving widespread coverage to the possibility of a link. As with the whole saga of the pill and breast cancer, Pike's material was followed with an avalanche of further papers refuting and questioning his findings. In 1986 the results of a large Swedish study conducted by Meirik were published. He found a doubling of the risk of breast cancer in those who used the pill for more than twelve years or for those who used it for eight years prior to their first full-term pregnancy.[18] In 1987 another paper from the Oxford/FPA study found a risk of breast cancer 2.5 times greater in women who had used the pill for four years or longer prior to their first pregnancy.[19] The most recent study (Pike, Chilvers, Peto, McPherson and Vessey) maintaining a link was published in early 1989. Since this is the latest pill scare it is worth looking at its findings in more detail.

The study involved 755 women diagnosed with breast cancer before thirty-six years of age and a similar number of healthy controls. It was found that among women who had taken the pill for four to eight years the risk of developing breast cancer before the age of thirty-six years was 40 per cent greater than normal, and among women who had taken the pill for more than eight years the risk rose to 70 per cent. In terms of actual numbers, the risk of developing breast cancer among non-pill-taking women under thirty-six is about one in 500. Among the pill-taking women in this study the risk rose to one in 300. The study concluded that about 20 per cent of the breast cancers in younger women could be attributable to the pill. While this data is worrying, it is also the case that most of the pill-taking women who developed a tumour in this study had been using one of the high-dose oestrogen pills available in the 60s and 70s, whereas 95 per cent of current combined pill-users take low-dose pills. The study estimates that among women taking low-dose pills the risk of developing breast cancer before thirty-six rises to about one in 400.[20]

Although the truth about breast cancer and the pill is still unclear, there is a fairly uniform view that the overall figures are reassuring and do not show an increase in breast cancer in all pill-users. Commenting on the latest pill scare, John Guillebaud maintained that the 'jury is still out', though he also suggested that the time might have come when GPs should at least raise the issue of breast cancer with women who request the pill.[21] Perhaps most worrying is that the risks of breast cancer seem greater for women who are under twenty-five when they begin the pill, and women who use it before their first pregnancy, since this is precisely the group who are most likely to be using the pill. Quite why it should have an effect here in particular is not fully known, but one explanation is that there is usually a period of time immediately after the onset of menstruation where there are relatively low levels of progestogen and oestrogen. Taking extra hormones at this point may be more damaging than later in life. It is also worth bearing in mind that the pill enables women to delay their first pregnancy successfully for as long as they wish. This means that many women move into a higher risk group for breast cancer simply by this delay.

The risk of breast cancer in relation to the pill at the other end of menstrual life is less well studied. Women who take the pill between twenty-five and thirty-five may even have a decreased risk of breast cancer due to changes in their hormonal milieu which are in fact favourable to them. More work needs to be done on age-specific risks for breast cancer and on the long-term effects of the newer low-dose pills before we can say for sure.

As we write, there are reports that the pill may perhaps be able to protect women from breast cancer. It seems that there is some promising early work which indicates that the progestogen gestodene stops the growth of breast cancer cells *in vitro*. Time will tell if this really is of any significance for breast cancer prevention.

Cancer of the cervix   About 50 per 100,000 of British women develop invasive cancer of the cervix each year. It is thought to be related to infection, with the papilloma or wart virus being the most likely source, probably picked up from a sexual partner. The disease seems to be more common in women who have their first sexual encounter at a young age and who have a number of partners. Fortunately the full-blown form of the disease can be prevented by regular cervical smears which detect pre-cancerous changes in the cervix and can be treated.

The link between pill taking and cervical cancer is by no means proven. While there are a number of studies that are broadly reassuring, there are also a significant number which do indicate that the pill increases the risk of cervical cancer.[22] Some of the earlier studies that were carried out were distorted by the fact that they compared pill-users with women who used barrier methods of contraception which may offer significant protection against cervical cancer. Moreover many studies partially or totally ignored questions of sexual practice in the women they studied, which may be one of the most significant predisposing factors in the development of the disease. Cigarette smoking may also have some effect on the risk of getting cervical cancer. Studies in the last few years have been careful to try and exclude any such factors that might bias the results and some of these have been reassuring.[23] Less reassuring however was the Oxford/FPA study. They published a paper in 1983 which concluded that there *was* an increased risk of pre-cancer and established cancer in pill-users.[24] Similarly, in 1988 the Royal College of General Practioners published a report which concluded that women who had ever used the pill had a significantly higher risk of cervical cancer than never-users. Women who used the pill for more than ten years had a risk of cervical cancer four times greater than never-users. However a recent epidemiological review of a number of studies concluded that the risk of cervical cancer in pill-users after ten years of pill use is only twice that seen in non-users.[25]

No doubt the debate will continue for a long time to come. If, as seems possible, the pill does increase the risk of cervical cancer, the likelihood of actually developing cancer can be greatly reduced by appropriate screening. All the long-term studies include women who have taken the old, high-dose pills and it remains to be seen what effect the ultra-low-dose level pills will have on the statistics.

Cancer of the endometrium and cancer of the ovary   The vast majority of cancers of the endometrium and ovary are in older women. An estimated 4,000 women die each year from ovarian cancer and just over 1,100 from cancer of the endometrium. Since both the ovary and the lining of the uterus are affected by sex hormones, they are potential candidates for cancers related to the hormones in the pill. Extensive studies have shown however that the risk of developing either cancer is significantly reduced among women who take the pill, and that this protective effect may last for at least ten years following pill use.[26]

The reduced risk of endometrial cancer as a result of taking the pill has been estimated as being as much as 60 per cent compared to never-users. This degree of protection takes about four years of pill use to develop, but even one year of pill use reduces the risk of endometrial cancer by 20 per cent. Ovarian cancer is difficult to diagnose, is often found late on in the disease and is very resistant to treatment. Studies show that women who have ever used the pill have a significantly lower risk of developing this cancer and that the protective effect increases with increasing duration of pill use. Estimates of the reduction of risk range from 30 to 80 per cent.[27]

The good news about the protective effects of the pill seem to have come under less intense scrutiny than the bad news of the possible increase in the risk of cancers of the cervix and breast. On the other hand, to make equations between the risks of a cancer on one hand and the protection from cancer on the other is not entirely valid. If a woman develops a cancer in which the pill may have played a part, it is very faint comfort for her to know that she had a lower risk of another tumour.

Other cancers   There are various cancers in other parts of the body that have been linked with the pill.

Hepatocellular adenomas is a benign liver tumour which can cause severe illness and even death. Though very rare, such tumours are thought to be very slightly more common in women who have used the pill than never-users, though the risk even as a pill-user is still less than one in a million.

Trophoblastic disease is a very strange condition which can become cancerous. It begins with the apparent onset of a pregnancy, though no embryo develops. Instead the uterus fills up with soft grape-like material known as a hydatidiform mole, which in time begins to bleed and an ultra sound scan reveals the fact that the pregnancy has not developed normally. A minor operation known as a D and C (dilation and curettage), is always necessary. This entails the gentle dilation of the cervix and the scraping out of the contents and endometrial lining of the uterus, which is usually performed under a general anaesthetic. After a short time the hormones in the blood (βhCG) which are detectable in a pregnancy test return to normal. If the hormone levels do not return to normal it indicates that choriocarcinoma, a type of cancer, has formed. This is usually successfully treated. The pill does not cause the development of a hydatidiform mole but women who have had this condition and who then take the pill before the βhCG reading is normal have a considerably greater risk of developing choriocarcinoma.

Other unwanted effects

The hormones of the pill have an effect on the cells of the liver which change the levels of many of blood-borne chemicals. The body is designed to compensate for this type of change and there are many biochemical actions which have been detected in women taking the pill but which as far as we know do not lead to disease. The influence of the pill on the body's handling of glucose is an example. Definite changes occur but despite persistent study no increase in the risk of diabetes in pill-users has been found. Diabetics may find control of their disease more difficult on the pill and should only use it with the help of a doctor.

Gall bladder disease   The reason for an increase in the risk of gall bladder disease in pill-users is not clear. Stones form in the gall bladder and tend to be made of fatty substances. It may be that the changes caused in the handling of fats by the pill are responsible for this. Some authorities think that the pill simply accelerates the development of gall stones in women who may have been prone to their formation at an older age.

In 1986 I stopped taking the pill in preparation for a cholecystectomy [removal of gall bladder]. I was only twenty-five years old and had three very large gall stones.

Vitamins   The handling of vitamins is altered by the pill, although the significance of this is poorly understood. Women with a low nutritional status, as may be seen in the developing world, do not seem to suffer any problems related to vitamin deficiency as a result of oral contraceptives. This crude observation is generally reassuring and it is thought that vitamin supplements are not necessary for most pill-users, but that a varied and healthy diet should be sufficient to maintain good health.

The measurement of the amount of an individual vitamin in the blood does not necessarily give a true picture of the amount of that vitamin available to the body, as the pill can change the storage of these (and many other) substances. It has been found that some women who become depressed while on the pill improve with supplements of vitamin B6 (pyridoxine). It seems that in this group of women the lowering of the body's vitamin B6 by the pill is significant to their health.

Vitamin C has a complex relationship with the pill. The blood levels of this vitamin are lowered by the pill. The blood level of oestrogen in pill-users is increased by vitamin C because of its effect on absorption in the gut. Women who take large amounts of vitamin C are effectively increasing the dose of their pill which, in theory, increases the likelihood of side-effects.

The level of folic acid in the body is lowered in pill takers. This may be of significance in women who become pregnant immediately after stopping the pill as there is some evidence that this may increase the very slight chance of having a baby with a neural tube defect. It is advisable to take folic acid supplements under these circumstances.

The levels of vitamins A and K are increased by the pill, while the levels of vitamins B12 and B2 are probably decreased. The significance of these findings is not known. The way in which excessive vitamin C supplements have a potentially harmful effect demonstrates that these changes should not be viewed in a simplistic way.[28]

Annoying side-effects

In this section we will look at the various annoying side-effects which have been attributed to the pill. They are usually genuine effects of the exogenous hormones that have been taken. Almost all of them lessen with time as the body adapts. Persevering for three months will often be rewarded with the resolution of the problem. The question of how many unwanted side-effects you can tolerate is a very individual issue. The role that the pill plays in the lives of different women differs considerably and may partially account for the differences in tolerance, though we have already seen there is a sound physiological basis for different effects on different women. A woman with four children and an unsupportive husband may be desperate not to get pregnant again and willing to put up with some problems. On the other hand, a woman who feels as if she has been coerced into taking the pill either by her doctor or partner may find that the problems arising while taking the pill are intolerable.

I started taking the pill later than most women I suppose, I don't know why I stuck with it then. I felt bloated and fat and I ached all over. In the first few months I was moody and spotty – I am surprised that anyone put up with me. It was like adolescence all over again.

In the following section, symptoms that may be improved by an oestrogen-dominant pill are marked * and those that may be improved by a progestogen-dominant pill are marked †.

Nausea† is a fairly common problem and can lead to vomiting in some women. On the whole the ultra-low-dose pills help to reduce this to a minimum and as our correspondent below found out, it usually improves with time. It is not really understood what causes the nausea, though in early pregnancy the heightened levels of hormone often produce the same effect.

I began taking the pill just a week before my wedding and felt so sick that I thought I would either have to cancel the wedding or stop the pill immediately. It was miserable. Miraculously on my wedding day itself I was fine, and the nausea definitely began to lessen with time.

Weight gain is a very common complaint among pill-users and is often accompanied by a bloated feeling. Some of the effects can be blamed on water retention†, which will tend to go away in the pill-free week, and will lessen with time. Other women experience real weight gain* which is related to an increase in appetite stimulated by the hormones in some pills. The problem may be improved by changing the pill, though some women find that they have to stop the pill altogether, or change their eating habits.

Breast enlargement† is a common effect which some women find disturbing and uncomfortable and others welcome. The change is usually slight and rarely continues after the second month on the pill. A different pill may help.

Breast tenderness† is less frequently seen and is usually absent in the pill-free week as it is often associated with fluid retention. Women who suffered with pre-menstrual breast tenderness before using the pill may find an improvement once established on the pill.

Headaches are quite commonly experienced by pill-users, particularly during the pill-free week, but it is important to talk to a doctor to sort them out. They are most often similar to a normal generalized headache, and usually helped by simple painkillers. If this fails, reducing the length of the pill-free week may be the solution though you should discuss this with your doctor. Anyone who develops migraine whilst on the pill or who experiences focal or severe headaches may be at risk of something more serious and should see a doctor. Migraine sufferers who use the pill should report any changes in their pattern of attack.

Dizziness† is a non-specific symptom which some women suffer while on the pill. This may decrease with time or be improved on a different pill.

*Depression** is less often seen with the low-dose pills, but it is still more common in pill-users than non-users. This may be partly related to aspects of lifestyle, but is almost certainly an effect caused by the hormones as well. Some women find that the pill relieves them of the anxiety of getting pregnant and without this burden they feel less depressed. In some women it may be resentment against the pill and its side-effects that depresses them. There may be resentment towards doctors, partners and society for the pressure to use the pill. One obvious solution is to stop taking the pill. Women who are depressed but keen to continue with the pill may be helped by taking 50 mg pyridoxine (vitamin B6) daily although it may take up to two months to improve the situation. Women with a history of severe depression may be advised against using the pill although, ironically for some women, pregnancy is also a cause of serious depression. The alternative method of contraception will need to be chosen carefully.

*Changes in libido** are sometimes experienced by pill takers. Some women find the release from the threat of pregnancy a liberating experience and enjoy sex more. Others find that despite the apparent freedom offered by the pill and the pleasures of a contraceptive method independent from intercourse, they have a decreased libido. This may be related to depression or other pill side-effects such as vaginal dryness, but there can also be a direct hormonal effect. Changing pill to an oestrogen-dominant pill may help.

I asked the doctor at the family planning clinic if there was any chance that the pill was having an effect on my libido. He said it was more likely to be time to change partners . . .

There is a possibility that decreased libido suffered by pill users may be due to the psychosexual effect of a very safe contraceptive method. Sex without possibility of pregnancy may seem to divorce intercourse too far from one of its original intentions – procreation. This is an important but little understood aspect of highly effective methods, including sterilization.

Pre-menstrual symptoms† Some women find that the symptoms such as irritability, mood swings, breast tenderness and swollen ankles which occur in the days running up to a period, are improved when their normal menstrual cycle is abolished. Other women find that there is no change and some develop PMT (pre-menstrual tension) for the first time when they start the pill. Once again the answer may lie in the exact composition of the pill, with symptoms tending to be worse on an oestrogen-dominant pill and with the phased pill. Juggling the formulation may help.

Cystitis is more common in pill-users and though this can usually be sorted out by taking a course of antibiotics, some women find that recurrences lead them to give up the pill. It is not really understood what causes more bouts of cystitis in pill-users. Some evidence suggests that a slight alteration in immunity may be responsible.

Vaginal infection Despite conflicting scientific evidence it does seem that candidiasis, or thrush, is more common in women on the pill. This condition, characterized by very itchy white cheesy discharge, can be a complete misery, especially as it tends to occur again and again. There is effective treatment in the form of vaginal pessaries and cream, or oral treatment by tablets which should get rid of any one episode but will not prevent its return. Some women who get repeated infections find natural yogurt on a tampon effective and more 'natural' – or at least a soothing temporary measure before they can see a doctor. The yoghurt helps to restore the acidity of the vagina and makes it less easy for the candida to grow. The other way of reducing attacks is to make sure that your partner is treated at the same time. He will have to wash thoroughly and use the cream on his penis for two or three days. Although thrush is not a sexually transmitted disease as such, men often carry the spore and particles of the candida yeast on their genitals. Despite having no symptoms themselves they will reintroduce the problem next time you make love.

The pill seems to offer some protection against vaginal infection caused by trichomonas vaginalis.

Pelvic infection There is some evidence that infection by the organism chlamydia trachomatis may be encouraged by taking the pill. If this is in fact the case it could be highly significant since infection by this organism is currently the most prevalent type of sexually transmitted disease. If it goes unrecognized and untreated, it can cause severe tubal damage which may affect subsequent fertility.

Vaginal discharge Some women get an increase† in vaginal discharge while on the pill. If this is white and inoffensive and simply an increase in normal discharge it is not usually a major problem and can either be ignored or improved by a change to a progestogen-dominant pill. Occasionally the discharge may be associated with a cervical erosion, the unnecessarily alarmist name given to changes sometimes seen particularly on the cervices of pregnant women and pill takers. An 'erosion' is where the lining of the cervical canal pouts out into the visible part of the cervix creating a slightly pinkish appearance. These lining cells produce mucus, hence the increase in discharge. Since they are also delicate they may sometimes bleed a little. It is essential to get any unexpected bleeding checked out even if you know you have an erosion.

Erosions can be treated if necessary by a process known as freezing. This is a quick, relatively painless procedure done in the out patients' department.

Some women experience a decrease* in vaginal secretions and complain of dryness. This may be helped either by the use of a lubricant during intercourse or by trying a different pill.

Irregular bleeding As discussed above the bleeding seen during the pill-free week is not a 'real' period and is generally much lighter and less painful than menstruation. In some women there is minimal or even no bleeding between pill packs. So long as there is no question of a pregnancy this is of no real importance. It simply means that the hormones are being particularly successful in reducing the endometrium to a minimum. If you do ever experience an absence of bleeding between pill packets it is important to have a pregnancy test.

Some women experience break-through* bleeding while taking the pill, especially in the first three months. In the majority this settles but some women may need to change the type of pill they are using. The use of the triphasic pill can solve the problem. Some doctors think that persistent break-through bleeding may be an indication that you have consistently low hormone levels in the blood. It may be due to erratic pill taking, or may be an indication that your body is too efficient in clearing the blood of hormones. In which case, if you are a regular pill taker, it may be appropriate to use a higher-dose pill. The levels that remain in your body will be no higher than the levels in a woman on a lower-dose pill with a more sluggish metabolism, but will be sufficient to give reliable contraception.

Skin problems Some women who find that their skin is sensitive to the changes of hormones in their menstrual cycle may also find that their skin reacts to the hormones of the pill. Their skin may become greasy* and spotty and some women may even notice a slight increase in body hair. Other women will find that their problem skin improves and a few women are even prescribed the pill more for its positive effects on the skin rather than its contraceptive effect.

Occasionally the pill causes a butterfly-like area of light brown pigmentation on the face. This is called chloasma and is the same as the 'mask of pregnancy' which some women develop during pregnancy. It is more common in women with darker skins and will fade slowly when the pill is stopped but may never completely disappear. The progestogen-only pill may be less likely to cause this problem, but for some women non-hormonal contraception is the only answer. The pill also predisposes some women to light sensitivity which may show up as rashes, while scalp hair loss is another unfortunate side-effect experienced by some pill takers.

Eye problems Contact lens wearers occasionally experience difficulty while on the pill. It is thought that this is due to a slight accumulation of fluid in the eye. Refitting may help but some women have to choose between the pill and contact lenses:

At the time I started the pill I had just been fitted for a new pair of contact lenses (hard) and began to experience extreme discomfort in wearing them – so much so that I found it impossible to wear them. Even when they were not in my eyes itched constantly . . . I didn't connect the pill with my problems and my doctor didn't suggest this as a possible cause when I visited him again. I felt rather foolish.

Leg pains may be serious and indicate that a deep vein thrombosis is forming in the leg, a potentially lethal side-effect of the pill. More often it will be a case of the aching legs or odd sensations which many women develop on the pill and which seem to have no serious consequences. It is very important to get medical advice, which will probably be reassuring. The aching may settle with time:

I took the pill on and off from about the age of eighteen but towards the end of 1985 I found that I experienced numbness in my calves and feet. As I found this rather alarming I discontinued taking the pill.

Despite this formidable list of problems, many women suffer no side-effects on the pill at all. Those who do have difficulties should see their family planning doctor or nurse who will help assess the severity of the problem and perhaps be able to suggest a solution. In many cases perseverance may help and in other cases switching pill types may do the trick. Within the range of low-dose pills, there are some which have greater progestogen effects and some which are more oestrogen-dominant. This division does not reflect the actual doses but rather the ways in which they are combined, and the type of progestogen used. The use of a triphasic combined pill may also be helpful in reducing side-effects because these offer the lowest total dose of hormone and attempt to mimic the natural changes in hormone levels.

Desirable side-effects
There are some 'minor' but to the user significant advantages in the pill which are often overlooked when balancing the pros and cons. Contraception is not the only plus point of the pill, but as with the problems not all women will benefit from all the good points. They are:

• Relief from heavy and painful periods

- Regular monthly bleeding (not real periods but at least predictable and controllable)
- Less PMT
- Improved skin with less acne
- Relief from fears of pregnancy

There are also some actions of the pill which significantly reduce the risk of some diseases:

- The overall risk of pelvic inflammatory disease in women using hormonal contraception is significantly reduced. This is thought to be due to the changes in cervical mucus which occur in pill takers which create a barrier to prevent the passage of dangerous organisms into the uterus. This is an important effect because it helps to preserve fertility by reducing the risk of tubal damage.
- There is some evidence that the pill halves the risk of women developing rheumatoid arthritis.
- Endometriosis is a condition of unknown origin in which patches of the endometrium, which usually lines the uterus, appear in other sites. This can lead to pain and can also compromise fertility. Oestrogen and progestogen can be used to treat the condition and it is thought that the pill may actually reduce the risk of developing it.
- The pill is excellent at preventing pregnancy and is equally effective at presenting ectopic pregnancies. It is therefore a very good method of contraception for a woman who has already lost one tube following a tubal ectopic pregnancy.
- Hormonal contraceptives also have the effect of reducing the risk of cancer of the endometrium and of the ovary. (This action was reviewed in the section on the pill and cancer.)

Effects on fertility and births

Women on the pill often wonder what, if any, long-term effects the pill may have on their fertility. Until relatively recently it was thought that the pill had none, but in 1986 some research material was published from the Oxford/FPA study that showed that ex-pill users may have to wait a little longer for a conception than women who have not used it.[29] Ex-pill users tend to take, on average, three to twelve months longer to conceive than ex-users of other methods. Among women who have already had a baby and resumed taking the pill, the impairment to fertility when they stop the pill in order to conceive again is very slight and short lived, whether the pill has been used for more than or less than two years, and regardless of their age. Among ex-pill-users aged twenty-five to twenty-nine who have never had children there is some evidence that conception takes a little longer to achieve though the difference is slight when compared to non-pill users, and has disappeared at the end of four years.

Only in women who are childless, aged thirty to thirty-four and who have recently stopped the pill in order to get pregnant does conception consistently take longer. Whereas three years after stopping contraception only 20 per cent of nulliparous non-pill users of an equivalent age had not had a baby, a little over 30 per cent of ex-pill users still had not given birth. And after four years 17.9 per cent of ex-pill users remained undelivered, compared with only 11.5 per cent of non-pill users. The research team concluded that there is evidence to suggest that impairment to fertility does occur in nulliparous women who have stopped the pill, and that this is greater in women over thirty. There is currently no evidence that the pill ever causes permanent sterility. The implications of these findings are significant for older women planning their first child over thirty. They may have to wait longer than expected for a conception to occur and may want to consider a fertility drug sooner rather than later to boost the activities of their ovaries if a conception does not occur. Nulliparous women over thirty planning a baby within a few years may want to consider switching to a barrier method to give their bodies time to return to a more regular cycle.

Another aspect of concern is the lingering effect of hormones on a developing fetus once a pregnancy has been achieved. It is almost impossible to prove conclusively that a drug or pollutant is or is not responsible for causing an increase in congenital abnormality because this type of problem is so rare that millions of pregnancies would need to be studied to exclude a small risk. Some work has looked at the risk of neural tube defects (spina bifida and hydrocephalus) in babies whose mothers used the pill three months prior to conception. There did seem to be a slight increase in the risk but these women lived in an area where the incidence of this problem is greater than normal anyway.

The trial did find a connection between vitamin levels and the chances of a neural tube defect, and as the pill does alter these levels to some extent there is a theoretical possibility of some pill effect. The study also found that vitamin supplements prior to conception reduced the risk of a neural defect.[30] Some authorities suggest that all women who have used the pill should make sure that their diet is vitamin rich before they conceive. The majority of work carried out suggests that the pill does not lead to any problems in a pregnancy which is conceived after taking the pill, though it is often recommended that you stop the pill and use a barrier method of contraception for three months before trying for a baby. This could have the benefit of reducing still further the *possible* slight risk of abnormality, but it has the more tangible benefit of making the dates of a pregnancy clear.

Another problem that needs to be considered is the possibility of a pill failure and a pregnancy occurring while a woman continues to take the pill. Some women have continued taking their pills through almost an entire pregnancy. In this situation the developing fetus is exposed to progestogens and oestrogens in the vulnerable first stages of pregnancy. Again it is almost impossible to prove either a positive or a negative effect on levels of abnormality. Animal research suggests that some sex steroids could cause abnormalities, and the tragic use of diethylstilboestrol (DES) shortly after the last war demonstrated this. DES is an oestrogen that was given to some women in early pregnancy which resulted in some of their female children developing a very rare cancer of the vagina in early adult life. The episode suggests that one should always be cautious about any drug in early pregnancy. However all the existing research on the combined pill is reassuring. The rate of birth defects in the Oxford/FPA and the RCGP studies following exposure in early pregnancy was no higher than in the groups expecting a planned baby. In fact since 2 per cent of all babies born show some abnormalities no woman can be promised a perfect child, whether or not she has used the pill. The Population Council's estimate that only in seven out of every 10,000 pregnancies could abnormality be attributable to the combined pill shows how very slight the risk actually is.

The progestogen-only pill

The progestogen-only pill (POP) or mini-pill as it is often called, is the most commonly used progestogen-only contraception used in Britain, but still accounts for less than 8 per cent of oral contraceptive users. In comparison to the combined pill there has only been limited research into its effects, and though available since the 1960s it is only just beginning to gain popularity. The general assumption is that the problems experienced by women taking the POP are similar to those experienced by users of the combined pill, but that they are experienced less often and the effects are less intense. Other progestogen-only forms of contraception currently available are the progestogen-releasing IUD and injectable contraceptives.

How it works
In the majority of cases the POP does not override the normal menstrual cycle in the way that the combined pill does. This means that most women continue to ovulate while they take it and the contraceptive

action exerted is more local. As far as we understand it, the POP works by preventing fertilization from taking place, and if it fails in that, by preventing implantation of the embryo in the endometrium. The POP has been likened to an orally taken barrier method which is a good description of one of the ways in which it works. Progestogens produce changes in the mucus made by the cells of the cervix which make it relatively impenetrable to the passage of sperm, overriding the normal mid-cycle thinning out of the mucus and isolating any egg waiting in the fallopian tubes. But this barrier effect is not 100 per cent effective and some sperm do appear to reach both the cavity of the uterus and the fallopian tubes. The second action of the POP prevents any resulting fertilization progressing further. The endometrial lining of the womb changes so that it becomes an unfriendly environment for a fertilized egg, generally becoming thinner the longer progestogens are taken. So, if a fertilized egg does arrive in the uterine cavity the chances of implantation are very small.

Another effect of progestogen involves changes in the fallopian tubes, though their exact significance is not clear. It seems that the number and size of the fine hair-like structures in the tube are reduced. As we saw in Chapter 1, these cilia are responsible for wafting the egg along the tube to the uterus. Under the influence of progestogen they may be less efficient at this egg transport. There may also be an effect on the muscular activity in the tube which normally contributes to the transport of the egg. Under the influence of the hormones of a normal cycle the egg matures as it moves down the fallopian tube; the exact maturity of the egg may be important for successful fertilization. An alteration in the length of time the egg spends travelling down the tube might produce a mismatch between the maturity of the egg and the site in which fertilization normally occurs, making successful fertilisation less likely. Unfortunately most of these mechanisms are poorly understood, but it seems that as well as their anti-fertility effect, they could contribute to the increased incidence of ectopic pregnancies seen among POP users.

The details of the way in which progestogens affect the pituitary gland and the ovary are complex and have not been fully worked out. About 40 per cent of women have basically unchanged menstrual cycles but at the other extreme some 16 per cent have their menstrual cycle badly disrupted. Among this group the progestogens seem to exert a more potent effect and they have little or no bleeding and do not ovulate. In between these two extremes there are women who experience a range of alterations to the menstrual cycle which we will look at in more detail later in this section.

Figure 8.5 Main action of progestogen-only contraception

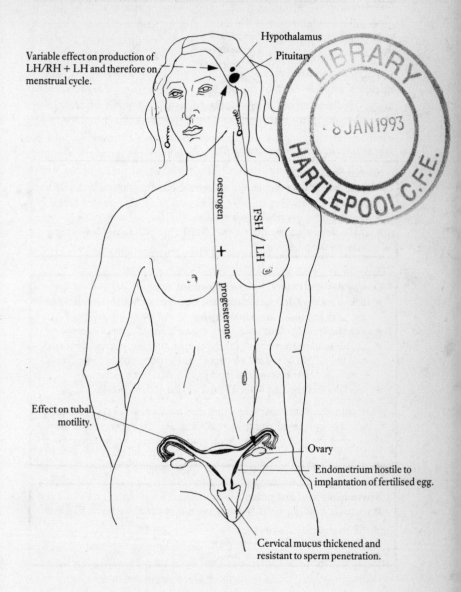

Hypothalamus

Pituitary

Variable effect on production of
LH/RH + LH and therefore on
menstrual cycle.

oestrogen

FSH / LH

+

progesterone

Effect on tubal
motility.

Ovary

Endometrium hostile to
implantation of fertilised egg.

Cervical mucus thickened and
resistant to sperm penetration.

Figure 8.6 Types of progestogen-only pill

	Progestogen type	Dose in mg
Neogest	Norgestrel	0.075
Microval	Levonorgestrel	0.03
Norgeston	Levonorgestrel	0.03
Micronor	Norethisterone	0.35
Noriday	Norethisterone	0.35
Femulen	Ethynodiol diacetate	0.5

How to take the progestogen-only pill

Starting pill taking
- Take first pill on day one of menstrual cycle (i.e. the first day of a period)
- Contraceptive protection is immediate
- If you are switching from a traditional type pill do not leave a gap between the pill packs

Day by day and month by month routine
- Take one tablet daily *at the same time every day*, preferably to within one hour and certainly within three hours
- Take tablet about four hours before your 'normal' time of intercourse
- Expect to have your periods at the normal time for you and continue with the pill while you are bleeding (your periods may become erratic but a missed period could be a pregnancy so check it out)
- You take this type of pill for 365 days a year with no breaks

POP effects peak at about four hours after taking it, so ideally follow this advice; it is more important to remember to take it at the same time every day so that the levels of hormone in your blood have no opportunity of falling off

Missed, late and lost pills
If you miss a pill, or vomit it up, or are more than three hours late with taking it:
- Carry on taking your pill normally
- Take extra precautions for two days

Does it work?
The POP has a failure rate of about 0.3–5 pregnancies per 100 woman-years (Oxford/FPA study) which makes it less reliable than the combined pill. Some sources quote a range from two to ten failures per 100

woman-years which would make it comparable with, or even less reliable than, barrier methods. The method is definitely not as effective as the combined pill even when used 'perfectly' and has a very much smaller margin for error, with a single missed pill giving a relatively high chance of conception. High failure rates tend to be found in women who find the exact timing required incompatible with their lifestyles. There is also an age effect on the failure rate, in that older women have a much smaller risk of accidental pregnancy than do younger women. Several reasons have been put forward for this. In general older women are less fertile, have less frequent intercourse, and are arguably more reliable pill takers. Moreover their menstrual cycles seem to be easier to upset so that the POP is more likely to prevent ovulation altogether. All this means that the failure rate is a very individual thing, the two most important variables probably being age and regularity in pill taking. A woman aged between twenty-five and twenty-nine has a risk of pregnancy of about 3.1 per 100 woman-years which falls to 0.3 at forty or over. The overall failure rate averages out at 0.9 per 100 woman-years (Oxford/FPA study).[31]

Side-effects of the progestogen-only pill

In general the side-effects of the POP are similar to those found with the combined pill, but fewer women get problems. The guidelines about who should take the POP are the same as for the combined pill although some people feel that this is over-cautious and reflects the general lack of data on these pills. Some women who are advised against taking the combined pill are often able to take the POP safely. Research so far indicates that the POP has little or no effect on blood clotting, carbohydrate metabolism, liver function, thyroid function and blood pressure. The balance of bloodlipids can be affected and there may be a slight decrease in the protective HDL which could theoretically increase the risk of arterial disease.

There is at present no evidence that there is any link between cancer and the POP though the lack of data on all aspects of this type of contraception means that no one can really be certain. According to our current understanding of the way the POP works it is a safer and better choice in oral contraception for women over thirty-five or those who smoke, are overweight, diabetic, have a history of high blood pressure or migraines, have sickle cell anaemia or who are breastfeeding. We look at some of its specific side-effects below.

Interruption of the menstrual cycle

What makes the POP unacceptable for many women is the effect that it can have on periods. Almost every irregularity of bleeding pattern may be experienced by a woman on the POP. The majority notice this at their first period after starting on the POP which is unusually long (although some women have a shorter bleed). Thereafter nearly a quarter of women will have more frequent periods and many will get bleeding between periods (though in general this is light). Many studies have found that the bleeding pattern improves with time and that the longer a woman is on the POP the less likely she is to have problems. Unfortunately they do not point out that at least part of this effect is probably due to the fact that women who have severe problems tend to drop out of the trials. About 20 per cent of women develop a menstrual cycle which lasts more than thirty-five days, and some women stop having periods all together. (If this happens to you remember that the cause could be pregnancy and you will need a pregnancy test.) Women who do not have periods on the POP (and are not pregnant) are very well protected against pregnancy and there is nothing unhealthy about not having periods in these circumstances.

The irregular bleeding seen with the POP is the single greatest reason for women wishing to stop using this method. Some women find that they can get used to and cope with erratic periods. Other women, particularly those with religious taboos relating to menstruation, find this side-effect unacceptable. On the other hand many women can accept some disturbance in their menstrual cycle, if they understand the reasons for it, so information on this is essential for POP takers. If the bleeding pattern is unacceptable, it may be worth trying a different brand of POP, either one with a different type of progestogen, or one with a slightly higher or lower dose as this can lead to an improvement.

Ectopic pregnancy

The POP is associated with an increased risk of ectopic pregnancy (a pregnancy outside the uterus, usually in one or other of the fallopian tubes). The chance of this is usually very low, with estimates in the region of 2.8 per cent ectopic pregnancies in POP users. (This compares with 0.8 per cent in the general population.) This is still a small risk but seems to indicate a definite association, though the reasons behind it are unclear and there is great debate about the subject. Some people think that the increased risk of an ectopic pregnancy is due to the effects of progestogen on the fallopian tube which changes the transit time of the egg along the tube, making implantation in the tube more likely. There are others who think that the apparent increase in ectopic pregnancies in POP users is due to the fact that it is not as effective at stopping tubal pregnancies as it is at stopping uterine pregnancies, leading to changes in the proportion of ectopic to uterine pregnancies rather than an actual numerical increase. Some studies compare ectopic rates in POP and IUD users with combined pill and barrier method users, but as barriers and the pill protect against ectopic pregnancies this is not a fair comparison. POP users should be compared to those who use no contraception.[32]

The fact remains, however, that if you use the POP you have a slightly increased chance of having an ectopic pregnancy and should be aware of the symptoms which are fully described in Chapter 7. Women who have had a previous ectopic pregnancy or damaged tubes are usually advised not to use the POP.

Luteal ovarian cysts

Women using the POP are also more likely to develop a luteal ovarian cyst. These small balloon-like structures are formed in the ovary at the site of egg release and are benign, usually coming and going without the woman's knowledge. Occasionally a cyst of this kind can cause pain which may create problems of diagnosis, since the symptoms may be similar to an ectopic pregnancy. Once the cause of the pain has been identified, painkillers and rest are usually all that is required. The reason for the increase in the incidence of this type of ovarian cyst in POP users is not known though it probably has something to do with the interruption in normal ovulation that occurs among some POP users.[33]

Effects on fertility and births

There is no evidence to suggest that the POP has any adverse effect on immediate or long-term fertility. Indeed the problem is rather one of accidental pregnancies while using this method. The return of fertility seems to be immediate in most women. Past use of the POP does not seem to have any adverse effect on the outcome of pregnancies. Obviously, the use of the POP after conception should be avoided and if a period is unexpectedly missed then pregnancy should be ruled out before continuing with the pill. While accidental use of the POP by pregnant woman has not been shown to increase the risk of fetal abnormality, it is always impossible to say that there is *no* risk. The possibility of an ectopic pregnancy should not be forgotten.

The POP is often prescribed to women who are breastfeeding. It seems to fill the gap at a time when the combined pill cannot be used because it suppresses milk production. The decreased natural fertility at this time also makes the POP a more appropriate contraceptive. The progestogen does cross into the breast milk in small amounts and the effect on the baby is not known. It seems likely that the minute quantities of this hormone which the baby gets (estimated to be a total of one tablet if you breastfeed for two years) are not harmful, but this is not proven.

Conclusion

The POP is rarely considered as a first choice method of contraception. Being less reliable than combined pills, it tends to get left out of lists of suggested contraceptive methods. In many women, however, the pregnancy rates are comparable to those seen in IUD wearers and yet some doctors seem keener to fit IUDs. There seems to be a tendency among medical professionals to provide contraception which is either 'safe' in terms of the risk from pregnancy, as with the combined pill, or at least works without the user having to do anything, as with the IUD. This attitude has arguably led to the under-use of a potentially valuable contraceptive. Many women who might well wish to try the POP do not even know about its existence.

As with any method of contraception the POP has side-effects, but on the data so far available it seems to be safer than the combined pill. The recurring statement in this section that the lack of data makes precise advice unavailable reflects a general lack of interest in the POP. Now that consumers are more concerned with safety there may be more interest in methods which are less reliable but have a lower price to pay in terms of risks to general health. Progestogen-only contraception may well benefit from this attention.

Injectable hormonal contraception

Oral contraceptives can only ever be as effective as the user makes them and they do not work if they are not taken properly. An unfortunate belief that women are irresponsible about contraception and can never be relied upon to take their pills or use their diaphragms properly made the development of an injectable contraceptive merely a matter of time. Indeed, many women might have supported the idea of a contraceptive they only had to think about every three months had not the unscrupulous use of Depo Provera in the late sixties and early seventies caused the whole idea to fall into disrepute. Indeed the very word 'Depo' has come to symbolize, for some women, the abuse of women by doctors in the name of contraception.

Depo Provera

Depo Provera is not the only, but is certainly the best-known, type of injectable contraceptive. It is an injection of long-acting medroxyprogesterone acetate (DPMA) which is a hormone of the progestogen type, formulated so as to be released slowly from the site of the injection. It was first used in trials as a contraceptive in the early 1960s, although its initial use was for the treatment of gynaecological disorders. In the late sixties and early seventies thousands of women were given Depo Provera in all parts of the world. In 1967 Upjohn, its manufacturers, applied to the US Food and Drugs Administration to extend the licence to include its use as a contraceptive. This was the beginning of a stormy period during which the use of DPMA became highly controversial. After seven years of considering the evidence the FDA gave their approval in 1974. This permission was hurriedly withdrawn following a public outcry.

In 1978 the Obstetric and Gynaecology subcommittee of the FDA recommended the approval of Depo as a contraceptive method but again even this informed advice was rejected due to further public pressure. Despite the strong move against Depo displayed in the USA, DPMA is licensed as a contraceptive in over eighty countries around the world, both in the developed and in the developing world. In the UK in 1982 the Minister of Health took the unprecedented step of turning down the recommendations of the Committee on Safety of Medicines and refused to grant a licence for long-term use of DPMA as a contraceptive. After a public hearing such use was approved – with certain provisos as to the way in which it should be prescribed.

The controversy

The use of Depo Provera is still bitterly opposed by many women. Groups were set up specifically to campaign against it, and they were successful in raising public awareness of the problems of this drug. There is strong feeling against both the drug itself and about the manner in which it is used. The accusation that the drug is under-researched and dangerous is one which many doctors would refute, though the claim that there have been abuses in the way in which Depo has been used is more generally agreed. When it was first available some women were undoubtedly given injections with little or no explanation as to possible side-effects and sometimes without proper consent. It remains a controversial drug and this has obscured the fact that for some women it is a positive choice, and that they may prefer to have to think about contraception only once every three months. For information on the opposition to Depo Provera contact the Women's Health and Reproductive Rights Information Centre (the address is given in Appendix 3).

The effects of Depo Provera

Depo Provera is given as an injection into the buttock. The injection, which needs to be repeated every twelve weeks, is usually given on day five of the menstrual cycle or five weeks after delivery. One of the attractions of Depo for many women is the pregnancy-rate of only 0.5 per 100 woman-years. Depo Provera has in fact only been licensed for long-term contraceptive use in cases where, after careful counselling, other contraceptives are contraindicated because they have caused unacceptable side-effects or have proved otherwise unsatisfactory. It appears to work by preventing ovulation, probably by a blocking effect on the LH surge. It is also thought to work in a similar way to the other progestogen-only contraceptives (see pp. 283–4).

As with the progestogen-only pill, many women on Depo lose less menstrual blood and some have less painful periods, while pre-menstrual tension is improved in some women. Another positive aspect of Depo is the protection it offers against pelvic inflammatory disease. The use of Depo Provera by women with sickle cell disease is said to decrease the number of sickling crises, although there is some question as to the validity of the research on which this is based.[34]

The contraceptive effects of Depo last for twelve weeks. Unfortunately any unwanted effects may also last at least this long. The main problem is one of disruption of the menstrual cycle, which can be so extreme as to be called 'menstrual chaos'. At one end of the spectrum women can lose their periods altogether, a condition known as amenorrhoea. The number of women in this group grows with duration of use, with most women being amenorrhoeic at the end of twelve months. Doctors tend to see this as a positive attribute but women do not necessarily agree. At the other extreme, a few women bleed continuously and many more have distressing spotting and irregular periods. If the length of period or the amount of blood lost is excessive, treatment may be required. Ironically one of the most effective treatments is the use of an oestrogen, the very thing that some women taking Depo were trying to avoid. Heavy bleeding is particularly common when the injection is given in the six weeks following delivery. There are also women who develop bleeding problems, which they attribute to the drug, after stopping Depo injections. Two studies have shown a 17 per cent and a 19 per cent drop-out rate in the use of Depo Provera which was due to problems of menstruation.[35]

The other side effects of Depo Provera are generally very similar to those seen with other hormonal contraceptive methods. Nausea, headache, a bloated feeling, breast tenderness, decreased libido and back pain are some of the more common problems mentioned. Weight changes seem to be a particular problem, with most sources claiming they are almost universal. Serious side-effects, such as an increased risk of cancer or cardiovascular disease, are not fully researched and are generally thought to be the same as for POP.

One problem specific to this type of injectable contraception is emerging. Depo may bring about very low oestrogen levels which may in turn lead to early menopausal changes in, for example, skin and bone. Depo Provera can also have a considerable effect on the time taken to conceive. One study found that only about 85 per cent of women had regular menstrual cycles at one year after stopping their injections, though a study in Thailand recorded a pregnancy rate of 92 per cent by twenty-four months after stopping Depo.[36] The data sheet on the drug produced by Upjohn states that '. . . transient infertility lasting up to two years or longer may occur following continuous treatment with Depo Provera.' Few women anxious to conceive would consider a stretch of two years to be merely transient.

Other injectable contraceptives

Norethindrone enanthate is a progestogen given by an intramuscular injection every eight weeks. It can be given on any of days one to five of the menstrual cycle and has a failure rate of 0.01–1.3 pregnancies per 100 woman-years of use. Unlike Depo Provera it is licensed only for short-term use, such as for the wives of men undergoing vasectomy. The advantages and disadvantages of this method are thought to be similar to those experienced by users of Depo Provera, though it has not been as fully researched as Depo.

The WHO is at present evaluating the use of a combination of oestrogen and a progestogen as a once-a-month injectable contraceptive. This could have less menstrual disruption than the progestogen-only injectables. Because of problems in developing long-lasting oestrogens and fears about exposure to continuous oestrogen, the time between doses is shorter than that possible with progestogen-only injectables.[37]

The future of progestogen-only contraception

Progestogen-only contraception seems to be a popular area for development at present and there are several trials under way which are looking at new ways of administering the hormone. One of the problems with the POP has always been the importance of absolutely regular pill taking to achieve reasonable reliability. The long-acting injectable progestogens avoid this problem but create new ones, especially since once given, the hormone could not be removed even if there were severe side-effects. The new ways of giving progestogen attempt to avoid both these drawbacks and to provide maximum contraceptive cover with the lowest possible dose. All of them aim for a constant release of progestogen over a period of time. This continual low level of hormone should provide better contraception than a pill which, taken once a day, gives peaks and troughs of hormone in the blood. The peaks mean that the body is relatively over-dosed with hormones and the troughs represent times when there may be too little hormone to prevent a pregnancy.

The simple-sounding aim of creating a constant release system has been found to be technically difficult, but the development of a new generation of plastics is finally beginning to make it possible.

Progestogen releasing IUDs
The idea of using a plain plastic IUD as a vehicle for an active substance began with the use of copper wire wound around the IUD. The use of new plastics has led to the development of the hormone releasing IUD. These have advantages over conventional IUDs, such as less bleeding, but at the moment require annual replacement. The inconvenience and discomfort involved is a distinct drawback. They also share some of the unwanted effects of the IUD (see pp. 235–6).

Implants
An implant is a small rod-like structure which is placed under the skin and is a form of removable injection. Two types of implant have been developed so far, one with a silicone-rubber capsule containing progestogen which needs to be removed once the hormone has been released, and one which is biodegradable and disappears as the hormone is released. The WHO is involved with large scale trials on this type of contraception but as the idea is still quite new there is still much to be learnt about the long-term effects. The only implant which is at present available is Norplant, but it is licensed for use only in Sweden and Finland.

It consists of six silastic rods each measuring 34 by 2.4 mm and each containing 36 mg of levonorgestrel. They are inserted in around fifteen minutes, usually into the apper arm in a fan-like pattern. Under local anaesthetic a single small (5 mm) incision is made and the capsules are placed just under the skin through a large needle. No stitches are required. Removal is similar but may take a little longer. The progestogen is released at the rate of 80 μg a day initially and then at 30 μg daily for about five years. During this time the release is equivalent to the dose used in the POP but since it is at a constant level its contraceptive effects are more reliable.

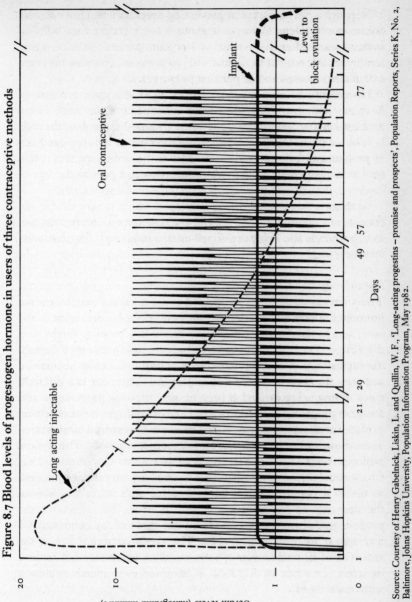

Figure 8.7 Blood levels of progestogen hormone in users of three contraceptive methods

Serum levels (nanograms/millilitre)

Days

Long acting injectable

Oral contraceptive

Implant

Level to block ovulation

Source: Courtesy of Henry Gabelnick, Liskin, L. and Quillin, W. F., 'Long-acting progestins – promise and prospects', Population Reports, Series K, No. 2, Baltimore, Johns Hopkins University, Population Information Program, May 1982.

Norplant is very effective at preventing pregnancy and has a similar failure rate to Depo Provera, at about 0.2–1.3 pregnancies per 100 woman-years. After the removal of Norplant, present evidence is that fertility rapidly returns to normal with 40 per cent of women pregnant within three months and 90 per cent by two years.

Disturbance of menstruation is once again the main problem of Norplant with two-thirds of women affected in some way. These problems can be severe and some women request removal of the rods because of them. Other side-effects are the same as for other methods of progestogen-only contraception. The only problem specific to this type of contraception is the risk of infection and pain at the site of insertion, though with correct insertion these problems are rare.

Norplant 2 is currently being developed which is very similar but consists of a two-rod system. A biodegradable system, currently known as Capronor, is also being developed using a single rod of the hormone levonorgestrel.[38]

Vaginal rings

Trials are currently being conducted using a vaginal ring to release hormones. These soft silastic rings are easily placed in the vagina by the user, and fit comfortably around the cervix in a position similar to a diaphragm. They release hormones which are rapidly absorbed through the vaginal wall. A constant blood level of hormone can be maintained and they are not affected by stomach upsets. There are two different types of ring being studied at present, one releasing progestogen and the other progestogen and oestrogen. The progestogen ring can remain in place for about three months and need not be removed for menstruation, though it can be taken out for intercourse if desired. The present prototype releases 20 µg of levonorgestrel in twenty-four hours and has a reasonable record of efficacy. This method is pretty much equivalent to the POP as far as problems associated with it go, but without the necessity of remembering to take it daily. The effects of the progestogen/oestrogen ring are more like those of the combined pill and appear to carry similar risks. The ring's advantage lies in the reduction of the total amount of hormone taken, which may well improve its safety. This type of ring must be removed every month to allow a withdrawal bleed.

Others

The search is always on for new ways of providing effective contraception, not least because success brings large financial rewards. Various other ways of taking hormones are being studied. An intra-cervical device which would sit in the cervical canal and release progestogen or a spermicide is one such method. Another method of hormone delivery recently brought out for hormone replacement therapy is a skin patch. These flesh-coloured sticky plasters release hormone on to the skin from which it is absorbed into the body. This could also offer a delivery route for contraceptive use. Similarly, bracelets rather like cats' flea-collars have been suggested. All these methods still rely on hormones for their contraceptive action and this means they all carry the health risks associated with taking exogenous hormones.

The problems associated with tampering with the finely tuned engine of the female body by the addition of extra hormones have not put off the researchers from coming up with more ideas which seem in some ways even more intrusive. There are trials underway looking into the use of analogues of LH releasing hormone as a possible contraceptive. These substances, which could be taken as a snuff, would break into the chain of events which lead to ovulation at an even earlier stage than the hormones used now, by suppressing the pituitary gland. The advantage to be gained from this could be a reduced impact on the hormonal milieu of the body which would, in theory, bring fewer side-effects. There are still many unanswered questions about this approach and we will have to wait to see whether it has real potential.

Anti-progesterones are already used in some countries and cannot strictly be called a hormonal method of contraception, more an anti-hormonal method! This method is described in the chapter on post-coital contraception.

The idea of a 'vaccination' against pregnancy may seem rather sinister to many women, though it may intrigue others. This is not a hormonal method of contraception but it does seem to fit in the continuum of the involvement in contraception of increasingly fundamental functions of our bodies. There are a variety of ways in which this might work. The basic idea is to give a vaccination which will promote the formation of antibodies to the cells or hormones which are necessary to some part of the chain of events which results in a successfully implanted embryo. One approach is to produce antibodies which inactivate hCG, one of the pregnancy hormones, which would prevent the body recognizing that a very early pregnancy had occurred. The menstrual cycle would then carry on relentlessly and wash away the pregnancy. Another strategy is to produce antibodies to the surface of either sperm or egg or both. This could be of particular interest as it might provide a method of contraception which would apply to men as well as to women. There is obviously concern about the reversibility of these methods, but work at present seems to indicate that vaccination can be a reversible method of contraception. It seems likely that our daughters' daughters will benefit from these developments. We can but hope that the relatively recent general awareness of, and concern for, our health and quality of life will ensure that these methods will have fewer of the problems which we are learning to expect from those of today.

Conclusion: changing attitudes to hormonal contraception

The pill, the flagship of hormonal contraception, has always been the subject of controversy. In the 1960s when it was first introduced it suffered from association with residual feelings that all contraception was slightly sinful; being invisible and so reliable it was doubly damnable, even more of a spur to 'sin without detection'. The great changes in sexual mores that took place in the 1960s have frequently been blamed on the pill. Undeniably, it must have helped, but by the time the pill was legally available to unmarried women in 1967, the era of free love was well and truly under way. The pill may have fuelled the fire, but it was already lit. Perhaps more significantly in the long run, the pill did much to bring contraception into the public arena, making women more aware of all forms of fertility control. For the first time, many women felt they had choices about their own fertility. Dilys Cossey, now chairwoman of the FPA, explains it like this:

Women then, if they were on the pill, could choose to have sex, which was one thing. They could choose when to have children or whether or not to have children. It actually made them exactly the same as men. Now that is deeply frightening I think to many people, and it was a revolution.[39]

With the eruption of pill scares and the growing women's movement in the 1970s, the pill began to be regarded in a different light. The idea developed that far from being a tool to liberate women the pill represented a threat to their well-being. The 'conspiracy theory of contraception' sees the pill as one more weapon developed by the patriarchy to make women sexually available to men at no cost to men and considerable cost to women. It was felt that this potentially harmful drug was released on unsuspecting women without enough care to ensure its safety. Drug companies were growing rich on the large pickings to be got from widespread use of the pill and, in the meantime, women found it difficult to get hold of any accurate information about the unwanted effects of this 'wonder drug'. Moreover the feeling was growing that sexual freedom was not perhaps all it had at first appeared to be. Sexual freedom might easily become sexual coercion. The pill simply took away one of the best excuses for being more discriminating. As one woman put it:

Looking back I think I actually had sex with people that with hindsight I wouldn't have bothered with. It was pressure of the time. It was all peace and love and yeah, you know, you can sleep with anyone and men expected it from you and I think the pill had a lot to do with those sorts of attitudes at the time, and of course once you had the pill you couldn't get pregnant, you didn't have that excuse, that was it, so off we all gaily trotted and I don't know for myself whether it was such a liberating thing.[40]

The pill certainly gave men more opportunities to exercise power over women. They were in a strong position to insist on intercourse regardless of the time of the month or other considerations, and without themselves being physically involved in preventing conceptions. If a woman got pregnant it was even less the man's fault than before, since women now had the power to prevent conceptions. There was a tendency to assume that all women would be on the pill and that as far as men were concerned contraception could be safely forgotten about.

At the same time as men became less involved in contraception in the private sphere, the largely male medical establishment took over almost all aspects of family planning provision. Having spurned it as irrelevant earlier in the century and been in the main quite uninvolved, the appearance of hormonal contraception and the IUD meant that it had become primarily a medical matter. Doctors are trained to diagnose disease and to treat it; many found it difficult to break out of this mould and tended to perceive fertility as a disease for which the appropriate cure was contraception, particularly the pill. In the 1960s very few doctors had been trained in family planning, and even as late as 1976 only 32 per cent of GPs had had any formal training in it. Despite this, the majority gave advice on contraception. This 'medicalization' had two major effects. The pill, being a drug, was a more familiar idea to doctors and reinforced their attitudes to illness. Methods such as the diaphragm required skill for fitting and was more difficult to identify as a 'cure'. These factors probably contributed to the huge and rapid growth in pill use.

Twenty years later these attitudes have not been entirely dissipated. While most GPs no longer see contraception as a cure for a female disease, the pill remains, as we saw in Chapter 2, the favourite method of contraception. A number of the women who wrote to us described the extreme reluctance of their GPs to prescribe anything else:

At least two of my friends have also had the pill offered to them when they've gone for treatment for something completely different. I understand that statistically it is the most effective method but many of my friends and I feel that doctors ram it down our throats as if we're such silly little girls that we can't be trusted to use anything else.

Having read a lot about the possible side-effects of the pill, I had decided to ask for a diaphragm. Since I did not know that much about the safety of any form of contraception, I asked the doctor which method he would recommend. Pen poised and prescription pad already in front of him, he promptly embarked on a song of praise for the pill . . . so I just gave in. Afterwards I felt defeated, and later on very angry. . . . Nevertheless I gave it a try, even though I hated myself for being so weak and letting an old man tell me what to do with my body.

For many, many women the pill remains a satisfactory and pleasant method of contraception. A number of the women who wrote to us thought that we needed to be given the positive side of the picture as well as the negative. The major differences between opting for the pill in 1989 rather than 1969 are that you can be sure to receive less hormone and that we have a clearer idea of the health risks that we may run while taking the pill long-term. Decisions regarding medicalized contraception can therefore be made with more of a grasp of both pros and cons.

I have been on the pill for eleven years and am very happy with it. The reliability of it is very important to us as we do not intend to have children. I hope that in a few years' time medical research does not show the pill to have side-effects manifesting in one's later years. This, however, does not cause me great concern. If it were not for the pill when I was unmarried I would surely have had at least two children by now and my life would have been totally different.

CHAPTER 9

Sterilization

Sterilization – what freedom. It was one of the most sensible things I ever did.

Vasectomy is the best method ever for married parents. Never have to worry about anything – brilliant.

Voluntary sterilization implies that no fundamental changes will be allowed to take place – life's die has been cast. It is the abandonment of management of one's own fertility and a regression to child status. Sterilization is not a substitute for contraception because it is the destruction of fertility: it makes as much sense as blinding a man who needs glasses.

Germaine Greer, Sex and Destiny

Sterilization puts an end to a person's ability to have children. Traditionally carried out by surgical methods and almost always regarded as permanent, it has now become the most common method of fertility regulation in the world. Germaine Greer cynically comments that '... among the dubious achievements of the twentieth century ... will go our character as the sterilizing civilisation',[1] citing as evidence the massive numbers of the world's women who have been sterilized – 75 million world wide when she published her book, and rising rapidly. However future generations choose to see us, it is true that sterilization now occupies a position of considerable significance in human efforts to control their fertility, and a special position in the range of contraceptive methods in that it is ideal for some and wholly inappropriate for others. It is equally unusual in that it can be chosen by women *and* men and, of the two operations, vasectomy is probably an older procedure than female sterilization.

Though references to vasectomy occur as early as 1775 it was not until the end of the nineteenth century that it was anything other than a crude and mutilating operation, often carried out punitively and including castration. In 1907 it became legal in the USA for eugenic purposes. Female sterilization was described in detail as early as 1834 but it is only recently that it has ceased to be a major abdominal operation with all the attendant risks. By 1934 the Report of the British Departmental Committee on Sterilisation began discussions on sterilizations for birth-control rather than eugenic purposes alone, and in 1935 in Aberdeen, sterilization was offered to women when there seemed no other way of controlling family size. Voluntary sterilization as a method of fertility control had begun.

The rise in popularity of voluntary sterilization was abruptly halted following the Nazi domination of Europe. Desire for racial purity coupled with horrifying mutilating procedures performed in concentration camps seemed to set sterilization back by decades. It was only just beginning to recover from these appalling associations when the Ghandhi government in India started its emergency programme of sterilization, which again had an effect on the wider acceptability of this procedure. In other countries, it has formed the backbone of national population policies. In contemporary China, for example, there is extreme pressure to undergo sterilization.

At present an estimated 95 million couples worldwide rely on female sterilization for contraception, and another 40 million on vasectomy. This means that about one in six of all the world's fertile couples are protected against pregnancy by sterilization. In the UK 27 per cent of women depend on sterilization to avoid pregnancy compared to only 4 per cent in 1970. It is the most used method of fertility control in Britain today, reflecting an anxiety over the safety of hormonal and intrauterine methods of contraception and the effectiveness of barriers. The current upward trend will in time level out since the number of people for whom a permanent method of contraception is appropriate is obviously finite.[2]

Attitudes to sterilization

If proof were needed of the importance of fertility to an individual then the intensity of some reactions to the permanent loss of that fertility by sterilization provides it. For many people, the links between sterilization, loss of virility, and castration remain strong. For equal numbers of other people, sterilization is a liberating and entirely positive development; the loss of fertility is not the issue, its control is. People who actively request sterilization are almost always happy with the resulting infertility; those to whom sterilization is suggested are far more likely to have regrets. The extremity of Germaine Greer's reaction is extraordinary in its failure to admit an individual's right to choose an end to the demands of fertility and live with that decision. It is not unlike the reluctance of some medical professionals to provide sterilizations because they cannot come to terms with their clients as mature adults who can take major decisions and live with the consequences. While Greer sees sterilization as abdicating responsibility and returning to a childlike infertile state; paternalistic medical professionals sometimes seem to be trying to protect unqualified, 'ordinary' people from such 'final' decisions. Both attitudes are unfortunate and both ironically seem to detract from a view of fertility control as being rightly within the province of the individual. A person's fertility is a highly significant aspect of their maturity, and they have a right to decide if or when the potential for reproducing themselves is no longer something they wish to keep central to their sexuality.

Until as recently as 1970 some hospitals used the so-called age-parity formula or 'rule of 120' for determining which women could be granted a sterilization and which refused one. By this extraordinary rule the woman's age was multiplied by the number of her living children. Women who achieved 120 or greater were considered to have done their reproductive duty and were 'allowed' to be sterilized. A woman of thirty who had four children would have been lucky; a woman of forty with only two offspring not so fortunate. It is not always easy to unpack attitudes to sterilization – they are not always so clearly displayed as this. Fortunately, any woman or man wanting a sterilization now has an opportunity to discuss the implications fully with a doctor and to clarify her or his own feelings on the subject before taking what is in the main an irreversible step.

Studies which examine the recipients' attitudes to sterilization all report that counselling can be very useful in reducing long-term problems. Some women and men have already worked through their decision on their own and counselling is less vital; other people need to talk through the facts of the operation and have all the possible pitfalls pointed out, particularly the changes in circumstances which might affect their desire for children. If you are thinking about the possibility of sterilization you will need plenty of time and the freedom, if you change your mind on reflection, to decide against it. The most frequent negative psychological reaction to sterilization is regret, apparently felt by up to 40 per cent of those who undergo the procedure.[3] Regret is far more likely if the decision was made at a time of change or stress, such as just prior to or after an abortion, around childbirth, or when a relationship is under threat. Similarly decisions made under any kind of pressure, whether from a doctor or from your partner, are more likely to be regretted. Sterilizations carried out for medical reasons are also more likely to bring with them regret. Sterilization is not a solution to unhappiness in a relationship, and divorce and a new relationship are common reasons for requesting reversal operations. The chance of satisfaction after the operation seems to be reduced if both partners do not agree that sterilization is the right choice.

No one can predict what will happen to them in the next five years. The chances are that you won't regret a sterilization, but because of the uncertainty that the future holds it is always best to make decisions about sterilization slowly, and well away from other major life events. An unwanted pregnancy now and a subsequent feeling that you will never want another child may precipitate a sterilization; a new relationship and a change in vantage points may make you wish you had at least held on to the option.

The majority of women and men express no regrets over the operation and many claim that their health and sexual life are unchanged or better. Some statistics show that the frequency of sexual intercourse goes up; although a few studies report decreased libido.[4] One explanation given is that some people miss the excitement brought by the risk of a pregnancy. You will get an opportunity to talk through all of these issues with a doctor or counsellor. Talking to someone you do not know can be a good way of trying out your own arguments. If you are still convinced by them at the end of your discussion – and some doctors and counsellors may question you quite closely to help you work out your own stance – the chances are that you will be happy after the operation too. It seems unfortunate that the care that is taken to help people make the right decisions about sterilization cannot be applied more generally to the contraceptive services.

The law and sterilization

The law has become involved with sterilization to an unusual extent. In the case of abortion the legislation surrounding it is felt to be important as there are the rights of the fetus to consider. In the case of sterilization, however, there is only the patient to consider and the risks to her or his life are no greater and often much smaller than many operations much more lightly undergone. The risk of abuse of this operation however has resulted in many countries setting up a legal framework within which health workers have to operate. Most important is the mandatory requirement for the patient's consent. In most European countries the law allows sterilization to be performed on anyone over the age of consent who is deemed to be capable of giving informed consent. There are some countries in which it remains illegal, often for religious reasons, while in others the patient must fulfil other criteria. In Egypt for example sterilization can only be performed on a parent who already has three children, one of whom is a boy.

In Britain cases in which individuals are not considered capable of giving informed consent, such as the mentally handicapped, frequently make headline news. It is vital that the handicapped have their fertility protected by the law if we are not to take a retrograde step towards earlier eugenic attitudes and practices.

It is no longer mandatory in the UK to have the consent of one's partner before having a sterilization. On the other hand if a partner is strongly opposed to the operation they have the right of action against the sterilized partner by, for example, making the operation the basis for divorce proceedings. One woman who wrote to us had the following story to tell:

It was on admission to hospital for the operation that my problems began. Not with the consultant but with his junior medical and nursing staff. You see I had decided that I would not consent to the hospital asking my husband for his signature to the sterilization form (it is customary, but *not legally necessary* to ask husbands). He knew my personal/political reasons and was entirely supportive. Twice therefore I was forced to argue my political case. Once with a woman junior doctor who tried to tell me that the government legally required my husband's signature – totally untrue – and secondly with the nursing staff on the ward. I told them all that under no circumstances whatsoever were they to approach my husband and that I would sign my Consent to Sterilisation Form. . .

In the end I had to ask the consultant to stop the harassment of me over the matter and he struck through the section on the form where husband's consent is mentioned. I signed the form publicly on the ward round.

Sterilization is also the subject of relatively frequent medico-legal cases. The bases for these cases are varied and include conceptions following sterilizations, sterilizations in the presence of an existing pregnancy and damage to internal organs which occur during the operation. Gynaecologists are consequently advised to warn patients about failure rates and the irreversible nature of the procedure, and most do so.

Female sterilization

All methods for sterilizing women involve blocking the fallopian tubes. Once the tube is blocked eggs from the ovaries cannot reach the uterus, and sperm cannot leave the uterus to get to the eggs. Conceptions can't take place. Instead of travelling down the fallopian tube, the microscopic egg falls into the abdominal cavity each month and is simply absorbed by the body. The mechanics are simple, but the fact that the ovary and uterus are abdominal organs makes female sterilization more complex than male. Until recently it was necessary to perform all female

Figure 9.1 Female sterilization techniques

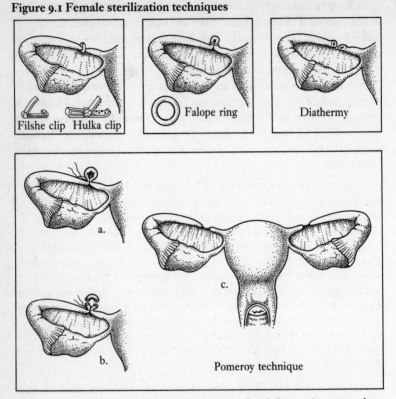

Filshe clip Hulka clip

Falope ring

Diathermy

a.

b.

c.

Pomeroy technique

sterilization operations through a large cut in the abdomen in a procedure known as laparotomy. A laparotomy is considered to be relatively major surgery, carrying risks both of the anaesthetic and the surgery, as well as being an uncomfortable operation to recover from. Fortunately, recent improvements in sterilization techniques have brought safer and easier operations.

The operation

In this section we will describe the types of sterilization now available. In all methods of sterilization the surgeon performing the operation needs to be able to see the fallopian tubes from the outside which means that he has to have access to your abdominal cavity. In order to achieve this, she or he can choose one of a number of techniques.

Laparotomy

This is the traditional form of the operation. The sterilization is carried out through a cut some 20 cm long along the 'bikini line'. This relatively long cut gives the surgeon a good view of all your abdominal organs, including your uterus, fallopian tubes and ovaries, and enables him or her to use a variety of different methods for blocking your tubes. The disadvantage is that the size of the operation will mean a stay of at least five days in hospital. The fact that your abdominal muscles will need to be cut makes full recovery slow and it may be as much as six weeks before you feel like resuming normal activity. The problems involved in this kind of operation mean that nowadays it is rarely done just for sterilization alone. Instead it may be used if you are already undergoing laparotomy for other reasons, for example, having a caesarian section or an exploratory operation for a gynaecological problem. Laparotomy can be performed under a general or an epidural anaesthetic.

Mini-laparotomy

Mini-laparotomy is a minor version of the full laparotomy as the incision is only about 3 cm long, made in the abdominal wall just above the pubic hair. A small probe is inserted into the uterus via the vagina so that the uterus can be moved about gently until the fallopian tubes fall into a position where they can be operated on through the small incision. Again, the surgeon can choose a variety of different methods for blocking the fallopian tubes, but will not be able to fully inspect the ovaries and other abdominal organs for signs of disease. Following the operation the uterus and fallopian tubes fall back into place again quickly. Like all operations, mini-laparotomy involves the risk of a general anaesthetic but because it is a smaller operation than a full laparotomy it can be done as a day case operation, so you can go home the same day. Alternatively you could have the operation performed under a local or epidural anaesthetic.

Laparoscopy

This is the method that has made female sterilization a far more popular and acceptable operation, since it is performed through minute incisions in the abdomen and the recovery time is very short. Nowadays it is probably the most frequently used method in Britain and is increasingly performed as a day case operation. The advantage of same day discharge, aside from its convenience for women, is that it is economical for the NHS, releases resources for more sterilizations and reduces waiting lists. Since sterilization is, as we have seen, the most popular form of contraception currently practised in the UK, short waiting lists are to everyone's advantage. The relatively detailed account given here will give you some idea of what to expect if you decide to opt for a sterilization by laparoscopy.

A detailed discussion of sterilization will normally be carried out in the outpatient department sometime before your operation. It should be made clear to you that the operation is essentially irreversible but that it does have a failure rate. This is estimated at 2 to 3 per thousand, with a three-fold increase if the operation follows a recent pregnancy.[5] You will be required to sign a consent form that says that you have understood these points and wish to undergo the operation. Your partner may also be asked to sign a form, though it is not mandatory to have his consent. Many hospitals are keen to involve partners but will not ask for consent from them. At the time of your first visit arrangements will probably be made for you to have a blood test shortly before your operation. You will also be asked to use some reliable form of contraception until you come in for the operation, which will ideally be in the first half of your cycle before ovulation, to reduce the risk of a pregnancy resulting from an egg released before your sterilization. Most women will be asked to arrive on the morning of the operation having had nothing to eat or drink since midnight. Other women are asked to arrive the day before, which may be simply because the hospital lacks the organization to cope with you on the day itself or because you have some slight complicating factor like asthma or heavy smoking, in which case your anaesthetic will take longer to sort out. Prior to your operation you will be seen by at least one doctor, and usually two. One will be a junior gynaecologist and the other an anaesthetist. They will listen to your chest and take a brief history of any past ill-health.

General anaesthetics are still used for laparoscopy though local anaesthetics are becoming more common. Once you have had your anaesthetic and are relaxed or asleep, gas – either carbon dioxide or nitrous oxide – will be introduced into your abdominal cavity through a large needle. The gas lifts your abdominal wall making it easier for the surgeon to see and manoeuvre your pelvic organs. A small incision of about 1–2 cm is made just below your tummy button and through this a tiny narrow telescope, the laparoscope, is introduced. It has its own light source and the surgeon will be able to see your fallopian tubes as he looks down it. The surgeon then makes a second small incision, usually at the level of your pubic hair. The instrument used to block your tubes will be inserted through this, while, as in the mini-laparotomy, another instrument is introduced via your vagina into your uterus to hold it steady during the operation. Once your tubes have been blocked off and the operation is completed, the gas is let out of your abdomen and dressing applied to the incisions. Sometimes a dissolving stitch is used to close the cut.

Waking up from the operation you may feel groggy and uncomfortable. The discomfort felt after a laparoscopy has been likened to the feeling of having been 'kicked in the stomach by a horse'. Other women find they do not feel anything other than rather bruised. You will be given mild painkillers and a rest in hospital which will last from a few hours to two to three days. You may experience some vaginal bleeding due to the manipulation of your uterus and cervix during the operation. Since the effects of a general anesthetic linger for about twenty-four hours, driving or any work with machinery is ruled out. You may feel like resuming normal activity after several days, or it may take a week to feel fully yourself again.

In skilled hands the risks involved in laparoscopy are very small. In about one operation in 500 a problem arises which requires a laparotomy to sort out. There could be damage to your bowel or pelvic organs while the initial needle is introduced to your abdomen since this is a 'blind' procedure. Occasionally a surgeon finds he is unable to complete a laparoscopy because the pelvic organs are scarred and the fallopian tubes inaccessible. In this case he or she might decide to sterilize you with a laparotomy or mini-laparotomy instead. If you think there is any chance that your surgeon might have problems using laparoscopy – for example if you have ever had a serious pelvic inflammatory disease – it may be worth mentioning this in advance and making your wishes clear.

Methods used to block the fallopian tubes

Once the surgeon has a good view of your fallopian tubes she or he has a choice of techniques available for blocking them. The older methods tend to be more drastic and less reversible, and involve cutting and tying the tubes. The newer methods aim for a high degree of effectiveness with the least possible damage, thereby improving the chances of a successful reversal. Rings and clips have been developed to this end. There does seem to be a pay-off in that the older, more radical methods do on the whole have a slightly lower chance of failure.

Salpingectomy is an extreme method in which the tubes are actually removed. The operation takes longer and has the risk of heavy bleeding. It is very effective and is impossible to reverse.

Tubal ligation involves tying and cutting the tubes. The best known version is the 'Pomeroy' where the tube is looped up and tied and the top of the loop cut out. The ties prevent bleeding at the time of the operation and when the tie finally dissolves the two parts of the tube separate. Spontaneous rejoining of the tube is very unlikely. This method of sterilization can only be performed by laporotomy or mini-laparotomy and reversal depends on how much fallopian tube remains. Sometimes the tube is simply tied and the success of the sterilization will depend on the scarring thereby produced. At other times the ends of the cut tubes may be buried in surrounding tissue, which is meant to prevent bleeding and increase reliability.

Cauterization involves burning the tube with a carefully applied electric current and was very popular a few years ago. While the tube is effectively blocked off, the damage done may be widespread and reversal may be very difficult. One of the main disadvantages of cauterization is that other structures may get damaged as well, either by the probe or by the hot fallopian tube once it has been cauterized.

Occlusive devices are the rubber or metal clips placed around the tubes to block them off. They work both by physically blocking the tube and by depriving the tube of its blood supply which in turn leads to scarring and permanent blockage. Most occlusive devices are designed to be placed on the tubes with a specially developed gun-like applicator which can be used successfully with a laparoscope. Falope rings (Yoon bands) are rubber rings placed over a loop of tube during the operation. Some studies have found that the use of rings results in slightly longer pain after this operation which may be due to the slow death of the portion of the tube which has been deprived of its oxygen. The length of tube destroyed is around 1–3 cm. Occlusive clips are devices which are like the jaws of a tenacious crocodile snapped shut over the fallopian tubes. The Hulka-Clemen clip, for example, is made of plastic held together by a gold-plated stainless steel spring. Another clip, the Filshie clip, is made of titanium lined with silicone rubber, has a high compression force and is particularly useful when the fallopian tubes are bulky. Clips are very effective but in order to work properly need to be placed skilfully. Their main advantage is that they only damage about 6–8 mm of tube and consequently give the greatest possible chance of successful reversal.

Which method and by what route?
The best method of sterilization for you may well be the one that your surgeon suggests since the safest and most successful sterilizations are performed when the surgeon is skilled and experienced. All operations require a knack and it is best for you if your surgeon does what she or he is used to doing. We think it is much better to find the right gynaecologist than to persuade a reluctant doctor to try out your chosen method. Find out from your GP which gynaecologists perform which

type of sterilizations and ask to be referred accordingly. If you feel strongly that you want a laparoscopy with clips tell your GP so that she or he can refer you appropriately. But remember that in 'choosing' the type of occlusive method to be used you have to accept at the beginning of the procedure that all sterilizations are considered irreversible. Never make a sterilization decision with the assurance of a successful reversal in the back of your mind since reversal is not always readily available on the NHS and is often not successful.

Since sterilization is much more of a life-changing event than the other methods of contraception we have examined so far, we are including a detailed first-hand account, to give an insight into how one woman experienced the procedure:

I made the decision to be sterilized while pregnant with my fourth child. It was an unplanned pregnancy and I wanted to make sure it did not happen again. My husband is a bit squeamish and felt unable to go through with a vasectomy. I discussed it with the consultant obstetrician, whom I was seeing in maternity outpatients, and he advised me against having the operation straight after the birth of the baby. Instead he suggested that it was done some four months later when it could be done by laparoscopy. I was put on the waiting list.

A letter arrived when Alice was six weeks old, requesting my admission at the end of July. I really didn't want the operation then as it was too soon after her birth and also just around the time of the school holidays. The date was changed to the end of September.

Meanwhile I was encouraged about having the sterilization by some friends and discouraged by others. One in particular put forward all the negative arguments with all the 'what if's': 'what if your husband died or you divorced and remarried?'; 'what if one or more of your children died?' and so on.

During the two weeks before the operation I worried and worried that I would feel different afterwards because an essential part of my body that was working well was to be deliberately damaged.

Common sense told me to stick to my guns. I was thirty-seven, had four children, with high blood pressure in all but one pregnancy. I could not cope with another one.

I felt sad when I went into hospital with Alice. I had a single room with a cot for Alice and a good friend stayed with me to look after Alice while I recovered. I was to stay in for just the day and as instructed I had not eaten or drunk since midnight. I was seen by the anaesthetist and the gynaecology registrar. The latter explained that nothing would change in my usual menstrual cycle and that contrary to some opinions sterilization did not lead to heavy periods. I did not find this difficult to accept as I could not see the link physiologically. The doctor explained that clips were used on the tubes to effect sterilization and that I needed to be aware that there was a one in 500 risk of pregnancy afterwards. I was surprised and also strangely reassured by this slight risk; it somehow blurred the finality of the operation.

Alice went to sleep and I went to the operating theatre. The anaesthetist was kind and my fear of not waking up from the anaesthetic receded a bit.

I woke up in the recovery room aware of an oxygen mask and quite severe lower abdominal pain. I looked at the clock opposite and thought that I must have been asleep for about half an hour. The anaesthetist came over and asked if I was in pain. He went to find a nurse to give me some painkillers. I remembered that the ward sister had told me to try and avoid having any Omnopon (synthetic morphine), as it often lengthened the recovery from the anaesthetic. However, I felt quite uncomfortable, so I decided to have it. I then tried to sleep.

It was a hot day and I slept fitfully. Alice needed breastfeeding often as she refused the expressed breast milk offered to her. I had a drink, felt very tired, and my eyes kept closing. I felt better by noon but I carried on sleeping on and off and I kept thinking that I would feel more awake soon. My head started pounding and I could only just stay awake long enough to feed Alice. By seven-thirty I still felt really drugged and just managed to go to the loo. The ward staff encouraged me to stay overnight. I did not want to and finally got ready to leave. However I felt so dizzy and sick that I went back to my room. A doctor that I had not seen before came in and suggested that I stayed overnight.

I and, fortunately, Alice slept well and I felt much better the next day. There was only mild discomfort as I had one umbilical stitch and one just above the pubic bone. My husband collected me and that day I got stuck into the normal family routine, but I did have a rest in the afternoon. I had some pain on passing urine which lasted about three days and there was a lot of bruising between the stitches. For a week I felt very tired.

Eight months later I am glad that I had the operation. Physically I feel no different than before and I feel satisfied that my family is now complete. I love little babies and I'm sure I will go on feeling broody when I see one until I am past the menopause. My husband also feels relieved as our lives are so busy with four children and we find it hard to give them each the attention that they deserve.

Failure rates

Sterilization is not 100 per cent effective. The Oxford/FPA study found that in the first twelve months the failure rate was 0.37 per 100 woman-years, falling after that to 0.10 per 100 woman-years. Life-table analysis of these results reveals that this means that for every 1,000 women sterilized, four would get pregnant after one year, eight after four years and ten after seven years.[6] The method of sterilization, the operator and the woman all have an influence on the risk of failure. The older methods of sterilization have a lower failure rate than the more recent developments of clips and rings.

Sterilization will certainly be unsuccessful if the wrong structure is operated upon. The uterus is held in place by two ligaments called round ligaments. These are not unlike the fallopian tubes in appearance, particularly after the delivery of a baby. Tying the round ligaments instead of the fallopian tubes is a recognized problem and is a particular risk with laparoscopy when the view of all the organs is limited. Sterilization may also fail if the tube becomes patent (open) once again. The tube down which the egg tumbles, may reopen, particularly if the tube is simply blocked but not cut. Or cut halves of a fallopian tube may miraculously find each other again and rejoin. Failures can occur at any time after an operation. Even if you have had years of trouble-free intercourse following a sterilization, a missed period could still be due to a pregnancy. Sterilization immediately after a pregnancy carries the greatest risk of failure because post-partum procedures, and those done at the time of an abortion, are technically more difficult. All the pelvic organs become enlarged and more fleshy during pregnancy which makes blocking the tubes more difficult and bleeding more likely. When the tubes return to normal size, ties or bands may become loose. For these reasons some gynaecologists are reluctant to perform sterilizations immediately after the birth of a baby.

It seems ironic that an operation which people are encouraged to consider as irreversible should also carry an appreciable risk of failure. You should always be alert to the possibility of a pregnancy since the earlier a pregnancy is recognized the easier it is to have an abortion if you wish to choose one. Most gynaecologists are very sympathetic to women with failed sterilizations and will do a repeat procedure at the same time as the termination if requested.

Side-effects of female sterilization

About one or two in every hundred women who undergo sterilization suffer from a complication. Death resulting from the operation is very rare: three to ten per 100,000 is the figure usually quoted and the majority of deaths are due to anaesthetic complications. Problems following a sterilization can be divided into immediate and long-term ones.

Immediate problems
The major complications of sterilization tend to occur either during the operation or immediately afterwards. Aside from the risks posed by all general and epidural anaesthetics, there are the risks of haemorrhage and infection. As we have seen, haemorrhage is more likely in the post-partum period when the pelvic organs have a particularly rich supply of blood. Infections can range from minor wound infections to more serious

internal ones. Since infections are treated promptly and effectively, any long-term consequences are very unlikely. Other complications could be due to damage caused to other abdominal organs during the operation.

Immediately after a laproscopic operation most women will feel some discomfort. You may feel shoulder pain, which is due to the effects of the remaining gas in your abdomen. If you have had rings put on your fallopian tubes you may have a lingering abdominal pain. Most postoperative pain only needs a paracetamol to sort it out. If you have persistent pain that is not controlled by mild painkillers you should see your doctor.

Long-term problems
Pregnancy is about the most unfortunate long-term problem associated with sterilization, particularly since women who do become pregnant after a sterilization have an increased chance of an ectopic pregnancy. The risk of a pregnancy in your fallopian tube seems to increase if your sterilization was performed by cauterization since occasionally this method damages your tubes but does not completely block them. It is important that you are aware of the possibility, however remote it may seem, of an ectopic pregnancy following sterilization.[7]

Many women believe that sterilization will affect the pattern of their periods. Usefully there has been a certain amount of research into this. Theoretically sterilization could interfere with the blood supply to the ovary which might result in a change in hormone production. The blockage of tube could also change the movement of chemicals such as prostaglandins along the tube, and both of these mechanisms could in theory result in changes in menstruation. Unfortunately to date most of the studies into menstrual problems have been rather short-term ones, slightly reducing the usefulness of their findings. However, their results indicate that 50–90 per cent of women experience no change in their menstruation, and of those who do report changes 50 per cent have an improved cycle and 50 per cent have problems.[8] This suggests random variation rather than an effect of sterilization. Among the longer-term studies, the Oxford/FPA study followed women for six years after their operations, and did report a slight increase in menstrual problems, though the statistical significance of this is doubtful.[9]

If the operation itself has a marginal effect on menstruation, the perception of changes in the pattern of menstruation may depend on the previous type of contraception used. If you stop taking the pill after your sterilization you will almost certainly experience heavier periods because you will be used to light withdrawal bleeds rather than a natural period. Conversely, if you have an IUD removed after your operation you will probably find that your periods are lighter. Another factor to bear in mind is that periods do anyway become heavier as you grow older; if you have a sterilization after thirty-five you may find that your periods grow gradually heavier, but they would probably have done so anyway. You may put it down to your sterilization, when it may be as much to do with the fact that you are beginning to approach the menopause.

The long-term psychological effects of sterilization are a very important parameter by which to judge this method of fertility control, but it seems that despite the finality of taking such a step there are surprisingly few such problems.

Reversal of female sterilization

A reversal is requested by as many as three out of every 100 women who have had the operation and it is estimated that from half to slightly less than three-quarters of these women will achieve an intrauterine pregnancy. The real figures indicating the success of reversals are hard to come by as the very rigorous selection procedure for the operation can lead to an artificially raised pregnancy rate. The skill of the surgeon is also an extremely important factor, some of the best surgeons achieving an 80 per cent success rate or more. However, they may only operate on women whom they consider will have a high chance of pregnancy, so it is not possible to extrapolate from such figures and say that every woman wanting a reversal will have the same success. Some surgeons are also reluctant to operate on a woman until they are sure about the fertility of her partner.[10]

One of the problems with reversal operations is that it is not necessarily enough simply to rejoin the two halves of the tube and make it open. Fallopian tubes are lined with fine hairs and have a muscular wall, both of which are important for egg transport. Small changes to this environment can interfere with the movement of the ovum. Sterilization creates scar tissue and interferes with the nerves and blood supply in this finely tuned organ. Fortunately the development of microsurgical techniques has improved success rates by enabling the surgeon to repair all the separate layers of the tube.

Various factors affect the success of the operation. There must be a sufficient length of undamaged tube to make a good repair possible. In one study of reversals all the women with 5 cm of tube remaining conceived while only 18 per cent of those with less than 3 cm were successful. Most surgeons consider that it is not worth operating if less than 3 cm of viable tube remains. Clip and ring sterilization offers the best chance of reversal, while electrocautery causes such widespread damage it is the most difficult to reverse. Other factors influencing the success rate of reversals include the point along the tube at which the blocking off occurs, the age of the woman and the length of time that has passed since the sterilization was performed. As we have seen, fertility naturally declines with age, but with passing time the condition of the tubes themselves may alter also making reversal much more tricky.

Reversal operations are done by laparotomy and take longer than sterilizations to carry out. Any pregnancies that occur subsequently are about twice as likely to be ectopic. Two women in 100 conceiving after a reversal may have ectopic pregnancies, though the figure is thought to be as high as 5 per cent if electrocautery was used to block the tubes.[11] If a reversal operation is not possible or fails, *in vitro* fertilization techniques offer an alternative chance of conception though this is by no means an easy procedure for a woman to go through and offers no guarantee of a successful pregnancy in the end.

The future

Developments in sterilization are taking two paths. One path pursues successful and easy reversal, and the other sterilization without abdominal operations. Trials have been carried out on non-surgical techniques of sterilization. Chemical tissue toxins are injected into the uterus via the cervix where they destroy the endometrial lining and can completely block off the cavity. While such techniques are by no means perfected, in one trial an estimated 98 per cent of women were made sterile after three doses.[12] The development was also proposed of tissue adhesives which are similar to 'superglue', though inserting them would require considerable skill, while another possible development for the future lies in placing plugs at the entrance to the fallopian tubes. Such plugs, made of silicone, have already been tested in clinical trials. They are created as liquid silicone and inserted into the fallopian tubes via a hysteroscope, a special magnifying instrument giving a direct view inside the uterus. Much more research is needed.

Male sterilization

I couldn't have it done, I'm afraid. I find it difficult to put my finger on what exactly it is that worries me about it. I feel I have to keep the life-blood of my family, my ancestors alive in my veins, though that sounds like nonsense. It is definitely something to do with 'male seed' and the masculine line, though.

My wife had always said that when she was thirty-five she was going to give up contraception and I had to take over. I was sterilized about a week after her thirty-fifth birthday and was amazed at how simple, painless and easy a procedure the whole thing was. No, I haven't suffered any ill consequences, and my wife certainly hasn't. If anything we make love more now than we did before.

I have had regrets. When I was forty-five my wife died and after a while I began a relationship with a younger woman. She was looking for a partner who would give her children. I obviously couldn't oblige her, and though we looked into the possibility of a reversal, something had already gone out of the relationship. My being sterile made me a much older man in her eyes.

My husband had a vasectomy privately in 1969 and we have had twenty wonderful years of 'sex without worry'.

Sterilization is the only method of contraception independent of intercourse that is available to men. It is the most effective male method presently on offer and is a simple operation which has very few problems associated with it. Something in the region of 33 million couples in the world now rely on vasectomy for fertility control, the majority of whom are in the USA, UK, India and China. Approximately 12 per cent of couples in the UK rely on vasectomy for their contraception, and though the operation has become slightly less popular recently there was a huge increase in the number of men undergoing vasectomy in the 70s and early 80s. The slight trend away from vasectomy may be partly due to the increasing availability of simpler and safer methods of female sterilization and partly due to the suggestions that vasectomy may carry long-term health risks.

Many men are uncomfortable or even horrified by the thought of a radical interference in their fertility. The fear of being made less 'manly', less whole, through sterilization appears to be deeply rooted, perhaps due to the complex relationship that exists for many men (and women) between fertility, sexuality and libido. While women are expected to be pleased to have the opportunity of reducing their fertility, it seems that many men see their own fertility as fundamental to their sense of manhood. There is also a strangely tangled relationship between castration and sterilization that prevents some men from considering vasectomy. According to Ferber et al, less than 50 per cent of men will tell their friends that they have had a vasectomy, and only 30 per cent are prepared to recommend it.[13] Perhaps men fear being blamed for the impotence of an associate. These peer group pressures are very powerful and contrast strongly with attitudes among women.

Women who have undergone sterilization are usually much more willing to admit it and to recommend it to friends if they feel happy with the procedure. The fear of the loss of potency following on from vasectomy is not confined to men alone. Many women say that they would not wish their partners to be sterilized and are prepared to put up with the more complicated procedure of a female sterilization instead. Research suggests that men who do have vasectomies are frequently the dominant partner and are used to taking responsibility for decision making, including contraception.[14] It will be interesting to see what male attitudes will be when, and if, a reversible male method such as the pill becomes available. Do men shy away from vasectomy because of the permanent nature of such a step or because they feel that their fertility and their bodies are too precious to interfere with? We suspect that the way the male-dominated establishment has dragged its feet over developing good safe male methods of contraception goes some way to answering this question.

Vasectomy

The word vasectomy describes the procedure involved in male steriliz-ation. The vas deferens is the tube which carries sperm from the testis where they are made to the penis from which they are ejaculated. The vas from each testis is interrupted or cut in a vasectomy so that the sperm created in the testicles cannot be ejaculated. Semen is largely composed of fluid from the prostate and other glands, and since these are not touched during a vasectomy there is no noticeable change in the amount of semen a man ejaculates after his sterilization. There is also no change in a man's ability to have sex; vasectomy has no effect on erections or orgasms. The testes continue to manufacture both male sex hormones and sperm so that apart from the fact that no sperm appear in an

Figure 9.2 Vasectomy

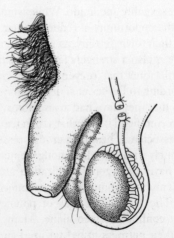

ejaculation there are no differences between men who have had a vasectomy and men who have not. The sperm are broken down and absorbed by the body, and do not just build up like water behind a dam.

Vasectomy is almost always performed under local anaesthetic and does not require a stay in hospital. Men who are particularly nervous can normally arrange to have a general anaesthetic if they want one. Firstly the hairs on the scrotum may be shaved or clipped, and the area thoroughly cleaned with an antiseptic solution. A local anaesthetic is injected with a fine needle into the skin of the scrotum, which may sting slightly. Once the skin is numb another local anaesthetic is given but at a deeper level. Next a small cut about 2.5 cm long is made in the skin of the scrotum and the vas deferens gently separated from the surrounding tissue. The surgeon then cuts the vas and ties the cut ends firmly, ensuring as far as possible that there is no bleeding from the skin or other tissue.

The surgeon performing the operation can use a number of methods to 'damage' the vas. The ideal method would be one which closes the tube completely, prevents bleeding and which damages the smallest length of the tube. The cutting and tying method is probably the simplest, but surgeons also use heat or electricity to cauterize the ends and more recently metal clips have been introduced. Once the tube has been blocked off the skin of the scrotum is closed with stiches, usually the dissolving kind, and the entire procedure repeated on the other side. While it is not painful, you may feel a certain amount of pushing and pulling. The operation completed you can usually go home within a few hours though you should not do any strenuous work for about a week. There may be some discomfort for a few days but simple painkillers like paracetamol are usually sufficient.

Unfortunately you cannot go home and expect to be instantly sterile. The whole procedure is not complete until all the sperm which were already in your semen have gone. In the UK you will usually be asked to have your semen checked for sperm, once at ten weeks and again at twelve weeks after the operation. If neither specimen contains sperm you can assume that you have been sterilized successfully. In countries where there are no facilities for testing semen men are told to have ten to fifteen ejaculations before they can rely on the operation for contraception. Most couples continue to rely on their previous method of contraception while waiting for the 'all clear'.

Success and failure

Vasectomy fails less than once for every 100 operations performed, a degree of effectiveness comparable to female sterilization. Failures are due to intercourse before the sperm count becomes negative, failure to achieve a negative sperm count at all, or sperm appearing in the ejaculate at some point after an apparently successful vasectomy. As with all operations vasectomy can fail because it is not done properly; sometimes the same tube is cut twice, or not completely shut off. The sperm counts should identify an operation that has gone wrong before a pregnancy occurs. A more unfortunate group of men are those who have a spontaneous reversal. Either the vas rejoins or a new passage develops and the sperm swim down it and into the urethra. Both events can happen at any point after the operation.

Short-term effects

The commonest problems experienced after vasectomy are bruising, swelling and pain, though they are usually minimal and wearing some form of scrotal support will usually help. Occasionally (in less than one in a hundred men) a haematoma or collection of blood develops in the scrotum. The treatment is rest, painkillers and good support for the scrotum, though occasionally it is necessary to drain the blood through a small incision. Another occasional problem is swelling and pain in the testes caused by the absorption of sperm not keeping up with production. The sperm builds up causing a certain amount of discomfort. Again the treatment is rest and support and the problem usually rights itself within a week. This build-up of sperm can occur soon after the operation or several months later. Infections are another potential problem, though rare, and are easily treated with antibiotics. Very rarely a hydrocele or build-up of fluid around the testes is formed. Sperm granulomas can also develop as a result of vasectomy. These are collections of sperm and cells which form as a result of sperm leaking into the tissue, causing inflammation but no infection. They can form either at the site of the vasectomy or in the epididymis (the coiled tube which joins the vas to the testes). A sperm granuloma is usually unimportant unless it causes pain. More significantly its formation occasionally allows channels to develop within the scrotum which restore the movement of sperm and hence fertility.

Long-term effects

To date there is no evidence that vasectomy produces any long-term effects on sexuality or has any significant psychological side-effects. Sterilization is, as we have seen, much less likely to be regretted if it is an entirely voluntary decision, and in this context it is interesting to bear in mind the fact that unlike women, very few men in Britain are likely to have the operation suggested to them by their doctors.

There is also no clear evidence that vasectomy carries any long-term risk to general health though there has recently been some concern about the possibility of it increasing the risk of developing atherosclerosis (fatty disease of the blood vessels) and making autoimmune disease more common. Autoimmune diseases are very varied in their symptoms but they are all caused by the mistaken identification of the body's own cells as enemy cells. Once the faulty identification is made the body sets out to eliminate these supposed enemy cells by producing antibodies and other hostile cells to attack and destroy them, much as it would defend itself from a bacterial invasion. Unfortunately this leads to the destruction of the body's own cells. In rheumatoid arthritis, for example, the body attacks and destroys the lining of its own joints.

There is a theoretical risk of developing an autoimmune disease after a vasectomy though, at the moment, there is no evidence to prove the risk. Many men develop antibodies to sperm after a vasectomy and since sperm share many characteristics in common with other cells in the body there is a risk that antibodies developed to fight sperm could also attack other cells in the body. To date the *only* effect which these antibodies have been shown to have is a reduction in the amount of healthy sperm available when a reversal of the vasectomy has been performed. The controversy in this area is largely fuelled by the fact that in experimental animals other effects have been demonstrated which may have an autoimmune origin, such as the higher incidence of atherosclerosis in vasectomized monkeys than in controls. Obviously this is an area in which much more research is needed.[15]

Vasectomy reversal

Inevitably some men wish to have their vasectomy reversed, though in the UK it is a surprisingly low one in 1,000. The reversal operation is not an easy one to carry out and may take a good three hours under a general anaesthetic. During the operation the scarred portion of the vas is removed and the surgeon rejoins the two ends, trying to ensure that the scar formed during healing does not block the tube again. Microsurgical techniques have improved the chances of a successful reversal, and various reports have put the percentage of men who regain sperm in their ejaculate at between 35 per cent and 91 per cent. The length of time between the original operation and the reversal seems to be an important factor reversals after ten years being relatively unsuccessful. Unfortunately even when there is apparent success and the man has a normal sperm count the number of successful pregnancies that result is disappointing. Different studies show this to range from a low 30 per cent to 60 per cent of couples where the man has had a reversal operation. Pregnancy-rates will depend on the skill of the surgeon, whether or not the man is producing antibodies to his own sperm and the fertility of the woman. The difficulty of achieving a completely successful reversal means that, like female sterilization, it is much wiser to regard vasectomy as permanent and irreversible.[16]

New developments

Research into improved methods of vasectomy have tended to concentrate on reversibility. A temporary plug for the vas has undergone animal trials which were sufficiently encouraging to make human trials the next step. The concept of a tap which could be plumbed into the vas deferens and turned on or off at will is an appealing one though achieving reliable infertility in the 'off' position is by no means easy to engineer. The wait for a negative sperm count after turning off the tap might also be a drawback. Another alternative being considered is the storage of sperm from men who are subsequently vasectomized.

Conclusion

Sterilization is an operation which provides a high level of contraceptive protection. It is equally applicable to men and women and is increasingly popular throughout the world. The permanent nature of the infertility produced by the operation sets it aside from all the other methods available and limits its appeal. Women and men who choose to be sterilized are, on the whole, happy with the consequences. There are at present long waiting lists in NHS hospitals for both male and female sterilizations, and for this reason many people have private operations performed. This can be arranged through your GP with a local consultant and will be done in the private hospital in your area. The cost of this is variable. There are three agencies which provide both counselling and arrange the operation which can be helpful if your own doctor has refused to refer you. They are:

Pregnancy Advisory Service, cost for female sterilization, £245
British Pregnancy Advisory Service, cost for female sterilization, £210
    (£110 if at the time of an abortion done at the BPAS), cost for male
    sterilization, £90
Marie Stopes House, cost for female sterilization, £210, cost for
    vasectomy, £95

The addresses for these clinics are given in Appendix 1. All prices given are for 1989.

CHAPTER 10

Post-coital Contraception

> *The most frequent eternal triangle*
> *A husband . . . . a wife*
> *and her*
> *fears*

Fewer marriages would flounder around in a maze of misunderstanding and unhappiness if more wives knew and practised regular marital hygiene. Without it, some minor physical irregularity plants in a woman's mind the fear of a major crisis. Let so devastating a fear recur again, and again, and the most charming and gracious wife turns into a nerve-ridden, irritable travesty of herself. Bewildering, to say the least, even to the kindest husbands. Fatal, inevitably, to the beauty of the marriage relation.

It all sounds very dreadful, doesn't it? But it needn't happen. The proper technique of marriage hygiene, faithfully followed, replaces fear with peace of mind. Makes what seems a grave problem no problem at all.

What is the proper technique? To my practice I recommend the 'Lysol' method. I know that 'Lysol' destroys germs in the presence of organic matter, not just on a glass slide. I know that it has high penetrating power, reaching into every fold and crevice. And I know with all its power, it is very gentle . . .

1933, *McCalls Magazine*

I think my worst experience of contraception was a post-coital one. Even though the regime is pretty simple – I think I had just four pills to take – I was terribly nauseated. Anyway, thank goodness, it worked.

The idea of post-coital contraception is as old as contraception itself but the techniques that make it more than wishful thinking are very recent. It has only been in the last twenty years or so that women who have been raped, or suffered from a contraceptive mishap, or simply taken a risk, have been able to do anything about it before a pregnancy becomes established. (Here we use the contemporary medical definition of the beginning of a pregnancy, namely when the blastocyst has implanted itself in the uterus, roughly five days after ovulation.) It is only about five years since post-coital contraception (PCC) became at all widely available. Yet throughout history women have douched, jumped backwards for seven magical steps, sneezed, held their breath, and performed 101 other rituals in the hope of warding off an unintentional pregnancy. Why has the idea of post-coital contraception persisted for so long, so much so that throughout much of this century post-coital douching with antiseptics such as 'Lysol', advertised above, really was an integral part of the sexual behaviour of many women?

One answer at least is that any method of post-coital contraception is likely to seem successful, at least for the first two or three times it is tried. This is, of course, due to the inherent extravagance of nature who wastes such a high percentage of fertilized eggs anyway, and not to the effectiveness of the post-coital method. Not surprisingly, if the chances of conceiving in any one cycle range from a very low 1–2 per cent to a still lowish 30 per cent, post-coital contraception, or indeed doing nothing at all, will have a reasonable chance of 'success'. Nature is prodigal with blastocysts, wasting as many as 40 per cent of those conceived.

Douching is still believed by many women and men to be a useful form of birth-control. Some American college girls apparently keep a bottle of Coca Cola by their beds for a post-intercourse douche. It is true that Coca Cola has spermicidal properties, but in order to have any effect it would have to be used within ninety seconds of ejaculation. It has been shown that the all-important mechanism for sperm survival, and hence fertility, is the behaviour of the cervical mucus. Sperm and mucus mix within ninety seconds and since, at the most fertile time of the month, once safely in the cervical mucus sperm can find a channel which will take them up into the uterus and fallopian tubes within minutes, douching is a little like shutting the stable door once the horse has bolted. At other times of the cycle, douching is like shutting the stable door when there is no horse anyway.

It was not until the 1960s that the first effective techniques for post-coital contraception were developed. A Dutch gynaecologist began to treat women who had been raped with high doses of ethinyloestradiol (the oestrogen used in the pill) which had the effect of preventing fertilized eggs from becoming implanted in the uterus. At the same time, other scientists were experimenting with DES (diethylstilboestrol), at first in monkeys and later with women, and they discovered it was effective post-coitally. The subsequent history of DES is documented elsewhere (see p. 283), and it is now never used post-coitally. Throughout the 1960s and 70s, high doses of ethinyloestradiol remained the choice for post-coital contraception, though the doses taken by women worked out at almost the same amount of oestrogen as is contained in approximately three years' worth of contemporary ultra-low combined pills!

Fortunately a major breakthrough in hormonal PCC began in the early 1970s when research was undertaken in Canada on the effectiveness of low-dose oestrogen/progestogen combinations. By the 1980s the Canadian gynaecologist Albert Yuzpe had developed what has become the standard hormonal PCC treatment, known as the Yuzpe regimen. It consists of four tablets of an ordinary contraceptive pill, containing 250 μg of levonorgesterol (the progestogen component) and 50 μg of ethinyloestradiol (the oestrogen) taken within seventy-two hours, or three days, of unprotected intercourse. This particular combination is found in Eugynon 50, or Ovran, both contraceptive pills which, since the arrival of the ultra-low regimens, are less commonly prescribed. The same formula is also marketed under the name 'PC4' by Schering. The dose is given in two lots of two tablets, twelve hours apart. In the UK, since 1984 when the Committee on Safety of Medicines gave approval for the use of hormones as post-coital contraceptive agents, this has been the accepted regimen, though some doctors may continue to prescribe ethinyloestradiol on its own. It is worth pointing out that *no other combination of combined pills works*, so borrowing a friend's pills will not offer you any post-coital contraception.

While doctors were experimenting with hormonal PCCs, other gynaecologists were discovering the effectiveness of the IUD when inserted post-coitally. The designers of two of the 'modern' IUDs, Tatum and Lippes, were the first to suggest using the IUD in this way. A copper bearing IUD can be inserted up to five days post-coitally and either removed at the next menstruation or left in place as a more permanent form of contraception.

In recent years more research has been undertaken into what has been called post-coital contragestion. Whereas traditional PCC has had to be started within five days of ovulation, the new range of drugs is designed to be used between days twenty-one and twenty-eight – the luteal phase – of the cycle. The fertilized egg, known as a blastocyst, settles into the wall of the uterus. It is entirely dependent on the progesterone produced by the corpus luteum for its survival. The development of anti-progesterones has provided a means of nullifying the effect of progesterone, causing a dramatic drop in the plasma levels of both progesterone and oestrogen. Without these steroids, the pregnancy cannot continue to develop and menstruation begins about two days after the administration of the anti-progesterone drug. At the moment there is only one drug being used in this way, mifepristone, known under its trade name RU 486. At the time of writing RU 486 was being used in France, America and other European countries. The French government has recently authorized RU 486 for public use. RU 486 is also used as an early abortifacient often combined with prostaglandin pessaries.

Developments such as RU 486 seem to be an indication of the way in which PCC will go in the future. Drugs that interfere with the corpus luteum, and drugs that affect the immune system are also being developed. There has been considerable interest in the concept of a once-a-month pill which would bring about a period when used, regardless of whether there had been implantation of a fertilized egg. RU 486 is a step in this direction and the next few years will almost certainly see the refinement and wider availability of such methods.

Hormonal post-coital contraception

Hormonal PCC seems to work in a number of different ways, depending on which point in the cycle has been reached when it is taken. If taken before ovulation, it appears that ovulation itself may be prevented. Research suggests that the positive feedback of the oestrogen rise is cut short, so that the normal peak in the luteinizing hormone does not occur. Without the LH peak, no egg can be released. If PCC is taken later in the cycle when an egg may have been fertilized, the hormones act by interfering with the corpus luteum in some way, causing it to malfunction and produce inadequate amounts of progesterone. Researchers have shown that the luteal phase of a woman who has taken PCC at or just after ovulation differs from that in a normal cycle. There is no rise in basal body temperature, and the luteal phase is often cut short, with a period arriving early. There also seem to be changes in the endometrium, or womb lining, making it less receptive to the fertilized egg. Finally there may also be changes in the transport of the ovum, or the fertilized egg, down the tube, though this is not fully understood.

In order to work effectively hormonal PCC needs to begin not later than three days after unprotected intercourse. If it is started too late the delicate but persistent mechanisms of fertility are much more difficult to interrupt. So far nobody has shown whether starting PCC within twelve hours of the first exposure to intercourse is significantly more effective than starting within thirty-six, forty-eight or seventy-two hours. It does seem to be the case, however, that hormonal PCC works best after a single sexual act. If there have been several days of unprotected sex, an IUD is likely to be a more effective option.

Hormonal PCC is very effective, with the high dose oestrogen regimen proving slightly more effective than the Yuzpe regimen. Taking ethinyloestradiol alone gives a subsequent pregnancy rate of less than 1.0 per cent. With the Yuzpe method the failure rate is around 1–2 per cent (1 per cent if the pills are taken properly), though one study has put the pregnancy rate at 5 per cent for mid-cycle exposure. A study carried out by the Margaret Pyke Centre in London put the failure rate at 2.6 per cent for women exposed to pregnancy mid-cycle (around days nine to seventeen, adjusted to take account of women's different cycle lengths). Albert Yuzpe, reviewing many studies, quotes a failure rate of 0.6–1.9 per cent per cycle, though he also points out that even these low figures give an annual failure rate of 7.8 per cent–24.7 per cent – considerably higher than other contraceptive methods.[1]

Post-coital contraception with IUDs

The way in which an IUD acts when used post-coitally will also depend on the point that has been reached in the woman's cycle. As we saw in the chapter on IUDs, recent research has shown that they work in a number of different ways (see pp. 231–4). This being the case, an IUD inserted just after an act of intercourse relatively early in the cycle, and before ovulation, may work in a different way to one inserted five days after ovulation. One of the advantages of using an IUD post-coitally is that it can be safely inserted up to five days after ovulation is presumed to have taken place. This is because it takes at least five days between the time of ovulation and the implanting of the fertilized ovum, at this stage called a blastocyst, into the walls of the uterus. An IUD placed in the uterus at any time before this will prevent a pregnancy establishing itself in 98–99 per cent of cases. After this point, use of an IUD becomes much more problematic. It is illegal to insert an IUD into a pregnant uterus, because it could be regarded as an attempt to procure an abortion. It is also extremely dangerous. Inserting an IUD into a pregnant uterus could bring with it a chance of a septic abortion, a life-threatening condition. This is why if you are seeking post-coital contraception in the form of an IUD it is important to be as clear as possible about dates. The doctor providing PCC has to estimate from your account the most likely date of ovulation and in the interests of your own well-being it is best to be as accurate as possible.

The IUD used post-coitally has a number of advantages and a number of drawbacks. Its main advantage is its effectiveness. In a review of the literature it was found that of 1300 women who were given IUDs post-coitally, only two became pregnant. This corresponds closely with effectiveness rates for the IUD when used as a long-term contraceptive. An estimated 1–2 per cent of women relying on the IUD become pregnant each year. A second advantage is that once an IUD has been inserted it can stay there for as long as is necessary. Many women choose to keep their IUDs as a long-term form of contraception. The IUD can equally easily be removed at the next period if that is what you wish. The third advantage has already been mentioned; IUDs can be inserted up to about day twenty of a twenty-eight-day cycle – or later if your cycle length is always longer than that. An IUD is also a good choice if you have had intercourse over several days before seeking PCC, whereas hormonal PCC works best after just one exposure to pregnancy. The other major advantage of an IUD is that it can be used where hormonal PCC is contraindicated – if you have high blood pressure, or a history of thrombosis, etc.[2]

The disadvantages of using an IUD post-coitally are more or less the same as its disadvantages as a long-term contraceptive. IUDs do bring with them a risk of an infection, and even though the risk is small, it is concentrated into the first few months after insertion (see pp. 241–5). The risk of an STD in IUD-users is higher among young unmarried women without children, and according to one study carried out in the Netherlands, 70 per cent of the women seeking post-coital contraception were nulliparous.[3] It is partly because IUD use does bring with it an increased risk of infection that doctors always carry out a thorough internal examination before fitting one. She or he will be checking for signs of an existing infection, but also making sure that you are not pregnant already from a previous cycle. Only if the doctor is convinced that you will not be put at any risk from an IUD will she or he agree to insert it.

Using post-coital contraception: for and against

There are a number of circumstances that could lead you to take steps to avoid a pregnancy after, rather than before, the event. One of the most common reasons cited by women seeking PCC is a contraceptive failure such as burst condoms. In one study two-thirds of the women asked said they had been the victims of burst condoms.[4] Sex with a new partner, first-time-ever intercourse, a reconciliation with a partner, sex under the influence of drugs or alcohol or spontaneous sex for any reason could lead to a situation where no contraception was used. If intercourse occurs around mid-cycle there is a definite risk of pregnancy. PCC is a much less traumatic solution than waiting anxiously for a period. The development of effective PCC has also been an enormous step forward in helping women who have been raped, particularly as there is some evidence (though it has been questioned) that they have a higher than expected pregnancy rate.

Many women find it very hard to approach their family doctors for post-coital contraception. They fear disapproval, particularly if the reason for their visit is that they simply did not use contraception. Quite why there should still be a censorious attitude among some doctors towards PCC is difficult to understand, but some of the women who wrote to us had had negative experiences with their GPs. Even if you have never been to a family planning clinic you may prefer to go there for PCC counselling since you are less likely to be given an unsympathetic reception. Some women find the very detailed questions that doctors ask at PCC counselling prurient and unhelpful. While it is not possible to vouch for all doctors, it is true that with PCC it is important for the doctor to get as accurate a picture of what has happened as possible.

She will need to know your age, whether you have any children, your relevant medical and reproductive history, the date of your last period, the details of your normal cycle, the calculated date of ovulation, the days on which you have had unprotected intercourse, the number of hours which have lapsed since the first episode and whether you use contraception. She will then carry out a pelvic examination, take your blood pressure and discuss the different types of PCC she can offer you. Most doctors will take time to discuss with you what you would do were the PCC to fail, including the (largely theoretical) risk to the fetus if you take hormones but none the less become pregnant. You will also get a chance to discuss your future contraceptive needs, particularly if you have not been using contraception recently or at all.

Depending on your circumstances and medical history, you and the doctor will decide on the next step. If you decide on hormonal PCC it's likely that you will be given the first dose there and then. It will consist of two small contraceptive pills. You will be given the next dose of pills (another two) to take with you, and told to take them twelve hours later. The chances are that you will feel sick, particularly after the second dose. An estimated 50–60 per cent of women feel nauseated to a greater or lesser extent by the pills, and about a third of women vomit. Your doctor may give you extra pills to take in case you vomit within two hours of taking them. Other side-effects reported by women are breast tenderness, headaches, dizziness and eye pains. Symptoms will almost certainly wear off within twelve hours of the last pill. You will be warned that your next period may be early, late or on time, and told that it is very important that you see your doctor for a follow-up visit – whether or not you have a normal period, or scanty bleeding. This is important since your doctor will need to double check that you are not pregnant. (Some women have a light period even though they are pregnant.)

If you are going to have an IUD fitted your doctor may do it there and then, or ask you to come back to see her or a colleague later in the day, or even the next day if it is still within five days. We suggest you read the section on having an IUD fitted (see pp. 226–9) so that you know what to expect. Again, a follow-up visit is important, and your doctor will want to see you either during, or just after your next period.

If, in spite of PCC, you do not menstruate, your doctor will test to see whether or not you are pregnant. Sometimes hormal treatment delays a period, but if you are pregnant, you will want to know about it as soon as possible so that you can plan what to do next.

The risk to the fetus if post-coital contraception fails

For roughly two out of every 100 women using post-coital contraception, menstruation does not occur. For whatever reason – PCC begun too late, multiple intercourse or just unknown factors – a pregnancy establishes itself, begins to pour out hCG into the blood stream and stops the next menstruation. If this happens to you, you will need to decide what you are going to do next. Most doctors will counsel you before they prescribe PCC, but if you are pregnant you may want to know whether the hormones or IUD could have harmed the developing embryo.

The short answer is that nobody knows for certain since very few babies have been born whose mothers took PCC. However, from all the evidence that we have to date the risk of fetal abnormality from both IUDs and hormonal contraception seems to be very small indeed. In the case of the Yuzpe method the amount of hormone taken is relatively small anyway – only four days' worth of the ordinary combined pill. Furthermore, since this hormone is taken before the blastocyst has had a chance to implant in the wall of the uterus the amount reaching it must be very small. Organogenesis (the development of the baby's organs) has not yet begun and there is evidence to suggest that until this process begins the embryo may be resistant to potentially harmful influences. As we have seen, women who become pregnant while taking the contraceptive pill, and continue to take it for several weeks into their pregnancies are considered to have an additional risk of an abnormal baby of about 0.1 per cent. It is important to put this in perspective. No one can guarantee any woman a 100 per cent perfect baby. About two women in every 100 will give birth to a baby who has some abnormality. With only an additional risk of 0.1 per cent many women who conceived while taking the pill decide to carry their babies to term. The risk for a woman who takes the Yuzpe regimen is considered to be less than that for a woman who has taken the pill into her pregnancy, but again, no doctor will be able to give you, or indeed any other pregnant woman, a 100 per cent guarantee that your baby will be normal.

Conceiving with an IUD in place presents a slightly different set of problems. We have reviewed them in the chapter on IUDs and recommend that you read pp. 245–8. At least if you become pregnant after having an IUD inserted post-coitally and decide that you wish to remain pregnant the chances of removing the IUD successfully are high. This is because you will know about the pregnancy very early on, before the uterus begins to enlarge at all. It is as the uterus enlarges that it tends to pull the strings of the IUD up and out of reach. Once the strings have disappeared into the uterus, it is very difficult to remove the IUD without also risking damage to the fetus, or inducing an abortion.

Using hormonal post-coital contraception on a regular basis

For women who make love only infrequently the idea of the Yuzpe regimen may seem attractive enough to use on a more systematic basis. The main drawbacks here are that you would have to make love very rarely indeed for it to be preferable to a barrier method or more regular pill taking. In the first place it is often not a very pleasant experience – too high a price to pay for 'spontaneity' for most women. And secondly it does not work for everyone – a pregnancy could still result up to 4 or 5 per cent of the time if intercourse occurred at the most fertile time. This is higher than the failure rate when using a barrier method carefully and considerably higher than the failure rate for normal use of the combined pill.

On the other hand, there is definitely something to be said for being forearmed if you are likely to find yourself in a situation where you might need PCC and cannot get hold of it – if you are planning to travel extensively for example. We know of a woman who was raped while abroad and though she was not taking the pill on a regular basis had taken a supply of Eugynon 50 with her, precisely for this kind of eventuality. Many doctors will be sympathetic to requests for PCC in advance. This is not to say however that self-dosing with hormones is a good idea at all. As will have been quite clear from the chapter on hormonal contraception, hormones are very potent drugs, and should always be used under medical supervision.

Conclusion

Some women are anxious about taking PCC because they think of it as abortion by another name. As we have already pointed out, PCC works in different ways, depending on the time in the cycle at which it is taken. If it works to delay ovulation, or to prevent ovulation from happening at all, clearly there is no interruption in the natural progress of a fertilization. The majority of PCC however is taken after ovulation can be presumed to have occurred and appears to act by altering the conditions in which a fertilized egg could settle into the walls of the uterus and begin its process of development. For the blastocyst everything depends on whether or not it implants in the walls of the uterus and begins to produce hCG in sufficient quantities to delay the next period and prevent itself being washed away by menstrual blood. We have already seen that nature is prodigal with blastocysts and at least 40 per cent fail to implant. PCC acts by adding to this process of wastage.

If you view any interruption to the development of the egg once it has been fertilized as early abortion, then logically post-coital contraception sometimes acts by producing a very early abortion. According to contemporary medical definitions however, a miscarriage, or abortion, cannot really occur until there is 'carriage' – i.e. until the blastocyst has at least implanted itself in the uterus. PCC is therefore accepted under the category of contraception, and not considered as abortion. If you feel unhappy about these definitions, then clearly PCC is not for you. Neither is progestogen-only contraception, or an IUD longer-term, since it is possible that these too work by preventing implantation of the blastocyst, even if only in a small percentage of cycles.

On the other hand, the ethical line between abortion and contraception is very much more blurred two or three days after unprotected sexual intercourse than it is two weeks later, when a period is a day or so overdue. This persuades some women that PCC is a useful option – as does the fact that it is quite likely that fertilization has not taken place at all: in two-thirds of the cases in which women take PCC there is no pregnancy to disrupt anyway.

CHAPTER 11

Abortion

No study of fertility and contraception would be complete without a discussion of abortion. Not only does abortion remain an important back-up in case of contraceptive failure, but historically it was the only recourse for women needing to control their fertility.

Abortion in the UK has progressed from what was essentially 'women's lore', through illegal abortion, to safe and legal terminations. While abortion seems to be as old as human society itself, until very recently procuring an abortion involved personal physical danger as well as moral censure and legal complications. That women persisted in seeking out abortions is testimony to their certainty that they needed them. Abortion decisions are now legally in the hands of the medical profession. In return for a safe, medicalized abortion women have traded in the hazards and unreliability of self-administered or illegal back-street abortions. That this shift has also involved a movement away from abortion as a relatively autonomous procedure has been much commented upon by the women's movement. The future of abortion may well see the circle complete itself with a return of abortion to women's control in the form of safe, self-administered terminations, carried out at home.

For the moment, however, abortion is still the most controversial area of family planning. Some commentators have pointed out that it was the last area to achieve academic recognition, clinical understanding and social acceptance. But in its curious blend of personal need and public and political control, abortion remains a signifier of broader issues in fertility control. Attitudes towards abortion sometimes, but not always, indicate attitudes to fertility control in general. Abortion is always the first option when a community first begins to control its fertility, and there is strong historical and epidemiological evidence that the substantial fertility decline that took place in Europe during the nineteenth and early twentieth centuries owed much to abortion. But despite its long history, abortion still rouses profound passions both in those who seek to defend a woman's right to choose abortion, and those who believe that no one is entitled to take the life of another even if that other is still invisible to the naked eye.

A short history

Women have always known how to prevent unwanted children from being born. Every society has known what herbs to take, which berries to infuse, which bark to pound. The danger surrounding these drugs was also well known and abortion has never been resorted to lightly. Chief among the traditional herbal remedies were ergot, rue, tansy oil and savin or oil of juniper, all potent abortifacients. Components of ergot are still used today in the drug egometrine, which is used to staunch bleeding in childbirth and abortion. In Britain, abortion was not illegal until the nineteenth century, providing 'quickening' or fetal movements had not set in. Once the fetus was felt moving abortion became illegal. Quickening was an important legal concept, for once a woman on trial had passed the quickening stage she could not be executed; special panels of women had to examine her and feel for the signs of quickening. The dangers of early abortion therefore related not to legal censure but to the risks involved in taking abortifacient drugs, for herbal abortions are capricious and their outcomes unforseeable. Their effects range from successful abortion, to nothing happening, to serious bleeding and death. Such randomness of action probably made the use of these drugs out of the question for regular contraception; they were rather a desperate stand-by for the unmarried. None the less the fact that there are so many historical references to herbal abortion suggests that they were hardly unusual.

In 1803 abortion became illegal at all stages in pregnancy, but there is plenty of evidence that it nevertheless continued to be an important means of fertility control. Some historians have suggested that however dramatic the increase in abortions after 1970 might appear to have been, it was not as significant as the first major increase in abortions that took place towards the end of the nineteenth century. This 'revolution' in the use of abortion to control fertility was made possible by the discovery of the vulcanization of rubber earlier in the century. By 1850 rubber catheters began to circulate, and abortionists used these to puncture the amniotic sac and then rotated them in the uterus until the fetus was dislodged. More significant still was the introduction of the syringe sometime around 1860. This made abortion an option for women who were not so desperate that they would choose it at any cost. Some historians argue that the drop in the birth-rate that began late in the nineteenth century and continued unabated until it had fallen to fourteen per 100 women in 1933 was largely due to abortion, and that the syringe played a considerable part in this.

Despite the risks of infection, perforation, peritonitis, severe bleeding and pain, syringes had become the most popular form of self-administered abortion by the first quarter of the twentieth century. Other techniques used in the same period were 'tents' or tightly rolled sticks of slippery elm, or seaweed of the laminara genus, which were known as laminaria tents. These were half the size of a matchstick and were inserted into the cervix and left. As they gradually absorbed the moisture from the cervix, it opened and an abortion followed. Laminaria tents are still occasionally used to dilate the cervix prior to an abortion. It was also in the first quarter of the twentieth century that 'D and C', or dilatation and curettage was introduced. Doctors could now induce abortion at a far earlier stage in the pregnancy, within the first two months, and the procedure became much safer. By the 1930s, given the discovery of asepsis, rubber syringes, uterine curettes, graduated dilators and seaweed tents, abortion had become a relatively well-established procedure. Women continued to take drugs as well, adding arsenic, lead and quinine to the list. These worked through their sheer toxicity and on the principle that, taken in small enough doses, they would kill the fetus before killing the woman.

These then were the techniques. It is more difficult to discover how many women availed themselves of abortions, and how many were done by doctors and how many by 'back-street' abortionists. Only with the recording of statistics after the 1967 Abortion Act do we have any accurate indication of the prevalence of abortion. Guesses have been made based on the rate at which the birth-rate dropped and on the number of reported post-abortion deaths or hospitalizations of women suffering from post-abortion infections. In Bradford, for example, the birth-rate fell from 24.9 per 100 married women aged fifteen to fifty-five in 1851 to 13.8 in 1901. This was a period in which birth-control was still limited and there is good reason to believe that a considerable proportion of this drop was brought about by recourse to abortion. At one extreme it has been estimated that the likelihood of a pregnancy ending in an abortion (including spontaneous abortion) around the First World War was as high as one in three. One working woman reported in 1914 that 'Six out of ten working women take something. . . . One woman said to me "I'd rather swallow the druggist shop and the man in't than have another kid." '[1]

Wealthier women, of course, could either attempt to abort themselves with a syringe or buy themselves an expensive and illegal abortion from a doctor. There have always been doctors willing to perform abortions and these were the safest. Throughout the twentieth century as procedures for D and C became safer, women who could afford it opted for such abortions. Other women opted for anything that was going regardless of the threat to their own lives. Potts and Diggory cite a study of illegal abortion techniques, based on admissions to a hospital on the outskirts of London between 1964 and 1968. Out of 734 women 381 were married (putting paid to the idea that abortion is only for unmarried women who get themselves 'into trouble'); the methods of abortion ranged from drugs (quinine, ergot), to transcervical injections of soap, potassium permanganate, toothpaste, whisky and brine; others had had a range of things introduced into their uteruses, from sharp objects such as crochet hooks and lead piping, to soft tubing, nylon cord and rubber catheters. Very few of the women had been aborted by D and C, perhaps because those able to obtain this technique tended to have safer and more hygienic abortions so were under-represented among the women who needed to be hospitalized because their abortions had gone badly wrong. One third of the women did not know how their abortions had been performed.

The hospital apparently admitted on average three women a week suffering from post-abortion problems. This surely says something about the number of women who were prepared to take the risk of having an abortion, since we can assume that the majority of them did not end up in hospital.[2] Various estimates have been put forward for the number of abortions carried out in the period immediately before the 1967 Abortion Act and it seems likely that there must have been over 100,000 carried out each year. Certainly the way in which the number of legal abortions in England and Wales rose to 100,000 within three years of the Act suggests that the number of illegal abortions must have declined rapidly. Deaths from illegal abortions fell from 108 in 1952–4 to four in 1976–8.

Following strenuous campaigning and a socially tolerant environment in the 1960s, the Abortion Act was finally introduced and passed in 1967. As we have seen, infections and deaths from abortions dropped off rapidly. Anti-abortion lobbies forced the Conservative government of 1971 to set up an Inquiry into the Abortion Act and, under the Honourable Mrs Justice Elizabeth Lane, it spent three years considering abortion from medical, psychiatric, legal and social points of view. The Inquiry came down firmly on the side of the current Abortion legislation, reporting that by 'facilitating a greatly increased number of abortions the Act has relieved a vast amount of individual suffering. . . . We are unanimous in supporting the Act and its provisions. We have no doubt

that the gains facilitated by the Act have much out-weighed any
disadvantages for which it has been criticized.'[3] Various attempts have
been made to amend the Abortion Act, most recently in the form of
David Alton's unsuccessful attempt to reduce the period in which
abortion can legally be carried out from twenty-eight weeks to eighteen
weeks. In fact as we shall see the proportion of abortions carried out
after twenty weeks is very, very small.

Abortion in Britain today: the facts

World wide there are now an estimated 30–35 million abortions
performed annually. More than half of these take place in developing
countries. Forty per cent of the world's population have access to
abortion more or less on demand, 26 per cent are allowed it for medical
reasons and for the rest it is illegal. Taken as a whole, such figures
suggest fertility control worldwide depends heavily on abortion. There
are now two induced abortions for every five live births, while in some
countries this figure has risen to one in two.

After the liberalization of abortion laws in the UK in 1967 the number
of abortions has shown a pattern of troughs and rises, though the general
pattern is upwards, and in 1986 reached 159,643 in the UK. Figures
11.1, 11.2 and 11.3 show the number of abortions carried out in England
and Wales among women of different age groups, the rate of abortions
per 1,000 women and the actual number of abortions performed each
year.

Following the introduction of free contraception in 1974 the number
of abortions carried out actually began to fall, though from 1977 the
numbers have begun to rise again. If we look at the rate per 1,000 women
aged fifteen to forty-four the trend is also upwards with the highest
rate being reached in 1986 at 13.5 per 1,000 women. A number of
explanations have been put forward for the continuous increase in
abortions since 1977. One is that the various pill scares have frightened
women into a rather precipitous end to their pill taking. It would only
take three women per 1,000 pill-users to stop taking the pill, become
pregnant inadvertently, and choose an abortion to create this rise.
However, an increase in the proportion of women having abortions in
their late teens during this period is probably equally responsible for the
rise, especially since the sixteen to nineteen age-group has a higher than
average demand for abortions.

The discussion surrounding the Alton Bill showed how little is known
by the public about the stage of gestation at which most abortions are
carried out. Figure 11.4 shows the spread of abortions according to

Figure 11.1 Legal abortion by age, England and Wales 1988

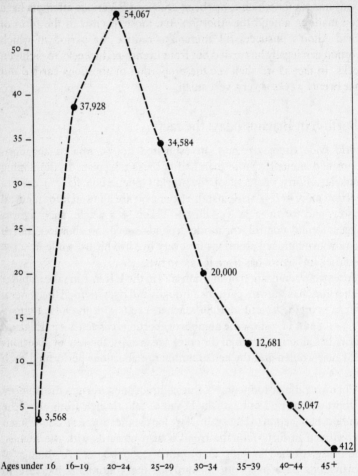

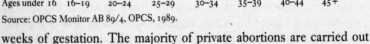

Ages under 16   16–19   20–24   25–29   30–34   35–39   40–44   45+

Source: OPCS Monitor AB 89/4, OPCS, 1989.

weeks of gestation. The majority of private abortions are carried out earlier than those done by the NHS. The private sector, which includes non-profit making advisory services such as the British Pregnancy Advice Service, does more than half of all abortions carried out in England and Wales. In 1983 more than twice as many non-NHS abortions were done within the first nine weeks of gestation (within five weeks of a missed period), and the difference would have been even greater if not for the fact that many women approach non-NHS clinics only after they have been turned down for an NHS abortion. It seems clear that bureaucratic delays are partially responsible for the later

Figure 11.2 Abortion statistics 1969 to 1987, England and Wales
Rate per thousand women aged 15 to 44

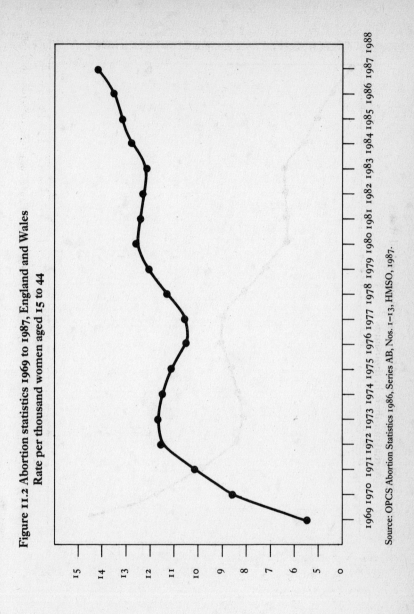

Source: OPCS Abortion Statistics 1986, Series AB, Nos. 1–13, HMSO, 1987.

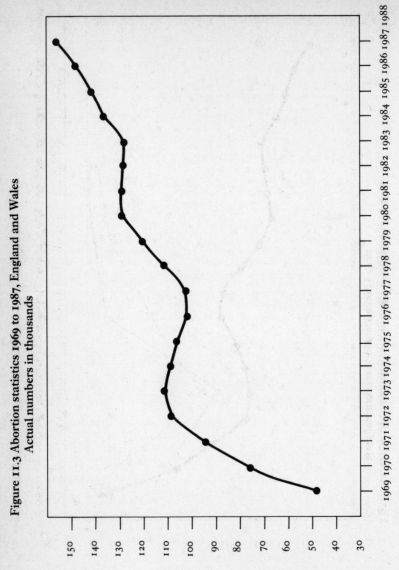

Figure 11.3 Abortion statistics 1969 to 1987, England and Wales
Actual numbers in thousands

1969 1970 1971 1972 1973 1974 1975 1976 1977 1978 1979 1980 1981 1982 1983 1984 1985 1986 1987 1988

Source: Ibid.

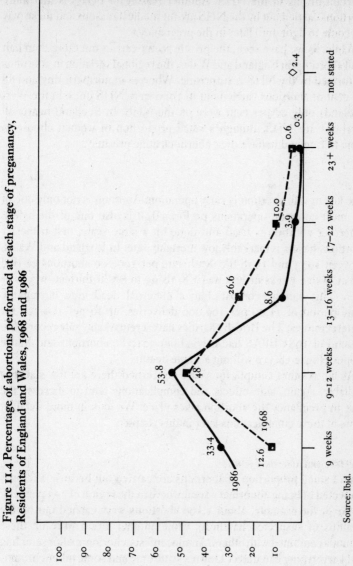

Figure 11.4 Percentage of abortions performed at each stage of preganancy, Residents of England and Wales, 1968 and 1986

Source: Ibid.

abortion profile of the NHS. Another reason for delays is that more abortions carried out by the NHS are for medical reasons and these may not come to light until later in the pregnancy.

While, as we have seen, the private sector carries out more than half of all abortions in England and Wales, the regional variation in abortions performed by the NHS is surprising. Whereas in northern England 88 per cent of abortions carried out in 1980 were NHS ones, in the West Midlands only 22 per cent were on the NHS. In Scotland nearly all abortions are NHS, though a small proportion of women choose to come to England to have their abortions done privately.

Safety

The key to safe abortion is early operation. Abortion is not only one of the most common operations performed, it is also one of the safest. Wherever abortion is legal and done on a large scale, first trimester abortions have a remarkably low mortality rate. In England and Wales, between 1973 and 1978 the death-rate per 100,000 abortions carried out at twelve weeks or less was 1.8, rising to 6.3 at thirteen weeks or over. This can be compared to a maternal death-rate during the same period of 11.00 per 100,000 deliveries, or 40 per 100,000 for hysterectomies. The British charities have a remarkably safe record. To the end of 1985 BPAS had carried out 321,389 abortions and Marie Stopes House 18,310 without a single death.

As far as other complications are concerned there are few statistics available. Again, side-effects and complications tend to increase the later in pregnancy the abortion takes place. We look in more detail at some of these complications later in this chapter.

Abortion and abnormal fetuses

Only a small proportion of abortions are carried out because a fetus is suspected of being abnormal – somewhere in the region of 2–3 per cent. In 1978, for example, about 1,500 abortions were carried out on the grounds of suspected handicap, while another 1,000 were on these grounds combined with others. Amniocentesis, chorionic villus sampling and karyotyping can detect Down's syndrome and some other chromosomally determined abnormalities. In Britain amniocentesis is now routinely offered to women pregnant for the first time over thirty-five, all pregnant women over forty and any woman whose fetus is at a particular risk of genetic abnormality. Amniocentesis can only be carried out after the sixteenth week of pregnancy, and since a second trimester abortion may not be ethically acceptable to all women it is obviously in everyone's best interests to consider this before embarking on an elaborate schedule of tests.

Repeat abortions

Repeat abortions account for only 9 per cent of all abortions performed, and there is no evidence, in the UK at least, to suggest that the availability of abortions persuades women to use them instead of contraception to control their fertility. Some doctors are not prepared to carry out repeat abortions.

The legal position

The current legal position regarding abortion in England and Wales is governed by the Abortion Act of 1967 which allows four reasons for having an abortion. The Act states:

1. A person shall not be guilty of an offence under the Law relating to abortion when a pregnancy is terminated by a registered medical practitioner if two registered medical practitioners are of the opinion, formed in good faith –
a. that the continuance of the pregnancy would involve risk to the life of the pregnant woman, or of injury to the physical or mental health of the pregnant woman or any existing children of her family, greater than if the pregnancy were terminated: or
b. that there is a substantial risk that if the child were born it would suffer from such physical or mental abnormalities as to be seriously handicapped.

The interpretation of the Act draws out four clauses. The first 'that the continuance of the pregnancy would involve risk to the life of the pregnant woman . . . greater than if the pregnancy were terminated' was intended to provide abortions for women who were suffering from some acute disease and whose life would be threatened by a continued pregnancy. In practice it provides a legal justification for abortions below twelve weeks since a termination before then is substantially less risky to the life of the pregnant woman than carrying a baby to full term and delivering it.

The second clause 'that the continuance of the pregnancy would involve . . . injury to the physical or mental health . . . greater than if the pregnancy were terminated' offers the legal justification for the majority of abortions. If a woman is suffering from anxiety and depression because of her pregnancy and abortion would reverse this process then it is legally justified.

The third clause that 'the continuance of the pregnancy would involve risk . . . of injury to the physical or mental health of . . . any existing children of her family, greater than if the pregnancy were terminated' means that if a woman already has children and feels they would suffer in some way from another pregnancy, the abortion would be legal.

The fourth clause (see b above) means that a woman can have an abortion if there is the possibility of an abnormality in the fetus – following rubella, or the discovery of Down's syndrome, spina bifida or some other hereditary disease.

Consent

If a woman is over sixteen and is not living with, or not supported by her partner, she can give consent. If a woman is over sixteen, is legally married and is living with her partner she will sometimes be asked to get his consent. If this consent is refused and there are medical grounds (see above) for the termination it can be carried out without the partner's consent. For girls under sixteen the consent of parents or guardians needs to be sought before an abortion can be carried out.

Although the Abortion Act legally provides for abortion up to the twenty-eighth week abortions are only carried out up to the twenty-fourth week. In practice, abortions are only carried out after the twentieth week in exceptional circumstances, such as the ill-health of the mother, or severe handicap of the fetus.

The ethics of abortion

Providing an overview of abortion and a way through the anger, polemic and confusion that the abortion debate has generated is one of the chief aims of this book. As Germaine Greer aptly comments, 'A genuine attempt to disentangle the complex ethical questions involved in pregnancy termination would benefit us all, for individual women are struggling, with very little help from their spiritual mentors, to confront a genuine problem.'[4] In fact much has already been written about the thorny ins and outs of abortion, by feminists, by medical specialists, by philosophers, by the pro-choice and anti-abortion lobbies; it would seem there is little more to add. Our aim in this section is to provide an overview of the territory covered so far in discussions on abortion, to chart the complexities of a matter at once intensely intimate and personal and, at the same time, the subject of national political agendas. The woman confronting an unwanted pregnancy was never far away from our minds as we wrote this, and we hope that this discussion may go some way to clarifying the issues involved in any abortion decision.

Abortion has become the most densely packed issue in the area of reproductive rights and fertility control. Regardless of which 'side' you are on, abortion may stand for a whole world view. Some have argued that freedom to choose abortion is 'the central feminist issue of our time',[5] while others see in the abortion of some 30 million fetuses a year only the depravity of late twentieth-century culture, the wanton destruction of the family and our moral bankruptcy. Many more would hesitate to take sides at all, believing that women confronting an abortion decision are not served well by the polemic, by marches or confrontational politics.

For a woman pregnant against her will both the moral absolutism that descends on her from one side and the marrying of the personal and the political on the other may appear distant from her own immediate problem. The irony of abortion is that it is rarely those who have faced an abortion who stake out the terms of the debate. If it were, abortion might well have been represented with more clarity and compassion than has often been the case both with anti-abortionists and pro-choice advocates. There is a paradox at the heart of the abortion issue. That abortion, unlike most other issues of such a personal bodily nature, can be abstracted from its immediate locus – the uterus of a pregnant woman – and its symbols paraded through the streets should be the first clue to the fact that it stands for more than the individual destinies of a woman and a fetus. Abortion is both an intimate and intensely private act and a national issue. In order to make sense of it we need to reconcile these two sides, the private and the public, which in turn leads us to questions of morality, or the construction of morality in relation to abortion decisions.

Those who would place themselves either strongly for or against abortion may not always even be conscious of why it creates such strong feelings in them. This section will attempt to show how and why an issue about which a woman may feel the most intense privacy (my body, my pregnancy) has been presented in the most overtly public and political terms, and why it is inevitable, but also right that this should be so. In order to describe the complex web of meanings that abortion has come to signify, we have arranged this section under the key concepts that crop up in abortion discussions – ethics, the fetus, mothering, sexuality and punishment, patriarchy, and religion.

Ethics

Anti-abortionists sometimes accuse those who defend a woman's right to choose abortion of evading moral issues. For anti-abortionists, abortion is a moral issue of profound gravity. But it is also an issue of profound gravity for many feminists and women seeking abortion. Anti-abortionists tend to believe that they are the sole custodians of the ethical issues, and that women who opt for abortions either do not recognize the seriousness of what they are doing or simply abdicate responsibility. Instinctively the majority of people sympathetic to tolerant abortion laws would perceive this to be a parody of the heart-searching that most women facing an abortion undergo, and while many anti-abortionists would share a compassionate view of the woman struggling with an unwanted pregnancy, they would none the less insist that the ethical issue of the status of the fetus be given prime consideration. Indeed, discussions have centred almost exclusively around the life or death of the fetus, and while feminists have agreed that a clear understanding of the status of the fetus is vital to any discussion of the ethical issues in abortion, they have also argued that deciding whether or not a fetus is a person does not 'exhaust the bases for moral enquiry about abortion'.[6]

Ethical objections to abortion seem to have three main aspects. Firstly, there is the view that fundamental to sexuality is the question of responsibility, and if a woman makes the mistake of getting pregnant, the only morally responsible thing for her to do is to have the baby. Cruder variations on this theme are 'she should have thought about that in advance' or 'pleasure has its price'. The philosopher Carol McMillan makes the point most forcefully, and with more sophistication, in her book *Women, Reason and Nature*:

... a fundamental feature of the sexual act is that it may result in conception. Feminists insist that women have the right to be agents. This is quite right. But it means that in so far as coition is an act between two people *qua* responsible agents – human life is never abandoned wholly to nature ... – and in so far as the sexual act *is* potentially a procreative act, the responsibility of a man and a woman for conception, that is the result of their sexual union, is theirs to accept and to acknowledge, whether they failed to abstain during the critical period when using the ovulation method or because the contraceptive device they used failed. Feminists believe that it is sexually responsible to make sure that one is using some form of contraception if a pregnancy is not desired. Hence they contend that if all reasonable precautions are taken against pregnancy, abortion may be regarded as a legitimate way out if the woman still becomes pregnant. This argument will not do ... the real point is that sexual responsibility means accepting the fact that the sexual act is, fundamentally and potentially, a procreative one. People who do not wish to accept this fact and the responsibility it entails should not have sex.[7]

McMillan's argument brooks no compromise. But by seeing sexuality as an entirely voluntary act between two consenting adults who despite all precautions to prevent a child would still welcome one, she takes her argument out of the realm of what 'is' into the morally absolute world of what 'ought to be'. She is writing from a stance which suggests that there are always the resources for one more, in which there is no

violence, no coercion, no confusion, no difficulty in negotiating the
tricky boundaries between adolescence and adulthood, between dependency and autonomy, no last-ditch attempt to hang on to a relationship,
no poverty, no rape, no sickness, no pregnant women abandoned by
their partners – none of the 101 reasons why a pregnant woman feels
she cannot go through with a birth.

Few could really tolerate the implications of McMillan's stance.
People who could not welcome a baby should not have sex, even if they
are using contraception, in case it fails. It would mean that women for
whom pregnancy would be a physical threat could not have sex; women
whose resources are stretched to breaking point; women in their forties
who certainly would not welcome another baby; handicapped women;
women with no resources at all. However even-handedly McMillan
spreads the responsibility between women and men, in the vast majority
of cases it is the woman who suffers the brunt of the pregnancy, whatever
its outcome. Since many men still regard contraception as women's
business they believe that unplanned pregnancies are not their responsibility. Other men take a different tack: Kathleen McDonnell, in her
book *Not an Easy Choice*, discusses men who demand that the woman
keep 'their' child; he may forbid the woman to abort 'his' child without
the slightest awareness of the responsibility that this position logically
demands of him.[8]

As we saw in Chapter 2, the reasons why people have sex may not
always be to do with passion and love. Petchesky, in her excellent book
Abortion and Women's Choice, cites a study of 150 American teenage girls
who were asked about their sexual experience. They never mentioned
anything concerning pleasure. The best they said was that it didn't hurt.
People may have sex for a variety of reasons; peer pressure when they
are young or as an act of defiance, a rebellion. Among teenage girls, at
least, the idea of 'penalty free sex' or 'pleasure without the cost' may
have little bearing on the complicated relationships they engage in.
McMillan's picture of entirely autonomous, morally free agents may
have little connection with the real-life tangles in which a young woman
finds herself. Among older women, too, the circumstances that lead to
the request for an abortion may have little to do with irresponsible sex
and the quest for pleasure. It is much more likely to be the result of a
contraceptive failure in the context of over-stretched resources that
leads a woman to opt for an abortion.

A second aspect of ethical objections to abortion concerns the right
of women to decide about abortion for themselves. Some would agree
that abortion is an issue of such moral profundity that it ought not to be
a decision left to individual women, but to professionals, be they

professional moralists (priests, popes) or doctors and legislators. Indeed, legally this is the case at the moment in the UK, as a woman needs the agreement of two doctors before being granted an abortion; for women opting for private abortions the procedure may feel less censorious. The feminist response to this is that abortion should be a woman's choice – summed up in the slogan 'Abortion: A woman's right to choose'. A section of anti-abortionists find the idea of a woman's choice very difficult to accept, in the belief that women 'choose' to have abortions because it is 'inconvenient' for them to have a child or because women have been infected by the 'throw away' mentality of consumer society. While other anti-abortionists would not be so glib, they are none the less unhappy about the idea of a woman's right to choose offering a justification for abortion.

The pro-choice lobby would raise a number of points in response to this criticism. First and foremost is the question of bodily autonomy. Pro-choice advocates have pointed out that for another to decide on an issue so private and bodily in nature is a violation of a fundamental right which in all other instances we would seek to protect. The issue is blurred by the manner in which questions about abortion are phrased. If, instead of asking, 'do you think abortion is morally right?' we asked (as Petchesky has suggested), 'do you think that whether you have an abortion should be up to your husband, boyfriend, parents or priest?', we would probably get a very different answer. Even while asserting that a fetus is a person, many people would also believe that an abortion decision should not be up to someone's boyfriend, parents or doctor.

And there are clear reasons why, at a practical level, this form of common-sense approach prevails. It is women who go through pregnancy, labour and birth and who are most intimately responsible for the child's care. The investment of time, of emotion, of energy in learning the craft of mothering rebukes those who would argue that motherhood is just a natural 'instinct'. In recognizing the commitment required, in taking mothering *seriously*, some women will decide that it is better to terminate a pregnancy at twelve weeks than shoulder a responsibility that they feel utterly inadequate to bear. If a woman is financially secure, in a happy and stable relationship with a loving partner committed to raising children and with plenty of resources to cope with the addition of a child, it is highly unlikely she will opt for an abortion even if the pregnancy was unplanned. Women who choose abortions are not often in this category.

Recognizing that women can indeed feel unable to bear children should cause us to reflect on the society in which this is possible. As Sarah Maitland bluntly puts it:

The real problem is a social problem, a reason why I wouldn't want to see the abortion law repealed because it does seem to me that it is the mother who has to carry the pain, all the emotional burden and most of the physical one, and if she decides she can't do it then it is nobody's business to tell her that she can jolly well pull herself together and have the child because Jesus loves her. If Jesus loves her then why the hell isn't she getting more support? It is one more sign of the sexism of things that so many women need to do this thing. They need to do it because society is bloody to mothers and babies and because the medical profession will not service our most primary demand which is for contraception which works.

Looked at like this, I cannot see why women must be looked at as solitary sinners if they choose abortion.[9]

While child allowances and maternity allowances are cut back, the provision of nursery schools woefully inadequate, and the negative attitude towards babies and young children prevails, while new mothers returning to work sense an immediate loss of status, there is little encouragement for women who feel that they 'can't do it' to change their minds. The pro-choice lobby has argued rightly that there are more ethical issues at stake than the personhood of the fetus. Caring for a child adequately is also a moral issue. As one writer has put it: 'There is nothing moral about giving birth to children we cannot feed and care for . . . It is precisely because women take life sacredly – our own as well as our children's – that some of us choose not to bring into the world those we cannot take care of.'[10]

The third moral argument, and for most anti-abortionists the bottom line of the whole debate, is that abortion involves taking another's life and is therefore murder by another name. Because the fetus is so helpless and innocent abortion is doubly awful. One extreme statement of this view appeared in a 1974 Declaration on Abortion by the Catholic church. It stated:

We do not deny these are very great difficulties. It may be a serious question of health, sometimes of life or death, for the mother; it may be the burden represented by an additional child, especially if there are good reasons to fear that the child will be abnormal or retarded; it may be the importance attributed in different classes of society to consideration of honor or dishonor, or loss of social standing, and so forth. We proclaim only that none of these reasons can ever objectively confer the right to dispose of another's life, even when that life is only beginning.[11]

According to Roman Catholic doctrine a fetus is a full human person from the moment of fertilization, and abortion is thus homicide. This is one end of a spectrum of views on fetal personhood, and the corresponding rights of the fetus to life. Practically speaking, few would condemn as an abortionist the surgeon who carries out a life-saving operation on a woman in danger of bleeding to death from an ectopic pregnancy, even if it means terminating the life of the fetus before nature herself does. Similarly, the lack of moral outrage against the progestogen-only pill and the IUD suggests that people do in fact make a qualitative distinction between the moral status of a three- or four-day-old fetus and a twenty-eight-week-old fetus or a new born baby. Germaine Greer makes the point with characteristic bluntness, 'A Catholic woman losing her blastocyst at menstruation has never been told of the possibility that a human life has just ended. It may seem very complicated to keep a jug of holy water to baptize sanitary napkins with . . . it would certainly dramatize the fact that Catholics take life before birth very seriously. The fact that they do not carry out rituals of this kind suggests that they do not really believe what they maintain in polemic.'[12]

But while the extremes of this moral position are easy to parody, the other extreme, adopted by feminists in the 1970s and early 80s, may be just as uncomfortable to live with. In response to pressure against the 1967 Abortion Act, the feminist movement as a whole played down the ethical issues in abortion. Abortion was simply a 'woman's right to choose'. Under the slogan, 'Abortion is a health issue, not a moral issue', feminists rejected any line other than that the issue at stake was a woman's autonomy over her body. McDonnell quotes one argument that was used at the time: 'If a clump of living tissues is a human being, then an acorn is an oak tree and an egg is a chicken.' Even if feminists marched under this line, it is also true that many felt less sanguine about the fetus being given no moral status at all. To many, abortion did not seem to be simply the moral equivalent of an operation to remove an appendix. McDonnell was one of these women and she points out in her book that the 'clump of tissues' argument justifies abortion by denying the fetus any status at all. The dilemma facing many women who choose abortions, whether they call themselves feminists or not, lies in the recognition of the fact that they *do* feel for their fetus, and believe it to have moral status, while at the same time they wish to assert the basic principle that they must be able to control what happens in their own bodies.

Anti-abortionists believe, often with great sincerity, that moral absolutes must come before all other considerations. The metaphysical takes priority over the physical; the importance of the life of the fetus even if it is only two weeks old carries a moral significance over and above the life of the woman in whose body it nestles. Against this, many women even while feeling that abortion is a desperate solution to the problem of unwanted childbearing, may still affirm the need to act according to the here and now needs of an individual situation rather than by some general principle. The material, tangible and touchable, takes primacy over abstract ideas. Patriarchal attitudes handed down over centuries have tended to dismiss, as an inferior form of moral development, the often complex dialectical manner in which women struggle to reconcile the moral rights of a situation with a 'feeling for the complexity and multifaceted character of real people and real situations'. For those who live in a black and white universe where moral absolutes prevail over the course of events, there will always be the danger of sacrificing people to 'truth' – which is, as the psychologist Carol Gilligan has pointed out, the danger of abstracting ethics from life. But many women are unwilling to make that sacrifice, recognizing the necessity of an 'ethic of care' which roots abstract principles of right and wrong in the firm, tangible ground of day to day existence.[13]

Women choosing abortions cannot be simply written off as moral opportunists or misled. They may well feel strongly about the moral status of their fetus and its claims upon them. Equally they may well face circumstances in which they recognize that abortion means taking a fetal life, but in full consciousness of this they still believe that an abortion is the only course possible – or the best course possible in the circumstances. McDonnell is worth quoting at this point:

What this acknowledgment of the fetus leads us to is a profound taking of responsibility for our choice, for the fact that we have, with full consciousness, terminated life. This is most emphatically *not* the same as blaming ourselves or burdening ourselves with an unnecessary load of guilt. It means, as one feminist who experienced post-abortion grief put it, 'not denying that there was something alive in you, and that you ended the process.' . . . Ultimately what we are talking about is an acknowledgment of the seriousness of abortion, an understanding that it is a choice that cannot be made lightly.[14]

McDonnell sees the 'multilayered, ultimately paradoxical nature of "letting in" the fetus and taking responsibility for abortion' as the crux of developing a feminist morality of abortion. Practically speaking this may be the best course too, for it allows women who have terminated their pregnancies the right to grieve. It recognizes the paradox of the situation – that you may choose to loose something precious – while at the same time accepting the need to take the moral responsibility for that decision.

Ironically, therefore, on this issue some pro-choice feminists (for certainly not all would opt for McDonnell's view of 'letting in the fetus') find themselves in agreement with anti-abortionists: that abortion is terminating life. The differences thereafter seem unreconcilable; for anti-abortionists no reason save perhaps the threat of life to the mother can justify abortion. The woman choosing abortion will believe that the circumstances in which she finds herself give her no other option.

Books such as *Mixed Feelings* by Angela Neustatter with Gina Newson give many examples of women unexpectedly facing a decision about abortion. The women we talked to had abortions for anything other than convenience or to get pleasure without paying for it. To suggest that women have abortions for trivial reasons is to discredit women's moral judgement. The anti-abortion lobby in its sincere anxiety to take the life of the fetus seriously sacrifices the seriousness of the moral autonomy of the woman and subjugates the complexity of her needs and life circumstances to the 'paramount' rights of the fetus.

While the anti-abortion lobby may seem to stand for nothing but the protection of the fetus, there are many ideological strands woven into its position. For a woman contemplating abortion it is important to be able to unpack these competing meanings. To understand the anger and passion that abortion raises we have to understand the threat it poses to cherished ideas about mothering and women, the significance of the fetus and the protection of the innocent, the role of sexuality, of fathers and of families.

The fetus

We have already looked at some of the arguments concerning the ethical status of the fetus. Here we intend to look at the way in which the fetus has come to symbolize much more than its own fragile personhood in the abortion issue. In its emotional appeal, the fetus stands for all that seems most helpless, most innocent, most in need of protection. The very meaning of the word fetus – 'young one' – invites our commitment to its survival. From conception onwards as it miraculously unfolds into life, it invites our identification, shows us something of our own unknown history. Fetuses are profoundly mysterious beings and anyone who has carried a child to term does not need to be told of the inescapably independent personality who begins to emerge long before birth. But the private relationship that develops between a woman and the actual fetus in her womb, and the public presentation of fetuses in the abortion debate are two very different things. In the latter we are presented with what Rosalind Petchesky has described as the 'symbolic' fetus. She demonstrates how complex a signifier the fetus has become in public discussions of abortion:

... the actual fetus pales next to the symbolic one, which ... has come to represent a whole series of losses – from sexual innocence to 'good' mothers.

... As this symbolic fetus becomes a more familiar presence – in civil courts ...
in hospitals (as patients), and in the media (as video stars) – its 'autonomy' from
the pregnant woman, along with her displacement from the centre of the abortion
issue, become cultural 'facts' that the feminist movement must counter.[15]

The fetus signifies many things, from the symbol of besieged patriarchy to our own feelings of isolation, vulnerability and alienation.
Presented on a screen, we see it only as an atomized, individual piece
of life, apparently floating free from all context (the sustaining uterus,
the body of the mother). Paradoxically we see it as both independent
and helpless. Its tiny fingers and toes invite us to identify with it, and to
believe in its autonomy, its life outside the pregnant woman's body. She
is displaced in this cinematographic affair. The problem with these
images, and their effect on us, is that we are attracted to what is essentially
an icon whose power is derived from our own nostalgia. The classic
image of the fetus in its little sac, floating free, slices up reality into tiny
bits, out of context, out of history, certainly out of any situation in which
a pregnant woman might recognize herself. Divorced from a woman's
body, blood, uterus, commitment, this view of the fetus represents not
the woman's standpoint, and certainly not the fetus's standpoint, but
that of a technician. Whether using ultrasound or sophisticated micro-
cameras, the technician abstracts the fetus into an apparent autonomy,
presents it as hero, and relegates the woman to the site of its play. Our
emotions provide the rest of the picture.

It is surely no coincidence that this bringing of the fetus out into the
light, so to speak, should go hand in hand with technical experimentation
and intervention in reproduction, described by the bioethicist Joseph
Fletcher as a 'steady movement towards converting the dark and ominous
secrets of biological life into lighted and manageable reality.'[16] As
Chapter 1 of this book makes quite clear, this is a view of reproduction
that we would repudiate.

The concept of an autonomous fetus as presented to the public is,
as we have seen, heavily dependent on sophisticated technologies.
Ultrasound and micro-cameras can open up the privacy of the womb to
all comers while other technologies can rescue the fetus should its
maternal environment fail from around twenty-four weeks. Traditional-
ists bemoan the beseiged role of the mother and look with horror on the
idea of artificial wombs. But the corollary to the autonomous fetus who
can be the object of a court case or the hero in a *Horizon* documentary
is precisely the erosion of and denial of the privacy of the maternal/fetal
dyad. The more the fetus is seen in isolation from the uterus of a woman,
the further diminished is the role of the mother *qua* moral agent.

Motherhood is thus diminished as an act of social and emotional commitment, will and desire, by being seen rather as a biological function. The irony is that motherhood, and all that is traditionally valued in the concept of the Mother, is fundamentally social and not biological in nature. As we argued in Chapter 1, although we know little of the conscious and unconscious influences at work on the fetus during pregnancy, we know enough to see that there are suggestive relationships between a woman's state of mind and health and the baby that is born. The child psychologist Penelope Leach writes that

The physical care and emotional sensitivity given to a baby interact with what he has already brought into life. As well as his genetic characteristics, including his sex, he brings a vast range of experiences in the womb and at birth. Many of these are still incompletely understood, but it is clear that factors such as the efficiency of the placenta and some aspects of the mother's health in pregnancy, together with the timing and nature of the actual birth, can all affect the 'kind' of baby who emerges . . . Every baby is part of a dyad from the moment of birth (quite apart from having been so *in utero*).[17]

There is not necessarily anything mysterious about this. The blood vessels in the uterus for example are intensely sensitive to stress. Stress makes them less effective in their task of supplying the baby with nourishment and oxygen. A woman suffering from stress may be affecting the fetus she is carrying. Once again, it seems, mind and body are profoundly linked.

The point of all this is to reassert at this end of the book that women do not get pregnant and give birth with the happy mindlessness of flowers producing seeds. Pregnancy is a process of which the psychosomatic elements are little understood, but clearly it is a process that is susceptible to the will of the woman in some way. Recognizing this leads us still further in the direction that it is right for women to determine the outcome of the conceptions that take place in their bodies. The growing tendency to educate the public in ways that show the fetus in isolation from the female body that is its home may be counter to a woman's best interests because it breaks up the maternal/fetal dyad which is still the absolute condition of sustaining fetal life until somewhere after the twenty-fourth week when a sophisticated incubator can take over. A woman's body is vastly more than a sophisticated incubator. The danger of playing on the emotional appeal of the fetus is that we risk seeing it as little more than this.

Mothering

Abortion throws deep seated feelings about motherhood into focus. Some of the anxieties that are expressed about abortion, though expressed in terms of protecting the fetus, are compounded with fears that women, if they resort to abortion, will cease to be mothers. Though many anti-abortionists may not admit to it consciously, motherhood implies unselfish self-sacrifice and if necessary total self-sacrifice to the fetus or the child created. As Petchesky writes, 'more ancient than the idea of the fetus as person, the primacy and necessity of woman as Mother has been a continuous ideological thread in anti-abortion pronouncements since the nineteenth century.' She quotes the Catholic theologian Bernard Häring, who states this passionate commitment to motherhood quite clearly: 'If it were to become an accepted principle of moral teaching on motherhood to permit a mother whose life was endangered simply to 'sacrifice' the life of her child in order to save her own, motherhood would no longer mean absolute dedication to each and every child.'[18] The use of the word 'child' here is unfairly emotive; few people genuinely fail to see a difference between a living child, surrounded by a web of relationships, and an eight-week-old fetus. While some, possibly most mothers would make profound sacrifices for their children, it is surely in a different league to lay down one's life for a fetus.

This may need qualification. One of the most unexplored aspects of pregnancy is the relationship which develops between a woman and her fetus. For many women the pregnancy takes on a quite different character as soon as the fetus begins to move. It suddenly becomes a baby. The attitude of a woman to her unborn child at thirty-two weeks is likely to be very different to her feelings at eight weeks. It is certainly not unheard of for women to delay treatment for life-threatening conditions in pregnancy in order to protect their fetus from any harm.

The threat that abortion seems to pose for motherhood comes from the implicit statement made by women undergoing it that mothering is not an absolute value in their lives to which all else must be sacrificed. It could be argued that in our deepest selves we retain our belief that this is what 'real' mothers do. Abortion would clearly threaten this cherished image, however irrational these feelings may be. Tied up with ideas about mothers as all-wise, all-self-sacrificing, are other ideas about women, with long and knotty historical roots. For whatever the changes that the last eighty years have brought about, with 60 per cent of married women in Britain working outside the home, beliefs that the *real* work of women is mothering, and that women will only be really fulfilled through mothering, cling tenaciously. And of course some women believe this, too. 'Girls are socialized from infancy to anticipate mother-hood. Women learn to like themselves in mothering roles, which allow them experiences of love and power not easily found in other situations.'[19] The fact that the anti-abortion movement contains so many women who have dedicated their lives to being good mothers suggests just how threatening it is when other women decide to affirm themselves in roles other than or in addition to their roles as mothers.

When girls or women decide not to become mothers, or to postpone their mothering role, or not to extend their mothering role to another child, seeking instead new identities through work or through education, they become threatening. By choosing an abortion and demonstrating their capacity to exercise control over life and death they become, in Petchesky's words, 'particularly, ineffably dangerous'. Closely allied to these feelings is the view held by some anti-abortionists that women who have abortions are in some way damaging themselves through a decision against motherhood. Obviously to deny that some women do find abortion traumatic and feel that they have made a wrong decision would be naive. Good counselling should enable women who feel ambivalent to determine either to continue with the pregnancy or to accept the decision that they have made to have an abortion. To claim that emotional damage and hardening are a necessary result of having an abortion is to disguise a paternalistic belief – that women are not capable of making important moral decisions – as an appeal to traditional feelings about mothers.

Those who argue that physically disrupting the relationship between the woman and her fetus necessarily damages the woman emotionally do not seem to have the facts on their side. There is very little support for women who have even late miscarriages and lose longed-for babies, which suggests that at a policy level at least, the mother/fetus bond is not taken very seriously. The vast number of embryos that silently abort before a woman even knows she is pregnant also suggests that very early abortion takes place without undue trauma. Arguments asserting that trauma necessarily follows abortion can only do so by playing down the role of social, personal and environmental factors in pregnancy.

A further anti-abortion argument derives its force from construing all abortions in the light of the 2.2 per cent of abortions carried out after eighteen weeks, ignoring the fact that 85 per cent of all abortions in the UK are carried out before twelve weeks, and 97.8 per cent before nineteen weeks. The fact that women who opt for abortions do so in vast measure before twelve weeks and that those who fail to do so are either impeded by hospital machinery, or are very young or disadvantaged in some other way, is evidence of a clear moral code among women. To try and suggest that women who have abortions are crazed baby haters, or morally bankrupt, or misled, or naive, are all ways of saying the same thing: that women who say 'no' to motherhood for whatever reason are deviant.

Sexuality and punishment
Some anti-abortionists worry about abortion not only because they care about fetuses but because the availability of legal abortion gives state sanction to non-procreational sex and sex outside of marriage. Some anti-abortionists would have fewer objections to abortion if it were still on the back-streets, because then it would be invisible and risky, as befits something as underhand as abortion. Abortion makes sex painfully visible. And because many anti-abortionists see nearly all abortions as the outcome of promiscuous sex they doubly condemn it. Here the issue at stake is less the life of the fetus than the sexuality of the pregnant girl or woman. If abortion communicates that women are having sex for its own sake, then the American writer Ellen Willis is right when she says that 'the nitty-gritty issue in the abortion debate is not life, but sex'.[20]

When the anti-abortion lobby loads the fetus with all the negative and ambivalent feelings it has about sexuality and disguises this under the 'protection of the fetus' stance, the only way for feminists to read its message is as a desire to control the sexuality of women. And it is difficult to avoid seeing this control as punitive, in that it puts the entire blame, or the whole consequence of unwanted pregnancy, on the shoulders of the woman. The sexuality of men is penalty free. A man who has 'got a girl pregnant' can disappear from the scene with nothing more than a guilty conscience. A pregnant woman, if refused an abortion in such circumstances, can only construe the refusal as an act of punishment for her sexual involvement. The onus is on the anti-abortion movement to prove that this is not in fact the case.

Patriarchy
The anxiety over sexuality displayed by many anti-abortionists is part and parcel of a complex set of attitudes towards abortion that can be called patriarchal. The sentiments about mothering and fetuses that we have already looked at are also part of the patriarchal complex. Disturbing evidence from surveys of anti-abortionists in the USA show how the opposition to abortion, far from being at one with a pro-life stance in other areas, is part of an essentially patriarchal view of the world involving capital punishment, military spending, support of American imperialism and opposition to arms control talks. The fate of the fetus is a badge of a movement that is not really about protecting vulnerable life at all.

Control over female sexuality, an assertion of male authority in state and home, and a return to traditional values are the real issues. Protecting the fetus is synonymous with reasserting control over the womb of a woman. While in the UK the anti-abortion movement is neither so clearly defined nor so politically coherent, the link between those who insist on protecting the life of the innocent fetus on one hand and support death-dealing technologies on the other needs careful scrutiny.

Clearly it would be absurd to argue that all anti-abortion sentiments spring from this patriarchal stable. There are probably equal numbers of anti-abortionists who are firmly opposed to patriarchal principles of military strength, male-headed families and the subordination of women, and whose anti-abortion stance springs from the 'sanctity of life' persuasion, which we look at next.

Religion
Many women contemplating an abortion believe that they would be condemned out of hand by most churches; and indeed most churches do little to prevent the guilt that may surround an abortion decision. Many Christians hold deep seated views about the sanctity of the life of the fetus and believe that only the most extreme threat to the life of the mother could justify termination. The belief that human beings are 'stewards' of their bodies, that in some way they are not their own, and, for Catholics at least, beliefs about the importance of baptism to the eternal destiny of the soul, means that abortion is a decision that should not really be left in human hands. It is for God to give and to take life.

Without questioning the genuine sincerity with which people hold these beliefs there are none the less other views than these within the gamut of Judeo-Christian thought. Some would argue that being fully human in a Christian sense means facing up to hard decisions including those about abortion. The 'knowledge' of abortion is with us, and can not simply be banished as we return to an age of innocence. Neustatter sensitively summarizes some other views of Christians on abortion, especially those who have stated that abortion must ultimately be a matter for individual consciences rather than an absolute or theological doctrine. She quotes the late Dr John Robinson as saying 'the Christian, more than anyone else must start from what "is" in a non-moralistic, non-judgemental way. . . . In the last resort the right to decide must rest . . . with the mother herself.' Similarly she cites another cleric who sees abortion as 'an area where God has put a moral choice in men's [sic] hands, and this choice must be exercised as responsibly as possible for the well-being both of the individual and the community. In the exercise of this choice there can be no moral absolutes. . . .'[21]

Some Christians would respond by claiming that abortion is a moral evil and the correct response is to ban it altogether. But as we saw in the section on ethics this is not a moral response at all, despite its apparent moral absolutism. For if the solution to the problem of abortion is simply to abolish it, there are, to quote Petchesky, 'no decisions to make, no hard choices, no ambiguities. But this is not morality because it absolves human beings, especially those lacking in patriarchal authority (e.g. women) of moral agency . . .'[22]

In conclusion to this discussion, it needs to be pointed out that we are well aware of the dangers of seeming to consign all anti-abortion voices to the same category of anti-women and anti-sexuality. It is not our intention to do this. Clearly there are already alliances in the anti-abortion movement between, for example, progressive elements in the church (those who support the Peace movement, women's ordination and so on), those supporting the rights of the disabled, and those who oppose abortion out of a genuine fear that the vale of human life is being ended.

The women's movement might well form alliances with such groups in supporting the rights of the weak and marginal in our society. But recognizing the rights of the disabled and other marginalized groups in no way undermines the necessity for women to control their own bodies and their own reproductive lives. That this control should occasionally take the form of abortion seems inevitable. We have already seen, and the evidence globally supports this, that if abortions are not legally available, women will seek out the most desperate measures in order to prevent the continuation of a pregnancy.

We would share the view of Adrienne Rich that abortion is a form of violence, done to the body and mind of a pregnant women, and, against the views of some in the pro-choice lobby, would see it as an extreme and unfortunate recourse for women wishing to control their fertility. The bulk of this book is precisely about trying to avoid the necessity of having to fall back on an abortion. None the less, neither do we underestimate the pain of becoming pregnant with an unwanted child.

The following section gives a clear explanation of what to expect if you decide to have an abortion.

Getting an abortion

Pregnancy tests

Pregnancy tests can be done very early in pregnancy. It is now possible to get a pregnancy confirmed within ten days of conception, before the first and most common sign of a missed period. This test is a blood test and is available from some GPs and family planning clinics and most pregnancy advisory services. The results are available in twenty-four hours. Other GPs will perform urine tests in the surgery and give results the same day, and these can be done as early as the day that a period is due. Occasionally these tests give false negatives, so if a test is negative and a period does not arrive within a week, it is important to have another test. There are a number of new early pregnancy testing kits on the market, but a doctor may want to re-confirm any results that you get from a test done at home. Unfortunately many GPs are still unable to provide fast and accurate pregnancy testing, with some results taking as long as a week to come back. Some doctors like to confirm pregnancy tests with internal examinations, though others consider this unnecessary. Some surgeries automatically give an appointment to women who have had a pregnancy test confirmed, but it may turn out to be an antenatal appointment on the day that the practice holds its antenatal clinic. It is always worth checking, and fixing an ordinary consultation if this is in fact the case.

Counselling

Finding out about a pregnancy brings with it a range of intense feelings. There is the feeling of amazement (especially if it is a first pregnancy) that it can happen at all. To have your fertility confirmed is an exhilarating feeling, even if it is followed by complete panic about the prospect of a baby. Some women who never intended to get pregnant feel almost instantly and instinctively that the pregnancy is right and that they will adjust their lives to a baby. Other women feel the opposite, and as signs such as nausea, breast tenderness and darkening nipples, tiredness and frequent peeing set in, feel that they simply cannot go through with it. The most important thing at this point is good counselling, and this can be from a professional counsellor or a good friend. A decision about an abortion is a permanent one. If you are pregnant it is vital that you make a decision that you can live with afterwards, whether you choose a baby or an abortion.

The first person you are likely to talk to is your doctor, or possibly a counsellor at a pregnancy advisory centre. Doctors vary in the skills that they bring to abortion counselling; some are excellent, others not so good. The aim of counselling is to help you to decide your best course of action, to decide what your real wishes are, to take responsibility for your own decision and so avoid serious regrets about it later. Many women need to work out why the pregnancy seems impossible for them, and how it might fit into the rest of life. They need to think through their own beliefs about abortion. An abortion counsellor is likely to want to discuss the context of the pregnancy: whether, for example, it occurred in a stable relationship, whether the pregnancy is one of a number of problems you are confronting at the moment; whether contraception is a problem. He or she will probably discuss alternatives to abortion – adoption or fostering or keeping the baby; there are now a number of books written about being a single mother if this is the choice confronting you. It is also important that you know about the practical details, for example where and how abortions are carried out.

Many of these issues are probing and personal; if you are facing an abortion you need to have time to think through them. Unfortunately it is also true that time is the enemy. A second trimester abortion is a different matter to a first trimester one (i.e. one within the first twelve weeks). The physical risks involved increase, though they remain small, but the emotional impact may be greater. All in all it is far better to ensure, if you can, that the abortion takes place in the first twelve weeks.

Where to have it done

Once you have decided to have an abortion the next step is for the doctor to sign the 'green form' (HSAI). She or he will then refer you to a gynaecologist at a local hospital, who will write to you with details of an out patient appointment. Before your doctor does this it is always worth checking that she or he is referring you to someone sympathetic, and that they know the system in the local hospital. Some women have had unfortunate experiences with consultants who have been insulting and have then refused to sign the form. If there are doubts, and it seems likely that having an NHS abortion in your area will involve unacceptable delays, the doctor should refer you to a charity such as The British Pregnancy Advisory Service, The Pregnancy Advisory Service or the Marie Stopes Clinic.

If your doctor refuses to sign the form, you have the right to seek a second opinion, and the GP should arrange this. Similarly, if the consultant refuses, she or he should also refer you to someone who is likely to be more sympathetic. If the consultant is willing to perform the abortion, she or he will sign the form showing agreement that your situation falls within the terms of the 1967 Act. Arrangements will then be made for the abortion – hopefully in the next week or so, but sometimes it takes longer.

You also have the choice of going straight to an organization like the BPAS. This will certainly save time and you will not have to trek from one doctor to another. You make an appointment at the clinic and see a trained counsellor. This is followed by an appointment with one or two doctors who will discuss the matter again. If they agree to the abortion, you will be given a medical examination and before you leave an appointment will be made for you in a nursing home, usually within a week or two. If you have the abortion privately it may cost around £160, £20 for the consultation and £140 for the actual operation. If the abortion is carried out after twelve weeks the costs go up accordingly. BPAS claim that no one is turned away because they cannot afford the help they need, and in some parts of the country BPAS works with the NHS to provide free abortions for local residents. We have already seen that more abortions are performed earlier by the private sector, and they are marginally safer.

Another factor in your decision may be the type of abortion being offered. Doctors working privately are more likely to perform abortions after twelve weeks using D and E (see p. 366) than are NHS doctors. NHS doctors more often resort to prostaglandins.

In 1984, 57 per cent of NHS abortions after twelve weeks were prostaglandin induced, with 32 per cent by D and E (and 11 per cent by other means). This compares with only 35 per cent of private abortions being prostaglandin induced, while 60 per cent were by D and E. Prostaglandin induced abortions after twelve weeks are more unpleasant for the woman, but D and E after twelve weeks is also more difficult to carry out. The next section explains in more detail what happens in an abortion.

Having an abortion: what happens

The first thing that will happen before the abortion will be a medical examination, which will involve an internal examination to check to see how many weeks pregnant you are. A medical history will be taken including questions about the pattern of menstruation that is normal for you, your contraceptive history, previous pregnancies, miscarriages or terminations, any major operations and anything to do with a history of thrombosis, epilepsy or any other physical problem. Blood pressure will be taken, and a urine and blood test, to check up on things like anaemia or a bladder infection. It is important to know your blood group in case you are rhesus negative; if you are, you will be given an injection called anti-D immunoglobulin to prevent you building up antibodies that might adversely affect future pregnancies.

Abortion – before thirteen weeks

The type of abortion you will be offered will depend on how many weeks pregnant you are. As we have seen, the vast majority of abortions take place within the first twelve weeks (85.4 per cent) and these are the simplest, least traumatic operations to carry out. There are basically two techniques used, one surgical and one medical. The medical technique involves giving prostaglandins which stimulate the uterus to contract. Prostaglandins are fat-like chemicals found in their natural state in the bodies of all men and women (though they were originally thought to exist only in the prostate gland of men). The trouble with them is that they produce side-effects such as nausea, vomiting and diarrhoea because as well as the uterus they also make the smooth muscle of the gut contract. Prostaglandins are used either for very early abortions or later ones. Before seven weeks of pregnancy some clinics use prostaglandin gel vaginally, supplemented with tablets taken orally. This usually stimulates cramping pains for several hours and then bleeding much like a very heavy period. However, this technique may not result in a complete abortion – it is estimated to be only 90–95 per cent effective.

Surgical techniques for early abortion (up to thirteen weeks) are carried out by gently opening the cervix and sucking out the contents of the uterus. If the abortion is carried out within seven weeks of the last menstrual period it is not even necessary to dilate the cervix. Most women choose to have a general anaesthetic, though a very light one, and lose consciousness for only half an hour or so. Other women opt for a local anaesthetic which is given in the form of an injection into the cervix. The advantage of a local anaesthetic lies in avoiding the unpleasant feelings on waking up from a general one, but for women feeling anxious and squeamish about the whole procedure, the choice of knowing nothing about what happens may be preferable.

When the abortion is carried out within seven weeks of the last period a soft, pliable tube, known as a Karman curette, is gently inserted through the cervix and into the uterus without dilating the cervix at all. This is attached to a source of suction, which may be electric or mechanical. In very early pregnancy a simple 50 ml syringe provides sufficient suction. This type of abortion can quite easily take place under local anaesthetic. It is necessary to lie on the operating couch with your legs in stirrups. The doctor will insert a speculum so that he or she gets a clear view of your cervix. This and the vagina are then cleaned with antiseptic solution to cut down the risk of infection. The cervix is held in place with an instrument called a tenaculum (the same instrument is used when an IUD is inserted). At this point the local anaesthetic injections are given, four of them usually, which may sting initially but will quickly numb the cervical area. The doctor then inserts the curette and checks how big the uterus feels; if it seems bigger than the dates of the pregnancy suggest, this technique may not be sufficient. Assuming all is well, the endometrium is sucked into the syringe along with the tiny bits of fetal tissue. The whole procedure takes only a few minutes, and while there may be some painful cramping, this is usually brief. Subsequent bleeding is usually minimal. If the bleeding does continue it is likely that the abortion was incomplete and so should always be checked out.

Abortions up to the thirteenth week of pregnancy are similar to these very early ones, but the cervix needs to be dilated and a suction pump is needed to empty the uterus. The cervix is dilated with a series of metal instruments called dilators. Dilating the cervix is a very delicate business, since it is possible to tear or damage its fine tissue. If you are nine weeks pregnant it will be necessary to dilate the cervix to about 8 mm, but the maximum dilation will only be 10 mm. Once the cervix is dilated, the dilators are removed and a soft vacurette is introduced to the uterus, and connected to a suction machine, the aspirator. The vacurette is moved gently in and out and round the walls of the uterus until it feels empty – though the doctor will always check the contents of the vacurette to ensure that everything has been sucked out. Vacuum aspiration is likely to leave you with painful menstrual-like cramps as the uterus begins to shrink back to its non-pregnant size.

Most women will experience some bleeding after an abortion of this nature, but it should be no heavier than a heavy period. Bleeding that seems very different from menstrual bleeding (for example bright red blood) needs to be reported to a GP or to the pregnancy advisory service at once – more on this in the section on looking after yourself.

Side-effects of early abortions
Complications during or following early abortions are rare but there can occasionally be perforation or incomplete abortion, infection or heavy bleeding. Very occasionally the abortion fails and the pregnancy continues.

Perforation is now much less common than it used to be because doctors use softer plastic materials instead of metal ones for performing abortion. A perforation will show up by heavy bleeding and the doctor performing the abortion will need to check the uterus with an instrument called a laparoscope. Small tears tend to mend on their own, though a larger tear will need to be stitched by the doctor. Estimates as to how often perforations occur vary; one estimate of 2.7 per cent of abortions is probably too high, while another estimate of 0.1 per cent implies very careful and skilled doctors. Perforation is less likely in early pregnancy; as the uterus enlarges it becomes softer and thinner and therefore more liable to damage.

An incomplete abortion occurs when some part of the placental tissue remains in the uterus. It usually shows up by heavy bleeding beginning a couple of days *after* the abortion, and occurs in about three to eleven of every 1,000 abortions performed. It needs reporting to a doctor and the operation has to be repeated again. Occasionally there is also a high temperature. This usually means that the retained tissue has become infected in some way. It is most important to see a doctor straight away so that antibiotics can be given and another operation arranged.

Heavy bleeding, as we have seen, can be caused by a perforation or an incomplete abortion. It can also be caused by damage to the cervix. This occurs more often in young women with small, tight cervixes than in women who have had children. Damage occurs to the cervix when it is dilated too fast or not gently enough. The doctor will sow up any tears in the cervix. Abortions carried out within seven weeks of pregnancy have the advantage of not needing to dilate the cervix and for this reason complications of this sort are rarer.

Infections can occur with or without heavy bleeding. As we have seen, incomplete abortions which produce heavy bleeding can also become infected, but any symptoms such as fever, abdominal pain, a yellowish vaginal discharge, nausea or flu-like feelings could be a sign of an infection developing, and it is most important to get medical treatment as soon as possible. Post-abortion infections are much less likely now than in the days of back-street abortions but even so, up to thirty-five women for every 1,000 undergoing an early abortion are likely to develop some symptoms of an infection.

Future fertility
Many women worry about the effects of an abortion on their future ability to have children. So far, despite strenuous efforts, no one has been able to prove conclusively that one early abortion carried out by vacuum aspiration has any effect on future fertility. Obviously if the abortion goes wrong, and results in a severe infection that is not treated in time, the uterus and fallopian tubes could be damaged, but nowadays this complication is very rare. The evidence on the effects on fertility when a woman has had more than one abortion is also inconclusive. The

suggestion is that dilating the cervix too many times 'unnaturally' may have the effect of weakening it or causing 'incompetence'. More research needs to be done on this.

Abortion after thirteen weeks

Later abortion, sometimes called mid-trimester abortion, is both medically more dangerous and emotionally more traumatic. Two techniques are used, dilation and evacuation (D and E) and prostaglandin induction. Performing a D and E after thirteen weeks is a difficult operation and is always carried out under general anaesthetic. The cervix needs to be dilated more fully (12 mm) and this brings with it an attendant risk of damage. The contents of the uterus are then dismembered and removed with forceps, and the uterus completely emptied by vacuum aspiration. Complications of bleeding and perforation are more common at this stage of the pregnancy. It requires great skill and experience to perform this procedure and, as can be imagined, it is distressing for the operator. Consequently there are not many doctors willing and able to do this operation in the UK.

More commonly after sixteen weeks, and especially in NHS abortions, labour is induced with prostaglandins. This abortion occurs in the same way that a full term delivery would, through contractions which dilate the cervix and subsequently expel the fetus. The prostaglandin is used in one of two ways. If the pregnancy has progressed beyond sixteen weeks a solution of prostaglandin F2 can be injected through the abdominal wall straight into the amniotic sac. A single injection is usually sufficient to begin labour which starts a few hours later. When the pregnancy is less advanced it is impossible to inject into the amniotic sac safely and so a prostaglandin solution is passed through the cervix and into the space between the uterus and amniotic sac, via a catheter. Frequent doses of prostaglandin are required and this is either administered by four- to six-hourly injections into the catheter or more satisfactorily by a continuous infusion via a small pump into the catheter. The time it takes to induce labour and the abortion varies as much as the length of full-term labours, but twelve to sixteen hours is usual. Many doctors administer oxytocin via a drip once labour is established to speed up the process.

Once the drug has been given it is a question of waiting for the contractions to begin. They usually begin mildly and build up into quite powerful contractions. The BPAS literature describes this form of induced abortion as 'a form of labour' and although the contractions may not be as painful as full-term contractions they will certainly hurt. However, if you are undergoing this kind of abortion you will be offered powerful painkillers and tranquillizers. It is very important that someone is with you throughout an abortion of this kind, not only because it can be painful and therefore frightening, but because emotionally it may be difficult. The fact that it is a late abortion implies that there was conflict in coming to a decision, or a battle with medical authorities, or that it was a wanted pregnancy with an abnormality diagnosed. Whatever the reason, the experience is similar enough to a full-term labour to make it emotionally distressing and it is important to work out support structures in advance.

Most prostaglandin terminations are followed by a procedure like a D and C to check that the uterus is empty. This is carried out under general anaesthetic as soon as possible after the delivery of the fetus. Following this brief procedure it is usual to remain in hospital for twenty-four hours to check that all is well. Few NHS hospitals perform abortions after sixteen weeks unless there are reasons such as suspected fetal abnormality, maternal ill-health, psychiatric disorder, or if the mother is very young. Late abortions are carried out by BPAS at their nursing home in Brighton and some gynaecologists will perform late abortions privately.

Looking after yourself after an abortion

Most early abortions are performed in day units nowadays, and clear instructions are usually given at the initial appointment as to the arrangements which you will need to make. After the abortion you will come round in the recovery room outside the operating theatre, and usually will go back to sleep for an hour or so while the anaesthetic wears off. When you wake up you may experience cramping abdominal pain, for which you will be offered painkillers. There will be some bleeding, so you will need some sanitary pads to wear to go home in. You will be encouraged to get up once you are fully awake and the nurses will want to check that you can drink without being sick, so you may be offered some tea. If all is well you will be allowed home within four or five hours. This system of rapid discharge relies on there being some support for you at home. Most places will insist that you are collected by a friend or relation and that you should not be alone that night. Although you may feel absolutely normal the effects of the anaesthetic linger for about twenty-four hours and your reflexes are dulled. Driving in this condition would be dangerous. Similarly if any complications arose such as heavy bleeding you would be less able to cope with getting medical help while still slightly fuddled from an anaesthetic.

There are many women who return to work the day after an abortion and many more who do not. This is usually due to nausea and general lassitude secondary to the anaesthetic rather than following any problems from the actual operation. All women lose some blood after an abortion but the amount and duration of this loss is very variable. It is difficult to lay down guidelines about what is normal. The most important pointer as to whether the blood loss is significant or not is the pattern of loss. If the loss is of dark blood, is not accompanied by pain and is getting less with time, even if slowly, then there is unlikely to be a problem. Any increase in loss or change from dark to bright red blood, or abdominal pain may indicate that a problem is brewing. It is always advisable to get advice if you are at all worried by bleeding following an abortion. Tampons are best avoided until after the second period following an abortion, due to the theoretical risk of an infection. Women with a regular cycle of around twenty-eight days should have a period within six weeks of the operation.

We have already looked at some of the other problems encountered after an abortion. If you have continuing pain, discharge, fever, or flu-like symptoms you should always seek medical advice promptly. Troublesome physical problems following an abortion are relatively rare and usually short lived. The psychological effects tend to be longer lasting. It has been said that the worst side-effect of an abortion is remorse. However compelling your reasons for a termination, and however convinced you are that this is the right decision for you, it is impossible to predict how you will feel afterwards. Good counselling before the operation and support afterwards will help. Post-abortion care tends to be overlooked within the NHS and it is therefore particularly important that you have friends you can turn to. You need to allow yourself space and time to grieve. Unresolved guilt, bereavement and grief can store up problems for the future, so if you are feeling unhappy it is best to face it straight away. There are self-help groups for people who have had abortions and it is worth discovering about these if you think it will help. Making adequate provision for your mental and emotional needs is probably the most important aspect of looking after yourself following an abortion.

Another important aspect of post-abortion care is getting yourself an effective method of contraception. Whatever the reason for opting for an abortion all women are advised to use contraception following the procedure. If you want to get pregnant again then a three-month wait is usually considered a good idea before trying again, though there is no overwhelming evidence that this is necessary from a medical point of view. Since the risk of a miscarriage is anyway quite high it is generally felt that a wait of a few months is sensible, so if you were to have a subsequent miscarriage you would be less likely to blame yourself. Many women who have an abortion have not been using any contraception at the time of conception. This may reflect ambivalence about the methods available, ambivalence about sexuality, or bad advice. An abortion offers no respite from fertility, so as soon as you become sexually active again you could find yourself pregnant.

Conclusion

Abortion is the darker side of human fertility. We started this book with a discussion of a perfect conception and the importance of fertility. Abortion is part of the spectrum of human fertility, though it involves a reversal of the outcome of the complex systems of physical maturity, sexual activity, conception and pregnancy. Abortion is an indicator of the extent to which human fertility is a social process and not merely a series of biological manoeuvres. Whatever one's views on abortion, if we forget this we risk confining women and their fertility within the category 'natural' and in so doing limit our understanding of the complexity of human relationships and their outcomes.

CHAPTER 12

Conclusion: Personal and Political

For too long the female body has been the very cage into which the whole sex had been forced. This body was fertile and fertility became the idyllized limit of women's opportunities . . . but fertility is never just 'fertility alone', there is no pure biology in the socialized world . . . But even though women have been, and still are, cheated by false invocations of their nature, there can be no liberation which is not based on their nature . . . 'liberation on the basis of nature' would mean developing the body's inherent potentialities. This development would once again be a social act . . . nature can only be realised through society.

Barbara Sichtermann, *Femininity: The Politics of the Personal*

At the end of this book we come full circle and return again to the fertile body and its potential, and the wider context in which decisions about fertility are exercised; in other words, we will draw the book to a personal and political conclusion. We argued in Chapter 1 that by and large western society does not value fertility highly, seeing it rather as subordinate to sexuality, and contraception as its antidote. Contraception in consequence has become largely a medical matter, a question of good health, and this in turn contributes to the picture of female fertility, particularly pregnancy and childbirth, as necessarily the province of health professionals. Until recently, feminist theory, in the few places where it considered women's bodies, tended to reinforce negative ideas about the limitations of reproduction; more recently, however, feminist 'essentialism' has argued that *only* on the basis of women's 'difference', (predicated on their reproductive role) can the change and transformation of individuals and society be brought about. We have argued for a middle way, fully acknowledging the dangers of defining women by their reproductive roles but equally agreeing with Sichtermann, quoted above, that there can be no genuine liberation for women which does not involve an affirmation of the female body. This involves an acceptance of fertility, which we define as the whole of the reproductive story of a woman's life. If a woman chooses to be sexually active with a man without wishing to conceive, contraception, whether 'natural' or otherwise, becomes essential. In making choices about contraception, however, a woman's reproductive life-cycle offers her potentials that can be developed or ignored. We have argued that there are positive gains to be made from developing them, and that not least among these is an opportunity to take responsibility for the way we live with our fertility, developing an awareness of what we are doing when we use contraception.

Learning about the particular pattern of one's own cycle may be a good starting point for reassessing contraception. We have suggested ways of experiencing fertility, by looking, feeling and touching. The process of observing, recording and interpretation can be an act of personal enrichment, as well as a useful foundation for deciding what you want to do when it comes to preventing pregnancy. Learning to like one's body and to respect its internal rhythms is a way of beginning to feel more in control. Whether or not you choose to try observing and recording the pattern of your own cycle, becoming more knowledgeable about the way in which your body works will at least enable you to understand more fully how contraception acts upon it. If you understand the action of hormones, for example, you are in a better position to decide whether or not the pill is the right form of contraception for you. Learning about your body may have still wider implications. In the introduction to *Our Bodies Ourselves*, the collective who wrote it explain that 'For us, body education is core education. Our bodies are the physical bases from which we move out into the world; ignorance, uncertainty – even, at worst, shame – about our physical selves create in us an alienation from ourselves that keeps us from being the whole people that we should be.'[1]

Clearly, if women want greater control over their lives, health and, in particular, fertility, they need information about how their bodies work and how different methods of contraception might work to their advantage and disadvantage. But this is not the end of the story. In the first place, knowledge is not enough: if women are really to have autonomy they will have to understand and be able to negotiate the health system which provides the goods. Moreover, knowledge inevitably has its limitations; in some areas, such as the very long-term effects of the pill, we still do not have enough experience to judge. In the second place, questions of an individual's fertility and health need to be understood in a wider context, which may, for example, involve ethical questions, as in the case of abortion, or questions to do with who controls the development of new contraceptive technology. The social and political context in which women make decisions concerning fertility was discussed at some length in Chapter 2. We argued for example that even if a woman seems to have a free choice in a consultation with her doctor about contraception, that doctor may be biased in favour of the pill if he or she has little experience or training in providing other methods. Women face many constraints in terms of the availability of certain contraceptives, in the timing of clinics and in the closure of clinics, aside from all the pressures that arise from their relationships and prevailing ideas about sexuality.

Taking responsibility in the area of fertility control means understanding your body, finding out the 'facts' of contraception, considering the broader issues, and beginning to negotiate any setbacks that may arise until you get what you want. For this you need self-confidence and a feeling of equality with health professionals. Knowing what you want and being well informed may be half the battle. For the rest, developing the assertiveness to cope effectively with this and all the other areas of life, whether at work or in personal relationships, is an issue on many a woman's agenda. Assertiveness training courses may be helpful, but are rather outside the scope of this book! Discussing contraception with other women may also be helpful. Many of the women who wrote to us commented on the fact that it was a relief to write down their experiences, and share their feelings with someone. Contraception, because of its intimate connection with sex, remains a taboo subject for some women. Finding ways of bringing it into the open and discussing your experiences and those of other women may be a good way of working out your own feelings on the subject.

Finally, it may be helpful to see fertility and contraception, however private and personal you feel it to be, as part of a still wider picture. In this book we have only concentrated largely on the personal dimensions of contraception and its immediate context. We have considered the structuring of its provision in the UK, its history and, in the chapters on different forms of contraception, the various controversies and issues attending different methods. We have looked at fertility and contraception in the context of health care in general, but have not considered in much detail the extent to which health care can be understood in the much larger context of a feminist analysis of society. If we had space to do so, we would look at the process of creating hierarchies and experts, those who have power and those who do not. Exploring this wider picture provides a further perspective in which to understand our own decision-making in the more intimate areas of our lives. This process of exploring broader issues and relating them to the way in which we perceive our bodies and make decisions is a little like building up a set of Russian dolls. From the starting point of the egg in the ovary – its significance to the individual woman and the complexities of her bodily history – we can trace a series of relationships: that with a partner whose sperm may fertilize the egg, or who may co-operate with the woman in preventing conception; that with family, friends and associates, whose opinions and expectations may shape the way in which she makes decisions concerning her fertility; that with society at large and its complex systems of education, health care, work, law and economy; and that within the global context, in which issues such as ecology, population and development come into focus. Whether one starts with the smaller doll and builds outwards or with the larger doll and builds inwards, the inescapable relationships of the different layers remain constant. The fertile body is at home in the fragile ecology of the earth. Pollution can lay its finger on the purity of ova and sperm as well as the water we drink and the air we breathe. Recognizing and making connections between our bodies and our environment is as much a part of learning to take responsibility for our lives as the kind of body education we have discussed at so much length.

Exploring the relationship between our choices (personal) and the forces that shape them (personal and political) is inexhaustible. Pursuing this interplay of personal and political in the area of fertility and contraception leads rapidly to questions such as why it is that some of the world's women have the opportunity to think about 'reproductive moments of being' as a source of personal enrichment, while for many others bodily autonomy and freedom to make decisions about childbearing remain a distant dream.

This book has focused primarily on the personal, because we have chosen – reflecting on personal experience – to unpack the Russian dolls, starting with the mystery of a woman's ova and the creative potential of her body. For others, the process of working out the significance of human fertility and its control may take quite a different route, but its importance and enormous interest remain undeniable.

APPENDICES

1 Drug Interactions with the Combined Pill

If you are using any form of hormonal contraception you should always remind your doctor of this, particularly if she prescribes any other medicines or tablets (drugs) for you. You may need to take extra contraceptive precautions (during the course of treatment and for seven days afterwards), take a slightly higher-dose COC pill, or possibly even reconsider your contraceptive method. This list gives *some* of the drugs with which the COC pill may interact.

Drugs which may make the COC pill less effective (increasing the risk of pregnancy)

Antibiotics
> Ampicillin (Ampicillin is a broad-spectrum antibiotic used to treat common infections and frequently prescribed)
> Tetracyclines
> Rifampicin

Anticonvulsants (used to treat epilepsy)
> Phenobarbitone (and other barbiturates)
> Phenytoin
> Primidone
> Carbamazepine
> Ethosuximide
> (Sodium Valproate is the only commonly used drug for epilepsy which does *not* reduce pill effectiveness).

Hypnotics (sleeping tablets)
> Chloral Hydrate
> Dichloralphenazone
> Glutethimide

Tranquillizers
> Chlorpromazine
> Meprobamate

Others
>   Griseofulvin
>   Phenylbutazone
>   Spironolactone

Drugs which increase COC pill efficacy (making your pill equivalent to a higher-dose pill)

>   Ascorbic Acid (vitamin C), in very large doses (0.5–1g daily)
>   Co-trimoxazole

Drugs whose action the pill may effect

>   Chlordiazepoxide
>   Diazepam
>   Some antidepressants (e.g. Imipramine)
>   Ergotamine (present in some migraine preparations)

Note:
The names used in this list are the proper or generic names of the drugs. You may be precribed a drug with a proprietary name; check with your doctor or pharmacist what the drug actually is.

2 Further Reading

Joseph Bellina and Josleen Wilson   *The Fertility Handbook*, Penguin Books, 1986

Elizabeth Clubb and Jane Knight   *Fertility, a Comprehensive Guide to Natural Family Planning*, David and Charles, 1987

Anna Flynn and Melissa Brooks   *The Manual of Natural Family Planning*, Allen and Unwin, 1985

Colin Francome   *Abortion Practice in Britain and the United States*, Allen and Unwin, 1986

Germaine Greer   *Sex and Destiny*, Penguin Books, 1984

John Guillebaud   *The Pill*, Oxford University Press, 1983

Contraception, Your Questions Answered, Churchill Livingstone, 1985

Frigga Haug, ed.   *Female Sexualization*, Verso, 1987

Ronald Kleinman, ed.   *Family Planning Handbook for Doctors*, International Planned Parenthood Federation, 1988

Nancy Loudon   *Handbook of Family Planning*, Churchill Livingstone, 1985

Kathleen McDonnell   *Not An Easy Choice: A Feminist Re-examines Abortion*, Women's Press, 1984

Mary O'Brien   *The Politics of Reproduction*, Routledge and Kegan Paul, 1981

Zandria Pauncefort   *Choices in Contraception*, Pan Books, 1984

Naomi Pfeffer and Anne Woollett   *The Experience of Infertility*, Virago, 1983

Rosalind Pollack Petchesky *Abortion and Woman's Choice*, Verso, 1986

Malcolm Potts and Peter Diggory *Textbook of Contraceptive Practice*,
  Cambridge University Press, 1983

Rose Shapiro *Contraception: A Practical and Political Guide*, Virago, 1987

Howard Shapiro *The Birth Control Book*, Penguin Books, 1980

Robert Snowden *The IUD: A Woman's Guide*, Unwin Paperbacks, 1986

Andrew Stanway *Infertility*, Thorson, 1984

3 Useful Addresses

National Organizations

Family Planning Information Service (FPIS)
  27–35 Mortimer Street, London WIN 7RJ. Tel. 071–636 7866

The Family Planning Association Regional Centres:
  27 St Peters St, Bedford MK40 2PN. Tel. 0234 62436
  13a Western Rd, Hove, East Sussex BN3 1AE. Tel. 0273 774075
  4 Barnfield Hill, Exeter, Devon EX1 1SR. Tel. 0392 56711
  6 Windsor Place, Cardiff CF1 3BX. Tel. 0222 42766
  20a Bridewell Alley, Norwich NR2 1AQ. Tel. 0603 628704
  5 York Rd, Edgbaston, Birmingham B16 9HX. Tel. 021 454 8236
  104 Bold St, Liverpool L1 4HY. Tel. 051 709 1938
  17 North Church St, Sheffield S1 2DH. Tel. 0742 21191
  4 Clifton St, Glasgow G3 7LA. Tel. 041 333 9696
  160 Shepherd's Bush Rd, London W6 7PB. Tel. 071 602 2723
  113 University St, Belfast BT7 1HP. Tel. 0232 22 5488

Irish Family Planning Association, Cathal Brugha Street Clinic, Dublin 1.
  Tel. Dublin 727276/727363

The Margaret Pyke Centre for Study and Training in Family Planning,
  15 Bateman's Buildings, Soho Square, London W1V 5TW.
  Tel. 071–734 9351

British Pregnancy Advisory Service (BPAS), Austy Manor, Wootton Waen,
  Solihull, West Midlands B95 6BX. Tel. 05642 3225

Pregnancy Advisory Service (PAS), 11–13 Charlotte Street, London W1P 1HD.
  Tel. 071–637 8962

Marie Stopes House, 108 Whitfield Street, London W1P 6BE.
  Tel. 071–388 0662/4843

Ulster Pregnancy Advisory Association Ltd., 719a Lisburn Road, Belfast
  BT9 7GU. Tel. Belfast 667 345

Brook Advisory Centres, 153a East Street, London SE17 2SD.
  Tel. 071–708 1234.

The National Association of Natural Family Planning Teachers, Natural Family Planning Unit, Birmingham Maternity Unit, Queen Elizabeth Medical Centre, Edgbaston, Birmingham 15. Tel. 021–472 1377 EXTN. 102

Natural Family Planning Service (Catholic Marriage Advisory Council), 15 Lansdown Road, London WI1 3AJ. Tel. 071–727 0141

The Association to Aid the Sexual and Personal Relationships of the Disabled (SPOD), 286 Camden Road, London N7 0BJ. Tel. 071–607 8851

Women's Health Concern, Ground Floor Flat, 17 Earl's Terrace, London W8 6LP. Tel. 071–602 6669

Women's Health and Reproductive Rights Information Centre, 52–54 Featherstone Street, London EC1. Tel. 071–251 6580

Women's National Cancer Control Campaign, 1 South Audley Street, London WIY 5DQ. Tel. 071–499 7532

Worldwide Organizations

International Planned Parenthood Federation (IPPF), 18–20 Lower Regent Street, London SWIY 4PW. Tel. 071–839 2911

The Family Planning Federation of Australia Inc., 24 Campbell Street, Sydney, NSW 2000, Australia

The New Zealand Family Planning Association Inc.
Correspondence: PO Box 68–200, Newton, Auckland, 1 New Zealand
Street Address: 214 Karangahape Road, Auckland, 1, New Zealand

Planned Parenthood Federation of Canada (PPFC), 151 Slater Street, Suite 200, Ottawa, Ontario KIP 5H3, Canada

Planned Parenthood Federation of America Inc. (PPFA), 810 Seventh Avenue, New York, 3NY 10019, USA

References

Two of our main sources appear so frequently that we have abbreviated references to them as follows:

John Guillebaud, *Contraception: Your Questions Answered*, Churchill Livingstone, 1985: to 'Guillebaud';
Malcolm Potts and Peter Diggory, *Textbook of Contraceptive Practice*, second edition, Cambridge University Press, 1983: to 'Potts and Diggory'.

CHAPTER I
1. Guillebaud, p. 1.
2. Joseph Bellina and Josleen Wilson, *The Fertility Handbook: A Positive and Practical Guide*, Penguin, 1986, p. 7.
3. J. D. Sherris and G. Fox, 'Infertility and Sexually Transmitted Disease: A Public Health Challenge', *Population Reports*, Series L, No. 4, Baltimore, Johns Hopkins University, Population Information Program, July 1983, p. l 124.
4. Germaine Greer, *Sex and Destiny*, Picador, 1985, p. 34.
5. E. Shorter, *A History of Women's Bodies*, Pelican Books, 1984.
6. *A Vindication of the Rights of Woman*, 1792, quoted in A. Rich, *Of Woman Born*, Virago, 1977, pp. 284–5.
7. Quoted in J. Sayer, *Biological Politics*, Tavistock Publishers, 1982, p. 8.
8. Sayer, op. cit., p. 10.
9. Ibid. p. 12.
10. Shulamith Firestone, *The Dialectic of Sex*, The Women's Press, 1979, p. 73.
11. Simone de Beauvoir, *The Second Sex*, Penguin Books, 1972, p. 64.
12. Carol McMillan, *Woman, Reason and Nature*, Basil Blackwell, 1982, p. 124.
13. Quoted in ibid., p. 75.
14. Mary O'Brien, *The Politics of Reproduction*, Routledge and Kegan Paul, 1981, pp. 46–8.
15. Quoted in Sayer, op. cit., p. 119.
16. Ann Ulanov, quoted in Penelope Shuttle and Peter Redgrove, *The Wise Wound*, Penguin, 1980, pp. 113–14.

17. Sheila Kitzinger, *Women's Experience of Sex*, Penguin Books, 1985, pp. 9–10.

18 Barbara Sichterman, *Femininity: The Politics of the Personal*, Polity Press, 1987, pp. 10–11.

19. Quoted in Rich, op. cit., p. 171 and pp. 181–2.

20. Shorter, op. cit., pp. 140 and 161.

21. Margaret Atwood, *Surfacing*, Virago, 1979, p. 80.

22. Margaret Mead, *Male and Female*, Penguin, 1976, pp. 250–1.

CHAPTER 2

1. Norman E. Himes, *Practical Birth Control Methods*, George Allen and Unwin, 1940, pp. 70–1.

2. 'Pregnancies in Britain' *Fact Sheet*, H3, Family Planning Information Service, January 1989.

3. Potts and Diggory, p. 388.

4. Quoted in Shirley Green, *The Curious History of Contraception*, Ebury Press, 1971, p. 23.

5. Quoted in Ruth Hall, *Dear Dr Stopes*, André Deutsch, 1978, pp. 17–18.

6. Christine Farrell with Leonie Kellaher, *My Mother Said*, Routledge and Kegan Paul, 1978, pp. 25–7.

7. Angela Willans, 'The Spin-off from Sex' in *The Consequences of Teenage Sexual Activity*, Brook Advisory Centres, 1981, p. 18.

8. Scarlett Pollack, 'Sex and the Contraceptive Act' in *The Sexual Politics of Reproduction*, ed. Hilary Homans, Gower, 1985, p. 70.

9. Malcolm Potts, *British Journal of Family Planning*, No. 12, 1986, p. 53.

10. Ary A. Haspels, *IPPF Medical Bulletin*, Vol. 22, No. 5, October 1988, pp. 1–2.

11. Robert Snowden, *Consumer Choices in Family Planning*, FPA, 1988, pp. 5, 7.

12. Farrell with Kellaher, op. cit., p. 169.

13. Ruth Coles, 'Acceptability and Use Effectiveness of Contraception for Teenagers', Brook Publications, pp. 3–4.

14. The Boston Women's Health Book Collective, *Our Bodies Ourselves*, Second American edition, Simon and Schuster, 1976, p. 183.

15. Germaine Greer, *Sex and Destiny*, Picador, 1984, pp. 42–3.

16. Quoted by Hilary Thomas, 'The Medical Construction of the Contraceptive Career', in Homans, op. cit., p. 53.

17. Snowden, op. cit., p. 15.

18. Kaye Wellings, 'Trends in contraceptive method usage since 1970', *British Journal of Family Planning*, Vol. 12, 1986, pp. 57–64.

19. Jill Rakusen, 'Depo-Provera; the extent of the problem', in *Women, Health and Reproduction*, ed. Helen Roberts, Routledge and Kegan Paul, 1981, p. 81.

20. Hilary Thomas in Homans, op. cit., p. 57.

21. Potts and Diggory, p. 323.

22. Rose Shapiro, *Contraception: A Practical and Political Guide*, Virago, 1987, p. 48.
23. Guillebaud, p. 40.
24. J. D. Sherris, S. H. Moore and G. Fox, 'New Developments in Vaginal Contraception', *Population Reports*, Series H, No. 7, Baltimore, Johns Hopkins University, Population Information Program, Jan–Feb 1984, p. H 172.
25. Guillebaud, p. 40.

CHAPTER 3

1. G. Howe, C. Westhoff, M. Vessey and D. Yates, 'Effects of age, cigarette smoking and other factors on fertility. Findings in a large prospective study', *British Medical Journal*, Vol. 290, 1985, p. 1697.
2. 'The legal position regarding contraceptive advice and provision to young people', *Fact Sheet*, F3, Family Planning Information Service, January 1989.
3. M. Eisner and M. Wright, 'A feminist approach to general practice' in *Feminist Practice in Women's Health Care*, ed. Christine Webb, John Wiley and Sons, 1986, p. 134.
4. Malcolm Potts, 'Counter reformation in family planning', *British Journal of Family Planning*, Vol. 12, 1986, pp. 50–6.
5. John F. Porter, ed., *The Control of Human Fertility*, second edition, Blackwell Scientific Publications, Melbourne, 1987, p. 157.
6. L. Ladanyi, 'Premenopausal fertility score as a guide to individual anti-conception', *Contraceptive Delivery Systems*, Vol. 5, No. 4, 1984, pp. 311–21.
7. David H. Kushner, 'Fertility in women after age forty-five', *International Journal of Fertility*, Vol. 24, No. 4, 1979, pp. 289–90.
8. Ronald Kleinman, ed., *Family Planning Handbook for Doctors*, International Planned Parenthood Federation, 1988, p. 193.

CHAPTER 4

1. Marie Stopes, *Contraception: Its Theory, History and Practice*, John Bale, Sons and Danielsson, 1926, pp. 86, 89.
2. E. Billings and A. Westmore, *The Billings Method: Controlling Fertility Without Drugs or Devices*, Allen Lane, 1981, p. 37.
3. John J. Billings, 'Cervical mucus: the biological marker of fertility and infertility', *International Journal of Fertility*, Vol. 26, No. 3, 1981, pp. 182–95.
4. Cited in John T. France, 'Overview of the biological aspects of the fertile period', *International Journal of Fertility*, Vol. 26, No. 3, 1981, pp. 143–52.
5. Eileen S. Gersh and Isadore Gersh, *The Biology of Women*, Junction Books, 1981, pp. 162–3.
6. John Billings, op. cit., p. 184.
7. Olive Schreiner, *Women and Labour*, T. Fisher Unwin, 1911, pp. 129–30.
8. L. S. Liskin and G. Fox, 'Periodic abstinence: how well do new approaches

work?', *Population Reports*, Series I, No. 3, Baltimore, Johns Hopkins University, Population Information Program, September 1981, p. I 45.

9. B. Kass-Annese and Hal Danzer, *The Fertility Awareness Workbook*, Thorsons' Publishing Group, 1986, p. 56.

10. Elizabeth Clubb and Jane Knight, *Fertility: A Comprehensive Guide to Natural Family Planning*, David and Charles, 1987, pp. 164–5.

11. Billings, op. cit., pp. 183–4.

12. Frank J. Rice *et al.*, 'The Effectiveness of the Sympto-Thermal Method of Natural Family Planning: An International Study', presented 23 June 1977 at the Scientific Congress held in conjunction with the First General Assembly of the International Federation for Family Life Promotion in Cali, Colombia, South America 22–29 June 1977.

13. Liskin and Fox, op. cit., pp. I 48–9.

14. Richard Hogan and John Levoir, 'John Paul II on family and sexuality', *Natural Family Planning*, Vol. 9, No. 2, 1975, pp. 144–67.

15. Rose Shapiro, *Contraception: A Practical and Political Guide*, Virago, 1987, p. 85.

16. Mary Shivanandas, *Natural Sex*, Hamlyn Books, 1980, p. 47.

17. Liskin and Fox, op. cit., p. I 49.

18. Anna Flynn and Melissa Brooks, *A Manual of Natural Family Planning*, George Allen and Unwin, 1984, p. 119.

19. Potts and Diggory, p. 103.

CHAPTER 5

1. Charles E. Flowers Jr *et al.*, 'The contraceptive aspects of the anatomy, morphology and physiology of the vagina', in Gerald I. Zatuchni *et al.*, eds., *Vaginal Contraception: New Developments*, Harper and Row, 1980, pp. 13–20.

2. J. D. Sherris, S. H. Moore and G. Fox, 'New Developments in Vaginal Contraception', *Population Reports*, Series H, No. 7, Baltimore, Johns Hopkins University, Population Information Program, Jan–Feb 1984, p. H 172.

3. Guillebaud, p. 39.

4. Norman E. Himes, *Practical Birth Control Methods*, George Allen and Unwin, 1940, p. 67.

5. Himes, op. cit., p. 81.

6. 'Contraceptive Usage', *Fact Sheet*, C2, and 'Contraceptive Trends in Great Britain', *Fact Sheet*, C3, Family Planning Information Service, January 1989.

7. Guillebaud, p. 38.

8. Germaine Greer, *Second Destiny*, Picador, 1985, p. 133.

9. Potts and Diggory, p. 134.

10. Bromwich and Parsons, *Contraception*, Oxford University Press, 1984, p. 70.

11. Walli Bounds, quoted by Louis Goldman in 'Cap is set to win US vote', *Doctor*, Vol. 18, No. 31, August 1988, p. 30.

12. Potts and Diggory, p. 128.

13. Quoted in Hilary Homans, ed., *The Sexual Politics of Reproduction*, Gower, 1985, p. 59.

14. Sue Craig and Sue Hepburn, 'The effectiveness of barrier methods of contraception with and without spermicide', *Contraception*, October 1982, Vol. 26, No. 4, pp. 347–59.

15. Louis Goldman, 'Cap is set to win US vote', op. cit.

16. Guillebaud, pp. 39–40.

17. Daniel Cramer *et al.*, 'The relationship of tubal infertility to barrier method and oral contraceptive use', *Journal of the American Medical Association*, May 1987, Vol. 257, No. 18, pp. 2446–50.

18. Sherris, Moore and Fox, op. cit., p. H 179.

19. *Pulse*, September 1987 and M. P. Vessey, 'Urinary tract infection and the diaphragm', *British Journal of Family Planning*, Vol. 13, 1988, pp. 41–3.

20. Sherris, Moore and Fox, op. cit., p. H 171.

21. Zoe Kopp, 'Cervical cap receives USFDA approval', *IPPF Medical Bulletin*, Vol. 23, No. 1, February 1989, pp. 3–4.

22. Rob Cagen, 'The cervical cap as a barrier contraceptive', *Contraception*, Vol. 33, No. 3, pp. 487–96.

23. Sherris, Moore and Fox, op. cit., p. H 162.

24. 'New Studies Find No Link Between Spermicide Use and Heightened Risk of Congenital Malformations', *International Family Planning Perspectives*, Vol. 14, No. 1, March 1988, pp. 39–40.

25. Patricia Scowen, 'Aids and Condoms', *Health at School*, Vol. 2, No. 5, February 1987, pp. 145–6.

—   R. Elgin, 'In vitro HIV antiviral studies with nonoxynol-9 and nonoxynol-11 spermicidal preparations', *British Journal of Sexual Medicine*, Vol. 16, No. 3, March 1989, p. 112.

26. Sherris, Moore and Fox, op. cit., p. H 179.

27. Walli Bounds and John Guillebaud, 'Randomised comparison of the use-effectiveness and patient acceptability of the Collatex (Today TM) contraceptive sponge and the diaphragm', *British Journal of Family Planning*, Vol. 10, 1984, pp. 69–75.

28. B. B. North and B. W. Vorhauer, 'Use of the Today contraceptive sponge in the United States', *International Journal of Fertility*, Vol. 30, No. 1, 1985, pp. 81–4.

29. Walli Bounds, John Guillebaud *et al.*, 'A female condom (Femshield™): a study of its user-acceptability', *British Journal of Family Planning*, Vol. 14, 1988, p. 83.

30. 'Femshield, the first female "condom" ', Medi News release, April 1988.

31. Walli Bounds *et al.*, 'Clinical trial of a spermicide-free, custom-fitted, valved cervical cap (Contracap TM)', *British Journal of Family Planning*, Vol. 11, No. 4, 1986, pp. 125–23.

CHAPTER 6

1. Quoted in Hilary Thomas, 'The Medical Construction of the Contraceptive Career', in *The Sexual Politics of Reproduction*, ed. Hilary Homans, Gower, 1985, p. 53.

2. Peter Elton and Andrew Blair, 'A contraceptive service for men', *British Journal of Family Planning*, Vol. 13, 1987, pp. 10–11.

3. Quoted in Peter Fryre, *The Birth Controllers*, Secker and Warburg, 1965, p. 25.

4. M. P. Vessey *et al.*, 'Factors affecting use-effectiveness of the condom', *British Journal of Family Planning*, Vol. 14, 1988, pp. 40–3.

5. Norman E. Himes, *Medical History of Contraception*, George Allen and Unwin, 1936, pp. 336–9;

— 'Contraceptive Usage', *Fact Sheet*, C2 and 'Contraceptive Trends in Great Britain', *Fact Sheet*, C3, Family Planning Information Service, January 1989.

6. John Bell, 'The thin latex line against disease', *New Scientist*, No. 1549, 26 February 1987, pp. 58–62.

7. 'Sexually transmitted diseases', *Fact Sheet*, D5, Family Planning Information Service, January 1989.

8. Potts and Diggory, pp. 115–16.

9. 'It's only condom sense' in *Self Health*, September 1987, pp. 10–15.

10. J. D. Sherris, D. Lewis and G. Fox, 'Update on Condoms – Products, Protection, Promotion', *Population Reports*, Series H, No. 6, Baltimore, Johns Hopkins University, Population Information Program, Sept–Oct 1982, p. H 131.

11. Guillebaud, p. 26.

12. Germaine Greer, *Sex and Destiny*, Picador, 1985, p. 110–11.

13. Potts and Diggory, p. 79.

14. Guillebaud, p. 28.

CHAPTER 7

1. Potts and Diggory, p. 216.

2. 'Contraceptive Trends in Great Britain', *Fact Sheet*, C3, Family Planning Information Service, January 1989.

3. K. Treiman and L. Liskin, 'IUDs – a New Look', *Population Reports*, Series B, No. 5, Baltimore, Johns Hopkins University, Population Information Program, March 1988, p. B 1.

4. Guillebaud, p. 209.

5. L. Liskin and G. Fox, 'IUDs: an Appropriate Contraceptive for Many Women', *Population Reports*, Series B, No. 4, Baltimore, Johns Hopkins University, Population Information Program, July 1982, pp. B 112–13.

6. M. E. Ortiz and H. B. Croxatto, 'The mode of action of IUDs', *Contraception*, Vol. 36, No. 1, July 1987, pp. 37–53.

7. Treiman and Liskin, op. cit., p. B 7.

8. Potts and Diggory, p. 219.

9. *Mechanism of Action, Safety and Efficacy of Intrauterine Devices*, Technical Report Series 753, World Health Organisation, Geneva, 1987, p. 13.

10. L. Liskin and W. F. Quillin, 'Long-acting Progestins – Promise and Prospects', *Population Reports*, Series K, No. 2, Baltimore, Johns Hopkins University, Population Information Program, May 1983, pp. K 37–8,
— Shapiro, op. cit., pp. 105–6.

11. Robert Snowden, *The IUD, a Woman's Guide*, Unwin Paperbacks, 1986, p. 76.

12. Jack Lippes, quoted in Potts and Diggory, p. 239.

13. WHO Technical Report Series 753, op. cit., pp. 46–7.

14. J. Hutchings, *et al.*, 'The IUD after Twenty Years: a Review of Worldwide Experience', in *International Family Planning Perspectives*, Vol. 11, No. 3, September 1985, pp. 78–9;
— Snowden, op. cit., p. 78.

15. Liskin and Quillin, op. cit., pp. K 37–8.

16. Snowden, op. cit., p. 81.

17. L. Westrom, 'Effect of acute pelvic inflammatory disease on fertility', *American Journal of Obstetrics and Gynaecology*, Vol. 121, No. 5, March 1975, pp. 707–13.

18. D. R. Mishell Jr *et al.*, 'The intrauterine device: a bacteriologic study of the endometrial cavity', *American Journal of Obstetrics and Gynaecology*, Vol. 96, No. 1, September 1966, pp. 119–26.

19. Treiman and Liskin, op. cit., p. B 12.

20. Ibid.

21. N. C. Lee *et al.*, 'Type of intrauterine device and the risk of pelvic inflammatory disease', *Obstetrics and Gynaecology*, Vol. 62, No. 1, July 1983, pp. 1–6.

22. Liskin and Fox, op. cit., p. B 122–3.

23. N. C. Lee, op. cit., pp. 1–6.

24. Liskin and Fox, op. cit., pp. B 123–4.

25. Howard J. Tatum, 'Intrauterine Contraception' in *Frontiers in Reproduction and Fertility Control; A Review of Reproductive Sciences and Contraceptive Development*, eds., R. O. Greep and M. Koblinsky, MIT Press, 1977, p. 199;
— Liskin and Fox, op. cit., pp. B 124–6;
— Snowden, op. cit., pp. 90–2.

26. Liskin and Fox, op. cit., pp. B 125–6;
— Anon, 'A rational approach to the IUCD', *Drugs and Therapeutics Bulletin*, Vol. 26, No. 16, August 1988, p. 63.

CHAPTER 8

1. Clifford R. Kay, 'The happiness pill?', *Journal of the Royal College of General Practitioners*, Vol. 30, No. 210, January 1980, pp. 8–19.

2. 'Contraceptive Trends in Great Britain', *Fact Sheet*, C3, Family Planning Information Services, January 1989.

3. General Household Survey, 1986, HMSO, 1989, p. 40.

4. A. D. G. Gunn, *Oral Contraception in Perspective*, Parthenon Publishing, 1987, pp. 85–113.
5. Gunn, op. cit., p. 136.
6. Potts and Diggory, pp. 144–5.
— John Guillebaud, *The Pill*, Oxford University Press, 1984, pp. 24–41.
7. M. P. Vessey, 'Female hormones and vascular disease – an epidemiological overview', *British Journal of Family Planning*, No. 6, October 1980, Supplement, pp. 1–12;
— Bruce V. Stadel, 'Oral contraceptives and cardiovascular disease', Parts 1 and 2, *New England Journal of Medicine*, Vol. 305, Nos. 11 and 12, September 1981, pp. 612–18 and 672–7.
8. Kay, op. cit.
9. F. M. Sturtevant, 'Smoking, oral contraceptives and thromboembolic disease', *International Journal of Fertility*, Vol. 27, No. 1, 1982, pp. 12–13;
— H. Ory *et al.*, 'The pill at twenty: an assessment', *International Family Planning Perspectives*, Vol. 6, No. 4, December 1980.
10. E. Eyong, 'Developments in new progestogens for oral contraception', *International Planned Parenthood Federation Medical Bulletin*, Vol. 21, No. 2, April 1987.
— Ken Fotherby, 'Oral Contraceptives and Lipids', *British Medical Journal*, vol. 298, No. 6680, April 1989, pp. 1049–50.
11. M. P. Vessy, op. cit., pp. 1–12;
— Ken Fotherby, 'Oral contraceptives, Lipids and Cardiovascular Disease', *Contraception*, Vol. 31, No. 4, 1985, pp. 367–89;
12. Ibid.
13. Ibid.
14. Potts and Diggory, p. 184.
15. M. P. Vessey, Sir Richard Doll and P. Sutton, 'Oral contraceptives and breast neoplasia: a retrospective study', *British Medical Journal*, Vol. 3, 1972, p. 719.
16. Potts and Diggory, p. 187.
17. M. C. Pike *et al.*, 'Breast cancer in young women and the use of oral contraceptives: possible modifying effect of formulation and age at use', *Lancet*, Vol. 12, No. 8356, 1983, p. 926.
18. O. Meirik *et al.*, 'Oral contraceptive use and breast cancer in young women. A joint national case-control study in Sweden and Norway', *Lancet*, Vol. 2, No. 8505, 1986, p. 650;
— M. P. Vessey, 'Oral contraceptives and breast cancer', *International Planned Parenthood Federation Medical Bulletin*, Vol. 21, No. 6, December 1987.
19. K. McPherson *et al.*, 'Early oral contraceptive use and breast cancer: results of another case-control study', *British Journal of Cancer*, Vol. 56, No. 5, November 1987, pp. 653–60.
20. C. Chilvers *et al.*, 'Oral contraceptive use and breast cancer risk in young women', *Lancet*, Vol. 1, No. 8645, 1989, pp. 973–82.

21. John Guillebaud, quoted in Jane Sullican, 'GPs plead for more balance in Pill debate', *Doctor*, 25 May 1989, p. 70.

22. D. Hellberg *et al.*, 'Long term use of oral contraceptives and cervical neoplasia: an association confounded by other risk factors?', *Contraception*, Vol. 32, No. 4, October 1985, pp. 337–46;

— Potts and Diggory, pp. 190–1;

— G. R. Huggins and R. L. Guintoli, 'Oral contraception and neoplasia', *Fertility and Sterility*, Vol. 32, No. 1, 1979, pp. 1–32.

23. E. Clarke *et al.*, 'Cervical dysplasia: association with sexual behaviour, smoking and oral contracpetive use', *American Journal of Obstetrics and Gynaecology*, Vol. 151, No. 5, March 1985, pp. 612–6.

24. M. P. Vessey *et al.*, 'Neoplasia of the cervix uteri and contraception: a possible adverse effect of the pill', *Lancet*, Vol. 2, No. 8356, 1983, pp. 930–4.

25. V. Beral, P. Hannaford and C. Kay, 'Oral contraceptive use and malignancies of the genital tract: results from the Royal College of General Practitioners' oral contraceptive study', *Lancet*, Vol. 2, No. 8624, December 1988, pp. 1331–4;

— J. J. Schlesselman, 'Oral contraceptives in relation to cancer of the breast and reproductive tract. An epidemiological overview', *The British Journal of Family Planning*, Vol. 15, No. 1, April 1989, Supplement, pp. 23–33.

26 Potts and Diggory, pp. 192–3.

27. The Centers for Disease Control and Steroid Hormone Study Group, 'Oral contraceptive use and the risk of ovarian cancer', pp. 1591–9 and 'Oral contraceptive use and the risk of endometrial cancer', pp. 1600–4, *Journal of the American Medical Assocaition*, Vol. 249, No. 2, 1983;

— Schlesselman, op. cit., pp. 23–33.

28. John Guillebaud, *The Pill*, op. cit., pp. 75–6;

— R. Hatcher, F. Guest, F. Stewart, G. Stewart, J. Trussell and E. Frank, *Contraceptive Technology 1984–1989*, Irvington Publishers, New York, 1984, pp. 284–7.

29. M. P. Vessey *et al.*, 'Return of fertility after discontinuation of oral contraceptives: influence of age and parity', *British Journal of Family Planning*, Vol. 11, 1986, pp. 120–4.

30. John Guillebaud, *The Pill*, op. cit., p. 110.

31. M. P. Vessey, M. Lawless, D. Yeates and K. McPherson, 'Progestogen-only oral contraception. Findings in a large prospective study with special reference to effectiveness', *British Journal of Family Planning*, Vol. 10, No. 4, 1985, pp. 117–21.

32. 'Minipill, a Limited Alternative for Certain Women', Population Reports, Series A, No. 3, Washington DC, The George Washington University Medical Center (Population Information Program), September 1985, p. A 57.

33. Guillebaud, *The Pill*, op. cit., p. 192.

34. Marge Berer, *Who Needs Depo Provera?*, Community Rights Project, 1984, pp. 14–15;
— Guillebaud, *The Pill*, op. cit., p. 151.
35. L. Liskin and W. F. Quillin, 'Long-acting Progestins – Promise and Prospects', *Population Reports*, Series K, No. 2, Baltimore, Johns Hopkins University, Population Information Program, May 1983, pp. K 26–7;
— John F. Porter, 'Steroidal Contraception', *The Control of Human Fertility*, ed. J F Porter, Blackwell Scientific Publications, 1987, pp. 115–17.
36. Liskin and Quillin, op. cit., p. K 29.
37. Peter Hall, 'Once-a-month injectable contraceptives', *International Planned Parenthood Federation Medical Bulletin*, Vol. 21, No. 2, April 1987.
38. Marge Berer, 'Norplant' Information Sheet, Women's Reproductive Rights Information Centre, London, 1986;
— Ronald Kleinman, ed., *Family Planning Handbook for Doctors*, International Planned Parenthood Federation, London, 1988, pp. 91–6.
39. Dilys Cossey, quoted in Sharon Goulds, Dee Bourne, Liz Kemp and Marilyn Wheatcroft, *Making History 5/Birth Control*, TV History Centre, 1988, p. 29.
40. Geraldine Rudge, quoted in ibid., p. 30.

CHAPTER 9
 1. Germaine Greer, *Sex and Destiny*, Picador, 1985, pp. 75–6.
 2. L. Liskin, W. Rinehart, R. Blackburn and A. H. Rutledge, 'Minilaparotomy and Laparoscopy: Safe, Effective and Widely Used', *Population Reports*, Series C, No. 9, Baltimore, Johns Hopkins University, Population Information Program, May 1985, p. C 127;
— 'Contraceptive Trends in Great Britain', *Fact Sheet*, C3, Family Planning Information Service, January 1989.
 3. Potts and Diggory, p. 265.
 4. Ibid., p. 266.
 5. C. J. B. Orr, 'Some medico–legal problems associated with contraception', *British Journal of Family Planning*, Vol. 13, No. 4, Supplement, January 1988, p. 38.
 6. M. P. Vessey *et al.*, 'Tubal sterilisation: findings in a large prospective study', *British Journal of Obstetrics and Gynaecology*, Vol. 90, March 1983, pp. 203–9.
 7. Liskin, Rinehart, Blackburn and Rutledge, op. cit., p. C 136.
 8. Ibid., p. C 146.
 9. Vessey, op. cit., pp. 203–9.
10. Liskin, Rinehart, Blackburn and Rutledge, op. cit., p. C 148.
11. Ronald Kleinman, ed., *Family Planning Handbook for Doctors*, International Planned Parenthood Federation, 1988, p. 185.
12. G. Marcus Filshie, 'Modern methods of female sterilisation', *British Journal of Family Planning*, Vol. 13, No. 4, Supplement, January 1988, pp. 9–10.

13. A. S. Ferber *et al.*, 'Men with vasectomies: a study of medical, sexual and psychological changes', *Psychosomatic Medicine*, 27, 1967, p. 354;
— John Bancroft, *Human Sexuality and its Problems*, Churchill Livingstone, 1989, pp. 652–3.
14. Potts and Diggory, p. 271.
15. L. Liskin, J. M. Pile and W. F. Quillin, 'Vasectomy – Safe and Simple', *Population Reports*, Series D, No. 4, Baltimore, Johns Hopkins University, Population Information Program, Nov–Dec 1983, pp. D 71–6.
16. J. Ross, S. Hong and D. Huber, *Voluntary Sterilization: An International Fact Book*, Association for Voluntary Surgical Sterilization, New York, 1987, p. 48.

CHAPTER 10
1. Guillebaud, p. 264;
— H. Albert Yugpe, 'Postcoital Contraception', *Clinics in Obstetrics and Gynaecology, Contraception Update*, Vol. 11, No. 3, W. B. Saunders, 1984, pp. 787–98.
2. Guillebaud, p. 264.
3. Ary Haspels, 'Post-coital Contraception', *International Planned Parenthood Federation Medical Bulletin*, Vol. 22, No. 5, October 1988.
4. Peter Bromwich and Anthony Parsons, 'The establishment of postcoital contraceptive service', *British Journal of Family Planning*, Vol. 8, No. 1, 1982, pp. 16–19.

CHAPTER 11
1. Quoted in Colin Francome, *Abortion Practice in Britain and the United States*, Allen and Unwin, 1986, p. 20.
2. Potts and Diggory, p. 282.
3. Hilary Homans, ed., *The Sexual Politics of Reproduction*, Gower, 1985, p. 89.
4. Germaine Greer, *Sex and Destiny*, Picador, 1985, pp. 161–2.
5. Homans, op. cit., p. 79.
6. Rosalind Pollack Petchesky, *Abortion and Women's Choice*, Verso, 1986, p. 327.
7. Carol McMillan, *Women, Reason and Nature*, Basil Blackwell, 1982, p. 147.
8. Kathleen McDonnell, *Not an Easy Choice: A Feminist Re-examines Abortion*, The Women's Press, Toronto, 1984, p. 59.
9. Quoted in Angela Neustatter and Gina Newson, *Mixed Feelings*, Pluto Press, 1986, pp. 104–5.
10. Petchesky, op. cit., p. 376.
11. Ibid., p. 333.
12. Greer, op. cit., p. 161.
13. McDonnell, op. cit., pp. 52–5.
14. Ibid., pp. 54–5.
15. Petchesky, op. cit., p. viii.
16. Quoted in McDonnell, op. cit., pp. 111–12.

17. Penelope Leach, *Babyhood*, second edition, Penguin Books, 1983, p. 108.
18. Petchesky, op. cit., p. 340.
19. Neustatter and Newson, op. cit., p. 6.
20. Quoted in Petchesky, op. cit., p. 263.
21. Neustatter and Newson, op. cit., pp. 104–5.
22. Petchesky, op. cit., p. 274.

CHAPTER 12
 1. Angela Phillips and Jill Rakusen, *Our Bodies Ourselves*, Penguin Books,
    1978, p. 12.

The authors acknowledge permission to quote from the following sources:
Abortion Act 1967, Crown Copyright; Margaret Atwood, *Surfacing*, André
Deutsch Ltd.; Simone de Beauvoir, *The Second Sex*, Jonathan Cape Ltd.,
1972, with acknowledgement to the Estate of Simone de Beauvoir; Mary
O'Brien, *The Politics of Reproduction*, Unwin Hyman Ltd.; Hélène Cixous,
The Newly Born Woman, Manchester University Press; Ruth Coles, *Journal of
Biosocial Science*, 1978, Supplement 5; Dilys Cossey and Geraldine Rudge,
quoted in S. Goulds, D. Bourne, L. Kemp and M. Wheatcroft, *Making
History 5/Birth Control*, 1988, reprinted by permission of the Television History
Centre; James Castle, 'Her Condom', *The Observer*, © Copyright The
Observer, London, 6th November 1988; Carl Djerassi, *The Politics of
Contraception*, W. H. Freeman and Co., 1982; Germaine Greer, *Sex and
Destiny*, Martin Secker and Warburg; Hilary Homans, ed., *The Sexual Politics
of Reproduction*, Gower, 1985; Norman E. Himes, *Practical Birth-Control*, Viking
Penguin; Ruth Hall, *Dear Dr. Stopes*, copyright © 1978, Supplement 5;
S. Kitzinger, *Women's Experience of Sex*, Dorling Kindersley; Erica Jong, *Fanny*,
Grafton Books, 1981; Penelope Leach, *Babyhood*, Penguin, reprinted by
permission of the author; Margaret Mead, *Male and Female*, Victor Gollancz
Ltd.; Angela Neustatter and G. Newson, *Mixed Feelings*, reprinted by
permission of Pluto Press; Malcolm Potts and Peter Diggory, *Textbook of
Contraceptive Practice*, Cambridge University Press, 1983; Adrienne Rich, *Of
Woman Born*, Virago, 1977; Barbara Sichtermann, *Femininity: The Politics of
the Personal*, Basil Blackwell; Robert Snowden, *Consumer Choices in Family
Planning*, The Family Planning Association; P. Shuttle and P. Redgrove, *The
Wise Wound*, Granada; Rose Shapiro, *Contraception: A Practical and Political
Guide*, Virago, 1987; Howard Shapiro, *The Birth Control Book*, St. Martin's
Press, Inc., New York; Ingrid Trobisch, quoted by Mary Shivanandas,
Natural Sex, Hamlyn Paperbacks, 1978.

Faber and Faber would by very pleased to be notified of any omission of errors
in acknowledgements, and will endeavour to rectify them.

Glossary

ABORTION   The expulsion of a fetus from the uterus at a stage before it is independently viable. If this occurs naturally it is then known as a miscarriage or a spontaneous abortion. If the abortion is induced it may then be known as an induced or therapeutic abortion or as a termination of pregnancy.

AMENORRHOEA   Absence of menstrual periods.

AMNIOCENTESIS   A diagnostic procedure which entails the withdrawal of a small amount of amniotic fluid from around a developing fetus.

ANDROGENS   Male sex hormones, the main effect of which is to encourage the development of male characteristics.

ANOVULATION   Failure to ovulate.

APGAR SCORE   A figure from 0–10 derived from five specific observations of a baby at birth and in the following minutes.

BIPHASIC CYCLE   A menstrual cycle during which the basal body temperature is low for the first part of the cycle, and then increases by about 0.20 at the presumed time of ovulation, and thereafter remains raised until menstruation.

BLASTOCYST   The ball of cells formed by the fertilisation of an ovum, which may implant in the uterus, and develop into a fetus.

BREAKTHROUGH BLEEDING   Bleeding which occurs between the monthly bleeds in women on the combined oral contraceptive pill, i.e., while taking the pill.

CAPACITATION   Changes in the membrane around the head of a sperm, which enable it to penetrate the ovum at fertilization.

CERVICAL EROSION   The appearance of the cervix when there is an area around the os which is covered by the lining cells, which are usually confined to the cervical canal. This may be seen in any woman but is more common in pregnant women and in some women on the combined oral contraceptive pill.

CERVICAL MUCUS   The secretions produced in the cervical canal.

CERVIX   The neck of the uterus, protruding into the vagina.

CORPUS LUTEUM   A group of yellowy cells formed from the remains of an ovarian follicle after ovulation has occurred. It produces progesterone and some oestrogen, and degenerates if fertilization does not occur.

COWPERS GLANDS   Small glands in the male urethra producing fluid which lubricates the passage of sperm.

DILATATION AND CURETTAGE (D & C)   A minor operation which entails the gentle dilatation of the cervix to allow the passage of a curette which is used to scrape the wall of the uterus.

DIZYGOTIC TWINS   Two babies born at the same time, as the result of the fertilization of two separate ova released at the same time. They do not share the same genetic make-up and are not identical.

ECTOPIC PREGNANCY   The implantation and development of a pregnancy outside the uterine cavity. It is a potentially life-threatening condition.

ENDOCERVIX   The lining of the cervical canal.

ENDOGENOUS HORMONES   The hormones produced within the body.

ENDOMETRIOSIS   A condition in which endometrial tissue develops outside the uterine cavity.

ENDOMETRIUM   The inner lining of the uterine cavity which develops during the menstrual cycle to be prepared for the implantation of a fertilized ovum. If fertilization does not take place this lining is shed at menstruation.

EPIDIDYMIS   Tubular structure connecting the testes to the vas deferens.

EPISIOTOMY   A cut in the lower vagina which may be made at the time of delivery to avoid tearing and to facilitate the birth of the baby.

EXOGENOUS HORMONES   Hormones which originate from outside the body.

FALLOPIAN TUBES   The pair of tubes which are attached to the upper part of the uterus and which transport the ovum from ovary to uterine cavity.

FERNING   The characteristic pattern made by fertile mucus when it dries.

FIMBRIA   The finger-like projections at the openings of the fallopian tubes which catch the ovum at ovulation.

FOLLICLE   The tiny fluid-filled sac in the ovary which produces oestrogen and in which the ovum may develop.

FOLLICLE STIMULATING HORMONE (FSH)   A hormone produced by the pituitary gland. In women this stimulates the formation of follicles within the ovary to produce oestrogen. In men FSH it triggers sperm formation.

FOLLICULAR PHASE   The first half of the menstrual cycle, lasting from the onset of menstruation (day 1) until ovulation.

GAMETE   A cell with twenty-three chromosomes, half the number of most human cells, and which can undergo fertilization, e.g. sperm and ova.

GRAAFIAN FOLLICLE   The follicle which produces the ovum.

HEPATOCELLULAR ADENOMA   A non-cancerous growth of liver cells.

HUMAN CHORIONIC GONADOTROPHIN (hCG or BhCG)   A hormone produced in very early pregnancy which maintains the corpus luteum. The measurement of this hormone is the basis for some pregnancy tests.

HYDROCELE   A collection of fluid around the testes.

HYPOSPADIAS   A congenital condition in which the male urethra opens out on the underside of the penis rather than at its tip.

HYPOTHALAMUS   A control centre at the base of the brain with many functions including the regulation of pituitary hormones.

HYSTERECTOMY   An operation to remove the uterus.

IMPLANTATION   The embedding of the blastocyst in the endometrium.

IN VITRO FERTILIZATION (IVF)   The fertilization of an ovum by sperm outside the body.

LAPAROSCOPE   A narrow telescope-like instrument with a light source, used to look into the abdominal cavity.

LAPAROTOMY   An operation to open the abdominal cavity.

LUTEINIZING HORMONE (LH)   A hormone produced by the pituitary gland causing ovulation and maintaining the corpus luteum.

LUTEINIZING HORMONE-RELEASING HORMONE (LH-RH)   A hormone produced by the hypothalamus which brings about the release of LH.

LIFE-TABLE ANALYSIS   A statistical method used to assess risk.

LUTEAL PHASE   The second half of the menstrual cycle, lasting from ovulation until the onset of menstruation.

MEIOSIS   The special process of cell division which results in the formation of gametes.

MITTELSCHMERTZ   The pain experienced by some women at the time of ovulation.

NEURAL TUBE DEFECTS   These are a spectrum of congenital abnormalities of the spinal cord and the brain. They include spina bifida and hydrocephalus.

NULLIPAROUS   Never having borne a child.

OESTROGENS   A group of closely related female sex steroids with similar properties. Oestrodiol is the commonest oestrogen produced by the ovary.

OOCYTE   Immature ovum.

ORCHITIS   Imflammation of the testes.

OS CERVIX   The opening into the uterus.

OVARY   One of the two female reproductive organs containing ova, situated close to the ends of the fallopian tubes. They are also responsible for producing sex hormones.

OVUM (single: OVA)   The female sex cell or egg, which when fertilized by a sperm is capable of becoming a new individual.

PAROUS   Having given birth.

PEARL INDEX   A score given to a contraceptive method which indicates the statistical risk of pregnancy associated with the use of that method.

PERITONITIS   Inflammation of the peritoneum, a thin layer of tissue which lines the abdominal cavity and covers the organs in the abdomen. This term is also used in a more general way to talk about generalized abdominal infection resulting from appendicitis, etc.

PROGESTERONE   The most common progestogen produced in the body.

PROGESTOGEN   One of a group of sex-steroid hormones which have similar effects on the body as progesterone. These may be endogenous or exogenous.

PROLACTIN   A hormone, produced by the pituitary gland, which stimulates the breasts to produce milk. It is also produced in small amounts in non-pregnant women.

PROPHYLACTIC   Something which prevents or protects from disease.

PROSTAGLANDINS Hormone-like substances produced in the body which have a wide variety of effects. Some prostaglandins cause uterine muscle to contract, and synthetic prostaglandins can be used to induce abortion.

PROSTATE GLAND A gland situated at the base of the bladder in men. The secretions from this gland give volume to semen.

PUDENDAL NERVE A nerve which supplies part of the vagina, vulva and perineum.

PULMONARY EMBOLISM A blood clot which becomes lodged in the blood vessels of the lungs.

SALPINGITIS Inflammation of the fallopian tubes.

SEMINAL VESICLES A pair of glandular structures behind the male bladder that produce secretions forming a large part of semen.

SEMINIFEROUS TUBULES Very small coiled tubular structures that make up about 80 per cent of the mass of the testes, in which sperm are made.

SEPTICAEMIA A generalized illness caused by the multiplication of micro-organisms in the blood.

SPECULUM A device used to obtain a clearer view of a body cavity.

SPERMATOZOON (SPERM) Male gamete.

SPINNBARKEIT The characteristic stretchiness of fertile cervical mucus.

TESTES (TESTICLES) The two male reproductive glands.

TESTOSTERONE Steroid hormone responsible for male sex characteristics. Small amounts are produced in women.

TRISOMY The condition whereby an individual has three identical chromosomes in each cell instead of the usual pair. The resulting type of syndrome depends on which of the 46 chromosomes is affected. An example is Trisomy 21, that leads to Down's syndrome.

TROPHOBLASTIC DISEASE A condition caused by abnormal development of a pregnancy, whereby the placental cells multiply rapidly, to fill the whole uterus with a soft grape-like growth. This condition is also known as hydatidiform mole or a molar pregnancy.

URETERS The tubes which take urine from the kidneys to the bladder.

URETHRA The tube which takes urine from the bladder out of the body.

URINARY TRACT INFECTION (UTI) Infection by a micro-organism of part or all of the urinary tract, comprising the ureters, bladder and urethra.

UTERUS The pear-shaped muscular organ in the woman's pelvis in which the embryo develops known as the womb.

VARICOCELE Varicose veins within the scrotum.

VAS DEFERENS The tube which passes from the epididymis to the prostate gland. Also known as the vas – hence vasectomy.

VENOUS THROMBOSIS A blood clot in a vein.

Index